The Merry Millionaire

*Entering into the spirit
of the Jazz Age
with gay abandon
a story based on true events*

J.A.Wells

Copyright © J.A.Wells 2016
www.johnwellsmurals.com.au/author

J.A.Wells has asserted his right to be identified as author of this work in accordance with the Australian Copyright Act 1968.

This book is a work of fiction and, except in the case of historical fact, any resemblance to actual persons, living or dead, is purely coincidental.

All rights reserved. Without limiting the rights under the copyright above, no part of this publication shall be reproduced, stored in or introduced into a retrieval system, or transmitted in any form or by any means (electronic, mechanical, photocopying, recording or otherwise), without the prior permission of the copyright owner.

Cover design by John Wells and Diane Challenor
Interior design by Diane Challenor

ISBN-13: 978-1530826582

ISBN-10: 1530826586

Dedication

I dedicate this book to the memory of Ronald Fry and Mervyn Watson and to my talented friend and mentor Diane Challenor, her husband John, and to my life long friend Bebe Bragg. To my ever loyal and supportive sister Kate and her family. Also to my darling mother and her valuable recollections.

About the book

The Thirties, a decade of decadence and depression, ending in war. This hardly has an effect on Ron and Mervyn, our intrepid pleasure seekers. Disregarding the rumblings of war in Europe, and dancing to a dying tune, they join the waning fast-set, cruising the Norwegian fjords on luxury ocean liners and sailing up the Nile on serene feluccas.

Explore the bygone age of first class sea travel and luxury oriental hotels, summer on the glaciers, and the heat of Cairo's social season. All seen through the eyes of Ron and Mervyn, the gayest pair of lotus-eaters you will ever encounter.

J.A.Wells has succeeded in painting a dense, yet frivolous view, of a time now lost to the journals of debutants and dowager duchesses. In the first of his duology, J.A.Wells uses his rich imagination, creating a colourful cast of living and breathing characters.

We will wonder what may become of the pairing of Ron and Mervyn, poles apart in age and class, yet similar in inclination.

About the author

The idea of a Renaissance man may be regarded as old fashioned these days, and rather a cliché, but the phrase can be forgiven when applied to J.A.Wells. After a twenty-year career as a professional actor on the British stage, and then a further twenty years as an artist, J.A.Wells has added storyteller to his list of talents.

In his two rollicking debut novels, The Merry Millionaire and its sequel, Pomp and Circumstance, J.A.Wells combines his gift for characterisation, and his sense of inspired visual imagery, as well as a delight in meticulous research, to bring to life long forgotten significant characters. 'Putting flesh on old bones' as he describes it. One thing can be said for J.A.Wells, he leaves no stone unturned, and is currently immersed in his next novel that delves into Australia's exciting and colourful past.

Author's Note

In most circumstances, at this point the author writes a disclaimer declaring that his or her characters bear no resemblance to people living or dead. However, in this case, most of the persons you will encounter in the story, once lived, but their names have been changed for reasons of expediency. I hope that by including them in this work of fiction I have given them the justice they deserve and have not sullied their reputations in any way.

Throughout this fictional memoir of a millionaire, using the voice of Captain Ronald Fry, ex army captain, scout master, philanthropist and benefactor, I tell how it was to be gay in the 1930's, when homosexuality was against the law and punishable with years of hard labour. To show one's true feelings, one ran the risk of blackmailers, entrapment, robbery, violence, and even murder.

Prelude

Tuesday, March 9th 1937
Hyde House, Wildsbridge, nr. Bristol. Somerset.
Dear Eric,

Yesterday, Mervyn and I returned to England on The Viceroy of India after enjoying a marvellous holiday in Egypt. We endeavoured to keep you up to date with our adventures. I hope you, Amy and Emily received the postcards; Cairo Post Office is most chaotic at the best of times.

Taking your advice, as you know I always have, I continue with my jottings as I call them, hoping they will amount to a memoir one day. Although I've no idea why you believe anyone will be interested in my paltry life.

Please note Eric, when you eventually read it, you will be immediately aware that I have told my story the way it is, pulling no punches so to speak. However, some revelations and descriptions of the way things are between my dear friend Mervyn Watson and I would be regarded as illegal in these present times. Although through my studies, I am aware that in Ancient Crete, Greece and Roman societies, a relationship between an older man and a youth was openly encouraged. I urge you to be prudent and hold off publication with the hope that, one day, the world will not condemn such men as he and I, and my work will be seen as an open account of how things are for the likes of him and I, and many others. I trust Eric you will not find particular passages in either tome offensive, or vulgar, since I have endeavoured to remain a gentleman in my descriptions and explanations regarding certain aspects that are dear to Mervyn and myself. I will not shy away from the truth of my life.

As soon as we arrived home, I was so enthralled and enthused by what Mervyn and I experienced of the antiquities of Ancient Egypt and the delights of Cairo in full season; I felt inspired to share them with you, and whoever else might eventually read my story. I've almost completed the two volumes, the first I've called The Merry Millionaire. For the second volume, I thought the title, Pomp and Circumstance, would be appropriate.

Now we are back in England we're looking forward to Coronation Day. What are you three doing on the day? Mervyn and I have front row seats in the grandstand beside Westminster Abbey. If you wish, I'll ask Keith Prowse if they have any near us still available.

We are both looking forward to seeing you all next week; Mervyn and I have presents for you.

***

This is how I found Ron's letter, unfinished and unfolded, lying on top of the second manuscript. He didn't send it! Ronald was entirely impetuous, a butterfly of a man, darting hither and thither endeavouring to fill every moment with activity and fun. More than likely he intended to post it, then distracted by something, forgot that he had ever written it.

Now everything is in order, and since I can call myself a progeny of Ron's, I feel justified as well as privileged to settle back and read what I urged Ron to write from the very start; **his memoir.**

Memoir of Captain Ronald Willington Fry
The Merry Millionaire

Volume One

Chapter One
Beginnings – Lost love

My name is Ronald Willington Fry. Henry Oliver Fry the third and John Bonny Willington were my paternal and maternal grandfathers, the first, a sugar manufacturer and millionaire of Bristol, the other a cotton spinner and factory owner from Skipton in Yorkshire. The Fry family business can be traced back three generations to the day Henry Oliver Fry first set up shop in Bristol and began his sugar business, a trade built on the backs of slaves.

My father, Stanley Fry, the youngest son of Henry Oliver Fry, was never closely involved with the firm. Having been educated at Clifton College and Trinity College Cambridge, he began his working life as a solicitor in Brompton Kent. However, as an older man he served on the board of Fry's Sugar.

I was born in Brompton on the twenty third of June, nine years before the turn of the century, the first child of Stanley Fry and Hilda Willington. My mother was proud to be a Willington, which is why my younger brother Wilfred and I share Willington as a middle name. There was another child born between Wilfred and myself. But sadly the baby died and we were never to know whether it was a boy or girl. Our family was small, Wilfred and I reared within a somewhat frigid atmosphere by a succession of nurses and nannies.

As the century turned, my father and mother moved to Bath, Somerset, taking up residence at Royal Crescent. However, as soon as

I was old enough, probably seven or eight, I was sent away to school, as was Wilfred I presume. My boarding school education began at Mount House in Plymouth, Devon, under the severe glare of the headmistress Miss Tubbs, who I believe was a distant relative. I remained at Mount House for the next four years until I was old enough to enter Farmborough College in Wiltshire.

Farmborough was my epiphany. Away from the world of little boys, schoolmistresses and matrons, I was now in a world of men; robust male teachers, hammering around rugger fields or demonstrating experiments in science class, also delicately handsome young men teaching Latin and Greek. Therefore as a boy of twelve, I was in heaven, surrounded by beauty on every side. I had crushes on senior boys and experienced such erotic dreams they caused me to wake in the middle of the night in a most embarrassed state, which I hoped would go unnoticed in the school laundry at the end of the week. Nevertheless, I was soon to discover I was not alone in my fantasy world. As I grew older, I developed physically. Moreover, I was tall for my age, therefore matured faster, which drew the attention of others less endowed. As a result, the crushes I experienced for older boys were now directed upon me and I discovered I had a foll wing of doting juniors. It became customary to spoil me with treat from the tuck shop, or some morsel a boy had received from hom

Yet to me thes rysts were meaningless, regarding them merely as rewarding the y 1g chaps for their efforts. My goals lay in greater and more chal ging fields. I became fascinated by the pursuit of the 'so called,' m aline boy. He, who was best at rugger, athletics and swimming. chap who made it clear that homos were weak and deserved rashing. These lads presented the most demanding pursuit. tealth and cunning, I cajoled my way into their favour, playin neir weakest instincts, their egos. It is extraordinary how far a flattery can go, a compliment about a performance during the cend match, or the afternoon trials. Also, because I was extr ly discreet with the juniors, my senior colleagues were un re my feelings lay on the opposite side of the fence. As a result, th took me entirely into their confidence so unknowingly played into my hands.

While in the upper fourth, one such conquest was a sixth form prefect, Anthony Goodfellow. He was beautiful, tall with hair like sunshine, his eyes as blue as the summer sky. He and I were in Cotton House, which in the years I attended Farmborough was the foremost house for sport. Of course, Anthony was top sportsman of Cotton House, excelling in rugby and every form of athletics and gymnastics. Although, it was swimming where he was most pleasing. I would quiz him as to when he would be training and sneak out of class on the pretence of using the toilet so I could watch him swim up and down the pool.

'Show me your dive again,' I would say, only so I could watch him climb out of the pool and stand on the side.

He was extremely fit and quite muscular for a lad of seventeen, with a broad chest and strong limbs, both developed from years of playing rugger. His torso, nor his limbs were never the centre of my attention however, and in that respect, I reserve my comments to your imagination.

Eventually, Anthony and I became pals and during his last year at Farmborough, he began inviting me to his family home for the holidays. The Goodfellows lived in Corsham, a few miles east of Bath.

At Easter, I decided to reciprocate but had second thoughts. The atmosphere at Royal Crescent was hardly conducive to young men having fun. My father was sickly and spent a great deal of time in bed, Mother saying he had a problem with his heart. So the house had taken on the atmosphere of a mausoleum, with the servants creeping about like mice. For this reason, when Anthony offered I decided to accept his invitation.

By now, I imagine you have reached the conclusion that I had already seduced my quest into submission. However, that was far from the case. I began to form the opinion that should I make an approach it would ruin our friendship. Surprisingly it proved not to be me that caused Anthony and myself to form an even closer bond.

Later that year, and during the summer holidays, I was again staying at Anthony's and since it was a hot and stuffy night, he suggested we sleep under the stars. Therefore, having gathered our bedding and a couple of pillows, we climbed the narrow stairs to the roof, where we removed our pyjamas and ducked under our eiderdowns.

Anthony's father was something in the city of London. Banking I think. Anyhow, the Goodfellow home, Hartham Park, was opulent and comfortable, standing in a hundred acres of farmland, with the area surrounding the house turned into parkland a couple of centuries earlier. I relished the grand rooms, the portraits, and the antique furniture, all of which Anthony took for granted. I suppose it was during those early days that my appreciation of beautiful things was spawned and has remained with me ever since.

There we were, on the roof, lying side by side, me the lanky youth and Anthony the Adonis. As we stared at the stars, sparkling out of a black sky, the circumstances could not have been more conducive to romance. Yet we had slept in the same room before, even lying together on Anthony's bed reading our books. I had grown used to restraining my emotions however, and hiding my excitement. Although on this night, it was not I who instigated a situation. Gazing up at the sky, we attempted to identify certain constellations, Anthony pointing out The Plough and The Great Bear, while I found The Little Bear. Well I thought I had, but Anthony challenged me.

"That's Orion!" he laughed. "Can't you see his belt? Look at those three stars."

"But I thought it was the bear's tail," I answered.

"You're a real duffer Fry." He always called me Fry, although I addressed him as Anthony. "I really don't know what's to become of you. If you didn't have a fortune coming to you I'd be worried how you'd get on after school."

"I'm going to Cambridge with you," I said. "We've discussed it. I wouldn't want to be there if you weren't."

"Of course," he said. "And I wouldn't either. There! I've said it."

"What do you mean?" I said, surprised by his sudden outburst. He never usually made any sign of affection towards me, or to anyone else for that matter.

"I don't know," he continued. "You're a good pal I suppose.

Almost like the brother, I never had. Sisters aren't the same."

Anthony was aware I had a brother. He always said how jealous he was of Wilfred and me; although I insisted my relationship with my brother was not one to be envied.

"What do you reckon to girls Fry?" Anthony suddenly asked.

Even in the darkness, I was aware that he was leaning on one elbow and so close I could feel his breath on my face.

"Not much," I replied. "Don't really think about them at all."

"Me neither," he said. "Although I should. I'm nearly eighteen. Girls are all the boys in the upper sixth talk about. They say some quite filthy things. Jenkins in my rooms has even had it off with his mother's maid. What do you think of that?"

The thought of a sexual relationship with any female appalled me, so I shook my head.

"Men can be relied on," continued Anthony. "They know how each other think and feel. Things go unsaid."

What could he mean? Was he trying to tell me something so private he hardly dare whisper it? Dumbfounded, I was unable to answer and there was a silence between us, broken only by the lonely hoot of an owl.

The day had been scorching, the sun searing out of an azure sky. As a result, the lead on the roof was warm, the heat slowly seeping into our bedding. Anthony was the first to throw off his eiderdown.

"Wow! I'm hot!" he exclaimed. "Aren't you Fry?"

He tugged at my cover, but I held it tightly.

"Come on," he said. "You must be roasting."

Without warning, the moon emerged from behind a cloud, flooding the chimneys and parapet with steely light and suddenly I was able to see Anthony beside me, his nakedness shining white against the grey lead on the roof.

"Go on! Throw it off."

He pulled at the eiderdown again and this time I did nothing to stop him.

"What's that?" he cried, seeing my embarrassment.

"Well!" I explained, covering myself with my hand. "It's natural. It just happens every so often. I can't help it."

Anthony laughed.

"Show me."

I took my hand away.

"You're not a tall lad for nothing!"

"Shut up," I said. "It's nothing."

"You call that nothing."

My heart was racing. The fantasy I had nurtured for months was rapidly becoming a reality.

"Compared to me, do you still say it's nothing?"

He had been lying on his stomach, but rolled over revealing his own part, which I thought at the time, was almost equivalent.

At this point, and for the sake of disgracing myself, and to save my own embarrassment as well as yours, I find it necessary to précis. Therefore, I will cease to tell you what happened next, although I can only admit that, at least everything for me reached a happy conclusion.

Anthony was not so gratified, quickly pulling his eiderdown around him and without a word or backward glance, disappearing across the shadowy roof and down the stairs.

For a moment, I sat stupefied, unable to fathom what had just occurred. Part of me was elated. At last, a dream had come true. Nonetheless, had what I feared and what had prevented me from making a gesture before, finally happened? Might I have lost my friend forever?

Still, why should I feel guilty? After all Anthony initiated everything. Had he not pulled off my blanket we would be asleep by now. It was no good feeling sorry I told myself. What happened, happened, and nothing we could do would change it. Therefore, I bundled up my bed and followed my friend back to our room.

After that night, things were never the same. At breakfast, the next morning Anthony hardly spoke, instead sat frowning, and never once looked at me. At one point, his mother asked if he was unwell, but he mumbled something and asked to be excused from the table.

Suddenly it felt odd being in the house without my friend associating with me. I wandered aimlessly, partly looking for him, even though something told me if I found him, he would still react in the same way.

Eventually, with a blood red sun setting behind the elm trees, I discovered Anthony in the temple beside the lake, a favourite place of ours. He was sitting on a stone seat, staring vacantly, so I walked inside and sat beside him. I thought he was going to get up and walk away at first, but something caused him to change his mind.

"I'm sorry," I whispered. "It was my fault."

"No," he said, shaking his head. "It's me. I've known all along but couldn't admit it. There's something rotten inside me. It's not natural. I've tried to smother it, but it won't go away."

"I'm the same," I said. "I know how you feel. But it's all right. We just have to face it and get on with our lives. There are lots of us at school. We're not the only ones."

Anthony looked at me with tears in his eyes.

"But those boys are homos. We're not like them. How can we be homo? We're normal."

A strong urge came over me to reach out and touch his hand.

"Of course we're normal," I said. "But it doesn't stop us being the way we are."

"I don't want to feel like this. I want to be like everyone else. To get excited when I see a pretty girl. Instead, all I can think and dream about is you."

"I don't believe it?" I said.

"I've never been a very jolly sort of chap," Anthony continued. "You're the opposite. Talkative and so much fun to be around."

I was stunned.

"But Anthony you're so good at rugger and everything. I can't believe you think you're shy."

"It's all an act! I am scared. Scared that one day someone will catch me out, and now they have."

"Don't be silly. I've told you. I'm the same. It'll be our secret."

There was a moment of silence between us, although I sensed he would never accept my sympathy or understanding.

"Why do we feel the way we do?" I said at last. "Do you think it's a kind of love?"

Anthony looked at me savagely.

"Don't be stupid Fry!" he shouted. "Love happens between men and women, not between men. It's unnatural. With men, it's lust. A desire that's spent in a moment then disappears into guilt. Now leave me alone."

He ran to the edge of the lake and left me sitting alone in the temple. I was helpless to know what to say or do. My heart yearned to hold him. To tell him that everything would be all right, but knew it would be hopeless. Therefore, with a heavy heart I returned to the house.

Later that evening, I asked Mrs Goodfellow if I could return to Bath.

"Are you boys alright?" she said, sounding concerned "You haven't quarrelled have you? I'm so pleased Anthony has finally found a nice friend. He's such a quiet boy. You seem good for him."

I assured her everything was fine and she arranged for the butler to drive me home.

Chapter Two
Tragedy and Trinity

There were still several weeks before school would begin, so I filled my empty moments by walking in Victoria Park, playing Patience, or swimming in the baths. But I was miserable and lonely without my friend. I considered writing a letter to Anthony, although worried it might be discovered by his mother, or even a curious housemaid, which would be disastrous. Therefore, all that remained was to wait until we were back at Cotton House before I could see him once more. One Friday morning, a week later as I sat at the breakfast table, my world came crashing down never to be the same again.

"Good Lord!" exclaimed my father. "A boy from your school."

It was one of his better days, when he was able to get up and come downstairs to read his morning paper.

"What a tragedy."

As I was born into the Victorian age, I have been taught to speak when I am spoken to and furthermore, never to ask questions.

"You might know him?" my father continued. "Goodfellow. Anthony Goodfellow."

My stomach lurched.

"Yes," I said. "He's in my house."

"He's been found dead."

My mind reeled. I wanted to snatch the newspaper from his hands and read it myself.

"The son of Geoffrey Goodfellow," my father read aloud. "A founder member, director and shareholder of Goodfellow and Charterhouse Insurance, was discovered yesterday at the family home, Hartham Park, near Corsham. However, after a thorough investigation, it is the conclusion of the police that Anthony Goodfellow's death did not involve foul play. The funeral is scheduled for Tuesday morning at St. Bartholomew's, Corsham."

Suddenly, I had an overwhelming feeling I was about to vomit my breakfast.

"How well did you know him?" father asked.

I swallowed hard.

"Not much. He was a couple of years above me."

"But isn't he the chap you've been seeing a lot of lately? I'm sure your mother's mentioned him."

I was stuck and had to confess.

"Yes. We were friends."

Having been a solicitor, my father still possessed an enquiring mind and I waited for his response.

"I assume the lad killed himself? Would you have a clue as to why?"

I shook my head, daring not to speak lest I began to cry. At that moment, the telephone rang in the hall, and shortly after our maid, Sarah, entered the room.

"It's the police sir," she said. "They want to speak to Master Ronald."

"I'll talk to them," said my father, and he left me alone at the table.

Frantically I wondered what I should say. At least I had a moment to gather my thoughts. Although in no time, father returned.

"They want to know whether you can shed any light on the matter."

I began blushing and knew my father had noticed.

"But don't worry. I said I'd spoken to you and you'd told me that as far as you were aware the boy was perfectly fine the last time you saw him."

My father could not let the matter drop completely.

"Had you a clue your friend might be depressed?"

"Not at all," I muttered. "He was a cheerful sort, and very good at rugger and swimming. I can't think why he should have done such a thing."

It was embarrassing talking so openly with my father. We were never close.

"Then not the sort to top himself?"

My stomach churned as he fired question after question until finally he seemed satisfied with the outcome of his examination and returned to reading his newspaper. I excused myself, left the dining room, and went to my room, where I fell on the bed and wept the silent tears of abandonment and loss.

Obviously, I expected Mr and Mrs Goodfellow to inform my mother and father of the funeral arrangements, but the weekend played out and Tuesday came and went with no invitation appearing. The following days and weeks passed with deadening monotony and sadness, until it was time to return to school.

Back in Cotton House, neither Mr Dickie the housemaster, nor any other master, mentioned Anthony's absence. Moreover, although he had been a primary figure in the sporting life of the school, any gossip amongst the boys regarding his disappearance remained minimal, proving to me the ephemeral nature of life at Farmborough.

Christmas came and went. Then spring and yet another summer, but the memory of my friend stubbornly remained. It dictated my reaction to any move towards potentially new comrades, as well as reduced to a minimum my once predatory advances toward hopeful new candidates. In fact, I became frigid and uninterested in anything regarding sex, which perplexed and annoyed the young fellows to whom I had previously granted favours.

In my state of limbo, I concentrated on cramming for my university entrance examination, thereby rewarded by a positive result. As a result, in the autumn of that year, I packed my bags and by way of London caught a train to Cambridge.

The first few months at Trinity were miserable since I was unable to get Anthony out of my mind. We had planned to be there together, to share the difficulties of life away from school. Instead, I was all alone to face the grown up world without him.

A young man from Skipton in Yorkshire and myself shared rooms, the same town in fact where my grandfather, John Bonny Willington, had a successful cotton-spinning mill.

My roommate, George Coleman, was a friendly giant of a man, a rugby full back from the top of his fair-haired head all the way to his massive feet. His shoulders practically filled our narrow doorway and his legs protruded at least a foot from the bottom of his bed.

George was full of fun and I have to thank him for shaking me from my melancholy and giving me back my usual cheery disposition. The son of a coalmine owner, he was educated at Rugby. Fortunately, though, the snobbery that sometimes accompanies middle class boys educated at boarding school seemed to have passed him by. He was as down to earth as any lad from the farm and I fell in love with him instantly.

Nevertheless, I was guarded in showing any sign of adulation. George was masculine to his fingertips. He drank in the Blue Boar Hotel in Trinity Street and chased the local lady shop assistants. In fact, by the middle of the term he had bedded two young things who worked at the Home and Colonial, and a hairdresser from across the street. George was a towering Don Juan and no girl could resist him. Oh! How I envied them as I listened to the stories of George's conquests.

Now that I had regained my old self, I was pleased to discover my interest in carnal pursuits had also returned, although to satisfy my desires in Cambridge was not as easy as it was at school. Clandestine, amorous encounters were normal but took place in dusk laden parks or murky public lavatories. Nevertheless, as the first term progressed, I discovered a well-guarded secret society within the university, which covered its covert sexual activities by masquerading as a political debating society.

Back in those days Trinity seemed to attract the bohemian and the outrageous but my star paled in the light exuding from the likes of Harry Philby or Ludwig Wittgenstein, the former would explore Arabia in later life, while Wittgenstein became a famous German philosopher.

At parties, I was the fellow who sat deep in a leather sofa, puffing on his pipe, listening but never remembering, instead of commanding centre stage with acerbic wit and loquacious machinations. Even then I realised I was hardly going to change the world with a personal philosophy or a political dictum. I was destined to be a follower and not a thinker or a leader of men.

During my second year at Trinity, and a month before I went down for the summer holiday, dramatic news from Sarajevo would postpone my academic life for almost a decade.

Chapter Three
Somerset Light Infantry - The Aquarium

It was a stifling day in early August when I enlisted into the Somerset Light Infantry, otherwise affectionately known as 'The Prince Albert's'. A church hall on the Lower Bristol Road had been requisitioned for the purpose, an orderly queue of potential conscripts formed outside. War with Germany had been declared and every man and youth was eager to join up, completely unaware of the terrible scenes of carnage and horror they were about to witness during the subsequent four years.

I found myself standing behind a young man who introduced himself as Conner Riddlington who, coincidentally, had skipped university to join up except he was an Oxford man. In addition, since he was a law student, we had a great deal to talk about as we drew closer to the door of the church hall.

On reaching the front of the queue, a gruff sergeant summoned me to a desk where a cheerful young officer recorded my name, age, address, as well as the address and name of my next of kin on a form. I swore the oath, and then joined my fellow recruits in an army lorry, which drove us to billets in Prior Park, south of the city, where we undertook basic training for almost three months.

My choice of regiment was The Somerset light Infantry for no other reason than pride for my county. Father always spoke proudly of 'The Prince Albert's' recounting some of the regiment's prominent conflicts over the past one hundred years. I hoped to see plenty of action when we finally joined the conflict.

Due to my university background and my status, after basic training, on the seventh of October, nineteen fourteen, I was gazetted, Second Lieutenant. Subsequently, on the twelfth of December, on a foggy morning, our company of four hundred men scrambled out of a train at Southampton Docks and climbed aboard the transport ship SS Saturnia, which would convey us to India. It was Lord Kitchener, I would discover later, who decided on our destination. He asked our commander, Colonel Hugh Frank Buckmaster, to form a second line battalion in order to relieve troops in India, thus enabling them to boost the forces fighting in France. This resulted in two years of comparative boredom until we were finally able to enter the thick of the action.

On the same day in October, there were seven other chaps gazetted to lieutenants and for the following month, we shared two cramped cabins until finally reaching Bombay. At this juncture, may I add that if you are wondering whether I enjoyed this close proximity to my own sex? I can tell you with complete honestly, it was possibly the worst, as well as the best thirty-six days I have ever spent.

When men find themselves in such circumstances all sense of respectability and dignity seems to vanish. Although my fellow passengers could boast a host of good schools and colleges, given the absence of land, also the company of women, they began to behave in a most abandoned and loutish way.

Alcohol was outlawed. Despite the ship's bar being fully stocked, no soldier of any rank was officially allowed to imbibe. In less than twenty-four hours at sea however, several of my chums had already bribed the steward to secrete a bottle of whiskey or two in our cabin. I must admit, I joined in the fun and even told tall stories of female encounters and conquests just so I might fit in.

The day began with reveille on the main deck. Six o'clock on a cold, dark, December morning, standing in a biting wind while the roll call is taken is not a pleasing experience. On any one of these mornings, as we navigated the English Channel and the Bay of Biscay, it was almost guaranteed to drizzle, so we were glad of our thick khaki great coats and peaked caps.

If the day brightened, the lieutenants took turns leading the men in morning exercise or gun drill, which passed the time until dinner. I might add the food was splendid. Our ship was a Royal Mail Steamer bound eventually for Australia. She carried fare paying passengers as well as troops; as a result, her larders and stores were crammed with the best produce to sustain her passengers and crew for the long voyage.

Officers took their meals in the first class dining saloon, therefore it was here at breakfast, and after our first night at sea, I met Fredrick Barnhoff, a captain in our outfit. Strangely, and in a beneficial way, his life would mingle with mine far beyond the present conflict.

"India's a bit out of the way Captain Barnhoff," I said as he and I devoured eggs, bacon and cups of sweet tea. "I hoped to see more of the action."

"I agree. But please, call me Fritz; everyone does. Since I resigned my commission in nineteen eleven, I've been sitting on my backside in my father's factory. When this blew up, I was pleased to join the old battalion again. But India! What are we going to do there?"

I shook my head.

"Sit it out till we're needed, I suppose. What's the factory?"

A steward was passing our table and Fritz snapped his fingers.

"Another pot!" he called and the steward hurried away.

"Soap Factory. Across the river, opposite where I live."

"Where's that?"

I have always been a curious, almost nosey, sort of chap. I put it down to my insatiable interest in my fellow man.

"Wildsbridge," Fritz said, "The factory's in Keynsham; on the other side of the Avon."

"I know Wildsbridge. Pretty village. Nice old church and a good pub. The Wheatsheaf."

The steward was back with a fresh pot of tea and placed it on the table.

"Would there be anything else Captain?" he asked.

"Yes. We'll have some more toast. You'd like some wouldn't you Lieutenant Fry."

"Yes please Fritz. But pardon me, as I'm on first name terms with you, could you call me Ron?"

"Of course my dear chap," Fritz laughed, "Ron it is."

There and then, a friendship was formed between us that would last for almost two years.

Since I had never been further afield than the occasional fishing trip to Norway, the exciting experience of seeing Gibraltar, Naples, Port Said and Colombo, was intoxicating to my young senses. Moreover, since our ship required coal, these ports were necessary stops, so the time given to refuel allowed us a few hours to explore.

Gibraltar reminded me of a minute version of an English country town, even down to the red telephone and post boxes. The Rock swarmed with soldiers and sailors, so for me, with a liking for a uniform of any description, there were constant distractions. I was cautious though not to allow my companion sightseers to see my attention drawn in that particular direction.

It would have been preferable to wander the narrow streets and secluded parks alone, with the hope of encountering a stranger who might have similar thoughts. However, the sane part of me realised how dangerous this might be, considering The Rock carried a strong force of Military Police. Consequently, as we toured the Gun Galleries and climbed, almost to the summit of The Rock itself, I stuck with my friends, while we explored the ruins of an old Moorish castle and found two massive guns, commanding the Straits of Gibraltar. We could easily see the coast of Africa from the galleries, as it was a lovely day, the distance across the Straits being just ten miles. Sooner or later, and practically exhausted we returned to the safety and security of the ship.

Several more days at sea and after a brief stop at Palma, we steamed into the Mediterranean. Here we experienced a marked change in the weather, as it turned balmy with cool mornings, but hot days and warm nights.

We navigated The Straits of Boniface, between Corsica and Sardinia, then, passing Elba, one time prison of Napoleon Bonaparte, and another island stronghold, Monte Cristo, made famous by Dumas, finally the ship entered the Bay of Naples, dominated and overshadowed by the vastness of Vesuvius. I considered this the most beautiful scenery I had ever seen. From the sea, the city looked pretty with a fortress and monastery on the crown of the hill, high above the harbour.

All these romantic judgments were suddenly marred however, as we passed the breakwater and nudged our way between vessels of all descriptions. There is an adage that immediately springs to mind, 'Smell Naples and Die', and I am afraid whoever coined the phrase is completely correct.

The ship tied up at the dock, where those of us who were going ashore surged down the gangway. As soon as we were on dry land, urchin boys and youths selling cheap souvenirs surrounded us. They looked awfully poor. Almost like beggars; some with nasty sores on their faces. I felt it would be unwise to buy a gift from any of them. I discovered I was standing beside Conner Riddlington, the young man who enlisted with me.

"Come on," he said. "Let's get out of here."

He seemed to know where he was going and swiftly ushered me on to a crowded omnibus pulled by a sullen horse. We paid the conductor and sat down. As our bus careered and rattled its way into the heart of the city, I noticed how dirty and decrepit the streets and houses were, commenting thus to Conner.

"Lately the city has suffered terribly from earthquakes," he replied. "Also, Cholera has been rife. For the most part, the people are extremely poor. They scavenge for anything they can get."

The shops and houses passing by, with their iron balconies and shuttered windows, were crumbling, some even encrusted with weeds. The streets were full of waste paper, rotting vegetables and heaven knows what else. Overwhelming everything was a pervasive stench of detritus, the odour so disgusting I have never forgotten it from that day to this.

Soon our omnibus left this district of the city and entered a more opulent suburb, the streets lined with grand mansions, villas, and parks. It was here that Conner nudged me, and he and I clambered off at the next stop.

While riding we spoke little, my attention taken by the people, sights and smells surrounding me. However, I did manage to glean something from Conner that hardly surprised me. He had visited Naples before.

"One summer a friend and I stayed. He was mad keen on Pompeii."

I remarked that I had only seen photographs of the hapless city, and how chilling it was to see the figures frozen in stone, demonstrating the agony of their last moments alive.

The road we walked was shady and lined with trees where I found the neatness of the villas impressive. The balconies, seen over their high walls and iron gates, tumbled with riotous bougainvillea and geraniums. So different to the shabbiness of what I had seen earlier.

A while later, arriving at the Opera House, judging by the grand hotels and smart shops, it was obvious we had reached the heart of the city.

"You'll like to see the Galleria Umberto Primo," said Conner. "If you wish to buy a souvenir, you'll find the best shops there."

As we strolled down the marble tiled arcade, beneath tiered limestone architecture and the fancy ironwork and glass roof, Conner and I chatted. Although I began to notice him continually engaged by the people passing by. Curiously, the focus of his attention and the reason for his obvious lack of interest in the conversation was not the items in the shop windows, but invariably handsome young men. For the whole time we shared a cabin it never crossed my mind I would have a like-minded fellow travelling companion. Whether or not they were soldiers, with over four hundred men aboard, it was more than likely one or two might share my sympathy. Nevertheless, I scarcely expected him to be sleeping in the bunk opposite to mine. As a result, I dared to broach the subject by making a rather brave statement.

"Dam good-looking these Latin men. Don't you think?" I said.

At first, Conner made no sign that he heard me and we continued walking, although, I did feel a kind of electricity suddenly happen between us.

"Yes," he said, as he stopped to look in a shop window at an array of coral and cameos. "Although the older men seem to coarsen with age. But the young are most handsome."

Almost immediately, we were outside the arcade and in a grand avenue of expensive shops seething with people, trams, and horse buses.

"This is the Via Roma," Conner said. "The finest street in Naples. I'll show you the Villa Nationale. It's only a little way away."

We continued in silence, as the hubbub of Neapolitan life teemed around us, until we reached a low balustrade bordering the entrance to a large park.

"This place is most agreeable," Conner said. "Let's see what we might discover."

By the tone of Conner's voice, we were hardly entering the park to find rare and exotic species of flora. Nonetheless, I remained silent and followed him through the gates and into the cool, lush greenery.

The paths were edged with flowers and shrubs, some of which were unknown to me. However, as we strolled, I quickly realised that all the passers-by were male and of a similar age. The park was a meeting place, a place of 'Dangerous Liaisons', of which I had been so afraid in the previous port of call.

"Conner! What are we doing here?" I asked, as another mysterious young man slid by. "Surely it's not wise. We don't know the language, and they might be in league with the police."

Conner laughed.

"As to the language Ronald," he said. "As you well know it's unwritten. But I do know a few words and phrases, although just a wink or a look is usually enough. Regarding the police, we'll have to look out, won't we."

We arrived at a wooden pergola, where at intervals, seats ranged along its length. The structure was completely enveloped in wisteria and several young men sat in the dappled shade of pale violet blossoms.

Unperturbed, Conner pushed on, urging me with his shoulder, until we were in the heart of the exotic, erotic tunnel. For me, looking back at this point in my life, and nowadays being a man of experience in such circumstances, I should have taken everything in my stride. Given it was a hot sultry morning in Naples however, a city whose ways and habits were entirely alien to me, I felt unprepared as well as a little fearful of what might occur.

Yet my friend was completely in command. He proved it by casually sitting down on one of the seats directly opposite two youths, who scowled handsomely in the sunlight. No one spoke, the sound of the cicadas in the surrounding trees, deafening. Several minutes passed, but I dared not look at my watch. My eyes were fixed on the ground or on Conner, who was brazenly staring at the lads. Despite Conner's obvious intention, their eyes never caught his. Rather, they shifted from left to right, or over Conner's shoulder, to a nowhere land amongst the greenery. It was Conner, who finally broke the stalemate.

"Boun Giorno," he said.

The youth's reaction was immediate and they nodded a reply.

"Il mio amico ed io," Conner continued, "ti piacerebbe essere le nostre guide turistiche?"

My Italian is far from good, but I think I understood him to say that he wished the young men to be our tour guides. The one who appeared to be the eldest smiled and made a gesture with his thumb and forefinger.

"He want's money," I said, rather naively.

"Certemente," Conner said, ignoring me. "Ma soprattutto vorrei che per trovare un posto dove il mio amico e potrei arrivare a conoscerti meglio."

What Conner said I had no idea, nonetheless the expression on the youth's faces confirmed that they certainly did, and glancing furtively about, they got to their feet and sauntered away. Reaching the end of the pergola, they stopped, which was obviously our cue to follow. So we left the seat and strolled towards them. However, as we drew closer they began to amble away and disappeared around the corner of a large building reminding me of a great white wedding cake.

"Do you like fish?" Conner mumbled.

"What do you mean?" I said, since it was early, and nowhere near lunchtime.

"This is the Aquarium."

There was a ticket booth inside the entrance, although maybe due to the hour it was un-manned. So Conner and I walked in unhindered, but the youths had vanished.

"Where do you think they've gone?" I asked, looking around.

Conner shrugged. "Strange. I'm sure I saw them go in."

Inside, we arrived at a lobby where, under a low stucco ceiling, vaulted galleries led off to all four points of the compass, where fish tanks glimmered green and eerily luminescent. For no obvious reason, Conner and I chose the northern gallery, and approached the first window.

"What's in there?" I said, staring hard through the glass and murky water, seeing a group of slimy rocks, a pipe lying on its side and some trailing weeds. Conner read aloud the sign above the tank.

"Grongo"

"What's a Grongo?"

"Conger Eel."

I looked again, but still saw nothing.

"There it is," Conner said, tapping the glass. "Inside the pipe."

He was right. A massive eel was lurking there, looking menacing, and by the size of its head, I took it to be possibly nine feet long.

"It says," Conner continued, reading the sign. "An eel reaches sexual maturity at fifteen years of age and can live to be extremely old."

I shivered at the sight of the creature's half-open mouth and the rows of needle sharp teeth.

"Come on," I said. "What happened to the boys?"

We continued down the passage, glancing at various aquariums as we went, some teeming with marine life, others appearing empty. The end of the passage opened into a hall, which seemed to be devoted to larger fish, since I saw silhouettes of huge sharks, rays and turtles swimming about, lit from above by what appeared to be a skylight. One side of the hall opened onto a terrace.

"There they are!" exclaimed Conner.

Through the glazed doors, I saw them, one leaning on a balustrade while the other sat beside him, his heels kicking a baluster.

"My friend and I thought we'd lost you." Conner said as we came out into the sunshine.

They seemed unable to understand, but smiled and nodded all the same.

The four of us were alone. Yet I hardly imagined we were in an appropriate place for what was intended. It was obvious the young men were well acquainted with the surroundings, because the seated youth flicked his head to draw our attention to a gentleman's lavatory, the entrance half hidden in a wall of ivy.

At this point, I have to admit I became rather afraid. It was some time since my last encounter in Cambridge, which was dangerous to say the least. But I was now in a foreign country, and dealing with foreigners. Therefore, it was with an equal amount of reluctance and anticipation that I followed Conner through the arch of ivy.

Once we were standing at the urinals it was clear the lavatory was filthy, the stench of urine and faeces almost unbearable. I felt a sudden surge of nausea. Was this sordid act and moment of ecstasy and excitement worth this? It would all be over in a moment and Conner and I would continue with the day. We might visit the museum or art gallery and take lunch in a smart street café? What was the point in degrading ourselves in this cesspit for the sake of seeing a young man's genitals and feeling the rush of an orgasm. As the boys joined us and began to undo their fly buttons, I shook my head.

"Sorry Conner," I whispered. "This is not for me. I'll see you outside."

I fled the pigsty into the sunshine of the terrace. Undoubtedly, Conner had a stronger stomach than I, and perhaps more resolve, because it was at least a quarter of an hour before he finally emerged.

"Come on then," he said. "Let's go."

Suddenly, Conner was in a hurry to get away, like a thief who suddenly feels the guilt of what he has done and wishes to run as far as he can from the scene of the crime. Saying nothing, I followed him back through the aquarium and into the park.

Our route took us through the pergola of wisteria again, where we avoided the stares of ardent youths who had appeared since we were last there. I tried to begin a conversation.

"I'm sorry," I said. "I lost my nerve."

Conner laughed. "Don't be silly. We can't all be the same. Anyway, it's all right. I got two for the price of one."

I laughed, pleased that we were back to our old selves once more, and the incident was never spoken of again.

At this juncture, sorrowfully, I must acquaint you with the tragic fate of Conner Riddlington, who remained with the battalion until India, but was seconded into the first. On the sixteenth of February 1916, he sailed to Mesopotamia where he saw fierce fighting against the Turks. On the eighth of March, at Es Sinn, during the relief of Kut, Conner was killed while gallantly leading his company against a Turkish position. Conner was greatly admired for the unselfishness and conscientious way he carried out his duties.

Chapter Four
Port Said

After the SS Saturnia left Naples, an extended period at sea began, the daily routine continuing with roll call, breakfast, lunch, and dinner. Then exercise, gun cleaning and drill.

As a second lieutenant, I was responsible for my platoon numbering forty men. Even so, Sergeant Bellow, a long serving bombastic chap, conducted all the various drills, which left time to handle administrative issues.

As the lads in the ranks and I became better acquainted, they began to regard me as a father figure or a replacement older brother. Quite often, I became embroiled in a family issue happening back home that might concern a young man. In fact, sometimes the lads even asked me for advice. Therefore, it was hardly surprising that I became rather fond of them. They were a cheerful bunch, well intended and terribly attractive in a down to earth kind of way. Perhaps because I have an open manner, of which I am proud, they seemed to take me into their confidence. Despite this, my relationship with the lads remained platonic, and I say lads, since they were raw recruits, some barely seventeen.

Of course, I refer to platonic in the classical sense. As a man who has always been interested in the well-being of young men, I was familiar with the writings of Plato and his philosophy to promote the emotional and beneficial relationship, between mature men and young men.

As a result, the long days at sea, between Italy and North Africa, were made less tedious by spending time with the lads.

At nine in the morning on Boxing Day, we birthed alongside the Quay El Sultan Hussein at Port Said. Seeing it was Christmas, our commanding officer, Colonel Buckmaster ordered the officers ashore while the ship was coaled. I tagged along with Fritz Barnhoff and a couple of other chaps, as I decided they would be less sensation seeking than my friend Conner.

Stepping ashore, I realised for the first time that I was abroad and beyond anything that seemed familiar. Gibraltar and Naples were foreign and colourful, but here in North Africa I was suddenly in a country where people practiced a different religion and appeared exotic and mysterious. The native men dressed in turbans and long flowing robes. The women wore black, and some females completely covered their faces. Donkeys and camels, led by their drivers, lumbered along the dusty streets laden with goods of every description.

Somehow, Fritz and I lost the others and wandered obliviously into the Arab Quarter where we were given our first taste of the marvellous Middle East. In this part of town, the streets are lined with houses, soaring four or five storeys, each having a disorganised array of decorative wooden balconies, which seem to have neither rhyme nor reason. Some are open, others shaded by colourful striped blinds or awnings. I could barely imagine the teeming mass of humanity living in these tenements.

Walking the streets was an ordeal in itself. Benches and boxes displaying the shopkeeper's wares often blocked the colonnaded pavements. Here a pile of carpets. There a tower of earthenware pottery. So one had little choice, as the alternative was to dodge the carts and horses in the street, as well as face the glare and heat of the sun.

It was particularly interesting to see the stalls displaying beautiful oriental daggers encrusted with jewels, while others sold hubble-bubble pipes of every size and shape. Occasionally, a breeze blew through the narrow streets, carrying the smell of the sea and reminding us that we were close to the harbour and the mouth of the Suez Canal. Furthermore, suffusing the air was the scent of spice, as well as the enticing aroma of exotic food cooked by street vendors.

At one point, Fritz and I saw a horse drawn omnibus with quaint cotton curtains shading the passengers from the sun. Jumping on board, we paid a paltry fare and let it take us where it would, until we saw a large hotel called The Great Eastern Exchange and hopped off and went inside.

"Do you know Fritz," I said, as we sat in the bar drinking glasses of cold beer. "I can't get over the fact it's Boxing Day. Who would believe that this time last year we'd be here! I wonder what the time is in England. What do you think our folks are doing?"

"Just waking up I should think. We're four hours ahead of Great Britain."

Fritz was a clever fellow. He knew exactly what, where, when, and how. In addition, unlike me, a Farmborough boy, he must have made the most of his Clifton College education. Invariably our conversation turned to Somerset as we swapped boyhood memories of Bath and the surrounding countryside.

"Father's German," Fritz said, as he lit our cigarettes. "Well Prussian actually."

"Is there a difference?" I asked naively.

"Of course! I reckon we were once aristocracy, but I've never gone into it."

At the time, I remembered thinking Fritz could well be correct. He did have quite an aristocratic bearing. He was tall, possessing a rather long face, hooded eyes, and a small neatly clipped sandy coloured moustache, which matched his hair.

"I've never been to Germany," he continued. "And, more than likely never will now all this has blown up. I'm only glad our surname doesn't sound too German. People think its Barnorth and I don't correct them."

There were few instances of racial disharmony at this early stage of the war. However, when the casualty lists began to be published the situation radically altered for Germans residing in Great Britain.

Soon it was time for Fritz and I to finish our drinks and return to the ship. So we climbed aboard another omnibus, which dropped us at the quay where, with coaling over, the last of the stores were coming aboard. With the ship still tied up, I spent the remainder of the afternoon reading in the cabin, and then headed to the dining saloon. However, in the early hours of the following morning I awoke to feel the vibration of the engines and the motion of the ship. We were under way once more.

The next morning the view through the porthole was strange to say the least, as all one saw from one's bunk was a great wall of sand slowly passing by. After breakfast, a few of us went on deck to watch the ship edge her way along the narrow waterway. We all agreed that the pilot was doing a tremendous job guiding us through without mishap.

It took most of the day to reach Suez where, by the evening, we entered the Red Sea, the scenery on either shore, spectacular; rugged mountains to port, towering above the coast of Arabia, while to starboard; Nubia and Africa.

Later, at Aden, we made our last coaling stop where it impressed me to see the town huddled inside the walls of a massive volcanic crater. Once refuelled, we sailed on, and several hours later, entered The Arabian Sea.

Not since the Mediterranean, had we been out of sight of land. Now however we were on the final leg of the voyage and we were well and truly at sea, with nothing but horizon for three hundred and sixty degrees.

The weather became warmer after Suez and we were relieved to exchange our heavy khakis for light drill. Even so, the air over the sea was thick and humid, the officers and men grabbing any bit of shade within which to sprawl as we endeavoured to stay cool. We were also grateful for the small, outdoor, swimming pool, which, needless to say, became very overcrowded.

Chapter Five
Bombay, Calcutta and beyond

Our first experience of Bombay was surprisingly not the sight, but the smell, coming to us on an easterly breeze, off an open sea and an empty horizon. The stench, which I can only describe as a mixture of drains, human effluent and curry, invaded the decks and the very bowels of the ship. I still find it strange to think that the visions and aromas of India would become so familiar to me, I would yearn for and endeavour to recall them for the rest of my life.

Eventually, on the morning of January eighth, the coastline of India appeared, like a stain between sky and sea. SS. Saturnia dropped anchor in Back Bay, before steaming around the point and into the harbour. We tied up at Alexandra Dock, where the remainder of the day was spent unloading baggage and supplies. In the evening, each Lieutenant mustered his platoon and the men marched down the gangway and assembled in ranks on the quayside.

Had I a camera, I would possess a treasured memento of that magnificent gathering. Except I only have memories to help describe the picture. Four hundred officers and men, each wearing cotton drill and white pith helmets, standing to attention, as the band played the regimental march, with the Sergeant Major barking his commands. Next, we marched to the Victoria Terminus Station of the Great Indian Peninsula Railway where we boarded a train. Tea was served to every man, and as no one had eaten since breakfast, we waited for something to eat; however, nothing materialised.

Finally, at almost midnight, we shunted away from the platform and began the long journey to Bangalore.

Once we left the outskirts of Bombay, the train took a gradual ascent into the surrounding hills. The route however, must have been arduous since our progress was terribly slow, with many twists and turns in the track. Sitting beside me, Fritz Barnhoff explained that, had it been daylight, we would have enjoyed the scenery, which he said was quite spectacular. He called the mountains The Ghats, explaining they were a huge range of mountains bordering the western edge of the Indian continent. Unfortunately, I could only imagine the deep ravines, tumbling waterfalls, numerous tunnels and lofty bridges that were passing us by in the dead of night.

As the train climbed higher, the colder we became, so we were grateful for the blanket we had scoffed at in the heat of Bombay. The wooden carriages were more akin to cattle wagons than a conveyance for human beings, every inch of bench space packed with hungry soldiers, huddling together, while the icy wind howled through every crack and crevice. It was a nightmare journey. We rumbled and rolled along, but no one slept as each man endeavoured to find a comfortable position.

Thankfully nightmares end, and at seven o'clock the following morning we arrived at our destination. Eagerly, yet exhausted, we piled onto the platform, where we formed ranks and were pleased to see tea and sandwiches being passed around. Sergeant Bellows mustered my platoon, and to the accompaniment of a native band, we began the three-mile march to the barracks.

The infantry barracks were as pretty as a picture. Two story stone buildings, possessing wide verandas, surrounded a sandy parade ground, all set in the midst of wide spreading trees. Infantrymen were quartered in barrack dormitories on the ground floor, while officers shared the accommodation above. Our rooms were sparsely furnished, with two iron bedsteads, folded sheets, two blankets and a couple of pillows. Everything piled on a flock mattress, while two cupboards and a washstand concluded the fittings; altogether, perfectly adequate for the needs of a soldier.

My colleague in the billet was Second Lieutenant John Gater. Since I was twenty-three at the time, and this was the beginning of the second year of the war, John was required to be at least eighteen to enlist. Yet, I suspected he was younger, as he barely needed to shave.

Even though five years separated us, and we had never spoken on the voyage or on the train journey, from that day on we became great pals.

"Where in England are you from?" I asked, as we unpacked our kit bags.

"Charlton."

"Charlton, Somerset?"

"My dad's vicar of St. John's."

"That's extraordinary!" I said. "I've bicycled through your village many times. The vicarage is between the church and the post office."

"Yes! How funny you should know it."

John stopped folding his shirts, and looking up at me he smiled and suddenly I saw a vision of a boy running through a summer meadow, the sun shining on his golden hair and flashing in his blue eyes.

"What was your school?" I continued.

"Farmborough."

"No!" I shouted. "Me too! That's ridiculous. Which house? Mine was Cotton?"

"Morris."

"You must have arrived the term I left."

This amazing coincidence so astonished us we stopped unpacking and sat on the beds. If we were both honest, although we were thousands of miles from home, it was a comfort knowing we shared places and memories that were entirely our own.

"I was ready to go up to Oxford," John continued. "And this happened. So here I am. Do you think we'll stay in India for long? I'd rather be in the action."

"Everyone feels the same. Who knows? But all the same; here looks pretty nice."

Since by now you know quite a bit about me, you would be

correct in thinking that I was beginning to form quite a liking for this handsome young man. However, at the same time, I told myself to be careful.

In the following months, while we carried out garrison duties, we were rarely out of each other's company, spending our spare time in the English Officers Club; drinking at the bar; playing billiards, or simply jawing.

If truth were told, life was entirely pleasant. So enjoyable in fact we were beginning to forget that, on the other side of the world, a vicious war was raging. Now and again, we would receive snippets of news by way of the newspapers, but we were hardly conscious of the huge losses the British and French were encountering over in France and Belgium.

In late July 1915, six months after our arrival in India, we heard from our C.O., Colonel Buckmaster, that our battalion of the Fourth Somerset Light Infantry was to be unbrigaded and join the Eighth Indian Army. Around this time, we were ordered to pack our kit bags and prepare to move quarters. Wherever we were bound, it meant another long train journey, except this time we were heading northeast.

Owing to his rank, Fritz Barnhoff had the ear of his superiors. Therefore, as John, a few other officers and I were in the same compartment of the railway carriage, Fritz let it slip that we were on our way to Calcutta. All of us agreed it was obvious the British Army had no idea what to do with us.

After the peaceful surroundings of Bangalore to find ourselves embroiled in the heart of a seething mass of humanity was a dreadful shock to the system. Still, as the battalion marched from the railway station to Fort William, it was a relief to see we were making towards the Maidan, a large park, well away from the squalor of the shantytowns.

Standing as it does on the eastern bank of the River Hooghly, Fort William is impressive, and especially so when viewed from the west. Built almost at the beginning of the British residence in India, there has never been a canon fired in anger or defence from its battlements. Despite the grandeur, after the informal atmosphere of

Baird Barracks in Bangalore, I considered Fort William to be rather overwhelming.

It was taken for granted that John Gater and I would share a room, although the quarters at the fort were far superior to Bangalore. We were surprised, as well as delighted, to discover our room possessed a ceiling fan and there were bathrooms on every landing.

While in Bangalore, John and I acquired a pair of bicycles. As a result, and mainly to relieve the boredom, once our garrison duties were complete, we escaped into the neighbouring countryside, where we were surprised to see how lush everything appeared. The reason being, the battalion had arrived between the bi-annual monsoons.

Large areas around Bangalore are utilised for grazing dairy cows, or growing rice and vegetables, with orchards abounding in a great assortment of fruits. Interestingly, throughout the region, there are countless lakes, called tanks, created by damming the waterways, the largest being Ulsoor Lake, a short distance northeast of Bangalore. Ulsoor Lake became a favourite destination for John and me, since surrounding it are numerous ancient temples, which had become our passion.

Once we were settled into our new Calcutta quarters, John and I decided to resume our excursions. Fritz Barnhoff had recently acquired a battered old motorcar, so one day I asked him if we might borrow it. As a result, with John driving, we were able to continue our explorations.

Somewhere in the scrub or forest, we inevitably stumbled upon an ancient temple, usually overwhelmed by vines and creepers. As a kind of diversion, I set us both a challenge.

Almost always, the crumbling walls were decorated with chiselled friezes depicting men and women in the act of lovemaking. So the contest was to find the most erotic scene, the man doing so, standing the other a drink in the club that night.

Being just twenty-three, I still had only a limited knowledge of sexual imagery. After every holiday, a boy at school, whose father was an ambassador in Paris, took the ferry across the channel, back from France to England. By some means, he was able to avoid custom searches at Dover and secrete French pornographic postcards in his luggage.

With an obvious eye for business, the lad rented out the images for cash, and as you can imagine the postcards became increasingly worn as the term continued. The boy was particularly popular and we could hardly wait for the end of the holidays to return to school for the latest consignment.

At Trinity, I became acquainted with the work of Baron Wilhelm von Gloeden. His impeccable photographs of Sicilian youths, striking classical poses were seen openly in reputable English photography magazines. However, the pictures displayed in German magazines were far more explicit and prized by undergraduate devotees of young male beauty.

One day at Cambridge, while a student colleague and I were studying in the Wren Library, he drew my attention to a very large book containing the illustrations of Aubrey Beardsley. Admittedly, I found them erotic but the exaggeration of certain parts of the human form, I thought rather fanciful.

Therefore, anticipating the first glass of cold beer, John and I would hunt through the undergrowth, pushing away branches and greenery to uncover the next lurid scenic act of love illustrated in stone.

One rainy afternoon in August, John and I returned from such an excursion to find the barracks in a frenzy of preparation. Apparently, while we were gadding around the countryside, the battalion received orders to get ready to ship out. This time we were joining a ship at Kiddapore Dock that would convey us to the Andaman Islands, which to be quite honest I had never heard of.

The voyage southeast across the Bay of Bengal took almost a week and was hot, humid and uneventful. The battalion eventually disembarked on Ross Island, the main island in the Andaman Group, where we were garrisoned in the barracks at Port Blair. Close by, was the notorious Cellular Prison where the British Government began incarcerating Indian political prisoners, provoking rumours of beatings, torture, suicide and illegal hangings. You might be right in wondering what the second battalion of the Fourth Somerset Light

Infantry was doing in such a place, and I can honestly say that we were asking ourselves the same question.

Despite our obvious dissatisfaction at the posting, the beauty of the island scenery, as well as the hospitality of the resident Indian and British ex pat families overwhelmed us.

Suddenly, we were in a tropical paradise with a sea the colour of turquoise, teeming with multi coloured fish swimming amongst kaleidoscopic coral. Beaches of white sand, bordering fringes of tall palm trees from which coconuts fell in abundance, while towers of limestone soared from azure blue lagoons. In fact, if the Garden of Eden was a reality, then Adam and Eve were Andaman natives. Although, in fact these were pygmies and the prettiest of people, with the blackest skin I had ever seen.

Yet there was an aspect of these natives that was even darker than their skin, since it was rumoured they were cannibals. Perhaps not the natives who lived on the main islands, and in close proximity to the Europeans. However, the Andaman's were extensive and we were told it was dangerous to go ashore on some of the more remote islands.

Regardless of the disadvantages, I soon saw the benefits of life on Ross Island. Ex-patriots, desperate for news of home, as well as the company of new faces, quickly swooped upon my fellow officers and me. As a result, there were invitations to balls; beach parties; tennis matches; dances, and dinner parties. By the end of the first month, we were quite exhausted.

The men in the ranks occupied the fort, while the officers were allocated bungalows and, since they were situated on the top of the cliffs, commanded delightful views over the Andaman Sea. Once again, John and I bunked together and enjoyed many evenings drinking whiskey and watching the sunset.

Life was extremely balmy, except, in the back of my mind, there was always a nagging guilt. In France, Tommy was taking it hard, facing bullets and shellfire, while we lounged in the club, drinking cocktails or swimming in the pool, and all because of a push of the pen in Whitehall. Our Eden nonetheless was not to last. The following January we received orders to return to Calcutta once again, packing our kit bags and marching to the jetty where a ship was waiting to convey us back to India.

We had only just returned to Calcutta when Fritz Barnhoff became ill, and was rushed to the Military Hospital. It appeared to be food poisoning, but that type of symptom is quite common in a country where the sanitation is poor and the local food is spicy. Truthfully, we suspected something more serious and waited anxiously for news.

Several days passed and we heard nothing. A fellow officer, Captain Foxcroft, visited the hospital, returning to tell us that Fritz was critically ill and was not expected to survive. Therefore, we prepared for the worst, which inevitably occurred.

At this point, I have to admit I used my influence and wealth to bring about an arrangement, which I never had cause to regret.

Since Captain Foxcroft was a friend of the Barnhoff family, he candidly told me after Fritz died, that he was unhappy for Fritz to be buried in a foreign grave. As a result, and unbeknown to the Captain, I had a word with the director of the Standard Bank, who kindly released to me an adequate amount of cash, enabling Captain Foxcroft to return Fritz to his family. It was embarrassing giving the money to the Captain, but he received it sympathetically and proceeded to arrange for Fritz to be embalmed and placed in a coffin ready to make the long journey home; such an unhappy end for a gallant officer and a fine comrade.

Sadly, I was about to lose another friend.

Several weeks later John Gater received orders to transfer to the Sixth Jat Light Infantry, an Indian regiment comprised of Sikhs.

John and I said a sad farewell at the station and I watched him board a train for Bombay and thence to Karachi, where he joined a ship that would convey him to Basra, in Mesopotamia.

At the end of the war, and after learning of John's death I paid a visit to his mother and father at Charlton to offer my sympathy. Reverend Gater read me a letter he had received from John's commanding officer, Major FME Kennedy. It told how the sixth Jats Light Infantry joined the Tigres Corp as part of the defence of Basra. On the 25th March 1916, during an attack on the besieged town of

Kut el Amara, John was killed by Turkish shellfire. He was nineteen years old.

Chapter Six
Citipur Flying School - Action at last - X Aircraft Park Abbassia

For the remainder of 1916 and part of 1917, our battalion was shifted from one outpost to another as various regiments were sent to France to increase the depleting numbers of soldiers. The Secretary of War, Earl Kitchener had been heard to say, 'I require white soldiers to replace white soldiers.'

In May, we travelled to Lahore where we remained until August. Then we moved to Poona, and subsequently Lucknow where, in September, the battalion received exciting news. We were to prepare to leave India and sail for the Middle East and Palestine. However, while stationed at Lucknow, I discovered a previously unknown talent and that was dissembling and assembling engines.

Not far from the city, in a town named Citipur, an Army Flying School had been established. In the war in France, aircraft were becoming increasingly important and it appeared the British Government considered India to have a suitable terrain where men could learn to fly. As a result, a squadron of BE2 Aircraft was flown to the school to provide training machines for new pilots. Because the Royal Flying Corp, as it was then known, was part of the British Army, the officers of our battalion, as well as those of the Royal Flying Corp, shared the same club. I became pals with a mechanic from the Aircraft Park and soon was stripping down aircraft engines during routine repairs and services. At last, I found an occupation that could while away the otherwise boring hours of garrison duties. I enjoyed the work so much that I asked my Commanding Officer if I could be seconded to the Flying Corp and to my delight, my request was granted. Consequently, when the Somerset Light Infantry quit Lucknow, I remained behind.

Remarkably, several weeks later, my new outfit received orders to train to Bombay where we would join my old battalion on a ship, which would take us to the Middle East.

The next phase of my war lasted a little more than a year, from September 1917 until Armistice Day on the 30th October 1918. It was 1919 however before finally I was put on the unemployed list and sent home; although, during those last thirteen months I contributed to the war in a far greater way than the previous three years.

In Palestine, by utilising his immense experience, General Allenby was proving extremely effective in his push north towards Jerusalem; on the 9th December, the third attempt to capture Gaza was successful, the Turks finally driven out of the city. Major T.E.Lawrence, who I had the great pleasure meeting in Cairo, with the help of the Arab League, had taken Aqaba and Damascus. Therefore, if truth were told, the British and French were doing far better in The Middle East than their counterparts in France and Belgium.

X Aircraft Park in Abbassia, between Heliopolis and Cairo, was a hive of activity, since stationed there was No 14 Squadron, Royal Flying Corp. Also No 1 Squadron, Australian Flying Corp, with further squadrons based at two large supply depots, Deir el Belah and Mustabig on the Mediterranean coast, east of Port Said.

My headquarters were in Abbassia, at the Aircraft Park in the Engine Repair Depot. I was in charge of supplies and a group of skilled aero engine mechanics. Since I was closely involved, I became friends with several pilots, one of whom was Australian, Lieutenant Adrian Cole.

On one occasion, while I was supervising the establishment of a new base at Ismalia, King Cole, as he was affectionately nicknamed around the base, asked whether I would care to join him on a dawn reconnaissance flight.

"You'll love it!" he shouted as we hurried to the airplane, while pulling on our flying helmets and goggles. "Have you been up before?"

"No!" I yelled. "I've no idea what to expect."

"There's a Lewis gun mounted in the observer seat. Use it if we meet any trouble."

Squinting in the early morning sun, I saw King clamber on to the wing of the RE8 machine and hoist himself into the cockpit, and doing the same I climbed into the seat behind him. King made this manoeuvre look easy, however, being considerably taller, my legs tangled with everything, until I finally settled into position.

"Ready!" King called to the three mechanics on the ground. One man pulled down the propeller and the engine burst into life.

"Take em away!"

The other two men dragged back the wooden wedges under the wheels and the plane began to move. With our speed increasing, we turned towards the rising sun and into the wind, while the ground passed faster and faster beneath us. All of a sudden, the vibration of the wheels stopped and I realised we were in the air. I felt exhilarated, letting out a great whoop of joy as my stomach hit the seat.

We climbed steeply, until I could see the rugged desert hundreds of feet below and distant mountains, miles ahead.

Once the plane reached altitude, King pushed the stick forward and we levelled out.

"Are you okay?" he yelled.

"Fine!" I shouted. "It's incredible!"

"Are you strapped in?"

"Yes. Why?"

"Watch out."

Without warning, King turned the plane into a steep dive, the engine screaming in reply as we dipped so low I saw our reflection in a wadi beneath us. Then up we climbed again and the sky was in front and above us, all the while my stomach doing cartwheels.

"My word!" I shouted, the wind attempting to whip my breath away. "Marvellous! When the war's over, I'm taking pilot training.

I've missed my vocation."

Whether King heard me or not I had no idea, because at that moment he looped the loop and once more headed towards the ground. At the exact last minute however, King pulled back the joystick and the plane responded by soaring upward, until we reached an altitude where I found it hard to breath.

"Just thought I'd give you a whirl, mate!" hollered King. "To give you a taster."

We flew on heading northeast, over rocky ranges, deep wadis and vast deserts, until King pointed to the horizon ahead.

"That's Tel el Sheria. It's a watering place held by the Turks. They want us to take photographs."

He turned and pointed to a box mounted on the side of the plane.

"It's a camera. The other bloke takes the pictures, so you may as well. Wait until we're close. They want to see the railway. When we're over it, take a few shots. The shutter lever's on the right side. I'll make three or four passes."

Keeping the sun to our right, we continued flying north. However, before long, several low hills appeared and finer details came into focus. A peaceful scene; one small railway station, a brick bridge across a wide valley, numerous bell tents pitched in the sand, many horses tethered together, and smoke from campfires drifting into the brightening sky. Although looking east and west it was disturbing to see the lines of trenches and heavy artillery disappearing in either direction.

"The Turkish Lines!" King yelled, over the noise of the engine. "Can you see the railway?"

He pointed beyond the guns to the terrain ahead, where a train track was under construction and vanishing behind a ridge.

"It'll link with the Gaza-Beersheba railway. If it's finished it'll connect with Shellal and be a vital supply line for the Turks. It's important we bomb it soon."

Our plane was almost above the half-finished track, so I put my eye to the viewfinder and my finger on the shutter lever. I was just about to take a picture when the plane shuddered violently as a shell exploded beneath us. King veered away from the shrapnel falling all around and made a sudden dive.

"Did you take one?" he shouted.

"No."

"I'll go around again. You'll need to be quick. The bastards have seen us."

As we made a second pass another shell burst, this time to our left, but I was able to click the shutter three times before King pulled us up and out of range.

"Let's have a go at them!" he yelled.

My body rattled with excitement. It had been three long years and I was about to fire a gun at last, and not just at a practice target, but also at the enemy.

"We'll dive!" King, yelled. "Are you ready mate?"

"Yes!" I shouted.

It was doubtful whether King heard me over the scream of the engine, so I grabbed the Lewis Gun clamped to the side of my cockpit, rammed the butt plate into my armpit, and found the trigger. With my eye on both the front and back sites, I saw the Turkish guns coming rapidly nearer, the gun crews scattering in all directions. We made a great sweep over their heads, I pulled the trigger, and the gun burst into life, firing round after round across the enemy lines.

King turned the plane in a great victory roll as we headed towards the cluster of tents and the tethered horses. The Turks were in a fright, scurrying around, endeavouring to organise themselves into an offensive. Unperturbed, King pushed the joystick to the left pointing us directly at the horses, and then dived so low I swore I could smell them. The terrified animals hurtled about, broke their tethers, and escaped the holding pens.

"Well done mate!" King shouted, as we soared into a climb. "Did you get any of them?"

"Don't know. Everything happened so fast."

King laughed.

"We better get back. We've got what we came for.

To be completely honest, I enjoyed the flight back to Ismalia more than I have enjoyed anything. By this time, I was so accustomed to the movement and sensation of weightlessness I was totally relaxed and confident, gazing around at the landscape passing below, all the while wondering at the beauty of nature. By now, the sun was higher and casting deep violet shadows across the arid yellow land, giving it an extra rugged appearance.

As we flew over the canal, I was quite sorry to see the smudge of Ismalia in the distance. Although King treated us to an exciting landing, crowning off the morning perfectly.

A month later, on the seventh of November, Tel el Sharia was the objective of a massive push by General Allenby to secure Gaza and onward to Jerusalem. The Australian Light Horse was involved in severe engagements with the Turks, in conjunction with the London Troops, capturing Tel el Sharia station with a bayonet charge.

Four weeks later, once Jerusalem was secured, the rout began for the Ottoman forces and they finally ceded defeat on 31st October 1918.

The following year, on a glorious day towards the end of August, myself plus three or four hundred soldiers boarded His Majesty's Transport 'Caledonia'.

The British Government was using every means possible to bring the lads home, since our ship was hardly large enough to accommodate the great number of returning forces. As a result, the quarters were overcrowded, even for the officers who in some cases were forced to share bunks. Despite the cramped conditions, the mood was jovial. We were going back to Blighty and the sea was kind. It was five years since my last encounter with the Mediterranean, consequently I was astonished to see the number of mines we came across, a few men having a jolly time shooting them out of the water.

Even so, the voyage was frustratingly slow, since the ship called at several ports to take on coal, plus further parties of soldiers. Eventually, conditions below decks became so bad a number of sergeants reported to their officers that their men were close to rioting. Fortunately, Malta was our last port of call before Gibraltar, where we only stopped for fuel.

Ten days later, on a beautiful September morning, we steamed into the English Channel, and my war was finally over. And, as my record states, on 19th October 1919, I officially joined the unemployed list.

Chapter Seven
Civvie Street - Hyde House

The station at Southampton's Ocean Dock was teeming with soldiers and unless one was ruthless and stood on the edge of the platform, it was impossible to get a seat on a train.

Luckily, I was in good company, since the day I left the Aero Supply Depot at Abbassia, my travelling companions were men from my unit. However, eventually it was time to say goodbye, since the train we crowded was bound for Waterloo and I had no desire to pass through London. As a result, I left my comrades at Winchester in order to make my onward journey to Bath.

It felt strange sitting alone in the first class carriage watching the English countryside go by the window. For five years I had been surrounded by my chums, hot sandy deserts, or open sea. Now alone, I was abruptly transported to a green land, which once was so familiar, but now appeared so strange.

Waiting on the platform at Didcot I was reminded how changeable the English weather can be, because it suddenly became extremely cold and began to drizzle. Therefore, I was prompted to join fellow travellers in the waiting room, and while huddling over a glowering fire I noticed I was the only man in uniform. Of course, I was proud to wear it, but was also keen to get back into civvies and on with my life.

Even though in a matter of hours, the day had changed from

sunny and warm, to cold and windy, the view from the window as the train pulled into Bath Spa station served to alleviate my gloom. After five years abroad, I had seen many marvellous sights, but had never forgotten how beautiful the panorama of Bath is in all weathers.

My reception at Royal Crescent was cordial. At Port Said I managed to post a card on an earlier ship, as a result, mother and father knew I was coming home. My brother Wilfred, however, was absent and on holiday from the Agricultural College in Cirencester, and away fishing in Norway.

Wilfred spent three years of the war in France, serving as a lieutenant with the Fifth Dragoon Guards. This surprised me since I never thought of him as an equestrian. He did see plenty of action nonetheless, as his regiment was responsible for killing over seven hundred German troops when they attacked a troop train at Harbonniers on the Somme. Wilfred was invalided out shortly before I returned. I am still not sure for what reason. He seemed perfectly fit and well when he came down the following Christmas.

For the remainder of the year I pitched myself into a daily routine, out of khaki and into tweeds. At eight o'clock every weekday morning, father's driver dropped me at Bath Spa station where I caught a train to Bristol's Temple Meads Station.

From there it was just a short taxi ride to the quayside and Fry's Sugarhouses.

Before my arrival from the Middle East, my father must have spoken to his elder brother, Sir George Fry, the managing director of the family business, Fry's Sugar, because there was a job and an office waiting for me on my return. Although he was my uncle, he was considerably older than father was and except for Fry social gatherings, I had little association with him. I was surprised; also, a little mystified to receive a memo one morning requiring me to visit him in his office forthwith.

"Take a seat, Ronald," said Sir George. "May I, on behalf of the family and the company, welcome you back to the fold after your gallant efforts. We can only thank our merciful saviour he has spared you in the struggle for liberty."

Immediately, I was reminded of my grandfather, Henry Oliver

Fry, after all, he was Sir George's father, the same short stature and round bearded face. The result of being born Victorians there was a hint of reserve about Sir George, an idiosyncrasy of my grandfather. In fact, during H O's time as director, he rarely spoke directly to any of his staff, preferring to send memos instead.

"Thank you Uncle George," I replied. "It's good to be home, although, with all the excitement of recent years it'll take a while to adjust to life back in Civvie Street."

"Quite," said Uncle George, offering me a cigarette. "Which brings me to why I've asked to see you this morning."

I leaned across his desk to light his, then lighting my own I sat down, intrigued to hear what he was about to say.

"I'm sure you're aware of the family's commitment to its staff and to the various institutions we support." Uncle George continued.

"Yes sir. Both my father and grandfather have been most generous benefactors."

"So now Ronald." He peered at me through his wire-framed spectacles. "It's time for you to do your bit. You were in Palestine were you not?"

I nodded.

"Magnificent job that Allenby did. His dispatches in The Times were most interesting. Did you have a good war Ronald?"

"Not bad sir. Rather tedious at the beginning but things livened up when we arrived in Egypt."

Never being known for his sense of humour, Uncle George appeared not to have heard me.

"While you boys were away the family continued to endow large sums to Bath hospitals, Bristol University, the local asylums, and Long Ashton Workhouse. It just so happens the chairman of governors of the workhouse rang me yesterday. He suggested one of the family's returned soldiers give a talk to the boys in the orphanage school. You immediately came to mind."

"Thank you, sir."

"They tell me you're a confident kind of chap. You'll be a jolly good speaker."

"It's kind of you to think so sir."

Uncle George and I shook hands and I returned to my office and my work. I say work, since the country was plunging into depression, with so many men now unemployed; it was rather a gesture giving the impression I was working.

My job was to manage the young office boys, whose task it was to put letters into window envelopes. To be honest, at the end of the week, I felt a pang of guilt each time I received a wage packet. After all, it was hardly necessary for me to work, since the shares I inherited from my grandfather, Henry Oliver when he died, were still worth a great deal and producing healthy dividends.

Despite this, I appeared every day, because it was better turning up to the office than loafing around Royal Crescent, getting under the servants' feet.

Then again, I rush ahead with my story and have almost forgotten to explain how I came to leave Royal Crescent and purchase my own home.

About a week after I returned to England, I had a sad duty to perform. As you may remember, Fritz Barnhoff, my fellow officer and friend, died in India from food poisoning and I promised myself, that on my return, I would offer my condolences to his widow.

My Father's driver drove me the few miles to Hyde House in the Somerset village of Wildsbridge, the Barnhoff residence, which immediately impressed me as a fine example of late nineteenth century Somerset architecture. Also retaining, just the right amount of quiet opulence to suit the unassuming Barnhoffs.

The butler led me into the drawing room, and left me alone while he informed Mrs Barnhoff of my arrival.

As I waited, I attempted to imagine my friend, Captain Barnhoff fitting into the chintz, walnut veneer, and porcelain of the room. Everything, from the wallpaper, upholstery, and draperies, was obviously inspired by a woman of taste. However, it was the view through the window that caught my attention. Beyond it, I could see a courtyard, entirely grassed, except edged by a paved pathway and low limestone balustrades.

Yet, what intrigued me most were two Doric temples at the northern corners since I had never seen the like and quickly decided they lent a pleasant, timeless serenity to the view.

"How do you do Captain Fry," Mrs Barnhoff said, hurrying into the room. "Please sit down. Do forgive me. I'm rather grubby. I've been in the garden, dead heading the roses. There's such a lot to do now autumn's here."

"Good morning Mrs Barnhoff," I said. "I was just looking at your garden. The temples are an interesting feature."

"Temple Court is one reason why Fritz and I were so taken with the house. That and the garden. Fritz loved roses you see. He planted the rose garden. It's been so lovely this year. He would have adored seeing it."

Mrs Barnhoff suddenly glanced towards the window, and I noticed her eyes had filled with tears.

"Thank you so much for your letter," she continued. "It was most kind."

"Not at all Mrs Barnhoff. I'm only sorry there was cause to write it. Your husband and I were good friends. All the officers were dreadfully shocked when Fritz passed away. It was so sudden."

Mrs Barnhoff smiled, and taking off her gardening apron, sat in an easy chair beside the fireplace.

"Please do sit down Captain Fry," she said. "I've taken the liberty of ringing for coffee."

Deciding the window seat would be an ideal spot; I sat down.

"I'm also given to understand Captain," Mrs Barnhoff continued. "We must thank you for getting Fritz home."

"Partly," I said, endeavouring to cover my embarrassment. "The C.O. decided to bury Fritz in Calcutta. But I pulled a few strings and managed to get him home. The memorial in the church and the statue over the grave are most appropriate."

"Then you've seen them."

"Yes. I asked father's driver to drop me off at the churchyard."
She smiled again.

"Please Captain. I'm sure if we had Fritz with us he would insist you call me Gertrude. If you and he were friends, then so shall we."

"Thank you Gertrude. Please call me Ron."

A maid entered and laid a tray set for coffee on a table in front of the window.

When we were alone Gertrude joined me on the window seat.

"Milk or cream?" she asked.

"Cream, thank you." I said, watching her begin to pour the coffee. "This is a beautiful house. There's a tranquillity about it."

"I agree. I'm sure it's because we're on top of a hill. Like Olympus. A haven for the Gods. Far from the hurly burly of the real world."

Gertrude gazed wistfully out of the window.

"After Fritz and I married it was difficult to live on a lieutenant's pay, so Fritz and I lived at Wildsbridge Lodge, the Barnhoff family home. We couldn't have afforded Hyde House without the help of my papa and Fritz's father."

"I remember Fritz saying he worked for his father at the factory."

"That's correct. Three years before the war he resigned his commission. He did this partly for financial reasons, although his father was getting frail and wished him to become more involved with the family business."

Another tear appeared in her eye and she sighed.

"Of course, I love Hyde House, but now there are too many memories for me to completely enjoy living here. I see him everywhere, especially in the rose garden and nowadays, with the boy away at school, there's just the girls and myself. We do rattle around in this big house."

"Forgive me for asking," I said. "Then are you contemplating living elsewhere?"

"To be honest. Yes. My mother and father are becoming feeble, so I'd prefer to be with them."

"I remember Fritz saying they lived on Bathwick Hill. He said you lived there before you and he were married."

Gertrude nodded.

"I can tell you were great friends. Fritz was never one to confide in just anyone. Yes. Bathwick Hill. The girls are at school on Lansdowne, so it would be sensible to consider a move."

Now it was my turn to put an idea into Gertrude's mind.

"At the moment I'm living with my mother and father at Royal

Crescent. But frankly, I'd prefer a place of my own. If the opportunity arose I would be delighted to buy Hyde House and make it my home."

Gertrude laughed.

"That will certainly make my decision a great deal easier. I promise I'll think over your proposal."

Gertrude and I drank a second cup of coffee and moved on to lighter conversation, during which I avoided any reference to India or Fritz. Subsequently, an hour later, we parted company the best of friends and have remained so ever since.

As regards my purchase of Hyde House, several weeks later, Gertrude rang me to say she had made up her mind to sell. Therefore, we arranged to meet at my solicitors, Thring, Sheldon, and Ingram, in Queens Square, to draw up a formal purchase agreement. Several weeks later, Gertrude and her daughters departed Hyde House and I prepared to take possession.

It was now that the fun began. Always having the opinion I had a good eye for a fine piece of furniture, here then was an opportunity to put my conviction to the test. I scoured the countryside thereabouts, attending every sale and auction in order to furnish my house appropriately as the residence of a country gentleman.

On two floors, Hyde House is large, boasting a handsome ballroom, which can easily double as a music room; plus a billiard room, two reception rooms, twelve bedrooms, six bathrooms, domestic accommodation, and a garage for five cars. There are also several cottages for the staff.

Since Gertrude was moving back to her parent's house, it was pointless taking some of the furniture. Consequently, we came to an agreement regarding the bedroom furniture in the servant's rooms, as well as most of the equipment in the kitchen. Nevertheless, I was keen to put my stamp on the house and began avidly collecting pieces of fine furniture and selections of antique carpets and curtains. I found a wonderful Elizabethan four-poster bed; an entire seventeenth century dining suite; an eighteenth century refectory table, and buffet tables, along with countless ornaments, paintings, and silver. At last, I was having fun with the money grandfather

Henry left me.

Now that you know how I eventually purchased Hyde House, I shall return to the thread of my story. You may remember my Uncle George calling me to his office one morning to suggest I conduct a talk to young boys about my experience of the war. Therefore, several weeks after I took up residence at Hyde House, my new driver Thompson, drove me to Long Ashton Orphanage where their Headmaster, Mr Edwards, greeted me.

Chapter Eight
Eric Harry White - Trinity again

Having returned to civilian life, I quickly became involved with Bath YMCA, and for fun, joined the local scout troop. As a result, my understanding of young lads and their affairs had greatly increased by the time I arrived at Long Ashton to make my speech.

For this reason, I made it purposely brief, being aware of the short concentration span of pubescent youths. The lads applauded politely at the end of my speech and their teacher, Mr Edwards, asked if any wished to ask a question. At first, I thought I would be let off lightly, however, a young chap put up his hand. He might have been one of the oldest, maybe fifteen, or so, with a pleasant countenance, fair hair and blue eyes.

Actually, I recognised him as the boy who responded when I asked if anyone knew where India was in the world, and he cleverly pointed to it on the map. His question was whether I met Lawrence of Arabia and Siegfried Sassoon while serving in Palestine. Of course, I was able to acquiesce to the former, but conceded on Mr Sassoon. Even so, I was immediately struck by the keen intelligence of the lad, completely unexpected in a lad from the lower classes.

When I finished my speech, Mr Edwards invited me into his office to take morning tea, and during our conversation, I mentioned the young chap.

"His name's Eric Harry White," Mr Edwards said, passing me a plate of biscuits. "It's a sad story. He was six and his brother Percival, four, when their mother and father died in a traffic accident. With no family to take care of them, they ended up here. They're not aware of each other. The board sees it best to keep their relationship a secret. Close companionship is not encouraged, in case of absconding."

"What's the lad's future?" I asked.

"He'll more than likely end up in a factory, or work on the roads."

"But with such an enquiring mind he should be instructed. Who knows what he might achieve given the right start."

"I agree," Mr Edwards said. "But scholarships are hard to come by, especially for orphan boys."

"It would be dreadful to allow such a bright lad to finish up in the mire of mediocrity," I said, rather melodramatically. "However, Mr Edwards, I've an idea."

Mr Edwards refilled my cup and sat back in his chair.

"How about I take him on," I continued. "Tutor him. If he turns out well, he might even qualify for university."

At first, Mr Edwards appeared hesitant to show enthusiasm for my notion. He referred to the fact that I was a bachelor and said he believed the lad should have a female influence in his life, as well as male. But when I guaranteed the boy would be in the care of my housekeeper, Mrs Lanesome, Mr Edwards seemed reassured.

The bargain was truly cemented on the suggestion that a sum of money might change hands in order the sudden disappearance of the boy might go unnoticed. Consequently, it was agreed that young Eric would be delivered to me at the end of the week.

For the remaining three days, I found an opportunity to acquaint my mother and brother Wilfred with my scheme. Therefore, on Wednesday, two days before Eric was due to arrive; I invited them to lunch. Curiously, I was surprised to find them less than excited, Mother thinking the idea silly and irresponsible, Wilfred appearing suspicious.

"Haven't you enough on your plate with the boy scouts?" he said.

"Phooey Wilfred!" I retorted. "I think it's a wizzo idea. At least I use my money to benefit others and not sit on it like some I could mention."

Wilfred has never been the generous type. In fact, I am unable to name one good cause with which he has been associated or made donations; unlike father and myself, who have been generous to a fault.

"People will wonder," bleated Wilfred. "Wildsbridge's a small village. Why don't you send the boy away to school?"

"That would be quite unfair," I replied. "Eric's had a rotten enough time as it is. With no mother or father, and a brother of which he's unaware. I want to look after him and make him feel safe, not throw him to the lions at some public school like Cheltenham or Farmborough."

"You mean you'll spoil him Ronald," mother said, joining in the quarrel. "You're twenty eight years old. You should find a nice young lady, marry, and have children of your own, instead of bringing waifs and strays into the house."

"Here we go again," I said. "It always turns into this. Why should a man be married to be respectable? Obviously, a nice young lady has failed to happen along, and may not ever. Moreover, mother! What about Wilfred? I don't hear you nagging him to get married."

"Don't be silly Ronald! Your brother's just twenty. Anyway, I don't think your father will approve of your venture. There's a limit to being a benefactor. I'll certainly mention it when I return to Yorkshire, although I wouldn't wish him to worry, considering his present state of health."

"I don't care what you both think," I said in exasperation. "I've made up my mind and I hope Eric proves you wrong one day. He's extremely bright. I believe he has a wonderful future. All he needs is a start."

As a result, the subject was closed and whether they changed their minds about Eric as they grew to know him, they kept it to themselves. In fact, in later years, mother occasionally invited Eric and I to Shamsworth, the house she eventually shared with Wilfred, who strangely to this day, has remained a bachelor.

Two days later, I woke to a glorious September morning, the kind that makes you feel good to be alive. Summer was barely over and there had been weeks of rain, but now the sun had returned to warm the sodden soil and rejuvenate the flowers.

Mrs Lanesome, my cook and housekeeper, was already in the kitchen, since as I lay in the bath I could smell my breakfast cooking.

During the war and the time I spent in India and Egypt, I had become accustomed to a traditional breakfast of bacon, eggs, and all the trimmings. Therefore, since joining my household, Mrs Lanesome rigorously conformed to my wishes, although continually reminding me of my fast expanding waistline.

After breakfast, I inspected Eric's room to ensure everything was in order, then went to the drawing room and rang Fortts of Milsom Street, to arrange the collection of cakes and sandwiches. My scouts were due at ten o'clock, so I quickly went to my dressing room and put on my uniform. When everything was complete, I endeavoured to relax by reading the morning paper, but in no time, I heard the car coming up the drive and hurried to the front door.

"Welcome to Hyde House," I called, as Eric stepped out of the Buick. "Come inside young fellow and let me show you to your room. Thompson will see to your things."

Naturally, the lad was nervous, which was hardly surprising since I imagine in his years at the orphanage, he had not left it too many times. However, despite his shyness he seemed pleased with his room and thanked me.

While we drank and ate our tea and biscuits, all provided by Mrs Lanesome, I acquainted Eric with my plans for his future and felt sure the boy was excited, although he appeared rather uncertain. When we were finished, I took Eric on a tour of the house to familiarise him with the layout, and it was while we were walking in the garden a charabanc arrived carrying my troop.

As you are already aware, during the war I gained valuable experience dealing with the affairs of young men. Therefore, on my return to civilian life I made a point of joining organisations, which solely involved the male youth movement. I became prominent in Bath YMCA, the Bath Boys Club, as well as a passionate contributor to the scout movement.

Eric's first day passed well and I was pleased when he decided to join my scout troop. The boys had a wrestling contest, which was won as usual by my biggest and fittest chap. The little ones followed a trail in the woods and then everyone enjoyed a tea party in a hired marquee pitched on the lawn.

Once my arrangement for Eric was finalised, I placed an advertisement in The Times, which was answered by Mr Chaston, a smart young man from Bristol, having been educated at Clifton College and at Oxford. At his interview he so impressed me with his innate passion for teaching, I hired him on the spot.

A bachelor, and with no ties to speak of, I offered Mr Chaston either a room at the top of the house and live in arrangements, or a lift to the station each night, and he sensibly chose the former. Mr Chaston became Eric's inspiration and I watched the lad blossom under his caring, sensible hands.

For me, the next few weeks were tremendously exciting. It was fun to see Eric adjusting to his new life away from the orphanage. He appeared happy, especially when he was at his lessons with his tutor.

In advance of any festering rumours, it was important the village understood about Eric living at Hyde House. By this time, Wildsbridge residents regarded me as their squire. Although Fritz's father lived at Wildsbridge Lodge, I was aware the villagers were never completely happy to regard Frederick Barnhoff as such, mainly because of his nationality, as well as his involvement in manufacturing. The people who mattered in the village were well aware Henry Fry was my grandfather and that I was of independent means. This became obvious because as soon as I was established as the new resident of Hyde House, Reverend Roach insisted I take the front pew in All Saints Church. It was there, on Eric's first Sunday, which happened to be Harvest Festival, when my plan began to take effect. Mrs Osterley, the widow from The Grange was sitting behind us, and I made a point of introducing Eric.

"Mrs Osterley. You've not yet met my nephew," I said. "Eric. Meet Mrs Osterley.

Eric gave me a queer look, but politely shook her gloved hand all the same.

"Good morning Mrs Osterley," he said. "I'm very pleased to make your acquaintance.

The old lady smiled, while quizzing Eric through her penc nez.

"Likewise, young man. Will you be staying in Wildsbridge for long?"

Eric glanced at me and saw me wink.

"I'll be here a while Mrs Osterley. You see my uncle is kindly educating me for Cambridge."

"How nice of Captain Fry," Mrs Osterley said. "But of course the Fry's are famous for their good intentions. I'm pleased for you young man and look forward to hear more of your progress."

The organ abruptly interrupted the conversation as it struck up the processional hymn.

"Hail thee festival day/ blessed day that art hallowed forever," sung the choir as it made its way up the aisle and into the stalls. I stood beside Eric feeling completely content and confident. Mrs Osterley was the voice and ears of the village. There was little doubt anyone who was anyone in Wildsbridge would know about Eric, as well as his relationship to me before the week was out.

Autumn became winter, Christmas came and went, and with spring around the corner, I was developing a tremendous fondness for my young prodigy. While Eric was at his studies, I spent my days dealing with my various charities, clubs, and institutions. There was always a letter to write and people to meet, much like my days as a lieutenant. However, in the evening, it was time for dinner and the moment Eric and I could relax. As I sat opposite Eric and Mr Chaston, happily listening to them discuss the day's lesson, I felt entirely pleased to have been the instigator of Eric's newfound knowledge.

Since he was almost seventeen, it would soon be time for him to leave Hyde House and take up residence at Cambridge, meaning I would only see him when he came down for the holidays. The thought caused me to feel quite miserable until I suddenly had an idea. You may recall that due to the war my time at Trinity was cut short by almost two terms. Why then not return to take up where I had left off? What a jolly time Eric and I would have sharing rooms, punting, picnics beside the Cam, and carols at Kings at Christmas. But when I put my scheme to Eric at breakfast one morning, he seemed less than enthusiastic, his response quite churlish and direct.

"Why should a chap as old as you want to spend time with a load of swotty eighteen year olds?'

The ingenuous young lad, who, two years previously, had climbed my front steps on a bright September morning, was no longer reticent and timid. He was a forthright young man, with a strong personality, and spoke his mind on more than one occasion, which, of course, I had aimed for from the start.

"Hey! I'm only older by thirteen years," I protested. "Thirty one's not old. Besides, this time I intend to enjoy myself. I'll not do stuffy law, which father insisted I do. I'll read ancient history. Since I've seen Egypt and Palestine it's right up my street. I'll become an archaeologist."

"Obviously, I can't stop you," Eric said, laughing. "But I'll be taking law, so I hope you don't get in the way of my studies. One day I'm going to be a politician. Maybe even Prime Minister."

My custom was to scoff when Eric talked about his ambitions. However, my show of disdain was really a means of encouragement. Perhaps, if I had done the reverse, ardently urging him towards a particular goal, he might easily have chosen the opposite way. Consequently, sticking stoically to my scheme, in September 1923, Eric, and I boarded a train to London; took a taxi from Paddington to Kings Cross Station where we caught a train to Cambridge.

It was exciting to be back after so many years and I felt invigorated and boyish as I remembered the happy times with my pals. However, my mood changed, when one day I happened upon the roll of honour, and realised how many of my alumni were no longer alive.

Weldon the head porter and I came to an arrangement for Eric and myself to room together. In addition, we were fortunate, since after a bit of monetary persuasion, the old man gave us a double, which meant we each had a bedroom, plus a shared sitting room, with the WC and the bathroom at the end of the corridor outside our door.

Despite my seniority, I was surprised how quickly I settled into academic life. I put it down to the youthful way I look at life, never taking things too seriously and always seeing the bright side. This attitude, however, was hardly conducive to study and I soon discovered archaeology was not going to be as exciting as I hoped. Maliciously, I mocked Eric as he ploughed through piles of musty books, since the reading list given to me by Hovell Minns, the Disney Professor of Archaeology, was equally ancient, as if it had been found in some mouldering Egyptian tomb. Thus, I quickly realised, if I were to survive Trinity for three years, I would need to do a considerable amount of bluffing.

This hardly dampened my insatiable thirst for a good time. Perhaps this 'joie de vivre,' stemmed from my restrictive army service, or because I was now free of the responsibilities of charity work and the role of the country squire. As a result, that first term I experienced a sense of freedom never before known. Back in 1911, when I came up to Cambridge as a boy fresh from Farmborough, I had less confidence. Now, I was self-possessed, with the understanding of five years of combat, as well as a rank of which I could be proud.

My self-confidence seemed to attract the attention of an element of young men, and I relished the adoration, flitting from one affair to the next with little concern for the consequences. Many of the young men were effete and not the sporty type who usually attract me. However, they served as a diversion, and made life entertaining. Visibly, Eric followed my pursuits with scowling disapproval. By now, he and I were quite open concerning my particular persuasion, even speaking often on the subject, although I remained unable to convince him that my urges were as natural to me as his were to him. Nevertheless, he did go along with me and kindly turned a blind eye if I brought someone back to our rooms.

It was around this time, maybe in the December of our first year at Cambridge, I began to notice Eric and Amy, the daughter of Fritz's sister, growing rather attached. Since my arrival in Wildsbridge, every Christmas time I was accustomed to receive an invitation to spend Christmas Eve with Amy's father and mother at Wildsbridge Lodge. Naturally, when Eric arrived, he too was invited. Since he and Amy were the youngsters in the party, every year they gravitated together, until it was plain to see how close they had become. As a result, during the spring term of our second year at Trinity, I began noticing discarded envelopes in the waste paper basket, franked "Wildsbridge, Somerset." I made little comment regarding this, although I was secretly pleased, hoping that the outcome would mean our families might be united in marriage.

It was then I realised Eric's identity might well become an obstacle. Ivor, Amy's father, was a conservative fellow and might easily find his prospective son in law's ignominious beginnings, less than worthy, causing embarrassment for the young couple. Consequently, one lunchtime, while Eric, myself, and a friend picnicked beside the Cam, I approached Eric on the subject.

"If you take my surname," I said. "You'll immediately become respectable."

At the time I realised how terribly snobbish this sounded, but there really was no other way of putting it.

"You're not suggesting I become your son?" Eric answered. "You won't get away with adopting me. For a start, you're unmarried and I'm still a minor."

"Not that old chestnut again," I said. "There are ways and means Eric. Things are simple if you can pull strings."

However, he was still unconvinced.

"I'll change my name if you like, but that's all. Actors do it all the time."

Then it was agreed by all parties and announced in the London Gazette that Eric Harry White relinquishes his name by deed poll, and henceforth will be known as Eric Fry.

Of course, this was no surprise to the village. They already viewed Eric as my nephew, having always assumed he bore my name. Amy understood my motives, and her father was satisfied his daughter was to marry into one of the most illustrious families in England. Before Eric could marry however, he and I must graduate. Yet, a small anomaly occurred which would delay us. There was a move to reduce the miner's wages, to which the unions refused to comply. As a result, in May, the miners were locked out of British coal mines, resulting in other unions calling out almost two million workers, culminating in a General Strike.

Eric and I did our bit, of course, and for almost ten days, we staffed the Cambridge Omnibuses, me as the ticket collector and Eric driving. We had tremendous fun and were quite sorry when the strike ended.

In July of the following year, my hopes for the couple came to fruition when, in All Saints Church, Wildsbridge, Eric Fry, and Amy Peters became Mr and Mrs Eric Fry.

Chapter Nine
Ham House for Eric and Amy

At the onset, I was keen for the couple to call Hyde House their home, however I soon realised, and for Amy at least, my house would only be a temporary residence. As Eric was now in London during the week, studying for the bar, Amy and I were spending considerable time together. We ate breakfast together and dined in the evening, however I found her difficult company. She was an educated young woman, but had little small talk, something at which I excel. I was just not intelligent enough for her. Gradually, our meals became quiet and strained, to the point that we could hardly wait for the cheese board to arrive so we could make our excuses and go to our respective rooms.

Each Friday night, Eric left London on the six o'clock train. However, the journey from Paddington to Bath sometimes took four hours, so he often arrived late and tired. It was on such an evening I was to receive some unhappy news.

"I'll have Mrs Lanesome do you up a tray," I said, as I greeted him at the door. It had been my custom to give Thompson, my butler and driver, Friday night off, and Amy invariably went to bed early.

"No thanks," Eric said, hanging his overcoat on the hallstand. "I had something on the train. Grilled plaice. Quite nice actually."

I said goodnight, and was about to climb the stairs when he called me back.

"Ron. Can I have a word?"

To me his words, as well as the tone of his voice, sounded ominous.

"Of course. Let's have a drink."

Eric followed me into the drawing room and sat down on the sofa, while I poured us each a scotch and soda.

"There you are."

I handed him his drink and slumped into a chair beside the fireplace.

"Ron," Eric said, once the whisky had settled in his stomach. "This is going to be most difficult. There's no easy way to tell you, so I'm going to come right out with it, and I apologise for both of us even now."

"Dear! Dear! Dear! Whatever can it be to make you apologise before I've even heard what you're about to say?"

"We've found a delightful house and we'd like to buy it."

Eric let out a great sigh.

"I've been worried about telling you all the way home and now I have. We both love you dearly Ron, but we must have a place of our own. It's only right. We'd like to start a family and Amy and I feel you mother us far too much."

I could hardly keep from laughing. All along, I had suspected this might be his news. You see I am a curious, snoopy kind of chap.

Secretly, I have always believed I would make an excellent detective, since I recently discovered 'For Sale' notices cut out of the Bath Chronicle. Obviously, as Amy found potential properties she posted them to Eric for his scrutiny.

"If I mother you, then I'm sorry," I answered. "I admit, at times I'm an old hen, but I mean well. You're my family. I've no one else other than mother and Wilfred."

Eric swallowed another mouthful of scotch. "Then you're not upset."

"Of course not. Where's the house?"

"Tisford. It's called Old Ham House. It's beautiful Ron. Sixteenth and seventeenth century, mostly. Awfully expensive though. We'll need to take out a loan."

"You'll do no such thing," I said. "See it as a present."

"Ron! That's outrageous! Amy and I couldn't possibly allow you to give us Ham House."

"Alright. You can pay me back. But it'll be free of interest. As I said, you're family and families stick together."

Although he was frowning, I sensed Eric was secretly delighted, after all, he knew there was nothing I enjoyed better than giving away money. Besides, what good is money to me, I have everything I ever wanted, and can go and do as I please. Then why should my friends not be able to do the same?

At breakfast the next morning, the atmosphere was excited and animated. Clearly, Eric had told Amy of the arrangement, as she was positively joyous.

"Ron! You're very naughty," she said. "How can we thank you? We fell in love with Ham the moment we saw it."

"Then you've already seen it?" I teased.

She and Eric glanced at each other guiltily.

"We drove over last Sunday. We told you we were visiting father. We're dreadfully sorry."

I laughed, and poured myself a second cup of tea.

"You're just like a couple of mischievous children, keeping secrets from old Ron. I'd like to see Old Ham House."

"We'll take a ride over this morning if you like," Eric said eagerly.

Accordingly, an hour later, we piled into the Humber and Eric drove us the thirty or so miles to Tisford in Wiltshire.

Old Ham House was indeed a splendid example of sixteenth century Elizabethan architecture. Constructed of local limestone, it possessed an imposing frontage of three gables, typical of manor houses of the period. Complete with tall spiralling chimneys and lead light, mullioned windows. It was easy to see why Amy and Eric had fallen for it.

Feeling confident my money was well invested, I instructed my solicitors, Thring, Sheldon, and Ingram of Queens Square, Bath, to begin the purchase agreement.

Of course, the couple had no furniture to call their own and Ham House was extensive, moreover it was important they were comfortable. Hence, with Eric hard at work at his studies in the city, Amy and I began choosing the various pieces that would turn Ham House into a home.

At last, we had something in common and could enjoy bidding at auctions and farm sales. We also discovered a similar appreciation of all things antique. Amy possessed a good eye for paintings; consequently, by the time she and Eric would remove to Wiltshire, they had acquired quite a collection. I gave them several beds that were stored in my outhouses, as well as the MG sports car, which I bought on a whim, and had never been driven. Therefore, on the day of their departure, Jolly's removal men had quite an assortment of odds and ends to load into their lorry.

Naturally, I missed them terribly. The house was suddenly dreadfully quiet. After all, Eric had lived at Hyde House for ten years, and Amy for three. I must admit, I felt lonely for the first time in a long while. I lost my appetite and found it difficult to relax. I suppose, nowadays, you would say I was depressed, but back then, such things were never mentioned. Despite my sadness, I plunged into the charity work and the pastimes that I loved, for example, the Young Men's Christian Association and Wildsbridge Boy Scouts. These distractions occupied several evenings a week and helped me adjust to the sudden emptiness in my life. However, around this time, one occasion gave me the greatest pleasure and served to promote me to every prestigious dining table in the City of Bath.

If you happened to open The Times in November of the same year, and glance at the Court Circular, you would have seen my name, prominently displayed beside that of my mother. Princess Helena Victoria, the granddaughter of Queen Victoria, was to visit Bath to attend the YMCA celebrations at The Pump Room, and officially open the Bath Royal Orthopaedic Hospital. Graciously, she gave mother and me the honour of accepting our invitation to lunch. Of course, the best people were also invited, including the Duchess of Beaufort; The Marquis of Bath; Lady Mabel Hamilton Stubber, and the Hon. Mrs Stuart Wortley, who was famous for her wonderful portrait by John Singer Sargent.

One month earlier, the world was devastated by the Wall Street

Crash, the Roaring Twenties; the decade of the Charleston; Al Jolson; Mickey Mouse; the Black Bottom, and Radio, coming shuddering to an end. Despite politicians warning everyone that a Great Depression was looming, the business of making sweets and confectionery continued, Fry's Sugar hardly feeling the sting of economic collapse other manufacturing industries were suffering. Although, by the end of 1930, two and a half million men were on the dole, they still seemed able to afford sweets for their children and put spoonfuls of sugar in their tea.

The year 1931 saw a cheerier event that would extend our little family by one. In March, after unsuccessfully trying to conceive for several years, Amy finally gave birth to a healthy baby girl. She was baptised, Emily Louise Fry, in Wildsbridge village church, and after the service the family returned to Hyde House for a jolly celebration.

Having given Eric the cash to purchase Ham House, I realised the benefit of investing money in property. Those early years of the thirties were financially difficult and rather than risk my fortune in a bank, as soon as my shares increased in value, I converted the profits into bricks and mortar.

Therefore, by 1934, I not only owned Hyde House, but Vale Manor, a rambling Tudor manor house near Colerne in Wiltshire and West Dockly, a modernised, West Country house, in Devon. It was never my intention to live in either, however, I enjoyed furnishing them elegantly, and then renting each home, which brought me a steady income.

In the same year, I was about to gain another acquisition, which would prove beneficial to me in a more private way.

Chapter Ten
Mervyn Watson - Oh! For the Wings of a Dove - Swindon Singing Eisteddfod - Cleopatra at the Forum

My involvement with Bath Boys Clubs invariably brought me in contact with an assortment of activities. The club could boast a football and rugby team, a cricket eleven, a group of extremely talented and attractive gymnasts, and of course, a swimming squad. It was to the latter that I gave my greatest support. At various times a year, I joined the lads and their coach, Mr Chittenden, when the club attended weekend swimming galas. While the lads changed, I would chivvy them along with my usual pep talk and promises of a tea afterwards. This also gave me an opportunity to appreciate the litheness of youthful young lads, a pastime of which I have never grown tired.

One such weekend in the month of October, the lads were to compete against the team from the Great Western Railway, the gala taking place at Swindon Swimming Baths.

Merrily, I accompanied the lads and Mr Chittenden in the charabanc that conveyed us to the town, some thirty or so miles northeast of Bath. As usual, we sang songs to pass the time, and since Gracie Fields was popular then, her hit song, 'Sing as we go,' was at the top of the list. Also George Formby's, 'With my little ukulele in my hand'.

In our seats behind the driver, Mr Chittenden startled me when he suddenly shouted, "Sing us a song, Watson!"

"Yes! Sing us a song Watson," the lads echoed.

Turning, I saw a lad stand up and move into the aisle. He was perhaps sixteen or seventeen, about five feet four inches tall, short fair hair, neatly combed, and wearing a faded brown jacket over a pair of camel trousers that appeared a little on the large side. Nevertheless, the lad possessed just the looks I found charming. I was immediately taken with this young man, he reminded me of Anthony Goodfellow, John Gater, and of course Eric. But when the lad opened his mouth to sing my admiration became adoration. His voice had broken, but with none of the squeakiness and unpredictability, that one usually hears in the voices of youths of a similar age. It was a steady tenor; smooth and soft; displaying an obvious ability to reach soaring notes by the choice of song he began to sing.

"Oh/ for the wings/ for the wings of a dove/ far away/ far away will I rove/ Oh! For the wings for the wings of a dove/ far away/ far away, far away, far away, will I rove."

The bus rattled along, dipping and swaying through the countryside, around bends and over bridges, but inside all was silent, except for the young man's angelic voice. From the very earliest days, my family have appreciated the sound of the human voice, encouraging the formation of choirs, as well as advancing the development of choral and church music. Therefore, it was hardly surprising I was moved to the point of being overcome by the boy's wonderful voice. Subsequently, once we arrived at the baths, and as the boys clambered out of the bus, I made a point of taking the lad aside to congratulate him.

"I know your surname's Watson," I said. "But what's your Christian name?"

"Mervyn sir," he answered.

"Mervyn! You've a marvellous talent. Have you considered having your voice trained?"

Mervyn shook his head.

"No sir. Dad and mum don't have that sort of money. There's all me brothers and sisters see. They're a lot to feed and clothe."

His Bathonian accent was exceedingly broad and he rolled his 'R's' like a country yokel.

"We might just see about that," I replied, as he and I followed the other lads up the steps and through the entrance.

Now at this point you may well say that what happened next is too much of a coincidence to be believed. Nevertheless, I say in all honesty, it actually occurred, because as Mervyn and I hurried past the ticket office, I happened to spy a poster, pinned to a notice board. 'Swindon Eisteddfod, Swindon Swimming Baths' it announced, 'Open to singers ten years and upward. Entry fee, two shillings, and six pence.'

"How about it," I said, as I drew Mervyn's attention to the advertisement. "Why not enter. You'd certainly stand a good chance of winning."

"Me dad can't afford two and six."

"I'll pay for you. Where do you live?"

"Swinbourne's Buildings."

"Alright. When we get back to Bath, I'll have my driver drive us to your house, and your father and I will have a chat."

In the changing room, I gave my usual rallying pep talk to enthuse the boys, promising a hearty tea when the competition was over.

The Great Western Railway boys did well at the outset, but Bath Boys Club pushed ahead during the senior races, bringing the teams level by the relays. Moreover, Mr Chittenden and I were thrilled when Bath raced ahead and eventually won the whole competition and the GWR Swimming Cup.

Once the boys from both teams had changed into their everyday clothes, the bus drove us all to the railway works, where the canteen had prepared a marvellous spread. As a result, and with our belts straining, we were a merry bunch on the return bus ride to Bath.

Thompson, my driver, was at the bus station to meet me, and Mervyn and I climbed into the back of the Humber and then drove through the city streets towards Julian Road. The lad was quiet and I imagine a little embarrassed to be alone in my company.

"How long have you lived in Swinbourne's Buildings?" I asked, endeavouring to break the silence.

"As long as I can remember," Mervyn answered. "Brother Harry was born there. Then me."

"How many brothers and sisters do you have?"

"After me, there's Richard, then Sarah, Ruby, Doris and little Eric. He's four."

"A big family."

"Yes, sir. The house is small, so it's a bit of a squeeze. It isn't much sir. Being the gent you are, I bet you live in a posh place."

His statement, I found difficult to quantify. I hardly wanted to agree and appear snobbish, neither to disagree, and tell a lie. Instead, I ignored it and changed the subject.

"You have a beautiful voice."

"Thank you sir. My grandfather lived in Wales once. Mum says Welshmen are good singers, so perhaps that's where I get it from."

"How about I take you on and have your voice properly trained?"

His silence and lack of a response told me that I should tread very carefully, where patronage was concerned. Consequently no further conversation occurred, until that is, Mervyn suddenly spoke out of the darkness.

"There's something else though, Captain Fry," said Mervyn,

He turned his steely blue eyes towards me, clearly visible in the lights of the dashboard.

"If you want a feel of it, go ahead. I won't holler. I reckon we both know what we want out of this, don't you? Me and you are the same I reckon."

Moreover, now, once again I will leave the entire incident to your imagination, as well as impress upon you that I was never the instigator of this intimate development in Mervyn and my friendship. Suddenly, I realised I was dealing with a young man who was entirely aware of what was expected of him, and me of him.

Should you ever wish to visit Bath one day to see for yourself the exact starting place of this important part of my story, you will see from the outside, Swinbourne's Buildings comprises a row of terraces lining each side of a cobbled street, joining Julian Road and Portland Place. Being almost two hundred years old, the houses were originally intended as dwellings for the families of the artisans who serviced the occupants of the opulent terraces and crescents in the surrounding neighbourhood. Nowadays, however, the street is reduced to a slum.

Living for most of my late childhood and teenage years in nearby Royal Crescent, I was quite familiar with the appearance of Swinbourne's Buildings. However, I never had cause to see the interior of the houses. Consequently, I was appalled by what I encountered when Mervyn's mother invited me inside.

"Good afternoon, Mrs Watson. My name is Captain Fry," I said, as Mervyn and I stood on the doorstep. "I hope you don't mind, but I brought your son home from the bus station."

Mrs Watson led us into a room barely the size of one of my bathrooms at Hyde House. The floor was bare-boards except for a threadbare rug in front of the fireplace and another under an old, scratched, black leather chaise lounge. Over the mantel, gas brackets flickered miserably, providing the only source of light other than a glimmer penetrating a pair of yellow stained lace curtains at the window.

"Please sit down Captain," she said, offering me a seat on the chaise. "It's kind of you to bring Merv home."

"Not at all Mrs Watson. However, there's another reason I'm here. I wish to speak with you and Mr Watson regarding Mervyn."

Hearing his name, Mervyn shuffled his feet nervously, obviously embarrassed by what I was about to say.

"Please sit down Mrs Watson."

Hesitantly she sat on the only other chair in the room that stood beside the fireplace.

"He hasn't done anything wrong has he?" she said. "Wouldn't you rather speak to his father? He won't be home until later. He's been called to Charlcombe Manor to mend a scratch in a dining table."

"Me dad's a French polisher," Mervyn interrupted. "So was his dad."

"How interesting," I said. "I may well need your father's services one day. All the same Mrs Watson, I can speak to you just as well, and you might relay our conversation to your husband on his return."

This seemed to assure Mrs Watson and she relaxed back in the chair.

"I'm sure you're aware that your son has a marvellous gift, and that's his singing voice."

"He takes after my father in that way," Mrs Watson said. "He could sing beautifully when he was young. But he doesn't do much singing anymore. Not very well you see."

"I'm sorry to hear it. However, I'd like to take your son on, if you and Mr Watson agree. With his voice trained who knows where he'll end up. Also, you needn't worry about the cost. I'll cover everything.

Mrs Watson smiled and I noticed her teeth were misshapen and stained. It was clear that this family was extremely poor and living on the breadline. Although, the Great Depression was officially over, times remained hard for the humble labourer. Wages were low, making it difficult to make ends meet.

All of a sudden, the front door opened and two small girls stood on the threshold, looking concerned.

"Mother! Is everything alright?" the older one said. "It's not the doctor or the undertaker is it?"

They sounded concerned, and understandably so. They must have seen the Humber parked outside, with my chauffeur standing beside it.

"No Ruby," Mrs Watson answered. "Captain Fry brought Merv home from the swimming. He's kindly offered to pay for your brother's singing lessons."

The little girls edged inside the door and smiled at me, shyly.

"Hello," I said. "I'm the Captain. I know your name's Ruby. But what's yours?" I asked the smaller of the two girls.

"Doris," she whispered.

"A pretty name for a very pretty girl."

Doris giggled, and hid behind her sister.

"Mervyn tells me he has three more brothers and another sister," I continued.

"Yes Captain," Mrs Watson said. "Our Harry's the eldest and serving out in Egypt. Merv's younger brother, Richard's thirteen and works on Saturdays in the greengrocers in Julian Road. Sarah's twelve. I daresay she's upstairs reading. You've met Ruby and Doris, they're eight, and six and little Eric's asleep in his cot. He's four."

At the time, I thought it a strange co-incidence, as the name Eric was uncommon, but refrained from saying as much.

"That's a lot of mouths to feed," I said.

Mrs Watson sighed. "Yes Captain. Father doesn't make much. People are keeping hold of the purse strings. But Richard helps out and I take in washing and scrub floors."

"This house is barely big enough for you all, Mrs Watson."

She nodded, and as her fingers tidied her hair, I noticed they were already showing signs of arthritis.

"Father and I are in the front, with Eric in the cot; we put up a screen in the back room so Merv and Richard can sleep in the bed on one side, while the girls are altogether on the other."

"You mean you've just two beds for five children."

She nodded again, giving me the impression she saw this arrangement as perfectly normal.

"It's made a big difference, Harry being away. Merv and Richard have much more room now. But of course, the devils keep growing."

I tried to laugh, but there was little humour in my voice. Suddenly, I realised I had never seen poverty on this scale, and was amazed with the dignity with which it was borne.

"Would you care for a cup of tea Captain?" Mrs Watson asked.

"No thank you Mrs Watson. I really must be going, except, there's something else I'd like to ask you. There's a singing Eisteddfod happening in Swindon in a few weeks time. Would you allow me to put Mervyn's name forward? Of course, I'd pay for his entry fee. I'd also be pleased to buy him a new jacket and trousers for the occasion."

"Of course Captain. Father and I would be honoured."

As I stood up to leave, I was suddenly aware of my height, appearing to tower over everyone in the room. Mrs Watson, Mervyn, and his sisters came to the door and waved goodbye as Thompson drove me away from the house.

For the next few days, I seemed unable to rid the memory of that Saturday afternoon from my mind. I sat alone eating my breakfast imagining Mervyn and his brothers and sisters crowded around the table. I wondered what their breakfast would be: eggs, bacon, sausage, tomatoes, and mushrooms? I doubt it. More like a bowl of porridge, or bread and drippings.

The more I thought, the more I became convinced it was my responsibility to do something to alleviate their plight, and in doing so, I might see more of my new friend, Mervyn. Later that day I telephoned the New Free Church, the fellowship that was organising the Eisteddfod, and sent them a postal order to cover Mervyn's fee.

The Saturday morning of the competition arrived and Thompson and I drove to Swinbourne's Buildings to collect my prodigy. It promised to be a lovely November day, the sky quite blue, with not a cloud to be seen; the air crisp and smelling of coal smoke and fried bread. Little Doris was sitting on the doorstep of number forty-nine and ran inside when the car drew up at the kerb. Mervyn was next to appear, beside him a handsome fair-haired lad.

"Can Richard come too?" Mervyn asked. "The greengrocer's shut for a wedding, so he's not able to work."

"Of course," I said. "The more the merrier. But what about the others? Don't they want to hear you sing?"

"We do!" Ruby and Doris screamed from inside the house.

"Then there's plenty of room for all. But where's your other sister?"

"She's upstairs reading," Mervyn said.

" Okay. The girls can sit up front with Thompson, and Mervyn and Richard can sit in the back with me. But what about your mother?"

"She'll need to look after Eric," Mervyn answered. "And dad's still in bed."

"That's all right Captain Fry," Mrs Watson said, appearing at the door. "You take them. It'll get them out of my hair. I always clean the house on Saturday mornings."

As we drove away, I watched the girls through the glass panel separating Thompson from the boys and me sitting in the back. Although they were fundamentally shy, Ruby and Doris occasionally glanced at each other and smiled, clearly excited to be riding in a motorcar, but also embarrassed to be sitting so close to my driver. Conversely, in the back Richard and I were having a jolly time. I asked him about his Saturday job and he proved quite the chatterbox as he explained his tasks, from the time he arrived at seven in the morning, until the shop closed its shutters at night. Consequently, although we had only travelled a few miles, I gained a great deal more knowledge about the greengrocery trade than ever I imagined I would.

All the while, Mervyn sat on the other side of me staring out of the window. I wondered what he was thinking. I must say though, seeing all the children together, I quickly came to the conclusion that they were an attractive family. There was, however, quite a dissimilarity between the brothers and the sisters. Whereas the boys were fair and had blue eyes, the girl's hair was dark and their eyes, green. I observed, at the outset that Mrs Watson's hair was white, not unusual for a woman her age, considering the circumstances of her life, as well as the fact that she had borne so many children. Therefore, I presumed the boys took after their mother, and the girls, their father, whom I still had yet to meet.

We arrived at the baths in good time to find seats a few rows from the front of the stage, which, I must say appeared most impressive, decorated with fresh foliage and flowers. Once we were seated, I teased the younger children by explaining that beneath the floor, under our feet, was the deep end of the swimming pool. It amused me to see their faces as they peered at the floor perilously. However, Mervyn was not amused at my joke, raising his eyes disdainfully.

Scrutinising the programme that I purchased at the door, I saw there were at least a dozen choirs, and more than twenty soloists, represented in various categories. Furthermore, as Mervyn was entered in the boys solo, fifteen to eighteen, and his name began with W, I realised it promised to be a long morning, and even a longer afternoon.

Once the third male choir had sung the last note of 'Jesu, Joy of Man's desiring', it became obvious that Ruby and Doris would never last the course; and Richard was beginning to fidget. Then I suddenly had a bright idea.

"Do you like ice cream?" I asked the young ones. "Oh yes!" they said in unison.

"Alright. When the next group has finished, I'll take you outside and Thompson will drive you to a teashop. Then, after you've had your tea, he'll take you home."

With the promise of sandwiches, cakes and ice cream, Richard, Ruby and Doris seemed hardly concerned they would miss Mervyn's song and happily tumbled into the car. I arranged for Thompson to return for Mervyn and myself, and as the car drove away, he and I returned to the concert.

The adjudicator of the Eisteddfod was famous Scottish composer and choral master, Sir Hugh S Robertson, and since he was responsible for founding the world renowned Glasgow Orpheus Choir, I was keen to hear what he thought of Mervyn.

The competition continued after an adjournment for lunch provided for the competitors and their families in the small swimming baths, which was also boarded over. However, with my stomach full of sandwiches, sausage rolls and tea, I must admit there were times during some of the women's more lyrical pieces when I could have easily fallen asleep. Nevertheless, a glance at the clock told me it was approaching four, and the designated time for the boys' solo fifteen to eighteen.

Earlier, a lady official, who happened to be from Wales, advised us that when the group of young singers was called, they were to assemble in the male changing rooms, where they would wait their turn to sing.

"Now don't be nervous my boy," I said, urging Mervyn out of his seat. "You know the song perfectly and sing it like an angel."

Nodding, he eased his way past the other people in the row, and just as he was about to duck through an entrance marked 'Men', he turned and smiled at me so charmingly I felt my heart leap in my chest. Mervyn's surname began with a W; consequently, with no other boy's name beginning the same, I had to wait right until the end for him to appear.

"Mervyn Watson, age, seventeen," the official announced.

Confidently, he strode onto the stage and across to the piano, and having given his music to the pianist, he walked to the front and waited for the introduction.

"O! For the Wings/ for the Wings of a Dove/ far away / far away /would I rove."

His voice soared into the iron framework of the vaulted roof, hovering there, while it filtered into every listening ear.

All of a sudden, I was weeping, tears stinging my eyes and falling down my cheeks. At once, I realised, if I dropped dead there and then, I would die a happy man to be in the presence of a sound so heavenly it would transport me to paradise. Not since the most famous choirboy of all time, Ernest Lough, of the Temple Boys Choir, made the sound recording, eight years earlier, had I heard the Mendelssohn song sung more brilliantly. In fact, I feel Mervyn has the edge on Ernest in the resonance of his top notes; although, I am not entirely an expert on the human voice and maybe a tiny bit biased.

However, the audience seemed to agree, because as Mervyn began the second verse, 'in the wilderness/ build me a nest/ and remain there/ forever at rest,' I glanced to my left and right to see people equally moved as myself. We were all experiencing the moment, a moment that would remain in our memories forever.

As Mervyn's voice faded away with the last chord from the piano, suddenly there was a great outburst of emotion as the audience applauded, some even getting to their feet. I could only wipe away my tears as my heart almost burst with pride.

It was then I made a promise. The population of Swindon and a Scottish adjudicator would not only hear this talent, but the entire country, with even the world recognising the voice of Mervyn Watson.

He was the last to sing, so while Mr Robertson decided the winner and wrote down his comments, the audience relaxed. Looking back at the entrance to the changing rooms, I saw Mervyn and the other contestants emerge and begin to find their way back to their seats.

"Who do you think will win," Mervyn whispered as he sat down. "The lad who sang 'Jerusalem' was good."

"His voice cracked once or twice," I commented. "Surely Robertson heard it. Are you hungry? Your brother and sisters would have had their tea by now."

"Now I've sung I am," Mervyn said. "I'm not usually nervous."

"Have a Fry's humbug."

We sucked on the sweets and anxiously waited for the results, until finally Robertson gave his notebook to an official.

"Ladies, Gentlemen, and children, here are the results of the boys solo, fifteen to eighteen years."

He began from the bottom place and proceeded upward, each time a name was read out, Mervyn and I breathing a sigh. Finally, it was down to the last three.

"Maurice Grant, eighty points, Mervyn Watson, eighty three, Ronald Selby, eighty four."

We looked at each other in amazement. One point and Mervyn would have tied; two and he would have won. Mr Robertson stood up and stepped onto the platform.

"Ladies, Gentlemen, and children, may I say how pleased and delighted I am to witness such high standards in the boys' voices, especially the first three. There was little to choose between each of them. Please boys, kindly step up to the stage."

Mervyn edged along the row and joined Maurice and Ronald on the platform.

"Well done," I heard Robertson say as he handed Mervyn his certificate. "A fine rendition of the Mendelssohn."

On our way back to Bath we were a jolly pair, chatting about the events of the day in the back of the Humber.

"I'm too excited to go home," Mervyn said. "Let's do something else."

"Alright. It's still early. How about the pictures?"

"Really! We don't go much. Dad can't afford it."

"What! A shilling?"

Mervyn shook his head.

"If he gives our Harry or me money, then Richard wants some; then our Sarah."

Clearly, when there is barely enough to feed your children, how then could a father provide treats?

"We don't need to worry about that," I said. "Cleopatra's on at the Forum. You've heard of Cecil B DeMille," Mervyn looked vacant. "He's a famous American film director. He made 'The Ten Commandments,' and, 'The Sign of the Cross,'"

"I've heard of that," Mervyn replied, eagerly.

I asked Thompson if he would like to see the film, but he declined, opting to stay with the car.

The Forum Cinema, having opened in May, was new to both of us. 'Cleopatra', starring Claudette Colbert and Henry Wilcoxon, was the latest smash from Hollywood and tipped to win the academy award. Resulting in a long queue formed on the pavement outside, and slowly edging towards the ticket window.

"Where would you like to sit?" I asked, as we drew closer. "Upstairs or downstairs?"

"Upstairs please! I've never been upstairs."

Suddenly I was overwhelmed. It was such a delight to give this lad pleasure. I was happy to give presents to Eric and Amy, or donate money to charities and institutions. Nevertheless this could hardly match the joy I felt, seeing the look on Mervyn's face as we sat down in the front seats of the balcony.

"It's beautiful," he whispered.

I had to agree. The interior of The Forum was without a doubt, beautiful. Stunning in fact, and a homage to the new design movement given the title, 'Art Deco'.

Around us, and surrounding the giant shimmering red plush curtains, the walls were decorated with motives and friezes, reminiscent of all things Roman, the concealed lighting giving everything a soft ambience.

While the cinema filled with people, unexpectedly, a spotlight appeared on the curtain as a giant Wurlitzer organ slowly emerged from an open trap door, and, as the organist played the opening chords of his first melody, he turned to the audience and smiled.

'When the red/ red /robin /comes /bob /bob /bobbing /along /along'.

Mervyn and I laughed as the audience began to sing to the tune, and naturally, we joined in.

Cleopatra was sensational: a film full of action and passion, the acting unparalleled, especially Colbert and Wilcoxon, the scenery and costumes, magnificent. At one point, as we sat there in the dark, watching a particularly stimulating scene in which Julius Caesar is seen in a Roman bath house surrounded by muscled soldiers and handsome young senators, all wearing nothing but skimpy pieces of towelling around their thighs, I suddenly felt Mervyn's hand arrive on my knee. Then, as we had seen in the previous scene, and reminiscent of Cleopatra's Barge floating up the River Nile, it took a slow course up my leg, eventually coming to rest against a long jetty. However, I forbade it to tie up, and sent it back to whence it came, after all, the picture house was packed that evening, people sitting to the left and right of us. Therefore, with the credits rolling, and once the curtain had fallen, both Mervyn and I agreed our favourite moment was when Mark Anthony visits Cleopatra's barge.

Once Mervyn and I were back in the car, I asked Thompson to stop at Fishy Evan's on our way back to Swinbourne's Buildings, and the three of us ate fish and chips parked in Milsom Street. It was almost the end of perhaps the best day of my life. However, I would discover many such days were yet to come.

Chapter Eleven
A deal's a deal - Christmas at No 10 Camden Place - Bedtime at Hyde House

Over the following weeks, I began to hatch a scheme, which on one hand would enable me to satisfy my philanthropic nature, as well as maintain my burgeoning relationship with my new young friend.

It was not until I saw a property for sale in the Bath Chronicle that I began to put my plan into action. With four bedrooms, a sitting and dining room, two bathrooms, a kitchen, a long garden, and a garage for two cars, for the cost the house seemed ideal. Subsequently, I instructed my solicitors, Thring, Sheldon, and Ingram, to purchase it on my behalf. Of course, the condition determined the price, since it was in sore need of renovation and decoration. With my usual panache, I pitched in, hiring painters, plumbers, and carpenters. As a result, and not before too long, number ten Camden Place began to appear entirely up to scratch.

It was now time to meet the illusive Mr Watson, and I must say I was a little nervous at the prospect. In addition, with no telephone communication, it was necessary to take potluck that I might find him at home. Consequently, a few weeks before Christmas, I paid Swinbourne's Buildings an impromptu visit, choosing early Saturday afternoon, thinking I might find him at home before he adjourned to the public house.

A serious teenage girl opened the door. She was an attractive creature, with a shock of blonde hair, despite possessing an unfortunate under bite, which was a dreadful shame.

"Hello," I said. "You must be Sarah. I'm Captain Fry. We've not met. Is your father at home?"

Sarah nodded. "Yes Captain. He's in the yard fetching in the coal. Mother and the others are at grandpa's. He's not very well. Would you like to come into the parlour?"

Clearly, Sarah was extremely self-assured for a girl barely fifteen; also bright, with a quick intelligence. Once more, I was impressed with yet another member of this family. I stood in the parlour as Sarah closed the front door, feeling again like the giant in the 'Jack and the Beanstalk', story. Almost immediately, the door to the kitchen opened and a small, spruce man entered, carrying a scuttle of coal. He put it down beside the fire and looked up at me.

"Don't tell me!" he exclaimed. "You're the Captain I've heard so much about. My kids can't stop talking about you."

"Then you're Mr Watson," I said, as we shook hands.

"Indeed I am sir. Also, I must thank you, as I understand you've already done my family proud with your gifts and such like. And what you have planned for our Merv."

"Mr Watson, it's nothing. I enjoy Mervyn's company. He has a great talent, which I wish to improve, with your permission of course."

Mr Watson sat down on the end of the chaise, and taking a poker from the hearth, prodded the fire, sending sparks up the chimney.

"Sarah," he called. "Put the kettle on. The Captain wants a cup of tea. Isn't that right Captain?"

"I wouldn't mind, because I've a special matter to discuss."

As I was still standing, and suspecting I would never be invited to sit, I sat in the chair beside the fire.

"What matter would that be Captain?"

Mr Watson piled a shovel of coal on the glowering embers, and then opened the damper in the grate.

"In the little time I've known Mervyn, and having been intro*d* to your family, I've been greatly impressed and would l all."

"Help us!" Mr Watson said coldly, turning away from the fire and looking at me keenly. "What do you mean, help us?"

A new tone was in his voice, a hint of anger, with a touch of sarcasm and suspicion.

"These are hard times Mr Watson. It doesn't take much to see you're struggling."

"You think you know about hard times," Mr Watson retorted. "You come here offering us charity just to appease your guilt."

"I've no reason to feel guilt Mr Watson. It so happens I have money. More money than I need, and I like to see it benefit people like yourselves."

He stared at me, his pale green eyes fixing me in an icy stare.

"This isn't really about us is it," he said coldly. "You're after something, I can smell it. I met your sort in the Army. I wasn't much older than our Merv is now. There's something about a short arse that attracts men like you."

"What do you mean?" I said, feeling anger rise in my chest.

"I was a corporal in the North Somerset Yeomanry," Watson continued. "My lieutenant had his eye on me. Always called me to his tent for some reason or another. He'd parade around with sod all on. Thought he'd entice me. Well no such luck. Anyway, my old ticker saw an end to my time in Egypt. I was invalided out. Bloody good job I reckon. Who knows what might've become of me."

I stood up to leave, but turned on him angrily.

"I'm not sure what you're driving at Mr Watson, but what you are inferring I regard as an affront to my person and good nature."

"Okay Captain," Watson said. "Perhaps you might have our best interest at heart; and our Merv's. So what's your proposal?"

Relieved that Watson appeared to have come to his senses, I sat down.

"My interest in young Mervyn is purely as a mentor," I said. "I only wish to bring out his best qualities and expose his gifts, which I believe will only happen in a more conducive atmosphere. This house is hardly adequate for you and your family. I could change all that."

"How?" asked Watson, suddenly interested.

"I've recently purchased a house in Camden Place, on Camden

Road, along from Camden Crescent. It would give me the greatest pleasure if you and your family would take up residence and called it home."

"Really! And how much will it cost?"

"Nothing. It's rent-free. See it as a gift. A Christmas present if you like."

Mr Watson suddenly stood up.

"Sarah!" he yelled. "Forget the tea! Bring me the Johnny Walker and two glasses."

"Yes dad!" she shouted from the kitchen.

"So what's the catch?" Mr Watson said.

"My only wish is to visit now and then. Just to see how you're getting along. I've had the decorators fix up the place and have made a few alterations. The bedrooms and bathroom at the top of the house I've turned into a little flat, which I thought would suit Mervyn. Also, somewhere to call his own, where he can begin his singing lessons."

"Nice and private you mean," said Watson coldly.

While I watched Mr Watson digest my proposal, Sarah came in carrying a whisky bottle and two glasses.

"Here we are!" Watson said. "Now we can get down to brass tacks. What you're really saying is that you want to visit Mervyn whenever you please."

Obviously, I had not been successful in convincing him that my interest in Mervyn was strictly platonic. Although, despite this, he seemed to have adopted a more casual attitude to the idea.

"He and I have become friends." I said. "I'll just be keeping up with his progress."

"And naturally you want mother and me to go along with this."

He poured the drinks, and for a while, we sat in silence, Watson slowly swallowing my proposal, as well as his scotch.

"Alright. If that's what you want, then we'll turn a blind eye. Mervyn's old enough to know what's what, so why should mother and I stand in his way. Just be careful though Captain. Should he come to me with any complaints, I'll be straight to the authorities, and the newspapers. They would be very interested to hear about the doings of one of Bath's famous benefactors."

Watson was far from silly. It was undeniable that he was attempting to blackmail me. However, I was being equally as ruthless by dangling the biggest carrot, a complete life change, which the crafty Watson clearly found impossible to resist.

"But what happens if things change?" asked Watson, pouring us another drink.

"Nothing. You can regard the house as yours."

He drank the second tumbler of scotch.

"Then I thank you Captain. My family thanks you. What concerns me though is how I explain this sudden change of circumstances to my mother, and brothers and sisters. They're bound to be curious."

"All you need say is that a rich benefactor, who wished to remain anonymous, mentioned Mervyn in his will. Mervyn then bought Camden Place. They can hardly question that."

"You're right," Watson laughed. "It shouldn't be a problem. The Mrs and I see hide nor hair of them anyway."

That was how the deal was made. It was agreed I would have access to Mervyn, while his family were set to live in comfort and security for the rest of their lives. Before I left that night, Watson and I set a date and time for them to take up residence at Camden Place.

"What belongings will we bring?" Watson asked, as he saw me to the door.

"Just your valuables and what you stand up in," I answered.

As Thompson drove away from Swinbourne's Buildings, I looked out of the back window of the car to see Mrs Watson pushing a pram up the street, with Ruby and Doris hanging on to the handles, while behind them, Mervyn and Richard were kicking stones.

I chose Christmas Eve to be the day Mr Watson and his family would take up residence, which I considered entirely appropriate. During the previous week, I became extremely busy raiding Jolly's auction rooms for tables, chairs, beds, linen, clocks, kitchen utensils, and pots and pans. In fact, everything the family would require to establish a proper home. Furthermore, I insisted all the furniture be brand new and modern, in a tasteful, country manor style.

***

As the day grew closer, I rang Caters, Stoffell, and Fortts, to arrange for their people to deliver enough groceries to stock the larder. Next, after advertising for a cook in the Bath Chronicle, I found Mrs Pratt, who agreed to live out, cook for the family during the day, and be present on Christmas Eve to take responsibility for the party food that Caters would deliver in the afternoon. My last task was to visit the fancy dress shop in Union Passage and hire a Father Christmas costume.

At last, Christmas Eve arrived with a hint of snow in the air, and at Camden Place, I waited expectantly for the family to arrive. Mrs Pratt was busy downstairs in the kitchen making sandwiches and opening boxes of cakes sent by the caterers. In the meantime, Betsey, the new parlour maid, was upstairs lighting gas fires and switching on lights in every room. At the same time as I was putting the final touches to the Christmas tree and lighting the candles on the mantelpiece, the Humber drew up outside.

"Come inside out of the cold!" I yelled, from the open doorway. "Merry Christmas! And welcome to your new home."

The children and Mrs Watson tumbled from the back of the car, while Mr Watson emerged from the front passenger seat.

"When you've parked, Thompson," I said. "Come in for something to eat."

Shyly, Ruby and Doris were the first inside the hall and their eyes widened when they saw the carpet on the stairs and the shining new paintwork.

"In you go little ones," I said, opening the parlour door, "There's a surprise for you."

Mervyn, Sarah, and Richard were next inside, looking smart in their best clothes. Sarah and Richard wore nervous expressions, seeming aware that something unusual was happening.

"We'll have such a jolly time," I said, reassuringly.

"It's like a fairy tale," Mrs Watson said, stepping over the threshold, Eric asleep in her arms. However, Mr Watson hesitated on the doorstep.

"Merry Christmas Captain," he said. "Well! Here we are. Just up and left the old place. Paid the last of the rent with the money you gave me. Packed a few things. Books, photos, mementos. They're in the back of the car."

"Of course. Come inside out of the cold Mr Watson," I said. "I'll have Thompson bring them in. Merry Christmas! Take off your hat and coat. Betsey will see to them."

A girl appeared at the bottom of the stairs. "Let me introduce your parlour maid, Betsey."

Betsey curtsied politely and then helped the adults off with their hats and coats, doing the same for the children. With the formalities over, everyone congregated in the parlour, where the gas fire roared comfortingly.

"I'd better show you around your new home," I said. "But first, let's have a hot toddy to warm us up."

The door opened and Betsey entered carrying a tray of glasses filled with steaming punch, giving one each to the adults and the five children.

"Don't worry Mrs Watson," I said, seeing her concern. "It's only raspberry juice, herbs and sugar. But Mr Watson. If you want something stronger, Betsey can bring you a scotch."

"Thank you Captain," he answered. "But I'm fine just for the moment."

Seeing the children's faces as they sat on the sofa, politely sipping their drinks, gazing in wonder at the pictures on the walls, the carpets, the clock on the mantle, the electric light chandelier, and the gleaming marble fire surround, I felt immensely pleased to be responsible for their happiness. Once sufficiently warmed, I marched everyone up the stairs to the first floor bedrooms, where, in the two front rooms I had placed three beds in one, presuming Ruby, Doris and little Eric would share, and another in the other, solely for Sarah. Also, there was a double bed in the rear bedroom intended for Mr and Mrs Watson.

"It all looks lovely," Mrs Watson said, peering into the rooms. "We only had two beds for the children. Now there are so many I've lost count."

Next, the family followed me up the further flight of stairs leading to the top of the house.

"So Captain, this is Merv's flat," Mr Watson said. "I've told mother about it."

"Correct Mr Watson. The three bedrooms here once belonged to the servants. But I've made a small room for Richard at the back and the other three into a flat for Mervyn. He has his own bathroom, a privy, and a telephone so he can ring down to Mrs Pratt for his meals."

"What a lucky fellow you are Mervyn. Aren't you going to thank the Captain?"

"Thank you Captain Fry," Mervyn mumbled.

The little flat was most comfortable, divided into two rooms, not including the bathroom and toilet. At the top of the stairs, three doors opened off the landing. The door facing the front of the house led to the bedroom and sitting room, both connected by a pair of sliding, oak doors. Each room possessed a large window, with views across the road towards the opulent villas on the opposite hill. Across the landing was the bathroom door and, seeing the house was on high sloping ground, commanding a spectacular view over the city and all the way to the Sham Castle. So extensive in fact, it felt a shame to use frosted glass in the window. As we are seeing often these days, I opted to have the water closet inside the bathroom, thus saving space for Richard's room next door, which also possessed a large window.

As to the furnishings, both upstairs and down, I spared no expense, having chosen everything with great care. Mervyn's bed was wider than the normal single. I selected it for this reason, also because the oak head and tailboard were carved with medieval designs consisting of roses and thistles. Soft Persian rugs covered the polished oak floorboards, while in the bedroom a chest of drawers, a large solid oak wardrobe, and a gentleman's dressing table, stood against the walls. In the sitting room, beyond the sliding doors, I gathered buttoned leather sofas, and easy chairs around the white marble mantelpiece, with small occasional tables beside them. Last but not least, a large sideboard stood against the wall opposite the window.

Wishing to create an atmosphere of quiet luxury, oil paintings depicting Scottish landscapes hung on the walls, their gilt frames sparkling in the light from table lamps placed about the room. The addition of porcelain figurines and a large sienna marble clock on the mantel achieved the desired effect.

"It's so lovely," Ruby whispered. "Just like a dream. It's real though isn't it Captain. You won't send us home when we've had our tea?"

"Of course not Ruby. It's real all right. I've also another surprise. Look in your wardrobe Mervyn."

Hesitating at first, Mervyn stepped up to the doors and pulled them open.

***

Throughout the week leading up to Christmas, and as soon as Mr Watson and I had come to our agreement, I rang the men's outfitters department of Jolly's in Milsom Street and gave the principal tailor a rough description of the height, set, and age of Richard, Mervyn, and their father. He then went ahead and compiled a collection of clothes for each of them, which I asked to see several days later. In addition, I requested he supply a selection of unshrinkable poplin shirts, ties and collars, as well as a dinner suit for Mervyn and Mr Watson, as no gentleman should ever be without a dinner jacket. Then it was the turn of the ladies, which was an entirely different proposition. Up until that moment, my mother was unaware of my plans for the Watsons so I could hardly ask her opinion. Anyway, her sense of fashion was pre-war and I hardly wanted to see the women of Camden Place dressed like Emily Pankhurst. However, once again Amy came to my rescue. Having already spoken to Eric of my scheme for the family, Amy was fully aware of my intentions and kindly agreed to drive over from Tisford. I think she thoroughly enjoyed choosing clothes for Mrs Watson and her daughters. Again, Amy and I collaborated successfully. As a result, by Christmas Eve, each wardrobe contained a set of clothes: Sunday best and summer coats and hats. Overcoats and scarves, gloves, shoes, boots and dresses.

"It's unbelievable!" gasped Mrs Watson. "Captain! We can't accept all this. You're much too kind."

"Not at all, Mrs Watson," I replied. "It's my greatest pleasure to see you happy. I want you to forget you ever lived in that dreadful slum."

"It wasn't that bad really," said Ruby. "People were nice. And we had lots of friends to play with."

"And so you shall in Camden Place. There's a nice school down the hill. I've already seen the Headmistress, so you and Doris start in the New Year. Also, I've arranged for Sarah to begin the term at Kensington High School, with Richard and Mervyn going to the Technical School."

"My word Captain!" Mr Watson exclaimed. "You've certainly been busy. You've left nothing to chance. We'll be beholding to you for the rest of our lives."

There was a note of sarcasm in his voice, which I chose to ignore.

"Come along everyone! Mrs Pratt is downstairs waiting to serve tea. She'll be wondering what's become of us."

At the party, I chose to gravitate towards Mrs Watson, Richard, Ruby, Doris, and young Eric, finding Mervyn, Sarah, and their father a little reticent to enjoy themselves. However, when I offered Mr Watson a glass of whisky he cheered up and even sang a couple of old music hall songs he told us his father sang to him. Obviously, singing was an important part of life in the Watson family.

Very soon, it was time for me to leave, since, by their bleary eyes, Ruby and Doris were ready for bed. Nonetheless, there was one question to ask Mr and Mrs Watson.

"Would you both do me a great favour," I said. "Would you mind if Mervyn stays at Hyde House tonight? There's something special I want to give him tomorrow. Don't worry. I'll return him to you in the morning."

They glanced at each other furtively and then smiled.

"Of course not," they said in unison.

Everyone, except for Eric, who had fallen asleep in his high chair, came to the door to wave goodbye, and soon Mervyn and I were alone in the back of the car.

"Are you real?" he said, as we left the lights of the city behind.

"What do you mean?"

"All this. You didn't have to do it you know. We could have continued to see each other some other way."

In the darkness, suddenly, I felt his hand on my knee.

"I know," I chuckled. "But I really can't resist a good cause when I see one."

Mervyn laughed. "Are you sure it's alright, me staying with you tonight?"

"Of course. Eric and his wife and daughter are coming for Christmas. I've told them about you and they're looking forward to meeting you."

"Who's Eric?"

"Just someone I took on years ago, when he was a lad around your age."

"Like you've taken me on. Then you've done this sort of thing before? So what's your plan for me then?"

"I really don't know," I said. "You've a lovely voice. I'd like to see you get on in singing. Maybe I'll turn you into a gentleman. But we'll just have to wait and see. There's plenty of time."

***

Eric, Amy, and Emily arrived later that evening, and we all walked to Wildsbridge Lodge, as Ivor, Amy's father, had invited us to Christmas Eve supper and drinks, just as old Mr Barnhoff and his wife did all those years ago. I was pleased to see Mervyn confidently mixing with the company, and when speaking, his voice even appeared to have developed a more cultured tone. Before we left for All Saints Church and Christmas carols, Mervyn delighted everyone by singing his Eisteddfod song. Now and then, Eric gave me the odd glance, but I smiled nonchalantly. Overall, by the time we arrived back at Hyde House, we were all tired and in need of sleep, so we said goodnight and I showed Mervyn to his room.

That's my bedroom," I said, pointing across the landing. "You've your own bathroom, and Mrs Lanesome's more than likely put a hot water bottle in your bed."

"Thanks Captain."

"And call me Ron, or Ronnie. No more of this Captain stuff. We're friends you and I."

"Okay Ron. Goodnight."

Quietly, so as not to wake anyone, I returned to the dining room and opened the door to the sideboard. Inside, I had hidden a dozen or so presents, each wrapped in festive paper. I stacked them in a pile on the dining table, and then carried them, one by one, into the sitting room, where I placed them under the Christmas tree.

Opening my bedroom door, my four-poster bed illuminated by the light from the hallway, I realised by the appearance of the eiderdown, that I was not apparently going to spend the remainder of Christmas Eve alone.

During the night, the sound of snow spattering my window pane presumably having woken me, I turned over, only to feel Mervyn fast asleep beside me, and I realised what had occurred just a few hours earlier had not been a dream but reality. I stared into the darkness trying to decide what to do. Allow this young man entirely into my life, or keep my distance and endeavour to stay strong and remain impartial to what my heart was trying to tell me. Although beautiful, Mervyn was cunning, no doubt inheriting this foible from his father. After all, who was it that instigated this further development in our friendship? Was he playing me for a fool, knowing full well I would give him the world if he had asked for it? Or was I the fool to think he would fall for a silly old duffer like me?

In the darkness, Mervyn stirred. Was he dreaming perhaps? Little did he know what surprises lay in wait for him on the morrow? It would be a dream come true for a young man. Whatever eventuates, one thing is certain, Mervyn is welcome to share my life as long as he wishes, and there, in the stillness, snow blowing hard against the windowpane, I said a silent prayer to the almighty that Mervyn felt the same.

Chapter Twelve
Mervyn's MG - Roast Turkey - King's Speech

Having packed Mervyn back to his own bed at first light, I threw off my blankets and hurriedly bathed and dressed, because, even as a boy, I could never stay in bed on Christmas morning. As I made my way downstairs, I noticed Mervyn was also an early riser, since, when I passed his door, I heard him singing in his bath; a comforting sound and one I was keen to perpetuate.

Everyone arrived at the table together, and we ate a hearty breakfast provided of course by Mrs Lanesome. Then it was time to open our presents. Eric and Amy gave me a nice foulard dressing gown, with the Fry crest thoughtfully embroidered on the breast pocket. Moreover, I was pleased because, although Eric and Amy had only known him a couple of days, they thought of a present for Mervyn, presenting him with a pair of gold and topaz cuff links. Eric's present from me was a pair of crystal decanters I found at Jolly's while searching for furniture for Camden Place. Mine for Amy was a bottle of Chanel No 5 purchased at Mr Breeze's perfumery in The Corridor. Emily was delighted with her doll, and immediately began to undress her.

"Mervyn," I said, once all the parcels were open. "Now it's your turn."

"What do you mean Ron?" he stammered. "I didn't get you anything. I wasn't expecting all this."

Eric and Amy laughed.

"You've a lot to learn Mervyn," Eric said. "Christmas is Ron's favourite time of the year."

"I'm beginning to see that," he replied.

"Come on everyone!" I shouted. "We'll need to put on our hats, coats, and gumboots, because what I have to show you is outside."

We were grateful to find that earlier, Mark Febrey, my gardener had cleared the steps and paths of snow, as a result our progress around to the rear of the house was considerably easier.

"I bet I know what this is," Eric whispered to Amy.

Since we were heading towards the garage, it was obvious what we might find.

"Open the doors Mervyn!" I ordered."

He did so, to reveal a bright, shining, brand new, black, MG NA Magnette sports car.

"Wow!" Mervyn gasped. "For me?"

"For you."

"But it's crazy. I'm too young to drive."

"I admit, you don't look your age, but anyway you're seventeen on the first of January. Thompson will teach you. We'll take it into the city later. I've some presents for your family."

Glancing at Eric and Amy, I read by their expressions, that they thought I had gone completely around the bend. But as always in such cases, I simply ignored them.

Later, with Mervyn squeezed into the back seat, along with a dozen parcels, and myself in the passenger seat, endeavouring to fit my long legs under the dashboard, Thompson drove us through the snowy lanes and into Bath.

The sun was shining from a clear blue sky, and I failed to remember Bath looking as pretty as it did that Christmas morning. A thick layer of snow covered the crescents, squares, and terraces, and even the stone carvings on the Abbey's great west front were frosted with ice. Clearly, there had been quite a blizzard during the night.

We arrived at Camden Place, and while Thompson and Mervyn tried hard not to laugh, I stood in the snow and changed into the Father Christmas suit, having the greatest difficulty fastening the black leather belt across my ample belly. Finally, I hooked the long white beard over my ears; threw the hood over my head; the sack over my shoulder, and marched up to the front door. I knocked three times and waited for a reply. Betsey the parlour maid had the day off and so it was hardly surprising when Richard opened the door. The look on his face when he saw who was standing on the threshold was worth all the tea in china.

"Ho! Ho! Ho!" I bellowed. "Have all the children in this house been good all the year?"

Richard was speechless, and could only nod.

"Then I've presents for all of them."

"Mother!" Richard yelled. "Father Christmas is at the door and he says he's got presents."

"Then let him in," Mrs Watson said, appearing at the parlour door, holding Eric in her arms. "He'll freeze to death out there. Doris, Ruby, and Sarah are in the garden making a snowman, Father Christmas. I'll call them. Go into the parlour and warm yourself."

"Thank you Ma'am!" I roared. "You're most kind."

Richard seemed hardly concerned that his brother Mervyn and a chauffeur had arrived with Father Christmas and trotted beside me as we entered the room. I sat in the big chair beside the fire, but no sooner had I put the sack of presents between my feet, then the door burst open and Ruby and Doris rushed in, eager to see the famous visitor.

"Father Christmas!" yelled Ruby. "You're really here."

"Yes my dear," I said, the beard tickling my nose. "And I've presents for everyone."

"Hooray!" cheered the little girls.

However, Sarah remained at the door, wearing a serious expression.

"Come in my dear," I chuckled, trying to reassure her. "But we've one person missing."

"Father's not up yet," Mrs Watson, whispered. "He did a little too much celebrating last night down at the Larkhall Tavern."

"Really," I said. "Then we'll put his present under the tree for later. He may well need a hair of the dog when he wakes up."

Beginning with the youngest, everyone watched Mrs Watson unwrap Eric's present.

"Toy soldiers Eric!" she said. "Aren't you lucky. Thank you Captain."

Doris opened her present to discover a doll, almost half her size, dressed in blue velvet with eyes that opened and shut, and rich brown curly hair.

"Tip her up Doris," I prompted.

She did so, and smiled when the doll said 'Mama'.

"Thank you Captain," said Doris shyly. "I'm going to call her Crystal."

Ruby's present was also a doll. Hers possessing blonde hair, blue eyes and dressed in pink satin.

"What will you call her Ruby?" I asked.

"She's Sandra Father Christmas. Just because she's so pretty."

Richard ran to take his present from his place beside Sarah in the doorway, which was obvious, since it is very difficult to disguise a football with Christmas wrapping paper. Sarah then was the last to receive a gift. I had purposely taken more consideration with her present, as she is a rather particular girl, no longer young enough to be happy with simply a doll. So I had taken the time to scour the shelves of WH Smith and sons, the booksellers in the High Street, and came up with two of the latest popular books for girls, 'Mary Poppins', by Australian writer PL Travers, and 'Ballet Shoes', a story of three children on the stage by Noel Streatfield. The look on Sarah's face as she tore away the paper was enough to convince me that I had made the right choices.

All the while, a delicious aroma wafted up the back stairs, the source, a huge turkey roasting in the oven. Mrs Pratt, the cook, had been hard at work since early morning, peeling potatoes, preparing brussel sprouts, parsnips, and carrots, all ready for Christmas dinner.

Then to follow there was to be a spicy Jolly's Christmas pudding and custard.

"My word!" I said. "That smells good."

"Stay for dinner Father Christmas," Ruby pleaded.

"I'm sorry my dear," I said through my whiskers. "I've many more children to visit today and wouldn't want to disappoint them. I wonder if you'll allow your son Mervyn, to come along with me Mrs Watson. He'll not be a hindrance and I'll return him to you later on."

"Of course, Father Christmas."

Mrs Watson and the young ones followed Mervyn, Thompson and I to the front door, and stood shivering on the doorstep while we scrambled into the MG. Strangely, neither Doris, Ruby nor Richard questioned why Father Christmas was leaving in a sports car. But that's children for you.

For the month prior to Christmas, the sale of radio sets at Duck and Son and Pinker, on Pulteney Bridge, had doubled. This was due entirely to the announcement that our beloved King George would make a Christmas address to his people, not only in Great Britain, but also across the empire. This unprecedented event had caused the rush to own a radio. We already had a set at Hyde House, but I saw to it that one was included in the furnishing of Camden Place.

Radio and the British Broadcasting Association, were fast becoming the opium of the masses, and nightly we listened to Jack Payne and the BBC Dance Orchestra, as well as programmes such as Toy Town and The Week in Westminster.

Back at Hyde House, Mervyn and I joined Amy, Eric, and Emily, making a jovial party around our own festive banquet.

Having eaten our fill of pork stuffing, turkey, roast and boiled vegetables, and Christmas pudding, we adjourned to the sitting room to listen to the radio.

Once it had warmed up and crackled into life, we heard a choir singing carols. Then the announcer introduced the William Walton Band. Next, the Cotswold Shepherd presented His Royal Highness to the world. We listened in silence to the King's Christmas message, since never before had a ruler of a nation been heard by his people all over the world, and at precisely the same time. I remember we remarked how genteel and genuine he sounded. Like everyone's grandfather. In fact, the entire experience was extremely moving.

To while away the rest of the afternoon, Eric, Amy, Mervyn, and Emily played charades, while I went to my room to take a nap.

***

Mother and Wilfred were due to arrive on Boxing Day and I was a little apprehensive. Neither knew about Mervyn so it would be interesting to see their reaction. I knew Eric could hardly wait to see their faces when my new prodigy was introduced. In fact, when the time came I was somewhat surprised, because after their response to Eric fifteen years earlier, I was expecting open hostility. However, despite my nervousness, almost everyone took to Mervyn immediately, except Wilfred of course, who looked down his nose disdainfully. Therefore, it gave me the greatest pleasure to see my new friend fitting so well into my little social circle.

Mother warmed to him, especially when he sang a rendition of Schubert's 'Who is Sylvia?', composed to accompany a song from Shakespeare's play, 'Two Gentlemen of Verona', the song being mother's particular favourite.

On the other hand, Wilfred was scornfully aloof to both Mervyn and myself, only speaking to me occasionally over the couple of days he and mother stayed at Hyde House, and certainly never attempting a conversation with Mervyn.

As I remarked earlier, fifteen years had passed since Wilfred challenged my motives in bringing Eric to live with me at Hyde House, Wilfred remaining, like me, a bachelor. Was there perhaps another reason for his resentment, and was that motive jealousy? It mattered little if Wilfred chose to behave so rudely. His attitude would not spoil my otherwise perfect Christmas.

***

Eric, Amy, and Emily said goodbye on New Year's Eve morning. Also, Mother and Wilfred left for Shamswell a while later, meaning Mervyn and I were alone in the house, except for the servants of course.

"It's your birthday tomorrow Mervyn," I said, as we sat down to lunch. "Don't you want to be home for your birthday? Your father and mother will miss you."

Mervyn shook his head.

"I like it here. It's warm and cosy. Besides I get to sleep in a lovely big four poster bed."

He gave me a cheeky grin.

"But what about the flat? You've not even slept there yet."

"There'll be time. Anyway, you're the one who wants me here."

"You're the one who won't go home, you mean. The maid will be washing your shirts and underpants next."

"That's alright. Thompson can get me a change of clothes tomorrow."

Clearly, the lad I plucked from destitution was fast becoming a Little Lord Fauntleroy.

"But can I stay tonight? After all, it's my birthday and I can do what I like on my birthday."

"Very well. But promise me you'll let Thompson drive you back to Bath after breakfast."

Seeing him smile, I began to realise that Mervyn knew exactly how the course of our friendship was going to run. Furthermore, I began to see him recognise how to manipulate and persuade me to do anything he asked. A talent he has utilised to its utmost in the years since.

Sitting beside the fire, later that evening, listening to the radio, Mervyn and I waited for the chimes of Big Ben, so we could toast the end of one year and the beginning of the next. Also, as the last chime faded, Mervyn became eighteen.

"Happy Birthday Mervyn," I said, as we said goodnight on the landing.

Then closed our respective bedroom doors.

Chapter Thirteen
RMS Viceroy of India - The South Atlantic - Tristan da Cunha

If you remember, a little while back I recalled the afternoon of the Eisteddfod, when I suddenly experienced a heart stopping moment as I listened to Mervyn singing his song. Well, since then I have continued to feel a fluttering sensation in my chest, and taking my pulse one day I realised that every now and again my heart misses a beat. Consequently, and without saying a word to anyone, I walked to the station and caught a train into Bath.

***

"You've developed an arrhythmia," Doctor Ingram said, once he had listened to my heart for several minutes. "It's barely noticeable, but your blood pressure's rather high. I'll give you something for that. Although, your weight concerns me. You really must try to shed some pounds."

"I know doctor," I said. "They do seem to have piled on in the last few years."

"Also, you smoke too much."

"Everyone says so."

"Both are bad for your heart. We don't want you to drop dead on us, do we?"

"No doctor. I think I've been overdoing it lately."

"Which might be the reason for the erratic heartbeat. I prescribe a rest. A holiday. Perhaps somewhere warm."

Doctor Ingram's suggestion started me thinking. Maybe a break in the sun. Greece possibly, or Morocco. Then one morning, I happened to see an advertisement in The Times.

'Winter in the Sun'

Cruise the South Atlantic in First Class Luxury

RMS Viceroy of India departs Tilbury, January 15th,

 on a month's cruise.

Ports of call, Lisbon, Madeira, The Canary Islands,

Tristan Du Cunha, And, Rio de Janeiro'

It sounded just the ticket, so I chased up to London to the Peninsular and Orient offices in Cockspur Street, and booked as well as paid for a birth.

***

"You're lucky," Mervyn said, scowling into the fire. "I wish I was going. I'm sick of this lousy winter."

I had invited him to Sunday dinner, taking the opportunity to tell him of my plans.

"It's impossible I'm afraid," I replied. "You started at the tech only a few weeks ago. It would be silly to miss a whole month. I didn't get you there for you to flunk your first term."

Mervyn was disgruntled, and it was written all over his face.

"I want to go home," he said, getting out of his chair. "Get Thompson to drive me."

"Don't be silly," I said, endeavouring to take the heat out of the moment. "When the summer holidays begin I'll take you on a cruise, I promise. Sit down and have a drink."

Mervyn slumped back in the chair.

"Anything I like?"

"Of course."

"Then I'll have what you have."

"Scotch and soda?"

"Yes."

Dubiously, I went to the drinks cabinet and unscrewed the top of the Johnny Walker bottle. However, keeping my back to him, I measured a thimble size tot of whisky into a glass, then half-filled it with soda from the siphon.

"Thanks," said Mervyn, as I gave him the glass. "If I'm old enough to drive, then I'm old enough to drink."

Recalling this scene, I now realise how spoilt Mervyn had become. Did I instigate this? On the other hand, had he always been that way? His precocious manner hardly concerned me. I was completely under his spell, and had he asked, I would have given him the world.

***

For the sake of repetition, I shall refrain from spending too much time describing my winter cruise. There will be further opportunities when other voyages prove more adventurous. I will recount one incident that sticks in my mind however, which I hope will be worth the telling.

We had been at sea for several weeks, having paid Lisbon, Madeira, The Canary Islands, as well as St Helena a visit, and were steaming leisurely south towards the island of Tristan da Cunha.

At the last count, there are just one hundred and fifty people living close to starvation on the north side of the island, in the tiny hamlet, Edinburgh of the Seven Seas. It appears that, if their potato crop fails, then the islanders have only their meagre supplies to see them through the long cold winter. The building of the Suez Canal is partly the reason for their plight, since fewer ships now navigate the southern ocean, meaning there is less opportunity for the islanders to trade their handicrafts in exchange for supplies from passing ships.

Our ship was scheduled to approach Tristan da Cunha in the early hours of the morning, so I made sure I went to bed early to be fresh and prepared to go ashore after breakfast.

At six thirty, my steward woke me with my usual cup of tea.

"Land in sight sir," he said, putting it on the bedside table.

Once washed, shaved, and dressed, I ordered a light breakfast in the veranda cafe, where I watched from my table a huge island appear; a great towering conical mass of rock, its peak shrouded by a blanket of cloud. As we drew nearer, I made out a cluster of small stone cottages above a jetty and a beach, the scene reminding me of the west coast of Scotland, where fishing villages huddle the shore, while the rugged Scottish landscape looms behind them. Other passengers had joined me, everyone keen to see the island so often talked about back in Britain. Nonetheless, by the look of the swell, I suspected we would not be stepping on the island that day.

"Look!" exclaimed a gentleman pointing toward the island. "They're coming out to meet us,"

Sure enough, squinting in the glare of the sun slowly rising behind the ship, I saw the hulls of maybe a dozen large rowing boats, heading out of the harbour and coming our way.

"Ahoy there!" a man shouted from the deck of the first to reach us. "Welcome to Tristan Da Cunha."

He was a swarthy fellow with a mass of black hair, reminding me of the men I saw in Naples.

"I'm Repetto! The headman."

"Come aboard," Captain Thornton shouted from the window of the bridge.

A rope ladder and line fell over the side and I noticed other boats arriving, each crewed by equally burly and bronzed men. There were also women aboard, wearing coloured headscarves and shawls. Unfortunately, some appeared quite seasick, vomiting over the side, causing me to appreciate how important it was to the inhabitants that our ship had stopped at the island. After all, what woman would dare to risk the heavy swell that morning?

Before long, Repetto's boat was alongside, and leaning over the gunwale as far as we dared, we saw Repetto haul on the safety line, tie it to his waist, grab the rope ladder, and begin the perilous climb aboard. Once we were certain he was safe, we hurried along the main deck in order we might see, and maybe meet, this romantic stranger. In fact, I was the first to reach the gangway gate.

"Welcome aboard The Viceroy of India," I said, as Repetto scrambled over the side aided by two sailors.

"Thank you sir," gasped Repetto, taking my hand in an iron grip. "It's kind of you to stop at Tristan. We'd no idea you were coming. But we keep a watch from the lookout just in case. Old Bob Grass saw your lights early this morning."

Repetto was as tall as I was, and there are few who can claim that. He wore a thick blue Guernsey, heavy corduroy trousers, and rubber boots to his knees. He may have been in his early thirties, but his face was tanned and weather beaten, giving him an older appearance.

"Good to see you're safely aboard, Mr Repetto," said Captain Thornton, having arrived on the deck. "I've mail from England for you all. I've also asked my first officer to see the companion way is put out so more of your people can come aboard. I doubt if my passengers will make it ashore in this sea."

Naturally, those of us hoping to go ashore were disappointed to hear the Captain. But when we saw more people climbing up the companionway, our disappointment rapidly turned to curiosity. While Captain Thornton escorted Repetto through the veranda café and into the smoking room, a couple of passengers and myself greeted the first of the female arrivals.

"You're very kind sir," a young woman said, curtsying. "We seldom have visitors. It's such a delight to see a new face."

Having introduced myself, she told me her name was Elizabeth. Although, I thought her manner and appearance old fashioned, she possessed a pretty face, made even more appealing by a red and yellow scarf covering her golden hair.

"How many of you are there on the island?" I asked, as we climbed the main staircase.

"I think someone said we were one hundred and sixty seven, at the last count, sir. Seventy six women and girls, and ninety two men and boys."

"It must be lonely for you all."

"Not at all sir. We're terribly happy. I wouldn't want to be anywhere else. Not that I've ever seen other places of course. But we all know each other and get on well. After all, each of us share seven surnames. If there's any trouble, our headman, Peter and his mother, Frances, sort things out."

"Is Peter his name?" I said, referring to Repetto, walking ahead of us with the Captain.

"Yes. I don't know why he's the headman. I think he was elected because the Repetto's are one of the three original families on the island."

"Apparently English soldiers were garrisoned on Tristan da Cunha in case the French tried to free Napoleon from his island prison of St. Helena."

"Really sir!" Elizabeth said. "Well I never! I know that many years ago, there were just three men on Tristan and only one had a wife. So the other two bargained with a passing sea captain to bring them a couple of women from another island."

"Then you would almost certainly be related to them."

"We all are sir. One big happy family."

Arriving in the dining saloon we found a long table set with silver tureens and warmers, each containing fried bacon and mushrooms, grilled sausages and tomatoes, devilled kidneys and black pudding. In fact everything one would find in an English breakfast.

Already there were considerable numbers of islanders on board, and although they were impossible to count, I calculated at least fifty; in effect, almost a third of the population of Tristan da Cunha. With everyone seated, bleary-eyed stewards began serving breakfast to each table, although some did so rather grudgingly, perhaps contemptuous at waiting on a class of person to which they were unaccustomed. There were six at our table, and I was sitting beside Elizabeth. And as we tucked into bowls of hot porridge, she told me a little about her life on the island.

"As a little girl, I remember our minister bringing a newspaper back from England. He used it to help us learn to read. Such tiny writing! You can imagine how battered it became as time went by."

"Some folks write letters in the British newspapers saying the people of Tristan suffer too much and should be relocated to a less isolated island."

"Sir, we would die if we left the island. How would we be with people we didn't know? It would be so strange."

"But what about the rats and the terrible weather?" How do you manage?"

"It's not true about the rats," interjected another Tristanite woman seated at our table. "When 'The Atlantis' called a few years ago, its captain wanted to know about our plague of rats. Admittedly, at one time there was more than usual, but it made us wonder how the rumour started."

"Do you grow crops?" asked a woman passenger seated next to her.

"Only potatoes madam," answered the woman. "We've made many attempts to grow other vegetables, when we've the seeds that is. But they've always failed. There's a small grape vine, a strawberry patch and a tiny fig tree in Frances' and Peter's garden. So you see the climate can't be too bad."

"In the evening we women fashion leather into moccasins," added Elizabeth. "The men polish horn, and the children make feather mats. We sell these to the passengers of the big ships so we've money to give the captain, in exchange for stores."

"But that's barely enough to purchase very much," I said.

"We manage. We've great hopes for our potato crop this year. If it's poor, then it'll be a bad winter for us. All we'll get to eat is fish, mutton, and beef."

"But you need your greens," interrupted, a woman passenger sitting opposite us.

Regardless of what I heard, looking around the saloon, the islanders appeared healthy and contented. Despite the dreadful winter weather and the constant threat of starvation, I realised the Tristanites were survivors. It was a pleasure to see them enjoying their breakfast. To be eating fresh fruit and newly baked bread must be such a pleasure.

Surely though there had to be a solution to their plight, a ship loaded with supplies could make a regular stop at Tristan. After all, Tristan da Cunha is a British territory; therefore, it is the responsibility of the Government to carry the expense. No wonder the cry in Parliament is to evacuate the island, thus ending the Tristanites happiness. I was determined to play a small part in alleviating a little of their deprivation and consequently began to hatch a plan.

With the last morsel consumed, Captain Thornton led everyone into the music room, where the stewards began to serve coffee. I think the women must have enjoyed sitting in the deep sofas and easy chairs, while the men stood about awkwardly, obviously unaccustomed to the opulent surroundings. It was then I noticed the men had the same Italian appearance as Repetto, with the same olive skin and jet-black hair. After all, every one of them was related to the three original Italian islanders. The women however were more diverse, some with fair hair, others brunette. In addition, the islanders struck me as being quite handsome, and considering there were just thirty-three families on the island there seemed little evidence of inbreeding.

As more of the ship's passengers arrived, I took the opportunity to draw Mr Evans, the Chief Purser, aside.

"I've a request Mr Evans. Might it be possible for me to purchase provisions from the ship's stores? I'd like to present them to the islanders."

"How much would you want to spend, Captain Fry?"

"Is five hundred pound a fair sum?"

"More than generous sir. But we've a week before we reach Rio and I'm worried such an amount might deplete our supplies. How about four hundred?"

"Of course. What could I buy?"

"Flour, butter, lard, bacon, salt, pepper, sugar, tea, and coffee."

"Do you have stocks of vegetables?"

"Only tins sir. Peas, carrots, beans and beetroot."

"That sounds just right. Could we load their boats before they leave?"

"Of course. I'll have a word with Captain Thornton."

"Thank you Mr Evans. Also, I'd rather my name's not mentioned."

Returning to my seat, I discovered the steward had replaced the empty coffee pot with a fresh one. However, I was just about to pour Elizabeth and her friend another cup, when Captain Thornton stood up.

"Ladies and gentlemen!" he said. "Can I have your attention, if I may? Firstly, let me say what a pleasure it's been for my crew, the passengers, and myself, to have you aboard this morning. Back in England, many people raise concerns regarding your situation here on Tristan da Cunha. They realise your isolation and worry you might meet with hardship. However, on our return I will be pleased to report that I found you well and happy."

The Tristanites smiled; some even began to applaud.

"I have one other important piece of news. One of our passengers, a most generous person who wishes to remain anonymous, has been so moved and impressed by your good nature and fortitude that they've spent four hundred pounds purchasing a quantity of the ship's supplies, which they wish to present to you."

Although there was an audible gasp from the people around me, I feigned surprise, and once Captain Thornton finished his speech, I invited Elizabeth, and several Tristanites, including two handsome young men, on a guided tour of the ship. Everyone was most impressed with the swimming pool, a luxury never before seen. I suggested I find the young men a bathing costume each so they could take a swim. Disappointingly, but hardly unusual for fishermen, they confessed to being unable to swim. By the time, my purchases were loaded they filled the decks of two fishing boats, and piled so high I feared the vessels would sink.

Then sadly, my fellow passengers and I watched the islanders descend the companionway and climb into their boats. My new friend Elizabeth and I said goodbye, after promising to write, and the last I saw of her she was waving from the boat as it struck out for the island.

Meeting the people of Tristan da Cunha I found moving as well as sobering, and I perceived my life very differently after that day.

Chapter Fourteen
Father's funeral - A summer cruise to Norway

On February 11th, our ship steamed up The English Channel and into the Thames Estuary. However, as we berthed at Tilbury, I received a telegram from my mother telling me that my father had died. Consequently, instead of returning to Somerset, I collected my brother from Whitehall Court in Westminster. Then taking a taxi to Kings Cross Station, we boarded a train for Skipton in Yorkshire, where a country taxi drove us the short distance to Elliston Hall.

Not surprisingly, I found it difficult to feel remorse at my father's passing. He and I were never close. Father was a cold man, showing little affection to neither his wife nor his sons. Nevertheless, I dutifully played the part of the sorrowing son, standing beside mother in Elliston village church, while Reverend Sumner read the eulogy. Subsequently, outside in the churchyard as the coffin disappeared into the grave. Yet I was interested to see Wilfred displaying a type of grief, since I always thought of him as a carbon copy of father in possessing little kindness or emotion. However, seeing him dabbing his eyes with his handkerchief, clearly I was wrong in my assumption.

Neither he nor I remained long at Elliston Hall since I was eager to return to Hyde House, and Wilfred was keen to return to the House of Commons, as he had recently contested and won a local Yorkshire seat.

Life resumed its congenial routine as winter turned to spring. Although due to my spell spent on an ocean liner, the experience of on-board luxury had rather spoiled me, and I found myself inclining towards the shipping news in The Times newspaper.

Accordingly, one day in early summer an advertisement caught my eye. 'Norway' it read, followed by a florid description of shimmering mirror like fjords, limitless waterfalls, and mighty glaciers.

RMS Viceroy of India, my favourite liner, was conducting a twenty-one-night cruise for first class passengers only, leaving Tilbury on 22nd June, and Leith in Scotland on June 23rd, the cost, twenty-one guineas.

By now father's will was settled, mother, Wilfred and I receiving an equal third of his estate. Of course, to me money was of little consequence. The thought of a large sum soon to be deposited in my account at Lloyds Bank in Milsom Street prompted me to think rashly.

After all, I had promised Mervyn, and a Fry never reneges on a promise. The tech would break for the summer holidays the week before, so I eagerly telephoned Thompson and asked him to drive me into Bath.

Since the beginning of term, Mervyn had been driving his sports car into the city, but the previous week he had a slight collision with a tractor at the bottom of the drive. Meaning the bumper required a small repair, so his car was at Mr Waite's garage. As Mervyn stayed the occasional night at Hyde House, Thompson was able to drive him to the tech in the morning.

Thompson and I waited outside the school, and just after four o'clock, Mervyn emerged accompanied by two friends.

Of course, I recognised them instantly. The tall lean fair-haired lad was Michael Pritchard and the shorter stockier lad, Edward Jacobs. I already knew them by their nicknames Mickey and Teddy, and aware from what Mervyn had implied during several conversations regarding his friends, that they were of the same inclination as Mervyn and myself.

Since Mervyn began attending tech, he had grown, not in stature, but in maturity. He was leaner, and had acquired a foxy appearance.

By that, I mean his face was thinner, his eyes keener, and with the aid of a newly grown moustache, had assumed a rather spivvy appearance, although he would have chastised me for saying so. He remained the apple of my eye however and could do no wrong.

"What's up?" he said, climbing into the back seat.

"Nothing," I said. "I thought I'd meet you because I've something to tell you."

He turned to me eagerly.

"Okay! What?"

Mervyn never dwelt much on ceremony.

"You remember I promised you something a few months ago."

"Now what was that? Let me think," he teased. "There's been so much! Oh, yes! You said you'd take me on a cruise."

"How good of you to remember, and now that father's money is settled, I think I can afford it."

Mervyn laughed raucously, even loud enough to cause Thompson to take his eyes off the road.

"Afford it! You were already a millionaire before your old man died. His money will make you a double millionaire."

By now, the Humber was travelling along the Lower Bristol Road.

"Where are we going anyway?" Mervyn asked. "I said I'd meet the boys later for a swim."

"To Norway."

"Not the bloody cruise. Where are we going now?"

"Hyde House of course. Don't you want to plan our trip?"

"So you've booked it. Just you and me."

"What do you mean?"

I knew what was coming and braced myself for a confrontation.

"Couldn't the boys join us?" Mervyn begged. "Isn't it boring with only me?"

"Of course not. But Mickey and Teddy are hard work. Besides, you're more than a handful on your own."

"Let them come. I'll get bored with all those toffs. Go on. It'll be fun."

Shaking my head, I realised he had cornered me once again. It was inevitable I would give way to him eventually. I always do.

"Very well. Although you and I will share a suite, while Teddy and Mickey will have a cabin each."

"They'll need new clothes. They're not as well kitted out as me. After all, won't there be parties and dances?"

"Almost certainly," I replied. "And we wouldn't want them to let the side down would we."

"Yippee!" Mervyn yelled. "I can't wait to tell them. They'll be tickled pink."

At this point, I took the opportunity to ask a question I wanted to ask for some time.

"How much do Mickey and Teddy know about us?"

Mervyn frowned. "About the presents you give me for being nice to you?"

"Yes. For instance, have you ever told them that I bought you a car and moved your family from Swinbourne's Buildings?"

"Of course not! I don't want them knowing my business. It's nothing to do with them."

"Then how do you explain the flat and all the expensive furniture?"

"I say what dad says, that a rich old chap left me loads of money in his will."

"Then it'll be up to you to buy your friend's new clothes. Tomorrow, we'll run into Bath and open an account for you at Lloyds. I'll arrange for a sum of money to go into your account each month. That way you can do as you please with a cheque book of your own."

"How much will I have to spend?"

Knowing Mervyn's liking for possessions the question was hardly surprising.

"Forty pounds a month. Except you'll need to be careful. There'll be no overdraft facility. When you run out, you're finished until the next month's deposit."

"Come on though. You'd help me out."

I shook my head. "It's about time you took on some responsibility."

As the realisation sank in, Mervyn began to smile. "That's nearly five hundred pounds a year. I wouldn't need to work. Then what am I doing at the tech?"

"Do you wish to be idle all your life? You need something to do. Besides, typing is a great skill to learn. Typewriters are here to stay."

Accordingly, and with his newly acquired chequebook, Mervyn took Teddy and Mickey to the gentleman's outfitters at Jolly's and kitted his friends with pairs of slacks, sports jackets, dinner suits, lounge suits, dress shirts, poplin shirts, collars, ties, sweaters and jumpers. As a result, a smarter pair of Bath dandies it would have been hard to find.

It fascinated me to see the effect this show of prosperity had on his friends. All of a sudden, Mickey and Teddy were aware that Mervyn was capable of generosity, which radically changed his standing within the trio. Mervyn became the leader. Mervyn could do no wrong. Of course, it was inevitable Mervyn would be altered by this sudden elevation in rank, and he became full to the brim with confidence, strutting around like a courting pigeon.

Meanwhile, it remained necessary to obtain permission from the lad's parents. Not surprisingly, Mr Watson was most compliant and agreed to all suggestions. Moreover, Teddy's mother was pleased to see her boy have a holiday, sadly, Teddy's father passing away from tuberculosis when the boy was barely seven.

It proved hardly as simple to convince Mickey's parents of my motives in taking their son on a cruise. When Mickey took me to his house in The Paragon, his mother and father frowned suspiciously, and were obviously distrustful of my intentions.

Of course, I was aware that cruising was far too expensive for most people's pockets. The lower and middle classes saw ocean liners exclusively as a means of getting from one place to another, with usually, in the case of emigration, no return passage. To regard a ship as a place of relaxation, pleasure, and sightseeing was completely beyond the capability and imagination of the majority of the population.

"There'll be other youngsters of his own age," I said, trying to avoid the couple's prying eyes. "It's a marvellous opportunity. The scenery of Norway is spectacular, especially the glaciers and fjords."

"Will there be someone aboard to supervise?" Mr Pritchard asked.

"My mother's coming along, and she's terribly good at keeping the young ones in order. There'll be excursions ashore, parties, and deck games."

However, the more I persisted with my vivid description of life aboard, the less convinced the Pritchard's appeared.

"Michael's a delicate boy," Mrs Pritchard interjected. "I'm worried his chest might return. Isn't Norway terribly cold?"

"Not in summer Mrs Pritchard. Besides, there's a doctor on the ship to take care of anyone should they become ill."

"Your wife and children will be accompanying you of course Captain Fry?" Mr Pritchard said.

It was impossible for me not to notice Mickey wince and begin to blush.

"As yet Mr Pritchard I remain unmarried. However, that is not for the want of trying."

He smiled at me witheringly.

"Very well Captain. I can't see any reason for Mrs Pritchard and myself to stand in the way of Michael's enjoyment. We only trust he will not be an encumbrance to you and your friends."

"Yes Michael," Mrs Pritchard interrupted. "You mind your P's and Q's."

"I will mother," Mickey, replied meekly, which was the first and only occasion I ever saw him display humility.

***

After father's death, Wilfred and I managed to persuade mother to leave Elliston Hall and return to Somerset. I realised it was hardly appropriate for her to live with me at Hyde House, as it would make Mervyn's presence almost impossible. Consequently, I telephoned Wilfred and suggested he accommodate her at Shamswell, a country house he had acquired with his share of father's estate. He reluctantly agreed, but added a proviso.

During a previous telephone conversation, I stupidly let slip my plans for the summer cruise to Norway, which he used as a means to postpone mother's move until Parliament recessed.

"Why not take mother," he said. "She's been through such a lot this year. She needs a holiday."

Desperately I tried to think of a reason why it was impossible for me to include her, but failed, and therefore conceded defeat. Moreover, this was hardly the end of Wilfred's guile, because the day I posted my cheque to P&O, the phone rang at Hyde House. It was Wilfred.

"No doubt you'll be pleased to hear I'm also joining you on the cruise," he said cheerfully. "It was mother's idea. She thinks it'll be good for us to have a long rest, so I booked our cabins yesterday."

I could do little to prevent them, so decided that if this were the case, the phrase 'the more the merrier,' would have to suffice. Why not provide the lads with some company of their own age. The children of my cousin Gilbert immediately sprung to mind, because they were the right age, twin girls of fifteen and a boy of seventeen. As the summer holidays were beginning, Gilbert and his wife would be more than willing to hand over their children for a lengthy holiday. Furthermore, they would doubly benefit, as I was the one to pay.

In order to add the new additions to my party, I travelled to London, and as the P&O office was in the city, I decided to surprise Eric at the Inns and shout him lunch.

After several glasses of wine, my enthusiasm ran away with my tongue, and I confessed my plan to him. His typically negative attitude was as I expected, and I immediately regretted my outburst. He even expressed an opinion that Mervyn and his friends would feel awkward and inferior around people of the upper classes, and virtually accused me of conducting a social experiment by exploiting children. Of course, I was terribly annoyed and told him so to his face.

Nevertheless, I remained unperturbed and continued to make my arrangements, telephoning Gilbert to ensure his children were at Tilbury by lunchtime on the morning of departure.

Chapter Fifteen
Up to Paddington - All aboard - A tour of the ship

The days hurried by, and at last it was time to pack our bags and catch the morning train to London. The four of us took up a first class compartment, and smoking my pipe, I relaxed into my seat, happy to watch the lads as they chattered excitedly, since the day they anticipated had arrived at last.

Neither Mervyn, Mickey nor Teddy had ever been to London, so it amused me to see their reaction when we eventually steamed into Paddington Station.

"It's huge," Mervyn exclaimed, as we followed a luggage porter to the taxi rank.

He was referring to the roof, which I might add, continues to be a wonder of construction, as well as a testament to the engineering genius of Isambard Kingdom Brunel.

My driver Thompson had collected Mickey and Teddy before breakfast that morning. As a result, by the time the taxi dropped us at the front of Fenchurch Street Station, I knew everyone was hungry so suggested we take lunch in the station buffet. Then it was merely a case of catching the boat train to Tilbury, a journey of three-quarters of an hour.

By this time, I was familiar with the sights, sounds and smells of the docks, but I still feel tremendously excited seeing the ship tied up at the quay.

As our train pulled into Tilbury Station, stores and provisions were being winched into the cargo hatches. Nevertheless, the gangways were in position, so I assumed we were able to board. Therefore, after seeing our trunks safely secured on a trolley, we climbed the gangway onto the ship, where a steward would show us to our cabins.

Since my Atlantic cruise, I was familiar with the layout of the ship; consequently, when I reserved our cabins, I made sure Mervyn and I had a pair of adjoining staterooms on C deck. My main reason for the preference was that they possessed a pair of sliding doors, enabling both occupants to share a large suite. Alternatively, I arranged for Teddy and Mickey to have single cabins on D Deck. I had no idea where mother and Wilfred were.

***

At this juncture, I feel I must break off the narrative and endeavour to provide you with a description of the ship, which was to convey us on our voyage. As you read the following paragraphs, you may well understand why I withheld an earlier description. RMS Viceroy of India is beyond compare, and well deserves a place in my story.

Initially named 'Taj Mahal', she was laid down in a Glasgow shipyard in April 1927. Then fitted out to the interior designs of Elsie Mackay, the daughter of the Earl of Inchcape, and subsequently launched on 15th September 1928 by the Countess of Halifax, wife of the Earl of Halifax, the then Viceroy of India.

Built for the Peninsula and Orient Steam Navigation Company, the ship was intended for the prestigious Bombay run. In addition, at the time of her launch, she was one of only three ships to be driven by the revolutionary and new, electric turbo power.

James Mackay the Earl of Inchcape, shipping magnate and chairman of P&O, was the first to envisage the idea of providing a single cabin for every first class passenger. It was his daughter, Elsie, however, who turned the dream into a reality. Tragically, Lady Elsie was never to see her wonderful interiors or even the launch of the ship she transformed into a floating luxury hotel. In March of the same year, she disappeared over the North Atlantic, attempting to fly from east to west.

Positioned on six decks amidships, the Cabins de Luxe are lavishly furnished with double oak bedsteads, flock mattresses, hardwood wardrobes and dressing tables. Also, and extremely modern for today, each includes a washbasin, with the luxury of hot and cold running water. Below the single first class cabins on decks A and B, is deck C, where thirty-two well-fitted staterooms are located, some with sliding doors, connecting one with the other. This enables passengers travelling in families the opportunity to share. In addition, two connecting cabins can share a private bathroom. Others on this deck are connected to smaller cabins for passengers who wish a maid or valet to be nearby.

Nothing is spared to provide an atmosphere of opulence and refined extravagance. As well as the furniture, light-brushed English oak panels the bulkheads, and expensive fabrics cover the beds and hang at the portholes.

Notwithstanding, it is the design of the public rooms where Elsie Mackay's deft hand and impeccable eye for detail really shines.

Spread between A and B deck, four large rooms are forward and astern, allocated for lounging during the day, dancing at night, or smoking, reading, and eating.

The George V Dining Saloon is situated at the forward end of A Deck, and directly below the bridge. This large airy, brilliant room lit during the day by tall leaded windows facing forward, port and starboard, is capable of seating four hundred and fifteen first class passengers at one sitting. Reflected in the crystal mirrored bulkhead, and seated at either round tables of eight, or square tables of four, a diner has a spectacular view across the ocean on either side of the ship, as well as to the bows.

Furthermore and an innovation, the Viceroy possesses a complex heating and ventilation system, unique to any other ocean liner, intended to navigate the Mediterranean, Suez Canal and the Indian Ocean. In addition to cruising the northern seas of Scandinavia and the South Atlantic Ocean, it is imperative the ship accommodates every type of climate. As a result, each public room and cabin in first and second class, as well as every living and working location throughout the ship, is heated or cooled by a change of fresh air every three minutes. Located above each dining table in the dining saloon are either four or eight moveable punkah louvres, enabling the diner to be comfortable whatever the temperature.

In the stern, and a little forward of the sports deck, is the smoking room, and it is here I feel most at home. Had I cruised on the Viceroy before purchasing Hyde House, I would have known how to furnish my new home. Every piece and design element of the smoking room is to my taste and has been thoughtfully considered, from the carved oak panelling on the walls and buttressed ceiling, to the hardwood timber floors.

With the furniture, fixtures, and fittings styled to appear late Elizabethan or from the time of James I, the ambience of the room is reminiscent of a baronial hall. At the forward end, around a stone and brick fireplace, a decorated oak mantel supports a severely carved royal coat of arms. Above the crest, the ceiling has buttressed oak beams, giving way to a brightly coloured leaded skylight, making the room feel airy and spacious.

It is the furniture that I admire most, however, as each piece is completely in tune with my personal aesthetic. In front of the fireplace, under the windows, and around a large carved table in the centre, are gathered high backed easy chairs, upholstered in red tapestry, as well as carved oak stools, small side tables and several writing desks. Light tan leather chairs and sofas make up the remaining furniture, while shaded table lamps and wall lights provide soft illumination at night. The final touch, and where Lady Elsie Mackay may have had her tongue a little in her cheek, are the pair of crossed sabres on the wall; one each side of the fireplace.

Overall, the room possesses an atmosphere of austere, but prepossessing grandeur, and entirely suitable for men who enjoy smoking, playing cards, reading, or simply discussing the events of the day.

Leaving the smoking room, and approaching amidships, you enter an oak panelled vestibule at the foot of a grand balustrade staircase. In addition, should you care to ascend you would reach a landing and be faced with two glazed bronze doors, flanked by a pair of palms growing in ornate porcelain pots. If you were curious to see inside, you might peer through the door's delicately fretted ironwork to see the music room, and the most forward lounge on the ship.

Here, the overall effect is Georgian, with lightly gilded Corinthian capitals, atop bronze, gold-dusted pilasters, appearing to support a central dome, featuring yet another coloured glass lead-light. Casement windows at the end of the sixty-foot room open onto an observation gallery, protected from the weather by sliding windows. Furthermore, at the same forward end, a handsome marble fireplace surmounts a brilliant cut glass mirror, featuring a jade border. The bulkheads are panelled in hardwood and painted in soft pastel shades between the windows, port, and starboard. Adding to the style, the recessed ceilings are bordered by subtle plaster mouldings and the dome is decorated with classical friezes.

Around and about the room is a selection of contemporary furniture. Armchairs; easy chairs; reading, and conversational tables; sofas and side tables, each chair or couch, deeply upholstered and covered in the finest of fabrics. As per the smoking room, the lighting is understated, with carefully placed shaded table lamps and discreet wall brackets. A large, English designed and manufactured, carpet covers almost the entire wood parquet floor; this easily removed should dancing be scheduled during the voyage.

Of course, any room calling itself a music room must possess a piano; as a result, a majestic Steinway stands beside a port side window should the resident pianist or a passenger wish to entertain.

Returning to the staircase, you would notice a pair of wrought iron lift gates, port and starboard, each lift capable of carrying passengers from the public rooms to the accommodation decks below. However, the port side lift descends, one more level, to E Deck and opens onto the pavement walk of the swimming bath.

Immediately astern of the entrance foyer on A Deck, and on each side of the ship, run corridor lounges leading to the reading and writing room. As in the public rooms, these are panelled in hardwood, enriched with soft green pillar casings and gilt frieze ornamentation.

The Reading and Writing Room itself is a fine example of Robert Adam style decoration, and here too, the panelling is in hardwood, painted in pastel shades, the furniture copied from some of the finest Thomas Chippendale of the late 18th Century. The mantelpiece is based on an original at Kedlestone Hall, the seat of that notable Viceroy of India, Lord Curzon, who sadly died a year before the ship was built and launched. Other details of the room are modelled on Harewood House, the Yorkshire home of the Lascelles family. A central dome forms the ceiling and contains oil paintings, while four large Wedgwood vases conceal indirect lighting.

Elsie Mackay's definitive feature, I have purposely omitted until last, because I feel it is here she really demonstrates her brilliance as a designer.

The swimming bath on E Deck surpasses any similar environment I have ever seen, deriving its influence from the lost Italian city of Pompeii. From stem to stern, the soft blue glazed tiled bath is twenty-four feet long and five feet deep. Above the changing cubicles, to port and starboard, the walls are a light cream, segmented by Ionic pilasters, which appear to be polished, tinted, terracotta marble. Wherever one looks one sees classical friezes and decorated architraves. Everything belongs to the Pompeian period of Roman history, from the low relief plaques, showing wrestling gladiators to the bronze railings fronting the cubicles and the spectator's gallery of the pavement walk above. Filled with seawater and heated to an agreeable temperature, it is a joy to swim in such an environment, and on my previous voyage to the South Atlantic, I took every opportunity to relish in my imaginary plunge into the olden times of ancient Rome.

In conclusion I must add, and I am sure it has also crossed your mind, since I have described in detail the luxury afforded a first class passenger, you might be wondering how the second-class voyager might fare on the magnificent Viceroy of India? Let me assure you, that the care and attention brought to the fittings and fixtures amidships, and in the forward parts of the ship are equally considered in the aft section, where the second-class public rooms are situated. Had I been ignorant of the facilities of first class, and unknowingly wandered into the public rooms in second class, I would have hardly considered them any less than first class accommodation on any other ship.

Consequently, I conclude my description of the splendid RMS Viceroy of India, which I hope will remain in your memory, so it will be unnecessary for me to pay elaborate attention to the surroundings as my tale continues to unravel.

Chapter Sixteen
All ashore who's going ashore - Happy Birthday Captain Fry

As a dockside crane hoisted our luggage aboard, Mervyn, Teddy, Mickey and I climbed the gangway towards the opening on E Deck where an officer was waiting to greet us.

"Welcome aboard Captain Fry," he said. "It's a pleasure to see you again."

I handed him our tickets and he noted our names on the passenger list fastened to a clipboard.

"Thank you," he said. "Which of you gentlemen is Master Watson?"

"I am," answered Mervyn.

"Then sir, you're on C Deck. Cabin forty-three, next door to the Captain. You're in forty-four Captain. Who is Master Jacobs?"

Teddy raised his hand.

"You're birthed on D Deck, cabin twelve, and Master Pritchard is in thirteen. Your luggage will arrive shortly gentlemen. Should you require refreshment the veranda café is open and serving tea."

"How about something stronger?" Mervyn interrupted.

"There's a wide selection of beer, wines and spirits available, which you may order from a steward in the smoking room."

"Come on lads," I said. "I know the way."

"I don't like the idea of being in thirteen," Mickey said, as we crammed into the lift.

"Don't tell us you're superstitious," Mervyn scoffed. "You'll jinx us if you go on."

"But in Norway aren't there icebergs in the sea?"

Mervyn and I laughed, although Teddy said nothing. I honestly believe he had no idea where we were going, or what he was about to see.

The smoking room was already peppered with an assortment of passengers, mostly male, although I did notice two young women huddled in conversation beside the fireplace, sipping cocktails, and smoking cigarettes in long cigarette holders. We found a couple of vacant leather settees beside a portside window.

"Would you care to order," a young steward asked, seeing we were comfortable.

By now, the boys were well accustomed to whiskey, although Teddy was less adventurous.

"We'll have scotch and sodas," I said, indicating Mervyn and Mickey. "You'll have cordial Teddy. Is that right?"

He smiled and nodded.

"And what shall we call you?" I asked, as the steward was about to walk away.

"Robert, sir. But the crew knows me as Bob."

He left us to fetch our drinks.

"I bet they do," Mervyn giggled.

"He's worth a shilling or two," Mickey added.

They laughed raucously, attracting the attention of several passengers, including the two young women.

Now, at this juncture, you are already aware of the true personalities of my companions and myself. I presume you have already guessed that behind my kindly and generous nature, I possess a secret, which is vital I keep hidden. Since, being the person that I am, and given my particular preference, at this moment in time any such revelation would result in extremely harsh consequences. However, may I assure you that my motive in bringing my young travelling companions along on the voyage is purely platonic and intended to be entirely out of friendship?

Naturally, you are probably aware that people can alter dramatically while cruising. Something about being out of sight of land and a 'life on the ocean wave' causes folk to become abandoned and gay. So much in fact, they easily lose perspective and a sense of reason. Therefore, I felt obliged to issue a few stern words of warning to qualm any initial high spirits, at least that is, until we were well under way.

"Now boys. Take it easy. We're aboard for three weeks. There'll be plenty of time for high jinx. But you better behave yourselves or the Captain will throw you in the brig."

Mervyn and Mickey sniggered, and in no time, Bob returned with our drinks.

Before long, I began to wonder about Gilbert's three children, so I left the lads to their second drink. Then returned to the gangway where the officer checking in passengers reassured me that Kathryn, Rowena and Gilbert Fry junior, were safely aboard and in their cabins. Relieved, I returned to the smoking room to find Mervyn and Mickey quite the worse for wear.

"When do we sail Ronnie, old chap?" slurred Mervyn.

"In an hour I think. Most people are already aboard."

"I don't feel very well," Mickey muttered.

He did indeed look rather green.

"We haven't untied yet and you're seasick?" Mervyn jeered.

"You both better stop drinking, otherwise neither of you will be conscious when we sail."

Along the portside corridor lounge, Bob was serving a group of passengers and I had a quiet word with him. From then on, he and the other stewards purposely ignored our table despite Mervyn's frantic waving and snapping fingers. It was obvious he was going to require a firm hand if we were to have a trouble free voyage.

"Ladies and gentlemen," an unidentified voice announced over the loud speakers. "All ashore who's going ashore, as we are about to sail."

It has always amused me to hear the word sail used on board ship. Despite the fact that a sail is never in sight aboard a modern ocean liner, there remains no other way to describe a ship that is about to weigh anchor and leave her moorings.

Hurrying the boys on to the sports deck, we leaned over the rail, just in time to see the gangway dragged free of the ship. Mickey and Mervyn seemed to revive once we hit the fresh air of the Thames and began cheering to the group of sightseers and well-wishers waving bon voyage from the quayside below.

It was then I caught sight of mother and Wilfred, further along the deck, mother looking happy as she threw streamers over the side. In fact, it was a long time since I had seen her so animated. On the other hand, Wilfred was not so abandoned, and waved, half-heartedly, when he saw us.

Unexpectedly, a great bellow issued from the ships foghorn, her funnels belching a pall of thick black smoke, as her gigantic turbine engines fired into life, while the massive propellers, deep under the water, began to turn. Then, once the ropes had fallen into the water between the dock and us, RMS Viceroy of India slowly edged astern.

We rushed across the lift vestibule to the port side rail in time to see four tugs steaming towards the ship, each preparing to nudge and guide us into the open water of the river.

"Wow!" shouted Mervyn. "This is fantastic! What lucky chaps we are! Thanks Ron. We wouldn't be here but for you."

When the ship reached midstream, and we had waved goodbye to the tugs, she picked up speed, although her progress remained steady so as not to cause damaging wash along the riverbank. When we finally entered the estuary, at last her engines were able to show us their power, as we cut a swathe towards The Warp and out into the North Sea. Next came boat drill and everyone assembled on the boat deck for instruction. Then it was time for dinner, so Mervyn, Mickey, Teddy, and I went below to change.

When we arrived in the corridor lounge an hour later, mother and Wilfred were already having cocktails. Therefore, once a waiter had taken our order, I gathered the lads together so we might join them.

Of course, seeing that it was the first time mother and Wilfred had met my new friends, Teddy and Mickey, I expected the atmosphere to be rather prickly, but was pleasantly surprised by mother's greeting. She particularly took to Teddy, due mainly I imagine to his hound dog expression, which he wore the majority of the time. In addition, and with Eric's warning sounding in my ears, I must say I was a little nervous as to how the lads would behave around upper class people, although they appeared relaxed and happily entered into conversation.

"My son tells me you're from Bath," mother said to Teddy and Mickey, as we sipped Manhattans. "I do so love the city. I'm so pleased to be living there again. My son Wilfred has a house in Shamswell, and he's invited me to live there. How is it you both know my son Ronald?"

While waiting for an answer, mother gave me a look that spoke millions. It was obvious she would have preferred to be with me at Hyde House.

"From Bath Boys Club and the YMCA," answered Mickey. "He takes a great interest in the young fellows."

"This is the first time any of us have been at sea," continued Teddy. "We're very grateful to the Captain for inviting us."

"He's a most generous man," mother said, "Aren't you Ronald. Too generous for his own good sometimes."

Wilfred screwed up his nose and twitched his moustache, as if he were about to speak, but thankfully remained silent. All of a sudden, the dinner gong sounded and the conversation ceased, as everyone trooped into the George V Dining Saloon.

Already the ship was way out to sea, steering a north-easterly course along the Essex coast, and by the motion of the soup in our soup bowls, experiencing a heavy swell. In the past, I have found that a steady eye on the horizon can be a means to combat seasickness, and I said as much as we began to eat. Despite my encouragement, I hardly think Mickey appreciated my words as his face turned a shade greener than his pea soup. As a result, I suggested he take some fresh air, so he asked to be excused and left the table.

"I'll see he's alright," Mervyn said, following him. "He'll be fine once he's been sick."

Realising the size of our party, the waiters put us at a table of nine, as our numbers had increased due to the addition of my cousin's three children. Although Mervyn and Mickey were absent, I took the opportunity to introduce everyone. The twins, Kathryn and Rowena, were terribly shy, obviously uncertain to be in the company of adults other than their parents. Gilbert junior, my cousin's eldest, however, was bursting with confidence.

"I've a place at Oxford this autumn," he said. "Magdalene. Papa's old college. I'm determined to win a blue. Did well at Henley this year in the under eighteens."

Smiling, I secretly wondered how the boys would react to young Gilbert, especially the sarcastic Mickey.

As Mervyn predicted, Mickey appeared revived when he and Mervyn returned. So much better, in fact, he made short work of the main course of roast beef, Yorkshire pudding, vegetables, and gravy.

"Let's hope the weather stays fine," Wilfred said, as we waited for dessert. "Knowing Norway as I do, it can be miserable in the rain."

This typically negative remark from my brother was hardly noticed by the rest of the company. Instead, I began to tell the young people what to expect on the voyage.

"Our first port will be Leith in Scotland, where I believe Wilfred, you fish. Then a few days crossing the North Sea to Stavanger. Up the coast of Norway to Bergen, then Molde."

Wilfred nodded solemnly.

"Next is Trondheim, then Tromse and the North Cape, where the sun never sets at this time of the year."

"How exciting," mother said. "Are there shore excursions?"

"It says in the itinerary that we'll visit peasants in Hardanger. Ride up a mountain on the funicular railway in Bergen and go fishing in Molde."

"There's thousands of fjords," Gilbert interrupted. "Which ones will we see?"

"Plenty I should imagine. But the famous fjord is Naero."

"What makes it famous?" asked Mervyn.

"As its name implies, it's narrow and deep, in places only four hundred yards wide. Also, the sides rise up to a height of two thousand feet.

Obviously, no one around the table had read the pamphlet that was placed in our cabins. However, they seemed interested, so I continued, despite sounding like a tour guide.

"We visit the town of Trondheim, which they say is quaint and picturesque, then we travel north into the Land of the Trolls."

"Oh dear!" put in mother. "That sounds most startling. Don't you agree girls?"

Rowena and Kathryn smiled, but remained silent.

"The pamphlet in our cabins," I continued. "Says our next encounter promises to be the highlight of our cruise. We'll actually walk on the Svartisen Glacier."

"Isn't that a bit dangerous?" asked Mickey. "Aren't there crevasses you can fall into?"

"Mickey!" Mervyn jeered, "Don't be such a wet blanket. You always think the worst."

"It's just that mother told me to be careful," Mickey whispered.

"I'm sure the Captain will make certain everyone's safe," I said. "It wouldn't be good for P&O if word got out someone's had an accident."

"Where will we go after the glacier?" asked Gilbert.

"Tromse. By then we'll be in The Land of the Midnight Sun. Here it appears we'll visit a Laplanders village."

"How marvellous!" exclaimed mother. "They're the people with the reindeer aren't they?"

"And they hunt Walrus and Seals," Teddy said, suddenly, surprising everyone by speaking. "I've seen pictures in a school book."

As I thought about it, the more I realised how little I knew about Scandinavia. I booked the cruise merely as a means to have some time and a bit of fun with Mervyn and his friends. Although reading the itinerary and hearing other people's responses, I saw that the cruise would be a revelation for me, as well as everyone else.

While the waiter put bowls of fruit salad and ice cream on the table, my mother asked the inevitable question, given we were to travel close to the Arctic Circle.

"I've often wondered. How is it the sun never sets?"

"It's all due to the tilt of the earth," Wilfred said, which pleased me, as I have always been rather a duffer at science.

"In summer the North Pole is closest to the sun, so as the earth rotates the sun rises in the sky to its zenith at midday, but never sets, and remains above the horizon at midnight. I hear it's a most disturbing phenomenon because people who experience it feel they cannot sleep."

"Does it mean the opposite happens in winter?" asked Gilbert.

"Correct," Wilfred said. "For a long period the Laplanders see no sun at all."

"How dreadful!" mother interjected. "Never to see the sun all winter. I would hate that."

"After Tromse, the ship sails on to North Cape," I continued. "The furthest point in the whole of Europe. Then we return to London via Leith."

Bob, our waiter from the smoking room, was serving at the next table and I noticed Mervyn had also seen him. Realising we were both looking in his direction Bob looked up and smiled. Could this young man be more aware than I gave him credit, or was he merely being friendly?

Dusk was falling as the lads, Wilfred, and I adjourned to the smoking room. However, before we settled down to port and cigars, Mervyn and I paused at the port side rail.

"Where's that?" he asked, referring to a string of lights brushing the darkening horizon.

"Yarmouth maybe," I said.

"Where will we be tomorrow morning?"

"Leith I expect."

"Will we go ashore?"

"No. The itinerary says we're taking on passengers."

Mervyn looked very handsome in his dinner suit, wing collar, and bow tie. It was the first occasion he had dressed for dinner since buying the suit at Jollys. I felt proud to be the instigator of his emergence, also amazed how far he had come in only ten months.

"Did you see Bob looking at me?" Mervyn asked. "What do you know? I think he's one of us?"

"Was he?" I said, suddenly feeling a pang of jealousy.

"I think I might be alright there," Mervyn added.

It was extremely silly of me to feel jealous at Mervyn's outburst; however, it caused me to sulk for the rest of the evening and prompted me to retire to my cabin before the others. It played on my mind nonetheless, and even the gentle rolling of the ship failed to lull me to sleep, causing me to toss and turn restlessly. Until around midnight, I heard a knock on the connecting doors.

"Ron!"

It was Mervyn and he was drunk. "Ron!" he shouted. "Let me in."

"Go to bed," I said, endeavouring to keep my voice down.

"What's up Ron? You're mad aren't you?"

"Just be quiet and go to bed. We'll talk in the morning."

However, my words had no effect.

"Let me in," he persisted. "I want to say sorry."

Clambering out of bed, I unfastened the doors.

"Come in for heaven's sake!" I whispered. "Stop making such a noise."

Dressed in his pyjamas, Mervyn staggered through the door.

"I'm sorry," he groaned. "I realised I'd hurt you as soon as I said it. Me and my big mouth! Let me be nice to you, like the way you like."

He made a lunge at my groin, obviously intending to grab me in a certain place.

"Come on. Let me see it. It's been too long. You've been funny about doing it for the last few days."

"That's because mother and Wilfred are with us," I whispered. "It just doesn't feel right to be carrying on with mother one side and Wilfred the other. You know what a row you make."

"Please Ron," Mervyn begged, beginning to pull off his pyjamas. "Look! You can see how keen I am."

Well what could a man do? The offer was there and I took it in both hands, and with my eyes wide open, although the moment of passion was short lived, since as soon as it was over Mervyn collapsed back onto my bed and the next second became unconscious and began to snore. So covering him with the eiderdown, I slid between the sheets and promptly fell asleep.

THE MERRY MILLIONAIRE

***

On the Viceroy, it is the habit of the stewards to wake passengers at a quarter to seven, as most wish to breakfast early. Accordingly, I anticipated Johnson's knock and woke Mervyn, bundling him into his own bed and shutting the connecting doors.

"We'll be entering the Firth very soon, Captain," Johnson said placing a cup of tea on the bedside table. "Perhaps you might wish to see the bridge sir. It's a sight to see."

"Thank you Johnson," I answered. "I've only seen photos. When I visit Scotland I always go up the other side."

"Then shall I run you a bath sir?"

"Thank you Johnson."

Since the day was rather special, seeing it was my birthday, I had no desire to waste a precious moment. Consequently, finishing my tea, I put on my foulard dressing gown, and collecting my shaving things from the dresser, went into the bathroom. I knew there was little point raising Mervyn since, unlike the early days; recently Mervyn had become a late sleeper, due mostly to his increased desire to get properly plastered by bedtime. His condition the previous night almost certainly meant it would be well into the morning before anyone would see him.

A spatter of passengers occupied various tables in the dining saloon, and as I began to eat my breakfast, I recalled the marvellous early morning feast laid on for the inhabitants of Tristan du Cunha. Was it really five months ago? I could hardly believe how time had rushed by.

Wilfred entered the saloon, and for a moment appeared about to sit at another table, but seeing me he changed his mind.

"Happy birthday Ronald," he said. "May I?"

How ridiculous! Having to ask permission to sit with your brother at breakfast. But that was Wilfred all over, precise and exact. A waiter took his order, while I poured him a cup of tea.

"Thank you for remembering."

Wilfred smiled wanly, spooning sugar into his tea.

"What was that raucous last night?" he said. "There was someone calling your name."

"Oh!" I said, nonchalantly. "That was Mervyn Watson. Drunk of course."

"But what did he want at that hour?"

"I've no idea. I ignored him and he went to bed. We'll be in Leith in an hour. Have you seen the Forth Bridge?"

"Of course. When I shoot at Archie's, I always take the train to Aberdeen."

"Do you know," I said, endeavouring to steer the conversation away from Mervyn. "What with last night's dinner, and now breakfast, I can feel the pounds piling on already. Doctor Ingram warned me about smoking and overeating at the beginning of the year."

"Funny you should say that," said Wilfred, devouring his second slice of buttered toast and marmalade. "He told me the same. Because father's heart did for him in the end, he said I needed to be careful."

"I went to him for that very reason," I confessed. "Mine was missing an odd beat now and again. It was rather alarming. But he put me on tablets, so now it doesn't happen as often."

It was rare for Wilfred and I to be so candid. We were poles apart in age, as well as temperament. Between having Wilfred and I, mother bore a child, but the baby died after a few days and she never said whether it was a boy or a girl. Perhaps, if it had lived it might have been a buffer between Wilfred and myself.

Wilfred remained a mystery to me. His life was far removed from mine. As I previously touched on, I never knew him to have a female friend, spending his leisure time shooting in Scotland or sailing his motor yacht, 'Frontera', to Norway, for the fishing. Sometimes, mother wrote to say he was in Spain or cruising in the Mediterranean. Alone, or with friends? We never knew. Wilfred hid his emotions quite like my father. However, as they say 'still waters run deep'. I fancied, either he led a secret life, possessing a similar persuasion as my own, or perhaps darker demons lurked within his soul.

After lunch, I took a quick nap, and as is often the case when one sleeps heavily in the afternoon, woke feeling rather groggy.

Consequently, I decided a swim was in order.

When last in Jolly's, Mervyn picked out a snazzy swimming costume for me; blue and white stripes; full in the front and rear, to accommodate my ample belly and behind; although it did flatter my legs. Nonetheless, as it was the first time I had worn it, and before putting on my robe, I had a quick look in the mirror to check whether it was too revealing.

With the sun dipping towards the disappearing Scottish Lowlands, by the motion of the ship, I realised we were underway once more. Having purposely put Mervyn out of my mind for almost half the day, I began to wonder about him and thought to knock on the connecting door. I changed my mind, and made my way to the lift instead, taking it down two levels to E Deck, and the swimming bath.

My concern for Mervyn was unnecessary, since I found him sporting in the water with Teddy, while Mickey skulked on a bench beside the change cubicle.

"What's the matter, Mickey?" I asked, removing my robe.

"Can't swim, can I," he moaned. "It's too deep. I'll drown."

"Don't be silly. You're a tall boy. Nearly six feet. It says on the wall the pool's five foot deep. With your feet on the bottom, your head will be well out of the water."

"Come on," I said. "Just climb down the ladder after me. I'll help you. Remember, I promised your mother, I'd look after you."

In no time, Mickey was splashing around with the others, while I methodically swam a few laps, at the same time enjoying the sumptuous surroundings of the Pompeian Bath.

Once I was confident I had swum off my breakfast and lunch, and the boys realised their hands and feet were becoming wrinkly, we dried ourselves and returned to our cabins to dress for dinner.

That evening I was surprised by a host of birthday presents. Mervyn, Teddy, and Mickey must have visited the shop on B Deck, because they gave me a silver plated eggcup and spoon, with an enamel picture of the Viceroy on each. Wilfred's present was a box of cigars, and mother's a framed picture of the ship signed by Captain Thornton. She must have also worked on Rowena and Kathryn as they were most animated describing their day. For the remainder of the night, Mervyn's attitude to me was conciliatory. He was obviously feeling guilty regarding his outburst and subsequent drunkenness, proving one is never too old to learn a lesson.

"Happy birthday Ron," he said as the lift gates opened onto our deck. "Leave the catch off tonight. I'd like to thank you for everything you've done for me and the lads."

"Just because you slept on my bed last night, don't think you're making a habit of it. Now go to bed."

Chapter Seventeen
Norway - After the Ball

The following morning I woke to the screeching of gulls, and looking out of the porthole, I saw cliffs disappearing into a wide dark waterway. Behind this appeared the harbour, red roofs, and spires of a city. All the while, a vast expanse of mountain formed a dramatic backdrop to the panorama.

"Where are we?" Mervyn said, opening the sliding doors.

"Stavanger I think. Go back to bed. The steward will be here in a minute."

Truly, it was a glorious sparkling morning, the crisp air tinged with the aroma of smoked fish. My entire party seemed to be of the same mind, as every chair at the breakfast table was occupied, perhaps the anticipation of going ashore encouraging everyone to rise early. I suggested we keep together when we embark the tender, so we might enjoy the sites of Stavanger together.

An hour later, the tender navigated the outer, then inner harbour, finally depositing us on the quayside, where our passports were inspected. We were instantly impressed by the quaintness of the scene; the wooden warehouses lining the quay, each painted in the brightest of colours and differing from one to another; numerous fishing boats bobbing casually in the glittering water.

Wandering the narrow streets, I realised that every house was built of wood, hence the reason numerous fires have destroyed the city over the centuries. Since the chief industry of Stavanger is fishing, the warehouses and factories close to the quay are concerned with processing fish. As a result, the air was heavy with the smell of smoked herring, which some found rather irksome, and others, appetising.

Eventually we stumbled upon the cathedral, which the pamphlet said was the oldest in Norway. Wilfred, mother and I were most taken by the pulpit, since it was a magnificent example of Norwegian Baroque. However, I felt the younger members of the party were rather disinterested, as there was little to hold their attention other than the points of interest I have already mentioned. Then, after discovering a little shop, we purchased postcards and mementos, and meandered back to the harbour, where the tender waited to return us to the ship.

Mother found the climb up the companionway to the opening on F Deck, rather difficult, which delayed our ascent. Although, when we finally arrived on board, the sight of a poster pinned to a notice board cheered us immeasurably.

There was to be a fancy dress ball the following night, costumes provided by P&O, a touch I found most generous. So, while the Viceroy steamed north, and away from Stavanger, this was the principal point of conversation as we sat down to dinner.

Next morning, there was quite a queue outside the cabin where we would select our costumes, an officer present should any quarrels occur regarding choices. Personally, I have never been one for fancy dress. There were some wild nights at Trinity where, dressed in bed sheets, we cavorted around as sex mad Romans, or crazed Arabs. However, those antics usually led to some kind of orgy, so I could see the point in dressing up. Parading about dressed as King Tut or the Prince Regent, just for the sake of causing amusement, holds little appeal for me. But rather than appear as a party pooper, I went along with the general enthusiasm.

Mervyn seemed to think I would make a good Nero, so I was back in a toga again, this time, with a wreath of laurel leaves and a fiddle. Mervyn chose a dashing red soldier suit, with a black shiny helmet and gold braid. Mickey found a mysterious Arab outfit, while

Teddy appeared most austere as a Spanish Don, in black doublet and hose, complete with beard and moustache.

We carried our costumes back to our cabins and then adjourned to the sports deck for games.

Here again, I was never much good. At Farmborough, I shunned the Rugby field, cricket pitch, and running track, only to skive in the lower third toilets. The games master knew me to be a duffer, and hardly expected me to show, so there were never any repercussions as to my absenteeism.

On my previous cruise, I did enjoy watching others playing deck and table tennis. In addition, the arranged tournaments of Greyhound Racing and Hunt the Spud were amusing and tremendous subjects for photography.

Mervyn was excellent at Ping Pong as he called it, and he and Gilbert Fry, who was no mean player either, began to challenge each other. I found this matching of the upper and lower classes most fascinating, as Mervyn seemed to hold his own bravely against formidable odds. I was reminded of my army days, when the officers mixed with the odds and sods, each benefitting from the association, as did Mervyn and Gilbert.

The chivvying began to occur at mealtimes however.

"You were pretty off this morning, Watson," Gilbert scoffed.

He was first to call Mervyn by his surname, the way boys do at public school, but I was pleased when Mervyn did the same, creating a kind of equality between them.

"I'll thrash you this afternoon, Fry. You wait and see."

"Okay boys," I said, in mediation. "I hardly think this is the time or place. Let's have lunch in peace."

Later that same afternoon, I took some candid photos of the spectators, rather than the competitors. Curiously, as I lined up the shot through the viewfinder, I could see that Mickey and Teddy were a little like me, finding games with balls rather beneath them, whether they were made of leather, cotton or plastic. Mickey was gazing at the action more interested in the aesthetic of the players, rather than the score, and Teddy just gazed, with nothing much at all on his mind.

He was an odd boy, as if some part of his personality was waiting to slot into place. I liked him, and wondered what kind of future he might have?

Mickey, I was sure, would marry. I could almost hear his mother and father insisting he find the right girl and settle down. Alternatively, Teddy was a mummy's boy, and being a widow, she would want to keep hold of her son as long as possible.

Being aware of their natures, I questioned how this might affect the remainder of their lives.

The married Mickey would lead a double life. On one hand, convincing his new wife that his lack of interest in the obvious area was due to low libido brought on by a childhood illness. All the while, encountering, anonymous strangers in dark secluded lavatories, or public parks, with always a wary eye open for the police. A sad, lonely, unfulfilled life.

Teddy I hoped might differ. He was sensitive enough to come to terms with himself and openly display his nature. This might attract others who shared a desire to lead a normal and honest life, as God made them. Despite having to be on his guard, I hoped Teddy would meet a person with whom he could share his life, until such time that is, 'the love that dare not speak its name' might one day be seen and accepted.

The fancy dress ball proved to be a splendid affair. We looked magnificent, and had there been a prize for the best-dressed table, we would have easily won.

Mother, sitting on my left, was dressed as Anne Boleyn, although she insisted she was Catherine of Aragon, because she said she had no desire to have her head chopped off. Appropriately, and beside her, was Wilfred, as Henry the eighth. Rowena and Kathryn made a delightful pair of can-can girls, with red ribbons in their hair and frilly petticoats. There was Gilbert, dressed as King Fuad of Egypt, complete with Fez and insignia, Mickey sitting beside him wearing his Arab costume, and Teddy as a Spaniard; then Mervyn, my gallant little soldier, and lastly me, Emperor Nero holding my fiddle.

Dinner was hilarious, where we positively roared at Teddy's antics as he endeavoured to eat his soup through his false beard and moustache. Then everyone promenaded into the music room where we danced to the music of the ship's orchestra until the early hours.

At one o'clock, which is considerably late for me, I said goodnight to my party and returned to my cabin.

How long I slept, I was unaware. Nevertheless, my travelling clock said almost three when I woke.

What had awakened me? I stared into the darkness and listened. There was the faint sound of the ship's engines and a spatter of spray on the glass of my porthole. On the other hand, might it be rain? It was then I heard a sound coming from close by. A gasp, or maybe a moan?

Horrified as to what I might find, I got out of bed, and crossing to the connecting doors, put my hands on the wooden panels. Opening them an inch and peering through the gap, I witnessed a sight, which I imagine will remain in my memory for the rest of my life. In the dim glow from the emergency light above the cabin door, I saw two naked males, writhing on the bed and in the throes of; well once again, I will let you use your imagination. Naturally, I recognised one of them since I could clearly see his face upturned against the pillow, but the other was hidden, with only his short fair hair visible.

Then, as the two of them changed position, his identity was revealed. It was Bob the waiter. I could barely breathe, my heart pumping so hard. I had to get out of the cabin. How could I remain knowing what was going on just a couple of yards away?

Not wishing to be discovered, I silently closed the door and sat on the edge of the bed.

My robe hung on the door, so getting up I hurriedly threw it over my shoulders and left the cabin, heading for the lift.

Up on the promenade deck, the air was crisp, the dark sky littered with a trillion stars. I have heard it said that on such nights, when the stars are at their brightest, one is closest to death. I shivered, and leaning on the rail, pulled my robe close, my heart still in my throat.

What should I do? My logical mind endeavoured to gain control, pushing aside my anxiety for a moment. Should I face him? Go back and interrupt their lovemaking, hence causing a scene and attracting attention. No. That would be disastrous. There were a dozen cabins on C Deck. If things became heated and Mervyn began to shout, it would wake people who would certainly complain that their sleep had been disturbed, which would result in Mervyn and I being questioned.

Might I casually let him know in the morning that I was aware of what had occurred, and chastise him, and let him apologise, all the while knowing he would do the same on another occasion? There were still many more nights after all.

Alternatively, should I say nothing?

Would I be able to live with myself keeping such a secret? The answer was 'Yes'. Mervyn and I have a special friendship, which I might lose if I become jealous each time he finds a young companion. Therefore, it was imperative I begin to understand that he is old enough to know whoever he pleases. I have no rights, or hold over him. It is necessary to come to terms with the fact that, although we have a deep friendship, and a strangely loving relationship, it is simply my generosity that keeps us together, and nothing more.

The wind in my face, as well as the sound of the water, hitting the side of the ship, seemed to calm my anxiety. I felt my pulse, and was happy to find it had resumed its steady pace. Nevertheless, I was still reluctant to return to my cabin. So finding a deck chair, I sat down and tried to relax. In no time, I was asleep.

***

"Where did you get to last night?" Mervyn asked at breakfast. "I looked in on you at four o'clock and you weren't there."

"I couldn't sleep. Too much excitement I suppose. So I went on deck for a breath of air and fell asleep in a deck chair. If a steward hadn't woken me, I'd probably still be there."

Mervyn laughed. "Wasn't it fun last night?"

"I'm glad you enjoyed yourself."

"Are you alright?" he asked, obviously puzzled by my coldness. "You don't seem yourself."

"I can't always be jolly old Ronnie. After all, this is the first time we've been in each other's company for five days at a stretch."

"If I'm boring you I'll leave you be. Don't worry. Fry wants to thrash me at Ping Pong. But we'll see about that. I've also promised to join him, Rowena, and Kathryn, in a doubles game of deck tennis."

"You've certainly got the day well mapped out. If you wish to find me, I'll be in the writing room. I've my diary to write up and letters to finish. We'll be in Bergen tomorrow, so I can post them. Have you sent your mother and father a card?"

"No. But I will. I've heaps to tell them."

He was becoming quite the young gentleman, the association with the Fry children obviously rubbing off. Again, Eric's warning echoed in my mind, causing me to smile. We finished our breakfast and went our separate ways, Mervyn to the sports deck, and me to my cabin to collect my diary, writing paper, and pen.

On the way, I ran into Bob carrying a breakfast tray. He smiled when he saw me.

"Good morning," I said as he passed. "Sleep well?"

"Yes. Thank you sir," he answered, clearly a little surprised by my question. "Very well."

There! I had spoken to both parties and by their casual reaction, could hardly believe I had witnessed a part of their secret night of desire. Clearly, the younger generation saw their lives and loves very differently than mine did in my day. This was rather a revelation and gave me much, 'food for thought'.

Chapter Eighteen
Bergen – Floybanen - Cupido

It was raining when we sited Bergen, which, during breakfast, Wilfred advised us, was hardly unusual. While we slept, The Viceroy of India navigated the narrow channels between several large precipitous islands, before finally steering on an easterly course towards the harbour. Once again, P&O were thoughtful to provide oilskins for passengers who wished to go ashore, which I for one was keen to do, despite the weather. Mervyn was also eager, which pleased me because he and I would spend the remainder of the day together, since the ship was due to sail at midnight.

We were moored at the end of a long jetty served by a lonely tram, which conveyed Mervyn, myself, as well as other intrepid passengers, into the city. This short trip introduced us to the busy harbour and the Bryggen, which the Norwegians call the colourful waterfront buildings. As we rattled along, Mervyn and I overheard a conversation between two gentlemen passengers. One was explaining to the other the reason for Bergen's high precipitation records. Apparently, the seven surrounding mountains act as a funnel, channelling all the moist, rain-laden, clouds into the fjord on which Bergen stands.

When we alighted from the tram and began our excursion, our oilskins proved good protection. Firstly, we consulted the map in our travel pamphlet, which pinpointed the places of interest. There were quite a few, including Bergen Cathedral, called Domkirken and the thirteenth century church, Karskirken. Also, the Bergenhus Fortress, which we had already seen at the entrance to the harbour; a counting house; Floyen Mountain; the German Quarter, as well as the German Church.

There appeared to be a good deal to cover, so I suggested we reinforce ourselves with a cup of tea. We discovered a quaint café in a narrow side street, behind the fish market, and shaking the water off our oilskins and depositing our umbrellas in a barrel beside the door, we went inside. Conveniently, the menu was in Norwegian and English, which we were grateful for, as the British find the pronunciation of the Norwegian language hard to master.

"Tea is Teen," Mervyn said, comparing one side of the menu with the other.

"And Kaffe is Coffee," I said. "That's easy."

"Kanne jeg hjepe du gentlemen?" a young woman asked, as she came through a door at the rear of the café.

Her words sounded typical to any question one might hear in a shop or restaurant throughout the world.

"Yes please," I answered. "Can we have a pot of tea? I mean teen, for two?"

"Alt a spise Herr?"

The waitress seemed to comprehend, obviously finding English easy to understand. After all, the Norwegians were Vikings at one time in their history, and since the Vikings invaded England, there must be a bit of Viking in all of us.

"Are you hungry Mervyn?" I asked.

"I am," he said, eagerly. "It's been a while since breakfast."

"What do you recommend?" I said, turning to the waitress.

"Rokt Laks," she answered.

Mervyn scanned the menu. "That's smoked salmon omelette," he translated.

"Anjos."

"Brisling, in a wine and herb sauce."

"That sounds nice," I said, realising I was also hungry.

"Surslid."

"Pickled Herring. I'm not sure about that," Mervyn said, wrinkling his nose.

"Brunost; Kvitost."

"Brown or white cheese."

"How extraordinary!" I exclaimed. "Brown cheese! Although, I'd like a taste. What do you fancy Mervyn?"

"Since knowing you I've grown used to smoked salmon, so I'll have the omelette if I may."

"And I'll have the brisling. One Rokt Laks please," I said, to the waitress, after consulting the menu again. "And one Anjos. Also, some brod and ost."

She seemed to understand, and smiling, disappeared once more into the kitchen. While we waited, I took out the pamphlet and glanced at the section on Bergen.

"It says we can take a train to the top of Floyen Mountain. Apparently, the views from there are spectacular. An opportunity to take some photographs."

"That must be the mountain we saw from the tram. Let's do that then. Better than seeing another old church."

"We'll do that too."

From our table beside the window I could see all the way to the quayside, where fishing smacks were unloading boxes of fish, presumably cod, since the booklet said smoked cod was Bergen's principle industry.

Over the centuries, Bergen, like Stavanger, has been devastated by a succession of dreadful fires, so I wondered why the people continued to choose to live in houses constructed of wood. Surely, it would be logical to find another source of building material. As I pondered this question, the waitress appeared carrying a tray of plates containing everything we ordered, the portions much larger than expected. The brisk morning air, however, and the vision of attractively presented unfamiliar food, gave us the appetite to eat almost everything.

My Anjos was delicious, and Mervyn enjoyed his salmon omelette so much he even suggested I ask Mrs Lanesome to cook it on our return to Hyde House. I said she would find it rather outlandish and we laughed. The cheese we found extremely smelly, and made us giggle as it reminded us of the odour of feet that have been in one's socks for too long. Nonetheless, the bread was wholesome and tasty.

It was so pleasant, just the two of us, enjoying each other's company, away from distractions and possible interruptions. So nice in fact, I had almost forgotten the circumstances of the night before last.

"Er du tar de Funicular?" the waitress said, as she cleared our table.

"Funicular?" I echoed.

Suddenly I understood.

"Funicular Railway. Yes. We are," I answered.

"Vil du like lunsj?"

"I think she said lunch," Mervyn whispered. "Under the breakfast menu it says Lunsj, which must mean lunch."

"That's an idea," I said. "A picnic! Yes, please. A selection would be nice."

Once again, I knew she understood me because she nodded and returned to the kitchen.

Carrying our basket between us, and using the map in the pamphlet, we navigated the narrow labyrinth of laneways, eventually arriving at the impressive entrance of the Floybanen.

By now you might be wondering how Mervyn and I paid for our tram ride and our breakfasts. The reason being, that once more P&O had thought of everything. The ships purser possessed a quantity of Norwegian currency, so all we need do before going ashore, was exchange our pounds shillings and pence for Kroner. I think the rate at that time was eighteen kroner to the pound. Therefore, each note was worth a little over a shilling. We were also amused to see some coins possessing small holes in the centre.

Mercifully, while we stood at the ticket window, the rain stopped and the weather began to clear, revealing a perfect blue sky. Quite a few people were waiting on the platform, including some faces we recognised from the ship. We acknowledged each other politely; however, that was all. The English abroad are a curious breed, opting to remain private when ashore, but terribly familiar on the ship.

At the end of the platform, two sets of rails disappeared into a tunnel, the sight of the moving cable in the middle of one track indicating the rail car was on its way down the hill.

"How does it work?" Mervyn asked.

Naturally, my answer was well prepared, as the information pamphlet thoughtfully explained in detail the mechanics of a funicular railway.

"A motor powers a cable that begins to pull the car up the mountain, while the car at the top slowly descends. Its weight helps the lower car rise, and dictates the speed of both cars. When we get back home, I really must write to P&O to commend them on their foresight in providing us with such a mine of information."

Suddenly and noiselessly, a bright red wooden carriage appeared from the tunnel, slowly coming to stop at the platform. A guard opened the doors and several people alighted.

"Welcome to the Floybanen," he said to us, using excellent English. "We will be leaving in three minutes. Have your tickets ready, please."

It was curious to enter an inclining carriage from the steps of a slanting platform. Undaunted, we climbed aboard and found two seats at the back where I imagined we would have the best view.

A bell sounded. The guard shut the doors and we were on our way.

Entering the tunnel at speed, leaving our stomachs on the platform, we rapidly grew accustomed to the upward motion of the train. Soon, the darkness ended as the car hurtled into the sunshine and began to wind its way up the incline, past elegant white wooden houses, clinging to the mountainside. The prospect of the city, fast retreating beneath us was breathtaking and Mervyn remarked how lucky we were that the rain had stopped. I took several photographs, one in particular of Mervyn leaning against the window with the panorama unfolding behind him. It has become a favourite of mine, since I eventually had it framed and it sits beside my bed at Hyde House.

Before long, the houses gave way to rugged mountain terrain and tall trees, while to the right a precipitous gorge tumbled away for thousands of feet into the valley below. After almost eight minutes, the car reached the top platform and everyone got off, only to discover a delightful restaurant, its picture windows commanding a glorious vista of Bergen, the glittering fjord and the mountainous islands beyond.

"How fantastic! What a view!" Mervyn exclaimed, while I sat down on a convenient seat in front of the restaurant. "It's endless."

It was indeed exhilarating. Almost like being on top of the world.

"It feels good to be alive," I said.

"In the pamphlet," I read aloud, "it says from here the adventurous can take many routes to explore the mountain."

"I don't think you'll be able to manage that Ron," Mervyn said. "You're a bit heavy for hiking."

Indeed, my weight did dictate how far I could walk; as it was clear from where we stood most paths would mean a steep climb. Mervyn was well aware of this and seemed content to sit down beside me and enjoy the scenery.

As we unpacked our lunch basket, and with the rain clouds gone, the sun on our faces felt warm. Nothing had been spared and we ate like kings, or should I say Vikings, feasting on cold cured meats, bread and Jarlsburgh cheese, slices of cucumber, little pickled herrings and sweet, tangy tomatoes.

"Do you know Ron," Mervyn said suddenly. "I can honestly say I've never enjoyed myself more. I'll remember this day forever."

"I agree," I replied, casting aside my doubts from the night before last. "We're good for each other."

He laughed. "At least you get some kind of exercise when I'm about."

He left off unscrewing the jar of pickled herrings, then turned and gave me a flirtatious wink, the sort I had come to love.

"But really Ron. You should think about losing a bit of weight. I've noticed, when we're walking, you sometimes find difficulty breathing. It's not good to have such a big tummy."

"Hey! You sound like Doctor Ingram. All right! When we get home I'll go on a diet."

"And I'll see you stick to it."

"We'll start walking," I said. "There're plenty of footpaths around Wildsbridge."

With our appetites assuaged, we packed the basket and walked back to the Floybanen, just in time to catch a returning car.

"What do you want to do this afternoon?" I asked when we reached the bottom of the mountain.

"How about shopping?"

The guard was about to ring the bell, however, as his English was so good I tested his knowledge of the city.

"Where may we find the best shops?" I asked.

"Strandgaten sir. It's west of the Vagen."

Consulting the map, I found the street. Then, after thanking the guard, and returning our picnic basket to the café, we headed in the direction of the harbour.

Clearly, Strandgaten was the Milsom Street of Bergen, although almost three times its length. Similarly, in Bath's Milsom Street, Strandgaten was filled with high-class shops. Mervyn and I counted at least six retail stores, as well as women's fashion shops, men's tailors, tobacconists, ladies hat shops and hairdressing salons. We only reached half way along the thoroughfare before we became quite overwhelmed. Nevertheless, we bravely negotiated one large store, emerging half an hour later with parcels containing a beautiful sterling silver Viking ship for me, a warm, hand knitted jumper for Mervyn, as well as a framed painting depicting the house of the composer Edvard Greig.

By three o'clock, we felt the need for liquid refreshment, so I suggested we duck down a side street leading to the harbour, where we might find a public house. Yet, I soon learned that the drinking establishments to which we Englishmen are accustomed do not exist in Scandinavia. In most cities in Northern Europe, places where one can imbibe seem to be in either hotels or back street bars. As our luck would have it, Mervyn and I chanced upon such a bar quite close to the fish market, its entrance in the wall of a warehouse.

"This looks promising," Mervyn said, pointing to a sign over the door depicting a flying baby holding a bow and arrow.

"Cupido," he said, reading the sign.

Before venturing inside, my natural apprehension made me wish to investigate the place a little further. But seeing there were no windows, I was a little timorous as to what we might find. We boldly ducked through the door however, exchanging the smell of fish for the acrid pall of strong tobacco smoke and an unmistakable aroma of cognac.

A short, narrow passage led to a room crowded with men, a few sitting at the bar, others talking in corners, or at small tables ranged around and about. All the while, a radio on the wall behind the bar blared out unrecognisable popular tunes.

Somehow, the dark mysterious atmosphere reminded me of a Hollywood film I saw last year, 'The Man Who Knew Too Much' immediately springing to mind. Even so, our entrance caused little disturbance, so we walked to the bar, where Mervyn ordered drinks. Whiskey seems to be universally understood and soda can be explained by making a swishing noise with one's mouth. As a result, in no time, and with drinks in hand, we looked around for a table. The only available seats seemed to be two stools at the bar, so we made ourselves comfortable and sipped our scotch and sodas.

Mervyn and I are quite open with each other regarding our natures. By now, he knew how it was with me, and me with him, so it hardly surprised me to feel him nudge my leg with his knee, seeing him raise his eyebrows and indicate a man sitting near us. In order not to appear too obvious, I glanced at the fellow just in time to see him wink at Mervyn. I quickly looked away in case I was seen, but taking a second glance, I saw him wink again.

How extraordinary! Was the man afflicted with Saint Vitas' Dance? Alternatively, some unexplained tic? On the other hand, was he openly making overtures towards my young friend?

The men in the bar were brawny and extremely masculine, so you might forgive me for being incredibly naïve. But then, and only then, did I realise by the intimate way they were associating that Mervyn and I, by some primeval instinct, had stumbled into a bar where we would feel most at home.

"Tourist ya?" the man suddenly asked Mervyn. "Not from Norway, ya."

"English. We're off a ship," stammered Mervyn.

"We're only here for a few hours," I interrupted. "We leave tonight."

All of a sudden, I realised how stiff, pompous, and terribly English I sounded.

"You like Bergen?" the man continued, his eyes finally leaving Mervyn to meet mine.

"Very nice," I replied, endeavouring to lessen my upper class accent.

He was very handsome, in a rugged kind of way. Fair hair and extremely blue eyes. How our English wenches must have swooned as hairy Vikings carried them back to their Long Ships.

"Are you all fishermen?" I asked, innocently.

The barman, who was listening to our conversation, laughed.

"Sure," The man at the bar chuckled. "Some fish. Some work in the market. Others in town. All sorts."

"You two?" the barman said abruptly. "You like this?"

He linked his little fingers, and then made a circle with his thumb and forefinger, poking the index finger of his right hand through the circle.

Naturally, I was stupefied, and noticed Mervyn blushing. Never had I been asked such a question in such a matter of fact way. However, by the men's reaction, the question appeared quite ordinary.

"We're friends," I said, warily.

"Ah!" they said, smiling and nodding.

"How did you find Cupido?" asked the man on the stool.

"Entirely by chance," I said, noticing several teenage lads amongst the crowd. "Cupido! Quite apt really. Do the police know about it?"

"Of course. Konstable Olav's over there."

By flicking his head, the man indicated the direction in which I should look, where I saw a giant of a man, standing near the door, drinking beer and talking with a young friend.

"How is it you can meet like this?" I asked. "In England such places would be raided and closed down. Since the war, men like us have had it tough. In the cities, plain-clothes policemen, working in pairs, trap us. While one seduces the innocent victim, the other waits to make an arrest. The guards from Knightsbridge Barracks prostitute themselves to anyone who can afford them, then attempt to expose the victim unless he pays more money. The police want to stamp us out, so to avoid a long prison sentence we have to be very careful."

To my surprise, I realised I had never spoken as openly, and at such length to anyone regarding the plight of homosexuals in Britain, and could see Mervyn was taken aback and listening keenly.

"Here we never have such a problem," the man said. "Nothing happens like you've described. We live openly, men with men, women with women. Of course, officially, our kind is illegal, but there's never been arrests or imprisonments. People know what we are, but turn a blind eye and leave us alone."

"Then you're very lucky," I responded. "One day I hope England will regard us as tolerantly, and we'll be able to express ourselves as freely."

It was so liberating to speak frankly about a subject so dear to my heart, that I ordered Mervyn and myself a second double scotch, along with a couple of schnapps for the man on the stool and the barman.

By the time we left the bar an hour later, we were both a little the worse for wear. So much so, we decided there had been enough excitement for one day and caught the tram back to the ship.

That night, as we slept, the Viceroy steamed away from Bergen, and by dawn had left the Fjords and was out to sea, heading north. Eventually, after half a day, her rudder conveyed us in an easterly direction, steering towards the coast, the ship entering a wide inlet between high mountain peaks. Considering I thought the previous scenery magnificent, nonetheless, the further we travelled into the labyrinth of Fjords, the narrower they became and the landscape more stupendous. Standing at the rail the following morning; seeing the towering cliffs of rock, forest and pasture, sea birds wheeling around the crags and crevices; I could well believe we had finally arrived in the Land of the Trolls.

Chapter Nineteen
Fjords and females

"What's a troll anyway?" asked Teddy, as we took tea that afternoon, in the dining saloon. "Are they real?"

Everyone laughed at yet another Teddyism, as we had come to call his outbursts.

"No Teddy," said Wilfred. "Trolls are part of Norse mythology. They're a type of creature, sometimes friendly, sometimes not. Much larger than human beings. As old as time itself, and exceedingly ugly."

Rowena and Kathryn shivered.

"You're frightening the children Wilfred," interjected mother.

"You've no need to worry though," Wilfred continued. "Lightening is known to kill them, and there are lots of thunderstorms in Norway."

"Where do they live?" Teddy asked, obviously not entirely convinced of the troll's non-existence.

"In the caves and crevices such as we're seeing now."

He pointed to the steep cliffs passing beyond the windows just a few hundred yards to port and starboard, and it was easy to believe them to be the dwelling place of monsters ready to eat one for supper.

Naeroyfjord is the darkest and narrowest lane of water in all Scandinavia, with its perpendicular walls of rock rising on either side to a shuddering three thousand feet. In places it is barely four hundred yards wide and is unnavigable in spring, since melting snow and ice causes huge rocks to fall into the water, some large enough to sink a passing ship. Perched on the cliff tops, almost two thousand feet above the fjord, cling eagle nest farmsteads, the inhabitants eking out an existence raising cattle, goats, and sheep.

The Viceroy weighed anchor in deep water at the head of the fjord, a little way off Gudvangen, a tiny village dwarfed by the enclosing mountains. Anticipating a tour ashore, Mervyn, and I went to our cabins to dress appropriately.

Since our party would board the tender on the surface of the fjord we need not have worried, because, as we descended the companionway the water was as tranquil as a millpond, hardly rocking the landing stage. Once aboard, the coxswain powered the engine and we began our trip to shore. Given the opportunity, I captured the scene with my camera. Although I wondered whether anyone at home would believe the sheer beauty and magnificence of what I saw through the viewfinder, the water resembling glass, mirroring the towering cliffs above. Furthermore, as I took a photograph of the ship, what I saw if I turned upside down, was a complete mirror image of that above, which might cause the photograph to appear most incongruous.

Approaching a stony beach and a small jetty, we saw the rooftops of a dozen or so cottages appear, then an imposing wooden building with a balcony, which was surely a hotel. Therefore, once we landed, it was towards the hotel that we headed.

My reliable guidebook informed me that during the time of the Vikings, Gudvangen was a busy market place, but when the Black Death arrived from England, everyone in the village died. The hamlet lay abandoned for several hundred years, until a community was established since it became a staging place for the postal service from northern Norway to Bergen. Subsequently, the village has become a popular destination for tourists, either returning by the inland route to Bergen, or visiting the Naeroyfjord.

Before we left the ship, an announcement over the ship's loudspeakers informed us that, since the ship would remain in the fjord for only three hours, should anyone wish to take the excursion to Gudvangen, there would only be a short period to see all the sights.

By the plentiful selection of picture postcards, trinkets, and souvenirs on display at the hotel counter, it was obvious cruise liners were frequent callers. However, I managed to steer our party away by drawing their attention to a poster fixed to the wall. It advertised excursions to Bakka, a village on the fjord, several miles north of Gudvangen, where the poster promised we would see peasants wearing traditional Norwegian costume.

Mother, Rowena, and Kathryn were keen, so I enquired at the counter as to when the next trip was scheduled to depart. The excursion was also popular with other passengers, as I noticed a queue forming behind me.

A ferry was due to leave the jetty in twenty minutes, so Mervyn and I left the group and walked down the lane towards a cluster of wooden houses huddled along the banks of a river. In front of each, we were intrigued to see collections of timber racks covered with rows of fish, each impaled on a metal spike.

"Why do think they hang them like that?" asked Mervyn.

"To dry them I suppose," I said. "You remember the dried cod in Bergen. The handbook says people hang their fish in winter, so by the late spring and summer they've lost almost all their water."

"Do they eat them?"

"Of course. I suppose they make fish soups and stews."

Mervyn made a face. "I wouldn't like that."

"Although, if the snow is deep and you can't leave your home, a bowl of fish soup might be most welcome."

We commented on how pretty the white painted cottages were. With bright red roofs and colourful floral window boxes, their wooden gables and window ledges carved into decorative shapes and fretted with patterns.

However, time flies as they say, and soon we turned back in the direction of the jetty just as the ferry appeared across the fjord.

A mile or so up the Naeroy, the village of Bakka is even smaller than Gudvangen, with just a dozen houses and a church. It appeared the entire population had turned out to greet us, everyone wearing

Norwegian national dress. The ferry drew alongside the quay, people with cameras having a field day capturing the scene, as women and children flocked around the female passengers, clearly shy of men, so few of them do they see other than their own relatives.

All the same, I managed to persuade some mothers to gather their children together in order I take a photograph. In the back row, Mervyn, Teddy, and Mickey, looked sullen, and Wilfred, towering over everyone, appeared his usual serious self. In fact, standing beside him, the only person seeming to be enjoying herself was mother. The children did not understand me when I asked them to smile. Nor did they know 'Cheese!' when I said it as a last resort, resulting in the final photograph being a little shambolic where the little ones were concerned.

For the sake of my female readers let me not leave here without giving you a quick description of the national costume. It consists of a brocaded, red velvet bodice, worn over a white, cotton blouse, embroidered at the neck. The skirt is black and reaches below the knee, over the skirt is worn a white apron embellished with delicate lace.

The ferry blew her whistle, so we hurried back to the jetty for the short return ride to Guvangen and thereafter to the waiting ship.

You might be forgiven if you are wondering how Mervyn was behaving since his dalliance with Bob the waiter. Naturally, I was alert for any association, except there seemed none. In the smoking room and dining saloon, Bob continued to serve us attentively and politely, and Mervyn at no time making special overtures to him, although this behaviour puzzled me. How could something so intimate have occurred between two people, and be so easily forgotten? As I mentioned a while ago, the post-war generation looked at life very differently.

On the other hand, Mervyn was having his own tribulations, and this time from the fairer sex. A certain young female passenger had taken quite a shine to him, and to his annoyance pursued him relentlessly around the ship. If Mervyn was playing ping-pong she was there cheering him on. Or else, should he be in the swimming pool cavorting with Mickey and Teddy, she was above on the pavement walkway gazing down at him with doe eyes.

Mervyn had always stated quite emphatically, that he was not entirely homosexual and was equally attracted to either sex. Therefore, seeing this was the first time a female had shown an interest I was keen to see his reaction. So one evening I made myself known to Jessica, as I found her name to be, and invited her to our table. As she sat down beside Mervyn, he shot me a daggered look.

"Did you know, Mervyn," said Jessica, excitedly. "There's going to be another fancy dress ball on Saturday night. I think you looked lovely at the last one. I wish you'd asked me to dance."

"I didn't know you then, did I," sniffed Mervyn. "Not like now. Of course I'll ask you to dance."

He glared at me across the table, while Mickey sniggered, and Teddy blushed, both keen to see how Mervyn would react.

In all my forty-five years, I twice found it necessary to fend off a woman's advances. The first occasion was when I was barely twenty and still at Cambridge. A certain country lad with whom I became acquainted lived in Fenn Ditton, a village a mile or so from the city. Almost every weekend I would ride my bicycle to his cottage and we would walk the lanes and byways, occasionally visiting an isolated barn or hayloft along the way. My friend owned a dog; an English setter called Richmond; an apt name for such a patriotic animal, and Richmond would join us. One Saturday, I arrived as usual. However, it appeared my friend was in bed with a cold, so I was about to head back to Cambridge when his elder sister, Rosemary, suggested she accompany me on my walk. Naturally, I was too much of a gentleman to refuse her invitation.

A storm had threatened all morning and, true to form, as we set out, the sky turned extremely dark. Despite this, and not wishing to deprive Richmond of his walk, we continued on our way. Although, by the time we reached the Cam it had begun to rain. I say rain; it was more of a deluge, so Rosemary and I looked around for somewhere to shelter until the storm passed. Luckily, we happened upon a boathouse along the towpath, and ran inside.

As we huddled in the doorway, watching the rain turn the river into a torrent, I suddenly felt Rosemary's hand brush mine.

"Don't you love the rain!" she said softly. "It always makes me feel so snuggly, especially when I'm in bed."

More than likely, I answered, although it was probably more of a mumble. My friend once told me that his sister was somewhat experienced in the ways of the world. Already, since reaching her teens, she had walked out with several country lads, although, I for one was certainly not going to fall prey to her enticement.

"It's kind of romantic Ronnie, don't you think?" she continued. "Here we are alone. No one to interrupt us. Why don't you kiss me? You know you want to."

"I'm sorry Rosemary," I stammered. "I'd rather not, if you don't mind."

Desperately, I struggled to think of an excuse for my disinterest.

"You've never done it have you? I can tell."

My eyes were on the river, even though I could feel hers fixed on me intently.

"You're a little forward for a girl of your age," I said. "Surely! Isn't it the man who makes advances?"

"If I waited for every boy to summon up the courage, I'd be all day. When a girl wants something she has to ask for it."

"Then I'm sorry Rosemary. I'm not your man."

"My boyfriend said, my brother told him you're a queer. I said you weren't. But I reckon he's right."

Suddenly, I was taken aback. My trust had been abused. I thought the relationship between her brother and I was a secret, but now I realised it was more than likely the gossip of the village. Ignoring her, I whistled for the dog.

"Don't be silly Rosemary. You can't believe everything you hear. I already have a girlfriend. We're almost engaged."

"Does my brother know?"

"It's my business. Nothing to do with him."

Thankfully, with the rain stopped, I hurried outside, found Richmond, and we continued our walk in silence. I never returned to Fenn Ditton, and my dog-walking days were over.

The second time where I found it necessary to defend my honour happened in Cairo at the end of the war. A few of us were on leave from Abbassia, and while we waited demobilisation, we put up at the Semiramis Hotel. The hotel boasted a first class orchestra, tennis courts, and an exotic roof garden. However, some of us craved something a little more ethnic, so we gravitated to a favourite Cairo night spot called the Kit Kat Club, situated in a small square across the Imbaba Bridge and close to the west bank of the Nile.

Here, at the finest nightclub in all of Cairo, one could see the best belly dancing, as well as the handsomest of Arab men; one reason I found it irresistible. Women also frequented the nightclub, accompanied of course by male partners. In addition, nurses from the army hospital at the Heliopolis Palace Hotel were frequent punters, intent on having a good time away from the horrors experienced on a daily basis.

One night, a few officer friends and I were enjoying drinks when a group of nurses sat down at the next table. They were a lively bunch and we were soon exchanging conversation. They invited us to their table and I sat down beside a young vivacious blonde, who told me her name was Sheila. She was Australian and typically loud and confident. I instantly took to her since she was witty and very entertaining.

As one did in those days, when the belly dancer finished her routine and the band began to play the usual dance music, everyone paired up and moved on to the dance floor.

I asked Sheila to dance, and that was how our friendship began.

Sheila and I met at the club quite regularly, and always danced together. I feel guilty admitting that I used Sheila as a smoke screen to maintain my reputation with my fellow officers, who all had steady girlfriends. I can honestly say that Sheila remains my greatest female acquaintance, her quick wit, and turn of phrase equalling mine. As a result, with our repartee quickly became the talk of Cairo, Sheila and I began to receive invitations to dances, dinner parties, tennis lunches and polo matches. Except one night at the Kit Kat, our bubble burst.

I remember, we were dancing a Fox Trot, doing our usual, Mervyn and Irene Castle impersonation when, all of a sudden, Sheila stopped dancing.

"I can't go on like this," she gasped. "I want you. I can't keep my hands off you. I love you."

At first, I thought she was joking, so I laughed.

"What me?" I exclaimed. "Silly old me! We're just friends. Let's keep it that way."

She looked horrified, burst into tears, and fled the dance floor.

Of course, I was unable to explain the reason I could never reciprocate her feelings, which hurt at the time. Later, when we spoke I feigned indifference, which angered her more, and so at that point, unfortunately, our beautiful friendship ended forever. I was demobilised and sent home and she, I presume, returned to Australia. I often wonder what happened to her.

So you see I was intrigued as to whether Mervyn might face similar dilemmas.

***

The fancy dress ball proved interesting to say the least, because it left me in no doubt that Mervyn's boast that he was neither one way nor another in his preferences, was pure fantasy. Firstly, instead of pleasing Jessica by repeating his toy soldier role of the previous ball, he put on the ugliest Arab outfit he could find, and covered his face with a large black beard, almost as if he wished to hide from her.

However, as I have discovered to my cost, when women set their sights on something, or someone, they are relentless in their pursuit. True to form, Jessica chased Mervyn all evening, seeming hardly concerned as to his appearance, until he eventually capitulated and danced with her.

By the end of the night, he must have given her the slip because, when I went to my cabin, I found him hiding in my bed.

The following morning, after leaving the fjords and heading north into open sea, the Viceroy steamed into Romsdalsfjorden, and turned her bows towards the city of Molde.

If you remember, Molde is Wilfred, my brother's, favourite holiday destination where, while Parliament is recessed, he spends the few months fishing in the rivers around and about, for salmon, sea trout, and char.

Molde is a medieval city, and was once most attractive, possessing luxurious hotels, quaint wooden houses, lush parks and gardens, pavilions and wide esplanades. In fact, it was reminiscent of Cannes or Nice in the South of France. In 1916, however, an unfortunate fire almost destroyed the playground of Kaiser Wilhelm and his cousin, Edward, Prince of Wales. Therefore, it surprised me to see how rejuvenated the city had become in nineteen years.

Naturally, we made our usual tour, this time in a horse and jig, which gave our blisters a rest. Then it was back to the ship for cocktails, dinner, and an early night.

Here began an extended period at sea, as the Viceroy steamed northward, taking two days and three nights to reach Trondheim. While it is incorrect to say nights, since from then on, we experienced the midnight sun, which turned out to be quite an eerie phenomenon. The sun hovers above the sea, doggedly refusing to sink below the horizon, giving one a feeling of timelessness. No one seemed to feel like retiring to bed. Instead, we danced, played cards, drank and smoked well into the night, until sheer exhaustion drove us under the covers, while the sun turned tail on itself and slowly rose, heralding a new day.

Chapter Twenty
Trondheim - Teddy tells all - Mother's adventure

By the time we steamed into Trondheimfjorden, by the look on his face when I suggested another tour, my senses told me that Mervyn was becoming somewhat bored with our customary shore excursions. So my choice was whether to go ashore alone, or find someone else to accompany me.

Mickey had become increasingly languid as each day went by, resorting to lounging in the smoking room, idly thumbing through magazines and getting through packets of cigarettes. Cruising sometime has this effect on people. Usually those you least expect discover, after a week at sea, the life boring and tedious. Personally, I am the opposite, since the further on we sail the less I want the cruise to end, so constantly make the most of everything, while remembering that all good things eventually end.

Mickey then, would hardly be my ideal companion, so I cast my thoughts elsewhere. I liked Teddy. He was like a sponge. Always asking questions, scrutinising the answers methodically in his mind. By this time, I had concluded that Teddy's education had been somewhat lacking. Perhaps being fatherless could be the reason for his absence of learning. A father should encourage and educate a son, more so than a mother, who simply loves and cherishes. I felt quite fatherly towards Teddy, even more than towards Mervyn.

Of the three friends, Teddy was the most aimless. Given that

Mickey was idle, and Mervyn played ping-pong with Gilbert Fry, or evaded Jessica's harrying; Teddy mused and wandered from place to place, wearing his hound dog expression.

Having given it some thought, I asked Teddy to join me on the tour, and he happily obliged. Therefore, armed with my trusty handbook, camera, and extra film, Teddy and I descended the gangway and boarded the tender.

By this time, we hardly noticed the smell of fish as we strolled towards the heart of the city. Instead, I consulted the guidebook and read passages aloud to Teddy.

"Trondheim harbour, as in most Norwegian ports, is bounded by colourful wooden warehouses. The city is located on a peninsula at the mouth of the River Nidelva, where it empties into the Trondenheimfjord. When he took the throne in the year 997, the Viking, King Olaf chose the city as his capital, becoming the first Christian King of Norway, building the country's first church. His statue can be seen on top of a tall column in the centre of the city."

Teddy seemed interested, so I continued.

"Principle sites are Nidaros Cathedral, Trondheim Bridge, Old Town, Kristiansten Fortress, Stiftsgarden, the largest wooden royal residence in Northern Europe, and the Trondelag Theatre."

"There we are!" I exclaimed snapping shut the guidebook. "There seems a lot to see. But this place looks nice. Shall we have coffee?"

We were standing in front of an impressive café, with 'Erichsen's' written over the door, and by the number of people sitting at the tables on the pavement outside, it appeared to be popular. Finding a vacant table, we sat down, the smell of roasting coffee completely intoxicating. In addition, the sight of the fancy pastries on people's plates encouraged me to forget I had only recently eaten a hearty breakfast, plus my promise to Mervyn to go on a diet.

"Two coffees please," I said to a waitress, hoping she would understand. "And a selection of your delicious pastries."

She smiled, and disappeared inside the café.

"What shall we do first?" Teddy asked, lighting a cigarette.

"Anything you like old chap," I answered. "It's a lovely day. The sun's shining. How about a walk in the park. We'll need it by the look of these cakes."

In the meantime, the waitress had placed a plate of fancies on the table, as well as setting down two cups of steaming coffee. The pastries were of every variety, from bite size buns, topped with icing sugar and glacé cherries, to a type resembling biscuits, very crunchy, and covered with crispy oats. Despite being stuck for choice, we decided our favourite was the simple chocolate cake, and in no time, the plate was empty.

"Ron, I hope you don't mind me saying," Teddy said suddenly, as we relaxed, while smoking and watching the world go by. "You spoil Mervyn."

I was taken aback. Such a comment coming from Teddy was rare indeed.

"Do you think so?" I said. "No more than I spoil you and Mickey. You're my friends, and what are friends for, but to give them presents."

"But he takes advantage."

By his expression, I could see the genuine concern in his eyes.

"You've no need to worry about me Teddy. I'm old enough to look after myself. I know what I'm doing."

"But he's going behind your back."

I began to feel the old anxiety appear in my stomach, but endeavoured to remain calm.

"What do you mean?"

Teddy looked away, obviously embarrassed to admit what was in his mind.

"Go on Teddy," I continued. "Have your say. I respect your candidness."

"You know the waiter…"

Here we go again, I thought. I was foolish to believe the dalliance was over.

"You mean, Bob," I said casually.

"Yes. Mervyn told Mickey and me that they meet during the day."

"Where?" I sighed.

"Around and about the ship. When I see you and Mervyn talking at mealtimes, you seem so happy, and I feel guilty that I know and you don't. You're so good to us. I think he's being very selfish."

Suddenly, I realised I was rapidly becoming rather bored with hearing about Mervyn's antics. Also, I felt less devastated by the news than at the initial discovery of his disloyalty.

"Thanks Teddy," I said. "I'm touched by your concern. However, who am I to tell Mervyn what to do. I'm not his keeper. He's his own man. But don't feel too bad. I've known all along."

Teddy and I suddenly saw the funny side of the situation and began to laugh.

"Don't tell him I know," I added. "It's our secret."

We finished our cigarettes; paid the waitress; then studied the map in the guidebook.

"By the look of things, the cathedral's a couple of streets away. How about we take a squiz."

Therefore, throwing care aside, we found our way into the main street and headed towards the cathedral, the green copper spire clearly visible in the distance.

Here again I apologise if I sound like a copy of the Baedeker, or Michelin guide, but I am unable to think of another way to describe what we saw over the next few hours.

Nidaros Cathedral particularly impressed Teddy and me. We were also very taken with the fantastic sculptures of the west front, as well as the tall spire. Built above the grave of Saint Olaf, the patron saint of Norway, between 1070 and 1300, the cathedral is a fine example of Romanesque and early Gothic architecture. Over the centuries, it has been subjected to many fires and was once burned to the ground, with only the stonewalls remaining. Nonetheless, sixty years ago, the cathedral was completely restored.

Next, we followed the map to the Trondheim Bridge, noticing it worked quite like Tower Bridge in London, and quite similar in appearance.

On a street strangely named Munkegata, it was necessary to jump on a tram to reach our next destination, which we chose to be Stiftgarden, a royal residence of King Haakon and Queen Maud of Norway.

The wealthy widow woman, who built it in the late eighteenth century, filled it with wonderful furniture, fabrics, and paintings, something that fired my imagination. The widow seldom resided in the house, instead using it as a residence for important visitors to Trondheim. Inside the palace, and using very good English, the guide informed us that the house comprised one hundred and forty rooms, and considering it covered an area of forty three thousand feet, it is the largest wooden construction in all Europe.

Teddy and I wandered through a few of the rooms open to the public, then after an hour, we decided it was lunchtime. The old town, which the locals call Bakklandet, is on the opposite side of the bridge, and here we found a café and sat down and ordered a meal. When it arrived, we were surprised to see it all together on one large plate; a selection of cured meats, cheeses, pickled fish and rye bread. It seemed we were expected to help ourselves. A novel idea we thought at the time and most civilised.

Once reinvigorated, we crossed the river again and simply followed our feet, discovering to our delight the pretty Trondelag Theatre, the oldest of its kind in Scandinavia.

At long last, and satisfied we had seen everything worth seeing, Teddy and I made our way back to St Olaf's Pier, where the tender waited to return us to the ship. On our arrival, I found Wilfred in a high state of anxiety.

"Mother took off with the twins late this morning, and we've seen neither hide nor hair of her since."

"Don't worry Wilfred," I said. "If I know mother. She's probably been side-tracked in some shop or other. She'll be along soon."

"But the ship leaves in an hour. What if she's lost track of time?"

In all honesty, I was also a little concerned, but hardly prepared to go ashore to look for her. Instead, while I ran a bath, anticipating a long hot soak, I sent Teddy to find Mervyn, and in no time, there was a knock on the bathroom door.

"Who is it?" I asked.

"Me."

Of course, it was Mervyn, and as he opened the door, I could see by his expression, he was anxious about me reproaching him about something.

"Mother's disappeared in Trondheim," I said. "Would you and Mickey go ashore and look for her? Wilfred's in a bit of a tizzy and thinks she might miss the ship."

"But I've a challenge match to play in half an hour. She'll be fine. You'll see."

"Please Mervyn. Go with Wilfred."

"But Ron! I don't know the place. Both of us stayed aboard. We're just as likely to get lost ourselves."

I could see his point and realised, reluctantly, that I should be the one to go.

"Mother's got a shocking sense of direction," said Wilfred, as the tender pulled away from the ship.

"I'm sure she'll have the good sense to ask someone the way," I said to reassure him.

Wilfred and I were well acquainted with tales of English women abroad, disappearing without trace. But I hardly imagined mother would appeal to a white slaver. She had simply become lost, and it was our job to find her. When the tender reached the jetty, Rowena and Kathryn were waiting to board.

"Where's mother?" Wilfred asked.

"We don't know," they said in unison, the way twins sometimes do. "We were over there, and she vanished."

They pointed to a curiosity market set up along the pier, selling everything from old clothes to antique furniture.

"What was mother wearing today, Wilfred?" I asked, as we jostled through the crowd.

"How do I know!" he barked. "The usual I suppose."

"It's sunny, so she would've worn a hat. She was fond of the large straw hat she wore at last month's fete."

We scanned the people wandering from stall to stall, but it was impossible to keep up with the milling throng. Then I had an idea, since I noticed the stall nearest the jetty specialised in porcelain figures, a particular favourite of mothers. Perhaps the woman minding the stall remembered her.

"Did you happen to see an English lady a while ago?" I asked, slowly and deliberately. "She might have been wearing a straw hat."

"Ya," the woman replied. "She bought two pieces."

"Really! Did you see where she went?"

"Ya. She caught the ferry."

"What ferry?" Wilfred snapped irritably.

"The ferry to the island." She pointed to the jetty.

"Silly woman!" Wilfred muttered. "Mother got on thinking it was the tender to take her back to the ship."

The stallholder was becoming annoyed at Wilfred's obvious rudeness so I became over polite.

"Which island?" I asked.

"Munkholmen. Perhaps she's visiting the prison."

"Do you mind?" Wilfred shouted. "The lady's our mother. There are no criminals in our family, if you please."

Exasperated, the woman threw up her hands and turned her back.

"Come on," I said. "Let's get to the jetty to check the time of the return ferry. She's bound to be on it."

Remarkably, this was the first time I had become aware of the tiny island of Munkholmen, but since it features in my story, I'll acquaint you with something of its history.

In the days of the Vikings, the island was a place of execution, the severed heads of the executed placed on stakes, facing outward towards the fjord, as a warning to strangers happening by. In fact, the story goes that visitors to Trondheim were forced to spit on the heads as a tribute to King Olaf the first. Several hundred years later Munkholmen became a monastery, then a fortress, and finally a prison.

Arriving at the ticket booth, we found the ticket window closed, plus the indicator board blank, and realised with horror that mother had unwittingly caught the last ferry.

"What'll we do?" Wilfred stuttered. "The ship sails in half an hour. We'll have to contact the island. If it's a prison, it's bound to have a telephone."

At this point, I too was beginning to panic, while looking around for a telephone box, but of course, had no idea what a Norwegian telephone kiosk looked like. With the tender waiting at the jetty, Wilfred and I came to a decision.

"If we don't catch it," I said. "We'll be in the same boat as mother."

Wilfred looked horrified. "We can't just leave her there all night. She'll get the ferry in the morning and find the ship gone."

"Don't worry, Wilfred," I said. "I've a plan."

When we arrived back at the ship, I asked an officer if Wilfred and I could see Captain Thornton, and he kindly escorted us to the bridge. If you have ever been on the bridge of an ocean liner, you will understand when I say that it is a remarkable sight. With shining brass instruments, rows of dials; levers; knobs; buttons and speaking tubes, it is a wonder how the officers know what lever to pull, or which switch to switch. Standing amongst all this technology was Captain Thornton; he smiled when the officer introduced us.

"Can I help you gentlemen?"

The previous night, Wilfred and I received an invitation to dine at the Captain's table, therefore I felt on familiar terms with him, having also taken his South Atlantic cruise earlier in the year.

"Very much Captain," I said. "Our mother, Mrs Fry, inadvertently caught the wrong boat at the jetty, and is at present marooned on Munktenholm Island."

"Dear me. I can see your dilemma," said the Captain. "Obviously, you wish me to make a call as we leave the fjord."

"If you please Captain. Wilfred and I would be extremely obliged."

Thus, we were able to breathe a sigh of relief, although still apprehensive and not entirely at ease until mother was safely back aboard. In an endeavour to relax, Wilfred and I adjourned to the smoking room, where we ordered two double scotch and sodas. Soon after, Mervyn and the boys arrived, hot and thirsty from a ping-pong competition.

"Did you find her?" Mervyn said, slumping into an armchair; while Teddy, Mickey and Gilbert Fry collapsed onto a sofa.

"Almost," I replied. "Although she's not on the ship."

"Where is she?" Teddy asked, sounding concerned. "They're about to take up the gangway."

"It's alright," said Wilfred, casually lighting a cigarette. "She'll be here soon."

It pleased me to see Wilfred playing along with my ruse, and nice to have a joke on the youngsters for a change.

"How's she coming aboard then?" Mickey asked. "By balloon?"

A great bellow from the ships foghorn drowned our laughter, announcing our imminent departure. So we watched through the windows the panorama of houses on the hillside slowly diminish as the ship drew further away.

"But what about Mrs Fry?" Mervyn said. "You can't leave her behind Ron! You wouldn't do such a thing. You're joking of course. She's on the ship."

Wilfred and I shook our heads, but remained silent, and having finished our drinks, I picked up the dinner menu from a side table. Today being Thursday, despite having been at sea for over a week, none of us had sat down to the same meal twice. On the menu that night was leek and potato soup, or smoked trout, followed by roast chicken, or salmon croquettes, served with seasonal vegetables. The dessert was apple pie and custard or Neapolitan ice cream and stewed pears.

"Roast chicken for me!" I exclaimed. "How about you Wilfred? Salmon?"

"Yes please. I fancy the salmon. If it's caught locally."

"Look at you both," Mervyn said. "How can you be so relaxed?"

Laughing gaily, I got up from my chair, and leaving the smoking room by the wrought iron gate opening into the veranda café, I sauntered on to the Sports Deck. It was pointless looking behind, because I knew everyone was following. By this time, the ship was well clear of the city, and glancing over the port rail, I saw the tender dogging our progress as we took a westerly course towards Munktenholm Island. The boys saw it too.

"Why hasn't the tender been winched aboard?" Teddy asked.

"For heaven's sake Ron!" Mervyn protested. "What's going on?"

Now it was Wilfred's turn to laugh, although to me it sounded more like hysteria.

"You'll see."

As we came abreast of the island, the tender pulled away, and made purposely in its direction.

"What's it doing now?" Teddy asked. But his question went unanswered, as Rowena and Kathryn, both eager to know the cause of the excitement, joined us.

"Fetch my binoculars Mervyn," I said. "You'll be quicker than me."

He did as I asked, and was back in a moment.

"Now we'll see."

Adjusting the focus, I found the tender just as she arrived at the island, and low and behold, there was mother waiting on the jetty, as plain to see by her straw hat. A seaman helped her aboard, and assisted her into a front seat. The sight of her sitting all alone caused me to laugh aloud.

"What's funny?" Wilfred asked, obviously frustrated he was unable to see what I was seeing.

"Nothing."

"Is she there?"

"They've just picked her up."

"Ron! Tell us what's going on," pleaded Mervyn.

"Mother took the wrong boat. She thought she was coming back to the ship, but instead went to the Munktenholm Island."

Everyone laughed, and at last we saw the humour of her predicament. Yet mother was still not aboard and would need to negotiate the companionway, which they were letting down at that precise moment. The tender approached the ship, and we watched it tie up at the bottom of the steps. It was a mercy the water was calm, even though, mother had difficulty breaching the gap. Finally, she alighted, and began the steep climb, while we all hurried to the lift and scrambled inside.

"What on earth provoked you to take the island ferry?" Wilfred asked, as mother reached the top of the companionway. "We've been so worried."

"Dear me!" she gasped. "Let me catch my breath. I'm in such a dither."

There was a chair beside the lift gates, so I urged her to sit down.

"Thank you, dear. I was so worried I'd drop them. It's almost impossible with one hand."

Under her arm, she clutched a package wrapped in newspaper.

"I couldn't believe it when I saw them," mother continued. "So pretty. How the woman hadn't seen the crossed swords I've no idea."

"What are you talking about?" asked Wilfred.

"Meissen dear! Two Meissen figures! Just sitting there. She wanted thirty-six kroner for the two. Look at them."

Carefully, mother put the package on her lap and began to unwrap it, while gesturing to us to come closer. The grubby newspaper fell away revealing a little porcelain man, dressed in eighteenth century clothes, wearing a wig, the colours so vivid you would have thought he was painted and fired yesterday.

"He's very rare," whispered mother. "I've seen him in the Victoria and Albert Museum, but never thought I'd have the chance to own him. He's called 'Les Marquis', and dates from around 1760. But who would have believed that on the table next to him was this."

Lifting away another piece of newspaper a figure appeared, caught in the throes of a dance.

"'Dancing Harlequin'. He's also terribly rare. How extraordinary to have two pieces modelled by Reinicke."

"Mother!" I exclaimed. "I never knew you were so knowledgeable about Meissen. You've been keeping us in the dark all these years."

"Ronald! You have your coins, furniture, and pictures, while I have my china. It just goes to show how blinkered you boys are. My collection is always on view if you care to look."

"Clearly," Wilfred said. "You were so taken by your discovery that you accidentally boarded the wrong boat."

"Yes dear. I suppose so."

With the excitement over, the youngsters drifted away, while Wilfred and I helped mother wrap the figures, then saw her to her cabin.

"I'll have a little nap," she said, before closing the door. "I'll see you at dinner."

"I don't know about you Wilfred," I said, as we returned to the lift. "I could do with another drink."

Chapter Twenty One
Find the Soap - Svartisen Glacier – Tromso - A Laplanders Village

The following day and night were spent at sea, so I usefully employed the time updating my diary, and writing postcards to friends and family. I was particularly eager to tell Eric, Amy, and Emily, about mother's adventure, as I knew they would find the story amusing.

Mervyn, Mickey, and Teddy also had a store of postcards, some they wished to keep as mementos, while others would be posted to their parents when the ship reached Tromso, our next port of call.

Prior to Tromso, we were to encounter one of the highlights of our cruise, the unforgettable Svartisen Glacier. At noon, the Viceroy made a sharp turn to starboard, and then began an easterly course between mountainous islands and dark inlets. She eventually entered a narrow, perfectly still, fjord, the cries of Guillemots and soaring sea eagles the only sounds accompanying the throb of her engines.

Lunch was served as the ship approached the head of the fjord, so our first glimpse of the Svartisen Glacier was through the windows of the George V dining room, making the meal doubly spectacular. A level area of land, plus a large emerald green lake, separated us from possibly the most amazing sight I had ever seen.

"It's vast," someone said, as we crowded at the windows to get a better view; and indeed, they were right.

Between two towering peaks, tumbled a great swathe of ice, dark blue in places, some parts grey, others white, ending in a sheer cliff, perhaps one hundred feet high above the shore of the lake.

"Ladies and gentlemen," a voice said over the loudspeakers. "Shortly, an excursion will leave for the Svartisen Glacier. All who wish to join must assemble at a quarter to two at the companionway on F Deck."

"That's not giving us much time," said Wilfred, hurrying his dessert. "We'll need to wrap up. It might be cold."

The tender could only hold twenty people at a time, and as there were many wishing to go ashore, I held back, using the opportunity to take photographs. The platform at the top of the companionway leading to the bridge was the best vantage point. Once there, I took several pictures, keeping the bows of the ship in view and the enormity of the glacier appearing in the background. Eventually, on our return to Hyde House, I developed the negatives, but realised I had inadvertently included several passengers sitting in deck chairs, sunning themselves on the deck below.

After a number of return trips, our party of nine boarded the tender, and once on the water of the fjord, we could fully appreciate the size and extent of the glacier. When we reached land, a number of horses and carts waited on the jetty, the old driver's tanned and wrinkled faces betraying their years of exposure to the elements.

We drove down a shale roadway to another jetty, this time on the edge of the lake, where a steamboat waited, already crowded with passengers. Once embarked, and to the shrill sound of a whistle, and a puff of smoke from her funnel, the steamboat chugged away from the pier, turning her bows towards the opposite shore and the enormous edifice of ice.

Once again I have cause to praise P&O's forethought in providing us passengers with such succinct information in their little tour booklet. This time I am able to acquaint you with a few statistics concerning the Svartisen Glacier before we brave the icy surface. In fact, apparently Svartisen is two glaciers. The east: Ostre, which is the fourth largest in Norway, and Vesta, the western and Norway's second largest. Together, they cover an area of almost one hundred and fifty square miles, rising from a plateau almost a thousand feet above sea level, although Svartisen is the lowest glacier in mainland Europe at just forty-five feet above sea level.

Drawing closer, we could see more of the glacier's structure, until the precipitous wall of ice towered above us, causing our little vessel to seem quite insignificant. Deep clefts, which could easily swallow a man, gouged the surface, as if a giant with a pic had attempted to cleave the ice apart to expose its heart. The clefts were an attractive shade of dark blue, at the same time, appearing rather menacing. Nearer the surface the colour of the ice became lighter, Officer Wickham, acting as our guide, explaining the colours were due to the density of the ice, the dark blue being older than the light blue, the lighter recently frozen snow still containing air bubbles.

The visual impact was not the only sense-provoking element of the glacier, since the smell of ice was extremely strong, and could only be described as the scent one experiences on a snowy winters morning, only intensified twenty fold.

Despite Wilfred's warning to wrap up, it was quite warm out on the lake, with the sun shining from a clear blue sky, its crisp light transforming the landscape into sharp focus.

When the steamboat reached the shore, everyone clambered onto a wooden pier, below an enormous flat rock shelf.

"Gather around ladies and gentlemen," Officer Wickham shouted. "Welcome to Svartisen Glacier. From now on, we'll make the remainder of the excursion on foot, so I need not enforce the importance of safety. Mind your step. There's no path over the rocks. Follow each other at will, taking the safest and easiest course. Once on the ice, remain together. Don't wander away from the party. In some places, the ice is steep, and should you fall, you might easily slide away for some distance. We would rather not rope you together, as should one go, then so do others."

His final statement caused some consternation amongst the crowd, a few people appearing shocked and worried, whilst others seemed amused and laughed, nervously. Remembering the fears Mickey expressed at the onset of the cruise, I glanced in his direction. But he also appeared to find the officer's statement funny.

"Keep clear of crevasses," Wickham continued. "Some are

extremely wide and deep. We don't want to return to the ship without you."

There was a further sprinkling of nervous laughter, and Mickey's expression changed.

With the safety lecture over, Wickham began to relate the glaciers statistics, much the same as I have already mentioned. Then, after giving directions, he sent us on our way.

The boys took off like lemmings, hurtling, and bounding over the rocks, from one level to the next, the twins following, rather less wildly. Naturally, Mother, Wilfred, and I found the going not as easy. Some places were steep, with the distance between one level and the next so wide, my brother and I needed to hold mother's hand while she attempted to cross. At one stage, the whole party came to a standstill on the edge of a torrent of melt water, which, over millions of years, had gouged a great channel in the rock, so narrow and deep it was necessary for everyone to hop over if we were to continue on our way.

At last, we arrived at the ice, which close too, resembled nothing I had seen before. To attempt to describe it would be almost impossible, but if you can imagine a giant meringue after someone has hacked it with a fork, then you would be close to understanding what I saw.

"Remember what the officer said," Wilfred cautioned. "Keep together, and try not to fall."

The dark clefts, we saw from the steamboat were now enormous fissures, some able to fit a large house inside. We peered into one to discover it had no end and I wondered whether the crevasses would be bottomless when we came to step on the glacier.

Contrary to Wilfred's advice, the heat on the ice was tremendous and I was tempted to remove some clothing, although I had second thoughts. This meant I would be carrying my jacket, which might hinder my way over the slippery surface. In addition, the glare from the reflected sunlight was so strong I wished I had remembered to purchase sunglasses.

Eventually, we were so far across the glacier we became engulfed by its enormity. The weird eroded ice sculptures reminded me of a photograph I once saw of Goreme, a place in Turkey, where time and weather has shaped the rock into strange conical mounds where people currently live.

Taking a moment, I gathered everyone together for the first of many photos, but rather than posing the group, I clicked the shutter informally, thus endeavouring to achieve spontaneity.

Folk began to feel less afraid as they became accustomed to the icy surface. But I did capture several spills as people tried to be adventurous.

Teddy made us laugh when he asked if he could take a piece of ice back to the ship as a memento. It was so enjoyable, pottering up and down the icy slopes, and quite a different experience to walking in snow, which can be hard when deep. With hardly a breath of wind, and the sun on my face, I became quite exhilarated, imagining that others felt the same. Once high enough, our view, down the fjord was breathtaking, including a magnificent image of the Viceroy at anchor, which was well worth photographing.

Mervyn, Mickey, Teddy and Gilbert junior took to sliding down the slopes on their bottoms, resulting in them having very wet behinds, which greatly amused mother.

Officer Wickham finally blew a whistle and brought everyone to attention. It was time to leave, so we left the ice and returned across the rocks to the pier where we boarded the steamboat.

That evening at dinner, all of us were enormously tired. Then at breakfast the following morning, everyone announced how soundly he or she had slept.

By now, we were well on our way to Tromso, the ship remaining under sail for the rest of the day and most of the night, which was fortunate since most were feeling the effects of their endeavours on the ice.

The best way to relieve the stiffness was swimming, and I advised the boys to follow my example. Therefore, we spent an enjoyable afternoon frolicking in the warm water.

That night, while we slept, the little town of Bodo slipped by unseen, and by the glow of the midnight sun, the Viceroy cautiously negotiated the narrow passages, and sometimes-treacherous tides between the islands of Tjeldoya, Senja, and Tromsoya, until finally, she saw the lights of a city twinkling beneath the distant mountains.

For some reason I woke particularly early that morning. My bedside clock said three, although, from around the curtains of my porthole peeked a glimmer of light. I got out of bed, and pulling them aside, saw we were anchored amid a large tract of open water, several hundred yards from a small harbour. The water was completely still, and I could see fishing boats and whaling ships, perfectly reflected. I presumed this to be Tromso, our last port of call before North Cape.

As usual, the sun hung stubbornly above the horizon. And since we were several additional degrees north, it was even higher than before. I could never imagine living in Norway, well not in the Norsland anyway, because I would never grow accustomed to seeing the sun twenty-four hours a day in summer, and the continual darkness in winter. As each day passed, I felt more confused, and for that reason, I was unable to go back to sleep, so instead, reached for the tour booklet on my bedside table.

It surprised me to read that Tromso is referred to as, 'The Paris of the North', the reason being that when the city became a tourist destination, visitors were pleased to find the residents less primitive than previously expected. Apparently, people presumed that folks living so near the North Pole would be primeval nomads.

The tour booklet continued to explain that Tromso is the principle-starting point for Arctic hunting parties, and polar expeditions. Famous arctic explorers recruited their crews in the city. Furthermore, Tromso is the centre for whaling in the region, an industry of which I have never really approved. We were also within the zone of the Aurora Borealis, otherwise referred to as the Northern Lights. Although, since it appeared during the winter, unfortunately we would be unable to catch the shimmering, colourful spectacle.

Eventually, after an hour I dropped off to sleep, and woke at six, feeling a little groggy, as one does when one has insufficient sleep. I decided to skip the dining room, taking breakfast in my cabin instead. So I rang the bell for the steward.

I was shaving when his knock came on the door.

"Come in," I said. "I'll have breakfast please, Johnson? The usual thank you."

"Certainly, Captain."

Surprisingly, the voice that answered was not as I expected, but belonged to Bob.

"Where's Johnson?" I asked, while feeling a little embarrassed.

"He's not well Captain. Stomach trouble. I'll be looking after you until he's better. Your usual is full English, isn't it Captain."

"Yes Bob. Thank you."

He left me alone, and I continued to shave. Johnson never called me Captain, so why should Bob? Then it dawned on me. Mervyn would have referred to me as the Captain. Although, it intrigued me to know why I should crop up in their conversation. In no time, Bob returned with my breakfast tray.

"Thanks Bob. I'll have it on the table under the porthole."

As I towel dried my face, I saw reflected in the shaving mirror, Bob place down the tray.

"Are you intending to go ashore Captain?" he asked, while setting the table. "It looks to be a fine day."

"I think I will, Bob. The cathedral seems worth a visit."

"It is Captain. I can confirm that."

"Have you been a steward on the Viceroy for long?"

"Since her maiden voyage Captain. Six years ago now. I was a bell boy."

"You must have been very young."

"Fifteen, Captain. They say I'm older than I look. Shall I run you a bath Captain?"

"But I'll need to be quick. Won't my breakfast get cold?"

"Don't worry Captain. It's on a warmer."

"Very well."

Peculiarly, I began to feel I was being purposely pampered. Johnson was never so obliging. As a result, I remained standing at the washbasin as Bob came into the bathroom, turned on the taps, and tested the water.

"You must have travelled many miles," I said.

"Certainly Captain. The Viceroy's been my home. The other chaps are like family you might say. We rarely get shore leave longer than a few days. Then she's away on a cruise or the Bombay run."

"It must be very exciting."

"Sometimes Captain. Only yesterday, we heard that when we get to Southampton, the Viceroy will be taking part in the Spithead Review for the King's Silver Jubilee. But like everything Captain, if you do it often enough, eventually it becomes boring."

Once the bath was half-full, Bob turned off the taps. However, as I removed my foulard dressing gown, even though the bathroom mirror was misting with steam, I saw him look up at me, taking more than a moment to glance at a particular part of my anatomy.

"You must meet some interesting people," I said, easing myself into the warm water.

"I do sir. Some more interesting than others, if you know what I mean."

His answer rather perplexed me, but as I began to wash, he commenced to tidy away my shaving things.

"How about I scrub your back Captain."

The question so surprised me I lost the soap.

"Well, yes!" I stuttered, desperately searching for it in the water. "Why not. I haven't had my back scrubbed in years."

"I would have thought your friend would do it."

"You mean Mervyn?" I replied, warily, still searching for the elusive soap. "I'm afraid he's not that considerate."

I looked to him for a reaction, and was pleased to see him smile as he picked up the scrubber from the bath rack.

"Do you have the soap Captain?"

"For the life of me Bob! I can't keep hold of it."

"Why don't I try?" he said, kneeling down beside the tub.

"The last time I felt it," I stammered. "It was somewhere near my feet."

At the time, I remembered thinking how silly the situation must have appeared, but in the next instant, Bob dipped his hand into the water.

Once again, I refuse to be graphic as to what happened next, and therefore leave the subsequent few moments to your lurid imagination.

A while later, I decided to go ashore alone, as the early bath and subsequent events had left me relaxed and in a contemplative mood, just the state of mind in which to visit a cathedral.

***

Tromso is located on the east side of Tromsoya Island and linked to the mainland by a ferry. To call it a city is a little overstated. Most Norwegian cities are only the size of English towns. Although, given the distance between them, they have great importance for the regions in which they are situated.

Surprisingly, I was the only passenger on the ten o'clock tender; perhaps people were becoming a little jaded by shore excursions. I regarded them as beneficial to the mind and the body. It is easy to become complacent when cruising, eating, lounging about, drinking, smoking, and reading trashy novels. Personally, I am pleased for the exercise, as well as experiencing the culture of a new location. So with the noisy seagulls crowding around the fishing boats, the tender dropped me at a jetty, where almost immediately I glimpsed the Cathedral through a narrow lane way between two warehouses.

After a short walk, I reached a square surrounded by colourful wooden houses and shop fronts. In the middle, standing in a pretty park, was Tromso Cathedral. I found it rather small and modern in comparison to other Norwegian cathedrals, except it does claim to be the only wooden cathedral in northern Europe, and perhaps the world.

Outside is painted a soft shade of orange, with details picked out in a bluish grey, the spire similarly, but capped with green copper. I climbed a short flight of steps and opened the door to discover an equally attractive interior, with pale orange walls, and woodwork a greenish cream. There is also an impressive gilded altarpiece, containing a very nice Resurrection. Despite the contrasting colours, they were agreeable to the eye. Although it suddenly struck me how aware, the Norwegians are of colour. Everywhere you look you see houses painted in vivid shades that might seem gaudy in other countries, except they are appropriate in Norway. In the north, for almost three months, the people never see the sun, so perhaps this might be the reason for the need of colour and brightness.

Since it was Monday morning, the streets were quiet, the people at work, and children attending school. Wandering at will, while looking in shop windows for presents for Mervyn's siblings, as well as Amy, Emily and Eric, I saw only the usual souvenirs. Dolls dressed in traditional costume, model Viking ships, knitted sweaters with fancy designs, trolls carved in wood, decorated plates and scrimshaw. After much debate, I chose a pretty tea service and a string of pearls for Amy, a doll for Emily, a Viking Ship with a pair of pearl cuff links inside for Eric. In addition, I purchased three dolls for Sarah, Ruby and Doris, a carved troll for Richard, and a troll stuffed toy for little Eric.

Exhausted by my rambles, and after discovering a newspaper shop and buying an out of date copy of The Times, I found a quiet little café, ordered a pot of tea, and lit my pipe.

Dated Friday, June 10th, over three weeks ago, having read this news before, I felt rather silly sitting there reading it again. However, at least I could catch up with the news, even if it was a little stale.

The events making news that day were hardly surprising, as the goings-on in Germany and Abyssinia, had been the main topic for most of the month.

Three years ago, under the leadership of Herr Hitler, the German Reich broke away from The League of Nations, since the country was not allowed to re-arm.

In March, Hitler introduced conscription, thus violating the Treaty of Versailles. Recently, there had been an alliance pact between France, Belgium and Soviet Russia, as well as Soviet Russia and Czechoslovakia. In England, the British parliament was debating the Anglo German Naval Agreement, to allow Germany to increase her navy by thirty-five percent. Accordingly, this was causing the French some concern.

Stories leaking out of Germany tell of the Nazi Party's discrimination of Jews, Hitler having incited the German people to hate the Jewish race. In addition, the Nazis are using this as a reason to hound and persecute them. The only Jews I know are Mr Rosen the watchmaker in the Paragon and old Mrs Goldstein, who owns the sweet shop at the end of Stall Street. Both are kind and gentle people.

In northeast Africa, the situation is fragile. Signor Mussolini regards himself as a modern day Julius Caesar, and in 1928, signed a friendship treaty with Haile Selassie, Emperor of Abyssinia. However, it is believed Mussolini has invasion plans in mind.

That day, the news in The Times focused on the Foreign Secretary, Anthony Eden's return to Paris from Rome. He reports to the French Prime Minister, Pierre Laval the result of his meeting with Signor Mussolini regarding the Abyssinia question. Parliament was still debating the Anglo-German Naval Agreement. The Nazis have banned public church and confessional meetings, as well as introducing compulsory labour service for boys seventeen and over.

On a lighter note, an article tells of the proposed visit to Belgium of the Duke and Duchess of York, and the little Princesses, Elizabeth and Margaret Rose. The Royal party will stay at the British Embassy in Brussels, and then at the Royal Palace, where they will meet the King and Queen of the Belgians.

Will there be a war? I hear you ask.

Personally, I think not. Herr Hitler has brought excitement; brown shirts; banners; bands, and rallies. However, has he brought bread? The people are near starvation. How can he increase the strength of a nation to the point of waging war on the rest of Europe, when he cannot even feed his people and find them work?

Having drunk a third cup of tea, and smoked a second pipe, I had read the paper and was partially informed as to the current affairs of the world. Furthermore, looking at my watch I saw it was time to meet the tender and return to the ship. When I arrived, I saw a great crowd assembled for the excursion to a Lapland village, so decided to give the trip a miss. My early morning bout of excitement, as well as the subsequent jaunt ashore, had left me tired and in need of a nap. Having skipped the excursion to the Laplanders' village, and wallowed in yet another bath, I hoped that at least one of my party might relate the experience to me on their return.

Later that evening, as everyone enjoyed a meal of roast beef, which by the way, Teddy suggested might be reindeer, the Viceroy steamed steadily north, away from the fjords, and into the Norwegian Sea. We were on our way to the last and most northerly destination: North Cape.

"Then you had a good time, Teddy?" I said, chewing on the succulent meat, while endeavouring to ignore his suggestion.

"Indeed Captain. The Laplanders bring their herds of reindeer down from the high pastures to trade with the folk who live in the lowlands, and beside the water. The tribes consist of family groups, sometime thirty or so in number. A respected elder called the Siida-isit regulates the daily affairs of the families. The Sami are very attune with nature and are careful not to over use their resources."

"My word Teddy!" I exclaimed. "You have been attentive to the guide."

"I took some great snaps Ron," interjected Mervyn. "I hope they all come out. There were some real characters, and they loved having their photos taken."

"The officer was most informative," said mother. "Really! There isn't much we don't know about the Laplanders, is there everyone."

There was a general nod of approval, although no one spoke.

Mervyn, in his usual place beside me, was tucking into the beef and roast potatoes.

"So! You had a good day?" he asked, between mouthfuls.

"I did," I answered. "In fact it began excellently, with Bob serving me breakfast. Such a delightful young man. Quite obliging and thoughtful. It's a shame he's away at sea so much."

Mervyn shifted uneasily in his chair.

"What do you mean?" he whispered out the side of his mouth. "Then you had breakfast in the cabin. That's why I didn't see you in the dining room. I even went to your cabin to look for you."

"What time was that?"

"About Ten,"

"I was well on my way into the city by then."

Lucky for me Mervyn was a late sleeper, otherwise there might have been a difficult state of affairs had he woken any earlier.

"Did you have a nice day?" repeated, Mervyn.

"It's been most pleasant. Bob brought me my breakfast, and then suggested I take a hot bath. He even offered to scrub my back, doing an excellent job. Such a considerate lad."

Mervyn squirmed, but remained silent. I felt smug. It was nice keeping a secret from the biggest secret keeper of all.

"So what else did you see Teddy?" I asked.

"A witch doctor do a dance, like in Africa," he answered eagerly. "But in Norway he's called a Shaman and is the priest of the tribe. You see Ron! The Sami believe every living thing has a soul. They think both good and bad spirits exist and play important roles in the lives of human beings. While we watched, the Shaman went into a trance. His spirit is supposed to leave his body and enter the spirit world. Then, by using animals as spirit guides and supernatural warriors to fight wickedness, he can treat sicknesses caused by evil spirits. The Shaman can bring messages from the supernatural and tell the future by throwing bones, or tracing the movements of rings on a magic drum."

"Amazing Teddy!" I cried. "Try to remember this and write it in your diary. Your mother will be fascinated to hear all about it when you get back to Bath."

Typically, Mickey Pritchard was not going to be left out when the compliments were being handed around.

"The Sami don't use money Captain," he said. "They barter their goods, exchanging one necessity with another. The Sami living on the coast exchange fish, vegetables, and corn, for meat from those living in the mountains, or in the high valleys, where they herd sheep and reindeer. The mountain Sami come down to swap. That's how we got to meet them."

Naturally, neither would Gilbert Fry remain silent if evidence of intelligence was to be shown.

"You see Captain," he said. "Each year, the reindeer migrate to the low country to have their calves. The people follow them to exchange meat, furs, and hides, for fresh supplies of stock fish and vegetables."

"So stock fish is the dried fish we see all over the place," I remarked.

"Wasn't the Laplanders' camp interesting boys," mother said. "Excepting, we're not supposed to call them Laplanders. They want to be called Sami's for some peculiar reason. We loved the reindeer, didn't we girls. They look so gentle chewing the cud."

As we pulled away into the darkness of the Norwegian Sea, I did some ruminating of my own. Say an Englishman from the modern world is suddenly exchanged with a Sami, and vice versa. Would they adapt to their new worlds? After all, they are human beings, although poles apart in their way of life. I wondered whether both would realise what they gained by the swap, and prefer not to return to their previous life. The Sami man would gain technology, communication and European culture, as well as a considerably more varied diet. On the other hand, the Englishman would enter an existence his ancestors would have known. A pure, down to earth, peaceful kind of life, free to wander the earth at will, breathing the fresh air and eating the fruits of nature. It was an interesting hypothesis and I put it to everyone as we enjoyed our dessert of poached pears and cream.

"Do you think there might be any like us amongst the Sami?" Mervyn whispered so only I could hear. "Because, I wouldn't want to trade places if there weren't."

A typical one-dimensional response from Mervyn; in contrast, Wilfred was most plainspoken.

"I believe the poor Sami would be completely disorientated," he said. "Look what happened to Pocahontas when she visited England. She died of a common cold. I'm sure such things would happen to the Sami."

Mother supposed the whole idea to be ridiculous. It would never happen. So why were we wasting time even talking about it.

Chapter Twenty Two
North Cape - Rough Seas - Fancy Dress - Home

At sunset and sunrise, the further north we travelled, the sun paused a little higher over the horizon each day, giving us an odd feeling of timelessness, as if one day was blending, seamlessly, into the next.

The considerable distance between North Cape and Tromso meant several days at sea. In fact, since the schedule said our only view of the Cape would be from the ship, Tromso would be the final location where any of us would go ashore until we arrive in Southampton. Unfortunately, once we left the coast, the weather changed, the ship subjected to squalls of rain and bouts of rough seas. Nevertheless, by then most of us had found our sea legs, and regarded the experience as amusing, if a little tedious.

Swimming in the swimming bath was an adventure in itself because, with the ship rolling from port to starboard then dipping from stem to stern, the water endeavoured to remain horizontal, causing much frivolity as it washed us from one end of the bath to the other.

Bob remained our steward for a further two days, but there was no repeat performance of his first morning, Johnson returning to us, his usual brusque self. Thus, Mervyn and I had to be content to watch Bob negotiate the dining room, tray in hand, while attempting to remain upright.

***

When we reached North Cape, the temperamental weather abated, and everyone was heartened to hear we were to enjoy another, and sadly our last, fancy dress ball. Again, we raided the purser's costume rail for the unusual or comical get up. This time, I chose to be a Bishop, complete with mitre and staff. Wilfred decided to opt out, saying all this frivolity was far too beneath him. Mervyn was a greasy Arab, along with Mickey, although Teddy became a very peculiar looking character, dressed as 'The Spirit of the North', wearing my trilby and heavy overcoat, all the while clutching a thermos flask and a hot water bottle.

It was a splendid party, everyone agreeing the ball was the best yet, maybe because we knew it to be the last before the ship steered west and began to head home. The evening culminated in a wonderful display of fireworks, appearing quite incongruous, exploding in a sky that still played host to a glowering sun.

North Cape was utterly stunning, the cliffs rising from the sea at least a thousand feet, concluding in a perfectly horizontal plateau. At the foot of the precipice, the Viceroy got as close as she dared to the rocks, so near in fact we could see hordes of sea birds claiming every nook and cranny of the immense face. In the past, there was no road up to the cliff edge, as a result, people wishing to access the top, needed to climb the cliff face. Famous visitors include the King of Sweden, and the King of Siam. The sheer enormity of the spectacle we found awe inspiring, but everyone agreed that seeing it from the ship was preferable to a perilous climb.

As well as adorable little puffins and unwieldy cormorants clambering over the rocks and diving into the black water, thousands of quarrelsome gannets clung to the cliff face; Mervyn even pointing out an eagle stalking stray chicks that may have left the nest.

***

The next day, it was full steam south to Trondheim, where the ship took on coal ready for the return voyage across the North Sea to Leith. It was pointless anyone going ashore, since refuelling would take barely three hours.

After lunch, as the last sight of Norway disappeared over our stern, I relaxed in the veranda café, catching up with my book, having taken a few candid snaps of the boys in their various pursuits. Mervyn and Gilbert were playing yet another game of ping-pong on the sports deck and I snapped Mickey idly smoking cigarettes, and Teddy sucking on his pipe, while leaning on the tender. A week later, after our return to Hyde House, I developed and printed this roll of film and was amazed to see how adapted these three working class lads from the back streets of Bath appeared, completely adjusted to the life of the upper classes. I resolved to rub such photos in Eric's face when next I saw him.

The sun was warm, the sea as flat as a millpond, the ship hardly making a sound as she carved a swathe through the dark water. At one point, I looked up from my book to see Wilfred standing at the bar.

"Like a drink Ron?" he asked.

"Thanks Wilfred. I'll have a Manhattan, if I may."

It was unusual for Wilfred to think of anyone other than himself. Maybe the tranquillity of the cruise was affecting him at last.

"Have you enjoyed it?" I asked, as he put the glasses on the table and sat down opposite me.

"Mostly," he said, taking a sip of Martini, then lighting a cigarette. "It's been good value for money. The cabins are top drawer. The excursions were interesting and informative. I couldn't fault the food, although the service might have been a bit better."

He was referring of course to Johnson, who was also Wilfred's cabin steward.

"How about you?"

"Very much. You know I'm in love with this ship. She's perfect in my eyes. The entertainment has been tiptop. I agree with you about the food. Officer Wickham was an excellent tour guide. The glacier was tremendous. The Midnight Sun thing became a little tedious, but the visit to the Sami people seemed to delight everyone."

Privately, I felt the cruise had been extremely beneficial to me mentally and physically, except I was hardly about to reveal that to

Wilfred.

We were lucky with the weather all the way back to Scotland, giving everyone an opportunity to get a sun tan and enjoy deck games, although I preferred to be an onlooker to both activities. I have never been keen to show myself semi clothed in public, having always been aware my body was never the most attractive part of my attributes. Maybe, when I was younger and slimmer, I was less self-conscious. But since then, my girth has increased and now hangs in front of me, resembling a skirt, supported by my long lean legs. The lard not only remains around my stomach, because my once manly chest now looks like a woman one might see in a painting by Rembrandt or Rubens. Consequently, I hardly dare enter the swimming baths before I make sure I am wearing a costume, which adequately disguises these unattractive elements.

Regarding ball games. As you will probably remember when I recalled my time at school, I admitted that I was never much good at games involving balls, the only exception being billiards, of which I am quite a fan and reasonably good. As a result, I leave others to run around chasing after balls.

The ship arrived in the Firth of Forth the morning of the twentieth day, anchoring in the exact spot as previously, where she waited while our Scottish contingent embarked the tender, which would convey them ashore.

Now that we were back in less northerly latitudes, at least we were able to watch the sun completely disappear over the horizon, then go to bed when it was night. Naturally, our final dinner was somewhat subdued, but I made a point of gathering everyone on the sports deck for a last photograph, including a very nice one of Mervyn and Teddy.

Although dinner was rather serious, nevertheless, I endeavoured to keep the conversation lively.

"What are you youngsters planning to do for the rest of the holiday?"

Mervyn was the first to answer.

"I'm looking forward to driving my car. It's been sitting in the garage for nearly a month."

Teddy smiled. "Are you going to drive Ron and me to Lairgs again Mervyn? There's a scout trip in August."

"So there is Teddy!" I exclaimed. "I'd completely forgotten. What a good idea. We had such fun last year."

"I could come this time," said Mickey. "I wasn't able to go last year. Mother and father took me on holiday."

With each youngster suggesting their plans, the gloom gradually lifted as everyone realised there were still several weeks before they would need to resume their ordinary lives.

The night passed quickly, and before we knew it, we were around the breakfast table and only a few hours away from our destination.

Up on the promenade deck, Mervyn and I leaned on the starboard rail, watching the Essex coast slipping by on the horizon.

"Isn't it odd," I said. "We've seen all those fantastic vistas and now we return to this?"

"Will anything ever be the same again?" responded Mervyn.

"It's as if it never happened," I mused.

"But we've photos to prove it did."

Mervyn was in a rare reflective mood. Perhaps, like Wilfred, the cruise had achieved its desired effect.

"Are you looking forward to getting home?" I asked.

He shrugged. "I suppose so. Everything will be just as we left it. Although, it'll be good to see Sarah, Ruby, and Doris again."

"Also, little Eric," I added, "And Richard, your brother."

Mervyn took out a packet of cigarettes and offered me one.

"I hope they like their presents," he said, lighting mine, then his.

"I'm sure they will. What did you get your father?"

"A pipe; plus a pearl necklace for mother. The one you picked out."

"With your gifts, plus mine to Eric, Amy, and Emily, we're going to be busy. Have you said goodbye to Bob?"

Mervyn looked at me sharply.

"I just thought you and he had become pals."

"What makes you think that?"

Mervyn tried to remain casual. However, I could hear from the tone in his voice, he was flustered.

They say, 'talk of the devil', well astonishingly, coming along the deck towards us, was the young man himself, looking spruce as usual. He smiled when he saw us.

"Good morning, Bob," I said, as he approached. "How long before we reach Southampton?"

"First Officer Metcalf said, the Captain says, we'll be home by teatime. The rough weather after Tromso set us back. But Captain Thornton's done a good job making up time."

"Then we'll not see you again. Mervyn! Aren't you going to say goodbye to Bob?"

"Bye," Mervyn, mumbled.

Bob saluted smartly. "See you next time," he said, and proceeded on his way.

After lunch, the ship became quiet as people adjourned to their cabins to pack. Considering we had been three weeks at sea and visited several Norwegian ports, as well as Naeroyfjord, the Glacier, and the Sami village, it was necessary not only to return our clothes to the trunks, but also to find room for a host of mementos and presents. Mervyn and I struggled to do up the clasps, eventually managing to clip them and buckle the straps. A knock on the door announced a seaman was there to collect them, and carry them to the hatch, where they would wait to be conveyed to the dock.

By the time we finished packing, the Viceroy had picked up the Sussex coast, and looking out of my porthole, I glimpsed Brighton, even seeing people gathered at the end of the pier, waving to the ship. It was then I realised I was home.

Soon the banks of the Solent grew closer to our port and starboard sides, the smell of land greeting us, a blend of seaweed, mud, coal smoke, and tar.

It was Friday afternoon, and the Southampton Dock workers had finished for the day, and no doubt quenching their thirst in the numerous public houses peppering the fringes. Sufficiently satiated, they would return home, give their wives their wage packets and sit down to tea, which, since it was Friday, would most likely be fish and chips bought from the fish shop on the corner. Although they say 'travel broadens the mind', having been away from home for a while, returning, you realise how deeply your country's culture is ingrained into your soul.

That evening, RMS Viceroy of India was not the only ship tied up at the landing stage, as several other liners were also disembarking passengers. Consequently, the quay was crowded with people.

"Now keep together everyone," I said, gathering up the youngsters. "If you get lost, go to the main passenger hall and wait under the clock."

In order not to crowd the gangway, each deck was requested to disembark separately and reversed alphabetically. Therefore, since Mervyn, Wilfred, mother and I were on C deck, and the others on the decks below, we watched Mickey, Teddy, the twins and Gilbert, hurry down the gangway and onto the dock, where we lost them in the crowd.

"Come on everyone," I said, as Deck C was called over the loudspeaker. "It's our turn. I daren't tell my cousin Gilbert I misplaced his children on the last day. I'd never be forgiven."

We hurried down the companionway and into the custom hall, where the luggage was appearing from a conveyor belt linked to the ship. And once an official had checked our passports, Wilfred, Mervyn, and I searched for our trunks.

"I won't be catching the train," Wilfred said, hauling his off the belt. "The Royal Review's on Tuesday and the lads have brought 'Merlin' from Cowes."

'Merlin' is Wilfred's newest motor yacht and his pride and joy. After father died, he purchased her with his inheritance, even crewing her with a permanent staff of five men, plus a lad. His other yacht 'Frontera' is moored on the Lambeth side of the Thames, opposite the Houses of Parliament. Wilfred can either stay at his flat at Whitehall Court, or cross Westminster Bridge to spend the night afloat. During Cowes week, he always races 'Merlin' on the Solent, and never misses the Henley Regatta with 'Frontera'. In summer, he often takes 'Merlin' cruising in the Mediterranean, just the crew and himself, with never a friend of either sex accompanying him. Overall, it is a splendid arrangement, and I am quite envious.

"No room for us I suppose?" I asked.

"Sorry Ron. Mother's coming. I really think you should get these lads home to their parents."

Chapter Twenty Three
Scandal

Of course, I was a little peeved by Wilfred's churlish reply. With the weather being most clement, surely a couple of the crew might give up their quarters for the lads and me, exchanging them for a place on deck under the stars. Then again, a portion of me agreed with Wilfred, since it was important I restore Mervyn, Mickey, and Teddy to their households. As a result, gathering my lads together outside the terminal building, I hailed a taxi that would convey us to Southampton Station.

"Teddy! When we stop," I said as the taxi drew onto the forecourt, "be kind and run to the newspaper stand and buy me an evening paper."

Once on the train and settled in our first class carriage, I sent Mervyn to find a steward in order to book a table in the dining car. While we waited for his return, I read out the proceedings for the following day's celebrations.

"The King, The Prince of Wales, the Dukes of York and Kent, will arrive in Cosham on Monday afternoon and embark the Royal Yacht Prince Albert, where they will spend the night. Then, on Tuesday, at one o'clock in the afternoon, a gun will fire to signal the review area is cleared of any unofficial vessels. At two o'clock the yacht procession will begin."

"I wish we could have seen it," said Teddy. "I'd love to see King

George."

"Sorry Teddy! But my brother seems to think you'll be wanted at home, and for once, I tend to agree, not that I don't adore your company of course

"But what about the Queen?" Mervyn asked, appearing at the compartment door.

"Sorry boys. It looks like she's not coming."

"Captain, have you ever seen the King?" Teddy asked.

"I have. He and his brother, Prince Albert Victor, visited Bath in 1911. I was your age at the time, and at Cambridge. Their carriage drove right by our house when my family lived in the Royal Crescent."

"I've seen his head on stamps, and photos of him in the papers," Mervyn said. "Has he always worn a beard and moustache?"

"As far as I know. It was the fashion, even when he was a young man. His father, Edward, always wore one."

"What about the Queen?" Mickey asked.

"She hasn't a beard," laughed Mervyn

"Don't be a dope!" Mickey snapped. "My mother says she's toffee nosed and never smiles."

"I don't know about that," I said, trying not to smile myself. "Sometimes people don't like to smile because it shows too much of their teeth. They say the old queen never smiled for that very reason, and she was usually a happy sort, that is until Prince Albert died."

"King George wasn't supposed to be King was he," Mickey put in.

"That's correct. How do you know that Mickey?"

"Father always says so. But he also says that if his brother had carried on to be King there wouldn't be a Royal Family, and we'd all be living in a Republic."

"How smart of Mr Pritchard. And of course, he's quite correct. I was completely unaware of the scandal making the daily news, since I was only a baby at the time. I would have remained so had I not bought a set of china while furnishing Hyde House, the set wrapped in an old copy of The Times, containing a full report in the law section."

The dining steward suddenly appeared at the compartment door.

"We're serving dinner, gents, if you'd like to make your way to the buffet car."

"What was the scandal?" Mervyn asked, as the four of us staggered along the corridor to the dining car.

"Something that would topple the monarchy if the word got out," I said.

"Come on Ron! Don't be a tease."

Having sat down, and after ordering roast beef all round, knowing I was about to tell a lengthy story, I gestured to the waiter to bring us a bottle of wine, since I would need a large glass once in a while to keep me fortified.

"Very well," I said, while sampling a particularly good French example. "As I unwrapped a china tureen, a headline caught my eye, 'Earl of Euston sues for libel'. Reading on, I discovered the Earl was embroiled in slanderous accusations made by a north London newspaper, the editor connecting the Earl to the goings on in a brothel in Cleveland Street, just behind Tottenham Court Road."

With our plates of beef, roast potatoes, cabbage and parsnips, now before us, of course, as soon as I uttered the word brothel I realised I had the lad's complete attention, since all three had ceased eating.

"Who's the Earl of Euston when he's at home?" said Mervyn.

"The eldest son of the Duke of Grafton. It appears Lord Euston was walking down Piccadilly one evening, when a tout handed him a card. On it was printed, 'Charles Hammond. 19 Cleveland Street, London,' and in italics, 'Poses Plastiques'"

"What's that mean?" asked Teddy.

"Living nudes, more or less," I answered.

"Women or men?" Mervyn sniggered.

"That's what Lord Euston was about to discover. He put the card in his pocket, although a week later curiosity got the better of him and he paid Cleveland Street a visit. Mr Hammond let His Lordship in and showed him into the parlour. When Lord Euston asked as to the nature of the Pose Plastiques, Mr Hammond told him in no uncertain terms. The Times reported the Earl saying in court, that he was disgusted by what he heard and that he threatened Hammond with violence, unless he let him out the door, immediately.

"So the living nudes were men?" Mickey said.

"There was no Poses Plastique. It was a ploy. Instead, the house was a place where Hammond's rich and titled clients could meet young lads."

"Did the boys make much money?" Mervyn asked.

"It seems the client was charged a sovereign, and Hammond gave the boy involved four shillings. That was a lot of money fifty odd years ago."

As my tale unfolded, the lads gradually resumed their dinner.

"Earlier that year, Constable Hanks, a policeman at the central London post office, was investigating a case of theft. A telegram delivery boy was discovered with fourteen shillings, a huge sum to possess for a working class lad of his age. Also, it was against the rules for messenger boys to carry money, so Constable Hanks' suspicions were aroused. Under examination, the boy admitted he was given the money by a Mr Hammond, at 19 Cleveland Street, as payment for allowing gentlemen to, 'Go between my legs, and put their person in me.'"

"Oh no!" Mervyn, Mickey, and Teddy exclaimed. "How rude!"

"Under duress, the lad named other messenger boys who frequented the house, and each was arrested. When questioned, they told Constable Hanks that a man named George Vecks procured them by means of a young male prostitute, Henry Newlove, who was also a telegraph boy. The boys continued to reveal the identity of some of their gentleman clients, which greatly interested the police, as the clientele came from the upper strata of society. Vecks and Newlove were arrested and tried at Bow Street Magistrates Court. And since they pleaded guilty, were sentenced to six months and nine months, respectively. The solicitor defending Newlove and Vecks was Mr Arthur Newton, a name you will hear later, since he was solicitor to Lord Arthur Somerset, another man you will hear a great deal of presently."

"That's not a harsh sentence, considering the crime," added Mervyn. "You're good at remembering the names Ron."

"Exactly. And thanks. Vecks and Newlove owned up to acts of

gross indecency. All the same, they still only received a mild sentence, as even back then, the crime was punishable by two years hard labour; and guess who paid for Vecks and Newlove's defence. Lord Arthur Somerset."

"Who's he?" asked Mickey, taking a bite out of a brussel sprout.

"The third son of the 8th Duke of Beaufort and his wife, the former Lady Georgiana Curzon. He was head of The Prince of Wales' stables, a major in the Royal Horse Guards. When I read about the boys involved, one name struck me as being very appropriate for a trial of this nature."

"Go on Ron!" urged Mervyn. "You're going to tell us of course."

"Thickbroom. Ernest Thickbroom."

Naturally, I knew the name would provoke hilarity and was pleasantly gratified by the howl of laughter it evoked.

"What were the names of the others?" giggled Mervyn.

"Charles Swinscow."

Further hysterical mirth.

"John Saul, George Wright, and Algernon Allies. All of them messenger boys at the Saint Martins le Grand post office. Although, Algernon seemed to be the one who most interested the police."

"Why?" asked Mickey.

"Because, when George Veck was arrested, he was found to be carrying letters addressed to Algernon and written by a Mr Brown."

The lads shook their heads, and looked at each other in mock horror.

"Although Inspector Abberline, the man now in charge of the investigation, had enough evidence to produce a warrant for Hammond's arrest, he dragged his feet due to the delicate nature of the situation, allowing Hammond time to escape the country, after being tipped off by Newlove."

At this point, I paused to take a swig of wine, giving the lads an opportunity to swallow the information so far.

"With the comings and goings at Cleveland Street now constantly under observation," I continued. "The police hid Swinscow, Allies, Newlove, and Thickbroom inside a hansom cab, in order to spot Mr Brown, which they duly did. Mr Brown was followed and traced to

Knightsbridge Barracks, where he was identified as Lord Arthur Somerset, a major in the Horse Guards and equerry to The Prince of Wales. All the same, there was no move to arrest Lord Arthur, although papers were sent to the Director of Prosecutions with a view to prosecuting him with the charge of buggery. Lord Arthur got wind of this, so he instructed his solicitor, Arthur Newton, to write to the Director of Prosecutions. The letter explaining that, should Lord Arthur be sent to trial it might be necessary for him to reveal that Prince Albert Victor, the son of The Prince of Wales, and grandson of Queen Victoria, was a frequent visitor to Cleveland Street."

Hearing this, Mervyn and Mickey's previous mockery turned to genuine incredulity

"This information seemed to stall the pending prosecution, giving Lord Arthur time to flee abroad, where he remained for the rest of his life, save for several clandestine visits. Meanwhile, with Algernon Allies in possession of damaging information, Inspector Abberline took it upon himself to see him safe from corruption or coercion by hiding him in a coffee house in Houndsditch."

"Crikey Ron!" interrupted Mervyn. "You really followed this case! Didn't you."

"Certainly. The old newspaper was most enlightening. For years, the Cleveland Street Scandal has been forgotten and swept under the carpet. Then, how is it I'd never heard about it until I discovered the newspaper?"

"Was Algernon the lover of Prince Albert Victor and Lord Arthur Somerset?" asked Mickey.

"Maybe. But that's never been proven, as the letters must have been destroyed. Although, I definitely believe Lord Arthur was. But people consider Lord Arthur's solicitor, Mr Newton, diverted attention away from his client, by spreading rumours Prince Albert Victor was involved. Nevertheless, the Prince's name was never officially mentioned in the scandal."

"How did the Earl of Euston fit into all this?" Mervyn said.

"Rumours of a royal connection with the scandal became rife amongst the public and aristocracy, especially when a letter revealed how important it was to keep (PAV) out of the picture. As the case unravelled in the courts, it intrigued the editor of a north London newspaper, Edward Parkes, as to why the rent boys were let off with such light sentences. As a consequence, he published an article, naming names, thinking he was safe to do so, believing the two men known to be regular visitors to the brothel in Cleveland Street had fled abroad. He was correct in thinking Lord Arthur was in self-exile in France, but was mistaken to presume, Henry James Fitzroy, Earl of Euston, was out of the country. When the Earl read the article, he immediately began libel proceedings against Parkes. At the trial, Parkes' defence submitted several witnesses, claiming to have seen Euston arriving and departing number nineteen on various occasions. However, his descriptions varied and failed to correspond, so eventually the Earl won the case, and Parkes was sentenced to a year in prison."

By now, we had finished dessert, and it had grown quite dark beyond the dining car window.

"I wished we'd stayed to see the review," Teddy said, as he lit our cigarettes. "But it's been a good dinner and a great story."

"It's not over yet, Teddy old chap," I said, laughing. "There's still another trial. This time involving Mr Newton, Lord Arthur's solicitor."

"Heavens Ron!" Mervyn exclaimed. "Will it never end?"

"Soon. I promise. But let's have port and cheese."

"Why was the solicitor on trial?" Teddy asked, as I waved a steward to our table.

"A piece of your very best Stilton, my man," I said. "And a slab of Cheddar. If it's mature."

Emptying my fourth glass of wine, I continued unabated, all the while relishing the scandalous nature of my story.

"You remember I mentioned Mr Arthur Newton a while ago, nonetheless, others were becoming involved in the investigation. Frederick Taylorson, Mr Newton's clerk, and Adolphus Du Galla, an interpreter, were summonsed to appear at Bow Street Magistrates Court on a charge of endeavouring to pervert the course of justice. They were accused of planning the disappearance of the witnesses, Thickbroom, Allies, Swinscow, and Perkins; also for arranging their passage from England to America, even providing them with clothes, payment for the voyage, and a weekly amount of money until they found employment."

"Lord Arthur was coughing up," said Mervyn. "That's tantamount to an admission of guilt."

"Remember though, Lord Arthur is in France." I responded. "Was it someone from an even higher position who was guarding the reputation of his son, and possibly the future of the British monarchy?"

I knew I had the lads spell bound by my story because, as they spread their Jacobs crackers, each hardly gave the slabs of cheese in the centre of the table, a glance.

"Frederick Taylorson met the boys in a public house behind Tottenham Court Road," I continued. "Here he told them that someone very important was looking out for them and wanted them to have a fresh start in life. The plan was for the boys to leave for Liverpool that very evening, and thence board a ship bound for America. Consequently, Taylorson suggested each lad write a letter to his father and mother explaining his intentions, and to say he would write, and not to worry, as he was being well looked after. Taylorson pocketed the letters and duly posted them. Had it not been for Algernon spilling the beans to Inspector Abberline, who knows what might have become of the lads? Mr Newton, his clerk, and the interpreter, were summonsed, tried, and sentenced to a short stay in prison. The scandal, then quietly vanished from the newspapers, with no further trials or reports."

Although the cheese had almost disappeared, I still had to finish the last chapter of my story.

"Nevertheless, Henry Labouchere, a Liberal member of parliament and the man we have to thank for the dreadful sentences men like us face today, thought the Cleveland Street Affair was conveniently covered up under the orders of a person from a very eminent position. In a seven-hour debate concerning the affair, Labouchere named Lord Arthur Somerset, Henry James Fitzroy, Earl of Euston, and (PAV) as being regular visitors to the brothel. Meanwhile, a royal tour of India was speedily arranged to remove

Prince Albert Victor from Britain, and the breaking scandal. From the Prince's letters to his cousin, Prince Louis of Battenburg, it appears he was completely oblivious to the gossip happening at home. All that concerned him was the failure of his engagement to Princess Alix of Hesse, who later married Nicholas, son of the Russian Emperor, Alexander the third, and we all know what dreadful fate awaited her and the rest of the Russian Royal family."

"Then what happened to Albert Victor?" asked Mickey. "Why didn't he become King?"

"The poor man died. He was all ready to marry Princess Mary of Teck when he caught influenza, which turned to pneumonia. Mary went on to marry George, our King. Britain fell into deep mourning, since Prince Albert Victor was apparently extremely popular."

"So people forgot he was linked to the scandal?"

"It appears so. But, they say his name is never spoken in Royal circles. Not openly, that is. I'm of the opinion the Royal Family would rather forget he ever existed. They must secretly have known the kind of man he was, and were privately pleased he was no longer around, because I think they knew he would have made a very unsuitable King."

Unanimously, the lads clapped their hands.

"Well done Ron!" Mervyn shouted. "That was an excellent story! And just the thing to end a splendid dinner. Brandy and cigars boys?"

Chapter Twenty Four
Rumours from Germany - Black Shirts in Britain – Abdications - Pork Pies and Pints

After our return to Wildsbridge and Hyde House, and as soon as it was convenient, one morning, Mervyn and I drove to Tisford to give Amy, Emily, and Eric the presents we purchased while in Norway. Of course, Mervyn elected to drive, nearly scaring the daylights out of me negotiating Wiltshire's twisting country lanes.

***

"Here you are everyone," said Mervyn, passing around the presents I had wrapped the night before.

"Thank you both. They're beautiful," Amy said, discovering the bone china tea set and the string of pearls. "You must have been so careful with the china, the way they handle luggage these days."

"As soon as I saw the cuff links Eric, I thought of you," I put in. "They'll look splendid with a dinner jacket."

"Thanks Ron. I've never seen pearl cuff links before. Most fetching I must say. And the Viking Ship will take pride of place on the mantel in the banqueting hall."

"Amy," Mervyn said. "I've a present for Emily."

"How thoughtful Mervyn. She's with Nanny, doing her studies. Although, I'm sure we can interrupt them. Come along! Let's go up to the nursery, and leave the men to talk."

"Would you care for a drink?" Eric asked, once he and I were alone.

"No thanks. It's still a bit early. Also if I have one it'll lead to another, then Mervyn will want one, and I'll not have him drive us home drunk. But you go ahead."

"Then let's go to the sitting room, and I'll ring for Bridgett."

We settled into the armchairs abreast of the fireplace, and waited for the maid to answer the bell.

"We're off to Scotland next week," Eric said. "Just a few days over Easter."

"Really! Whereabouts?"

"We thought we'd play it by ear. Although Amy wants to see John O'Groats, where all the elopers go. You know what women are. Seeing you've made the trip annually for several years, do you have any hotels you'd recommend?"

"Certainly. As you're travelling north, there's the Old England at Windermere. And once you've reached Lairg, I recommend the Sutherland Arms Hotel, right on the shore of Loch Shin. You'll be amazed at the view from your window. John O'Groats House Hotel is on the beach. Emily will love it. Mind you, if the weather turns nasty, it can be a bit bleak."

"I'll need to write these down." Eric said, laughing.

There was a knock on the door, and Bridgett entered the room.

"Yes sir?" she said, curtsying.

"I'll have a Manhattan please Bridgett. Are you sure you won't Ron?"

"Go on then. Twist my arm. But I'll have a scotch and soda. One won't do any harm."

Bridgett curtsied and left us alone.

"While you were away," Eric said. "A bit in the Bath papers had me worried. I think you should hear it from me, so you'll be prepared if anyone tackles you."

"What on earth is it?"

"It concerns Mr Bulleid."

Suddenly my heart missed a beat, the first occasion since the cruise to the South Atlantic.

"What about him?"

"There've been complaints in the 'Letters to the Editor' column. Nothing came out to point the finger. But Bath Boy Scouts was mentioned, although not Bulleid personally."

Lawrence Bulleid was an eagle scout in my Bath scout troop.

"I take it you mean objections from parents."

Eric nodded.

"The lads have gone home and told tales. If anything comes of this Bulleid could name names and drag people into it."

"Don't worry Eric. Poor Bulleid."

Eric frowned. "Don't be so blasé Ron. As they say, 'there's many a slip'."

To my great relief the conversation was interrupted as Amy, Emily and Mervyn entered the room, Emily obviously pleased with her present.

"Look Uncle Ronnie! Mervyn's given me a lovely doll, dressed like a little girl from Norway."

"It's very kind of you Ron," Amy said. "You can see she's delighted."

After a while, I was able to steer the subject towards Hyde House, and before Mervyn attempted to ask for a drink, we said our goodbyes. Returning to the car, we sped away down the drive, heading for the Warminster Road.

"How about a drink and a pork pie," I suggested as we passed through Tisford, "The Old Bell is always a sure bet, and it's just on opening time."

Of course, Mervyn agreed, so he parked the car outside.

Entering the deserted public house, we headed for the snug, finding it empty. Therefore, while Mervyn settled on a bench seat, I went to the bar, where a woman was polishing glasses.

"Two whiskies and sodas please," I said. "And a couple of your best pork pies."

"You're early birds, gents," she said, with a smile. "Strangers round here, ain't you. Travelling far?"

"Just to Bath."

She took down two large tumblers from a shelf and filled them half-full from a bottle of Johnnie Walker.

"The soda's on the bar, sir. Help yourself."

When I returned to my seat, Mervyn was smoking a cigarette and gazing through the hatch at two young farm chaps leaning on the counter in the public bar.

"The English are more handsome than any foreigner," he said. "They're swarthy. I like that."

"You're saying the Norwegians are too clean cut?" I said, lighting myself a cigarette. "If you prefer them swarthy, then you'd like the Egyptians."

"Funny you should mention Egypt. Yesterday afternoon, Mother told me something that's had me worried."

The publican's wife suddenly appeared with our pork pies.

"I've put a bit of Coleman's on your plate, sirs," she said. "I dare say you'd want some."

"What did your mother tell you?" I asked when we were alone again.

"Harry's not happy."

"Your brother in Egypt?"

"He doesn't want to be in the army anymore."

"Not much he can do about that, old chap. Once you've signed up, you're there for the duration."

Eating his pork pie, Mervyn looked at me, wearing a familiar expression.

"Mother asked if you might help."

"Totally out of the question, my boy. There're some things even old Ronnie can't do."

"But she said it's possible to buy someone out of the army. Couldn't you pull a few strings?"

Mervyn was like a dog at a bone, as usual attempting to manipulate me into a corner. All the same, I was well aware of his tactics, so I steered the conversation onto another subject.

"By the way you drive, if we leave once we've finished our pie, we'll be in Bath by four o'clock."

"But aren't you having another drink?"

"No. And neither are you. I want to see Thompson and Mrs

Lanesome in one piece, even if you don't."

As we drove out of the town, by the atmosphere Mervyn was generating, I was aware he was sulking. I also preferred to be quiet. As a result, the remainder of the journey was spent in silence.

***

Our lives resumed their usual routine, the excitement of the early and middle part of the year exchanged for mundane repetition, until we were exchanging one year for another, which proved to be equally ordinary.

Although 1936 was uneventful for Mervyn and I, it proved to be gripping in other respects.

On 20th January, our beloved King George V, died at the age of seventy, after several years of ill health, his eldest son Edward, Prince of Wales, succeeding him. As a result, the country was plunged into mourning.

Unbeknown to Mervyn and I, and certainly almost the entire British public, behind closed doors, a constitutional crisis was quietly occurring of which we only became aware at the end of the year. His Royal Highness, King Edward the eighth, the most popular monarch of Great Britain and the Empire there had ever been, was about to do battle with Parliament for a cause concerning the woman he loved.

At the cinema, during August, we thrilled to watch the Pathe News as Great Britain and Northern Ireland won two gold medals and four silver, in athletics at the Berlin Olympics. A gold medal was awarded in the four by four hundred metres men's relay, the other in the fifty-kilometre walk. The silver medals went to the men's four hundred metres; the men's one hundred metre hurdles; the marathon; the women's high jump; also three bronze medals in eventing, yachting, and cycling. As usual, the United States excelled. However, the newsreel showed the German Chancellor, Adolf Hitler, leave the Berlin Stadium, protesting against the Negro, Jesse Owen, winning the gold medal in the men's two-hundred metre race.

Later, the same month, Great Britain and Egypt signed the Anglo Egyptian Treaty that required British troops to withdraw from Egypt, all except those who were necessary to protect the Suez Canal. A further condition of the treaty was for Britain to supply and train Egypt's army, as well as assist in its defence in case of war. Perhaps, this might mean an end to Mervyn's brother's plight and Harry might return home. Even so, he would still be a serving soldier, and therefore should be ready to go wherever he is sent.

As the year passed, through occasional reports and articles in the newspapers, I noticed that the rise of Hitler and fascism was causing unease amongst ordinary Germans. This was exemplified at the beginning of October by The Battle of Cable Street.

Four years previously, Sir Oswald Mosley, an English aristocrat, Labour politician, self-confessed fascist, and Hitler sympathiser, founded the British Union of Fascists. Mosley instigated a corps of uniformed parliamentary stewards, nicknamed 'Black Shirts', who quickly became involved in violent confrontations with Jewish and communist groups, especially in London. Two years ago, during a fascist rally at Olympia, the hecklers were violently removed by 'Black Shirts', causing mass brawling amongst the crowd.

This, along with reports from Germany of political murders, and the violent anti-Jewish behaviour of Hitler's 'Brown Shirts', led to the loss of mass support for the British Union of Fascists, the party then unable to fight in last year's election.

Mosley would not be discouraged and began organising marches through London, especially the East End, the home of a large population of Jews. One such march was organised for Sunday, 4th October, in Cable Street. It was well publicised, giving Jewish, anti-fascists, anarchists, Irish, and communist groups, an opportunity to organise a protest demonstration, many people arriving in the East End by buses and the underground.

An estimated three hundred thousand anti-fascists turned out, and proceeded to build barricades across Cable Street in order to prevent the British Union of Fascists march occurring. Ten thousand police, including four thousand on horseback, attempted to clear the way for the march to continue. However, the protesters fought back with anything that came to hand, including sticks, rocks, and chair legs. Women even threw rotten vegetables and the contents of chamber pots at the police from the upstairs windows of houses along the street. After several running battles, and many injuries, Mosley agreed to abandon the march and most British Union of Fascists marchers dispersed to Hyde Park. There were numerous arrests amongst the demonstrators, who later reported harsh treatment by the police.

During the months after these worrying events, and given the similarity of circumstances happening in Germany, parliament has debated the issue, hence the Public Order Act that was given its Royal assent in December. The act prohibits the wearing of uniforms associated with political parties or events, and gives police the power to bar any political demonstration, unless given its consent.

The day after the battle, and nearly three hundred miles to the north, a little over two hundred miners from Jarrow began a walk to the Palace of Westminster in London to protest against unemployment and poverty in the northeast of England. Throughout the route, which took in Darlington, Harrogate, Leeds, Nottingham, and Luton, the men received enormous support, given shelter for the night, food and drink, and even new boots to replace those that were worn out by the toil.

Arriving in London on the 31st October, the miners headed for the Houses of Parliament armed with a petition signed by twelve thousand supporters. Nonetheless, its announcement in the House of Commons caused little comment, Prime Minister Stanley Baldwin refusing to see the marcher's representatives, saying it would set a dangerous precedent. Although the march made the headlines, it did nothing to alter life back home, and after each man received a pound to help pay for his rail fare, the men returned to Jarrow disillusioned and defeated.

On a lighter note, 1936 saw an invention that would ultimately change our lives. On November 2nd, the BBC launched the world's first regular television service, and anticipating the coronation of a new King, I purchased a receiver for one hundred and twenty guineas, a vast sum of money, considering my Norway cruise cost twenty-one.

From a position in a shady part of the sitting room, the walnut cabinet and nine-inch cathode tube soon became the focal point of the room.

On that afternoon, last November, Mervyn, Thompson, Mrs Lanesome, and I, peered at the flickering grey image on the screen as Mr Norman, the chairman of the BBC, officially inaugurated the first television service in the world, using the term, 'viewers,' for the first time. Then, after lengthy, rather boring speeches by the Postmaster General, a man from the Baird Company, and a director of EMI Marconi, we settled back to watch a transmission of the British Movie Tone News.

Next, the announcer informed us we were to hear, and see, a concert given by the Vienna Symphony Orchestra. The works included Mozart's Haffner Symphony, conducted by Oswald Kabasta. Mrs Lanesome chose to return to the kitchen, and Thompson said he needed to wash the car. Therefore, Mervyn and I were alone in the tranquillity of the sitting room, engulfed in the sound and vision of violinists; cellists; horn and harpsichord players.

In the spring of the same year, and still completely unaware of the machinations occurring between King and Parliament, I had the honour to attend a special Boy Scout event at Windsor Castle. Here, King Edward the eighth joined over one thousand scouts, and their officers from all over Great Britain, in a National Scout Service held in Saint Georges Chapel, Windsor.

We assembled in the Riding School, marched to the cloisters behind our county flags, and regrouped on the lawn, large cheering crowds watching the procession and King Edward passing amongst our ranks.

Standing bareheaded in the bright, yet chilly, sunshine, His Majesty addressed us from the steps of the chapel. Firstly, he welcomed us to Windsor, then reminding us that, for many years, he had the honour to occupy the rank of Chief Scout for Wales. The King explained, how during his travels throughout the world, he had many opportunities to become acquainted with the work and activities of the scout movement, in promoting comradeship and good fellowship. He urged the boys to remember when they were grown up, with their scouting days behind them that the example set by the selfless dedication and leadership of countless scoutmasters throughout the globe, would assist them as they took leading roles in the affairs of the world.

'I wish you a safe return to wherever your homes may be,' the King concluded. 'Also, I would like you, when you get back, to give my best wishes to all Scouts for the future, whatever it may be.'

That day, everyone felt moved by His Majesty's words, and anticipated him reigning over us for many years to come. Little did we know, however, that in just eight months, we would listen to him make an altogether different speech.

At one point during the same year, my village of Wildsbridge received its first red telephone box, and much consternation it caused amongst the inhabitants. Almost everyone had the opinion that the colour was grossly out of keeping with the surroundings. Personally, I could see the sense in having such a receptacle so brightly painted. Should there be an emergency, a traffic accident, for instance, or a house fire, then it was important a telephone be found quickly. Our box is situated where The Barton meets Wildsbridge Lane, and close by the post office and the village shop. For a while, it was an oddity, gathering a crowd of curious onlookers. However, in time, everyone became accustomed to its presence, until we hardly noticed it at all, except that is, when it was necessary to use it.

As if a portent of things to come, on the night of the 30th November, the glorious relic of the Victorian age, The Crystal Palace, burnt to the ground, and as the smouldering rubble cooled, a certain Bishop of Bradford, Doctor Alfred Blunt, was preparing to make a speech at a Diocesan conference. His words would rock the world and change the lives of a contented family forever.

For months now, the news of King Edward's amorous involvement with one of its female citizens had been making American news. Yet despite the rumours leaking across the Atlantic, only a few discreet members of the press and the British public were aware of the case. They were keeping the knowledge close to their chests; with the hope the situation might resolve itself positively, sooner rather than later.

Had the Bishop of Bradford not voiced his opinions regarding the King, the inevitable would have happened nevertheless. Baldwin and his cabinet were determined His Majesty would never marry the recently divorced, Mrs Wallis Simpson, and were resolute that neither would she become his queen.

Consequently, nine days after Doctor Blunt's revelation in the press, at his home, Fort Belvedere, and in the presence of his brothers, the princes, York, Kent and Gloucester, King Edward the eighth signed an instrument of abdication.

Thus, by signing the hurriedly passed Act of Abdication the following day, His Majesty performed his last act as a monarch. That evening, with a million people listening throughout the nation, His Royal Highness Prince Edward, as he was now to be referred, broadcast his decision and the reasons why he was handing over the crown to his brother, Albert.

Of course, for those of us who were ignorant of the rumours, his departure came as a dreadful shock, since it had been a certainty that Edward, Prince of Wales, would become our reigning monarch. Now it was necessary to regard the little known, extremely private, Duke and Duchess of York, and their two young princesses, as the new occupants of Buckingham Palace. Furthermore, a new line of succession would begin; meaning Princess Elizabeth would become next in line to the throne.

On Friday, January 1st, 1937, Mervyn became nineteen and was free to come and go as he pleased, although he behaved just the same as he had as an eighteen year old. Without any encouragement from me, he virtually deserted his family at Camden Place, preferring to reside at Hyde House.

Mervyn's bedroom faced north and overlooked the Temple Court. He ate his meals with me; drove to college during the week, and on Sunday mornings, picked up Teddy and Mickey, ending up in some village pub, propping up the bar, puffing on his latest passion, a Birchwood pipe. It amused me to see him desperately attempting to grow up, as it only seemed yesterday he had been the lad from Swinbourne's Buildings.

Yet, the old chestnut of Mervyn's brother Harry remained a cause of disagreement. Almost every week, Mr and Mrs Watson received a postcard or letter from their son pleading to bring about his release from the services. Regularly, the phone at Hyde House would ring, and by the tone of Mervyn's voice as he took the call, I knew instantly his mother was on the end of the line. Ultimately, I realised that yet again I would need to come to the rescue. However, the mission I faced would be fraught with challenges, and pitfalls of which I was soon to discover.

Chapter Twenty Five
Packing again - The Last Days of Pompeii - RMS Orontes – Confessions

"His letters say that he's in a hospital," Mervyn said one morning at breakfast. "But they don't say what the matter is."

"But what are the army doctors doing?" I asked.

Mervyn shrugged. "Who knows? Harry just might die."

***

With this conversation echoing in my mind, a few days after Mervyn's birthday, my eyes were drawn to the shipping news in The Times, where I noticed the RMS Orontes was to sail for Australia in a fortnight, Port Said being her fourth port of call.

"Another voyage!" Eric's voice boomed through the receiver. "You're obsessed, Ron!"

"But this isn't for pleasure," I replied. "It's a mercy dash. Mervyn's brother could be very sick."

"What makes you think you'll do any good? It's virtually impossible to buy a man out of the army."

"My cousin Gilbert's in Egypt. He'll be my introduction to Harry's superiors."

"Does he know you're coming?"

"No. I thought we'd surprise him."

"So Mervyn's going too!"

"Of course. He is his brother after all."

"Well you better keep him well out of the way. Gilbert's no fool. He's bound to wonder what you're doing travelling with an eighteen year old boy."

"He's nineteen. And he's not a boy Eric," I retorted. "I'm not a complete fool. Mervyn's quite grown up these days. He's got a mind of his own. He picks and chooses what he does or doesn't do."

"So are you going to pass him off as your nephew to Gilbert? He isn't Wildsbridge village Ron. He's family."

Suddenly, I felt a strong urge to put down the receiver, but restrained myself, taking a few deep breaths instead.

"Sometimes Eric, by the way you speak to me, I believe you've forgotten who you are. If it wasn't for me, Eric Harry White, you would be earning a wage in a soap factory in Keynsham, instead of strolling around Lincoln's Inn Fields wearing a wig and gown."

There was a deathly silence at the other end of the line.

"Furthermore," I continued. "To be quite honest Eric, what I do is really none of your business. The voyage is already booked and paid for. We leave on the 16th."

I heard a click, and the phone went dead.

Why do some people try to organise other people's lives? I constantly find persons close to me attempting to order me around, with the opinion they know what is best for me. I am my own master, old enough to make my own decisions. Perhaps, because I am tall, and a bit of a dumpling, maybe they see me as vulnerable and soft, giving them the idea I am incapable of thinking and doing things for myself. Well, take this as a fact. I am not as they might think. I will be forty-seven in June, and well able to conduct my affairs responsibly and with candour. There! I have had my say, and will now return to the story.

***

Eighteen months have passed since Mervyn, Teddy, Mickey and I returned from Norway, and to be honest, more than once, I have looked yearningly at advertisements promoting cruises, yet resisted temptation. But here was the chance to once more venture upon the high seas, so I eagerly planned an itinerary to follow once Mervyn and I arrived in Cairo.

"We'll catch the train from Port Said," I said, as we sat beside the fire listening to a concert on the radio given by the BBC Symphony Light Orchestra. "I can't decide whether we'll stay at Shepheard's or The Continental. Both are excellent hotels."

Mervyn had his nose in a large book he recently borrowed from Bath library.

"It says here Giza's a must," he said.

"Of course. That's where you'll find the Sphinx and the Pyramids."

"I want to ride a camel," Mervyn said, eagerly. "Promise me I'll ride a camel."

"Before leaving Egypt, at the end of the war," I said. "I noticed archaeologists were excavating Karnak and bits of Memphis and Heliopolis. It'll be interesting to see how the temples look now."

Since returning to Cambridge with Eric, and studying Ancient History, I had developed a tremendous appreciation for timeless antiquities.

"What about King Tut?" Mervyn said, lighting his pipe with a taper from the fire. "Can we see him?"

"I think he's in the Cairo Museum. Once we've seen my cousin Gilbert and everything's in motion, we'll have lots of time to explore. You'll find Cairo fascinating. The dragomen and donkey boys are most helpful and can make excellent guides."

"Donkey boys!" sniggered Mervyn. "I assume they're called donkey boys because they look after donkeys and not because of other things."

I chose to ignore his lewd allusion.

"You've told your mother and father I take it. How were they?"

"Fine. By now, they're used to me gallivanting about with you. As long as everything stays the same, they're happy. Anyway, father's busy in the newspaper shop you bought him. So he can't complain"

"You mean you bought him? He doesn't know it was me, does he?"

"Of course not. You told me not to tell him."

Since I opened Mervyn's account in the bank, he had accrued a considerable amount in a year and a half. Moreover, I advised him to invest some of the surplus. He drew my attention to a news agency business for sale, across the river, in Twerton, and asked whether he might buy it. Mervyn explained how his father needed an occupation to keep him away from the public bar at the Larkhall Inn, where Mervyn caught him making eyes at the barmaid. I saw the business as a wise investment, and endorsed a cheque for two thousand pounds, which Mervyn withdrew from the bank.

"Who do they think is paying for Harry's release?" I asked.

"I told them I was," answered Mervyn.

It was incredulous to think Mr and Mrs Watson naively believed their nineteen-year-old son was able to afford such a thing. Obviously, they knew where the money came from, but chose to think otherwise.

"And that's how I want the story to remain," I said. "The less I'm involved, the better."

Saturday 16th January dawned brightly, with a chill in the air that forecast snow. If true, then I was pleased we were heading to warmer climes. I have never been a tremendous lover of the white stuff.

Mervyn and I travelled up to London from Bath on Friday afternoon, catching the midday train. At Paddington, we caught a cab to the Midland Grand Hotel at Saint Pancras Station, and settled into a pair of deep leather armchairs in the smoking room to discuss our evening entertainment.

"'Balalaika', at the Adelphi looks good," I said, scanning the entertainment section of The Times.

"Really. Who's in it?"

Mervyn was thumbing gold flake tobacco into his pipe.

"I don't know. It doesn't say. The Coliseum, the Embassy, and Palladium, all have pantomimes."

"Can't stand them."

"How about Shakespeare? Laurence Olivier is doing 'Hamlet', at the Old Vic. Wilfred saw it and said it was tremendous. It's a fantastic cast. Marius Goring, Michael Redgrave, and Robert Newton are also in it."

"If you're trying to educate me again, then it's a no. After you trailed Teddy and me along to Bath Theatre Royal to see 'Julius Caesar', I said I never wanted to see another Shakespeare."

"Alright. How about an operetta? 'Careless Rapture', is on at Drury Lane, with Ivor Novello and Dorothy Dickson."

Mervyn scowled and shook his head, at the same time puffing on his pipe, filling the area around us with grey, acrid smoke.

"How about a film."

"We're stuck for choice there. 'Charge of the Light Brigade' is on at The Carlton."

"Who's in that?"

"Errol Flynn and Olivia De Havilland. 'Last Days of Pompeii' is at the Court. Or we could see 'The Great Ziegfeld' at the Empire. You love American musicals."

"I rather fancy 'The Last Days of Pompeii'. You said we'd visit Pompeii when we arrive in Naples."

"That's true. Very well. 'Last Days of Pompeii' it is."

The film began at ten past six, which gave us time for tea, a quick wash, and brush up, and the ten-minute cab ride to Sloane Square.

In my student days, I often attended matinees at the Royal Court, as it was known then. The plays of George Bernard Shaw were often staged there. However, signs of the times had led the owners to believe there was a greater future for the place as a picture theatre. But as our taxi drew up under the brightly lit canopy, I was pleased to see once more the red brick exterior and the marble clad steps.

As we climbed out of the cab, and after paying the cabby, it was hard not to miss the great advertising placard fixed to the building, picturing the film, its garish colours lit by a hundred light bulbs. With Vesuvius erupting in the distance, panic takes over the populace as temples topple, lava streams, and people flee in terror as the city is engulfed in ash. The stars of the film are seen, their heads, perhaps ten feet high, appearing petrified, yet stalwartly facing the fate awaiting them.

Released at the beginning of the year, the film's popularity had not waned, so there was a considerable queue at the ticket window. I paid seven shillings and six pence for two tickets; we climbed the stairs to the dress circle, and found our front row seats.

"Who're the stars Ron?" Mervyn asked, lighting a cigarette.

Purposely, I suggested he refrain from bringing his pipe. For my part, I think cigars or pipes have no place in a picture house, their smoke is so thick it can sometimes interfere with the quality of the image on the screen.

"I recognise Preston Foster from the poster," I said. "You know! The Chain Gang man, plus Alan Hale and Basil Rathbone."

"I've heard of him. Isn't he Sherlock Holmes?"

"Correct. I've not heard about any of the others. The book's in the library at Hyde House, but I've never read it."

Pathe News began the programme, and we saw newsreels ranging from the gloomy activities of Germany in French Morocco; women in a Blackburn factory making filters for gas masks; the construction of the keel of the White Star Liner, No 552, in Clyde bank and intended to be a sister ship to the Queen Mary. Also, the King and Queen, visiting Buckingham Palace, before they officially take up residence. The cock crowed for the last time; the lights came up, and the curtain went down.

Then, after a few seconds, no doubt while the projectionist changed the film, the footlights glowed once more and the curtain slowly rose as the British Board of Film Censors certificate appeared on the screen, informing us that the film we were about to watch was rated U and suitable for all ages.

Synchronising perfectly with the dimming lights, the opening music surged through invisible sound speakers as the film title appeared.

"Wow!" Mervyn whispered. "I certainly know I'm watching a film in London. It's never like this at Bath's Little Theatre."

Quickly, I realised this was a first for Mervyn. He had never seen a film in London, and as such, I tended to agree. There is a particular professionalism in the metropolis that you do not see in the provincial towns. Admittedly, Bath Forum Picture House does a decent job. However, nothing beats a London Picture House for atmosphere and class.

The film had a slow beginning while setting up the story.

Consequently, after half an hour, I noticed Mervyn shifting uneasily in his seat, obviously becoming bored with the talking and little action. So I offered him a cigarette, which seemed to calm him down.

"When are we going to see the lava and ash, and people turned to stone?" Mervyn muttered, after another half an hour.

Being we were in the dark, I shrugged and shook my head. But still the film went on.

At last, the action began, the volcano spewing its lava, temples toppling, and folk engulfed in fiery ash. The hero dies after finding redemption in the eyes of God, the credits roll and the lights came on.

"That was good," said Mervyn. "The ending was fantastic. Do you think we saw a real volcano erupting?"

"It certainly looks genuine," I answered. "But all the falling buildings must have been modelled."

"How did they do the lava?"

"I've no idea. It looked like burning porridge. They're clever with the effects these days."

Outside in Sloane Square it was dark and raining. So, rather than join the majority of the audience hurrying to the tube station, I hailed a taxi, asking the cabby to take us to the Midland Grand. The route took us along Eaton Gate to Eaton Square. Then down Grosvenor Gardens, through Grosvenor Place, keeping the Royal Mews to our left, ultimately entering into Buckingham Palace Road. I knew the way. But Mervyn was mesmerised by the lights and the magnificent houses we passed.

"You'll see the front of Buckingham Palace soon," I said.

Sure enough, in a moment, the shape of the royal residence suddenly loomed to our left, although the windows were dark, their Royal Highnesses still living in their house in Piccadilly.

"I wish it was daytime," Mervyn said. "The place is as black as pitch."

"When we get back from Egypt it'll be just two months until the Coronation. You'll see it then. And I promise it'll look very different."

On either side of the Mall, the streetlights shone out of the darkness, revealing dozens of scurrying people under umbrellas, the scene mirrored in the wet pavement beneath their feet. Suddenly, Admiralty Arch swooped over our heads and we were heading into Trafalgar Square.

"There's Nelson on his column," Mervyn said, eagerly pointing at the statue far above us, standing in the glare of a floodlight.

Across the square, our taxi made a left turn into Saint Martin's Lane, plunging us into a world of sparkle and electricity. We were on the edge of theatre land, otherwise known as The West End. It was still early and the shows were yet to begin, as a result, the street teemed with people either eagerly queuing at the box offices, arriving by taxi, or emerging from Leicester Square underground station. Undaunted, and keen to be out of the rain, they hurried across the road, braving the queue of traffic as it nudged its way towards Seven Dials.

At Shelton Street, we turned right, and then left into Endell Street, at the end stopping at a set of traffic lights.

"Can you see the old school?" I said, pointing to a brick edifice through the rain-streaked window of the taxi. "There's a basement next door and a door leading to the infamous Caravan Club."

"Infamous!" asked Mervyn. "Why? What went on?"

"What didn't go on, you mean! About three years ago, if you were the way we are, then the Caravan was the place to go in London. There you could drink, relax, dance, make new friends, and see a live show. No holds barred."

"How do you know? Did you ever go?"

"Once or twice. Around the time I met you."

"You sneaky beggar!" Mervyn said, laughing. "Hey! If it's so good, why don't we pay the cabby and go in?"

"The police closed it down. I was there the night it was raided, and one of the seventy seven men arrested."

"You! Arrested!" Mervyn exclaimed. "I don't believe it."

"Why not? I've led a life Mervyn! I'm not as fuddy duddy as you might think. The rest of the chaps and me were herded together, then crammed into the back of police vans and taken to Bow Street Police Station. I was put in a cell with a chap with one leg shorter than the other and a young man, whom the others called Cyril de Leon."

Mervyn guffawed so loudly the cabbie turned to look at us through the glass partition.

"He sounds like a female impersonator," Mervyn chuckled.

"He was. They arrested him in full slap as they say in the theatre world."

"The man with the short leg turned out to be a phrenologist."

By now, Mervyn was in a helpless fit of the giggles.

"What's that, for heaven's sake?"

"A person who reads bumps."

"Whereabouts?"

"Not where you're thinking," I laughed. "Bumps on your head."

"Did he read yours?"

"Do you mind? I don't have any. We were crowded into cells, a dozen at a time, and seeing it was one o'clock in the morning when the police burst into the club, most men were much the worse for wear. You can imagine the conditions. I don't think I've ever been as intimate with a group of people, and hope I never will again."

"What happened next?"

The taxi sped away from the traffic lights, took a left turn at the Princes' Theatre, and headed for New Oxford Street.

"The following morning, everyone appeared at Bow Street Magistrates Court, and we were asked to give our names. Obviously, if my name had made the papers it would have been devastating for the family, so I chose to give a false one. I think the judge was so overwhelmed by the sheer numbers of the queerest folk he had ever seen, he cleared the public from the court to give us room to stand. While the judge retired to his chambers, two fellows, one of them my phrenologist friend, were detained in the dock, while we crowded around it, or took up positions in the public gallery. These two chaps were the owners. The judge returned, and set bail for the couple. Then surprising most of us, after hearing the proceedings, he dismissed almost everyone, me amongst them, and I left the court a free man."

"Very exciting," Mervyn said. "I've a notion I'm the only one to know about this. I can't think of anyone else you'd tell."

"Of course, stuffy old Eric would have been mortified and quite disgusted had he found out. Mother, more than likely would laugh, and Wilfred, well, I can just hear him chiding me. In fact, I think it's done me good telling you. I've always felt guilty keeping it a secret."

"I'm honoured you feel you can take me into your confidence," said Mervyn, "and that you trust me enough to tell me. I know how well you guard your family's reputation. Don't worry. From now on, it'll be my secret too."

As usual, High Holborn was heaving with traffic, since the tail end of the evening rush hour was still in progress. The wet road shone like glass, reflecting street lamps and blazing shop windows, the light reflected off the sleek black and coloured shells of cars, taxicabs, and omnibuses. Our taxi turned into Kingsway and motored up Southampton Row, the shops exchanged for Georgian terraces and Government Offices, the windows of the former shining with warm light, those of the latter glowering, dark and grim.

"Okay Ron, as you've decided to delve into your shady past," Mervyn said. "What other hangouts have you been arrested in?"

To tell the truth, and in hindsight, I enjoyed opening up to Mervyn that night. Although, I am quite happy in my skin, there have been events in my past I am rather ashamed to disclose. However, Mervyn and his generation consider such activities as quite normal, and talk more freely about them than the likes of mine ever do. This gave me confidence to reveal some more of my secrets.

"Come on! Spill the beans," he coaxed.

"Lots went on at Cambridge in the twenties," I began. "But it was the bright lights of scandalous London that would always attract. When I was an undergrad after the war, Wilfred's rooms in Whitehall Court belonged to my father, so it was easy to come down to London on a Friday night, knowing I had a place to put my head."

"Unless of course, it was someone else's place."

"That would never be," I said. "Far too dangerous. Like nowadays, blackmailers were ten a penny. Plus policemen in plain clothes could seduce the unsuspecting and lure them to some place where another uniformed officer was waiting to arrest the poor gullible man. No! It was far better to remain clandestine, otherwise meet in establishments where it was safe to conduct oneself in the way ones nature intended."

Mervyn laughed. "Ron! You have a clever way of avoiding saying the obvious, which by the way, I've always admired you for."

Indeed! Could I be in for a promise later? Mervyn must be in a good mood.

"Just behind Regents Street, there used to be a popular basement club, terribly chic and bohemian," I continued, "I must admit to feeling a little out of place at 'The Cave of the Golden Calf'. The clientele were awfully hoi-polloi. Maybe because the place was owned and run by August Strinberg's widow. You saw musical entertainments, dramatic tableaux, poetry readings, and of course, dance with your partner without any prejudice."

"We could go there tonight."

"I'm afraid not my lad. It just about lasted the war and then closed. On Sunday afternoons, in the twenties, there was always the Long Bar at the Trocadero. But you needed to be on your guard. Piccadilly boys knew the Troc as the place where well to do gentlemen looked for young lads. You could easily be minus your wallet before you could say Jack Robinson."

"They were rent boys. Did you ever approach one?" Mervyn asked.

"Yes. But not in the way you think. I took pity on a lad one time. He was down from Liverpool and fed me a sob story about how his mum had thrown him out when she discovered him larking with a friend. Since he said he was going to sleep on the street, I offered him a bed for the night at Whitehall Court. Naturally, it was mine, as there's only one bedroom. But, I assure you, nothing occurred. You never knew what you might catch playing around with rent boys. In the morning, the boy had a wash. I then I sent him packing after giving him his fare back to Liverpool. I had a shave, bathed, and returned to Bath the same day. But I soon realised the little rascal had given me something."

"Oh no! What?"

"Scabies. I'd heard of it, of course. It was rife in the ranks during the war. But I'd never experienced it. So at first I had no idea why my skin was burning and I was scratching like a madman."

Suddenly realising we were approaching the hotel; I curtailed my story and prepared to pay the driver.

"Thanks gov. You're a gent," he said, seeing I had tipped him sixpence. "Goodnight, gents."

Mervyn and I entered the lobby, and after collecting the key to our room, took the elevator to the fourth floor.

Our suite looked over Euston Road, south in the direction of the city, over the rooftops of Fitzrovia and University College Hospital. As a consequence, when we opened the door, the glittering panorama through the windows was quite breathtaking.

"Come on Ron. What happened next?" said Mervyn, still waiting to hear the end of my story.

Suspense is the key to good storytelling. Therefore, stalling a little while longer, I rang for room service.

"It's Friday Mervyn, so we'll have fish," I said, "For dessert, would you like crème caramel, lemon tart, or spotted dick?"

"Spotted dick please."

"Two lemon soles, and a couple of spotted dicks please. Room 441."

Putting down the receiver, I saw Mervyn had slumped on a sofa, so I joined him.

"Funny you requested spotted dick," I laughed. "It was that which eventually convinced me to visit the hospital."

"Really Ron!" shrieked Mervyn. "You're outrageous!"

"No my boy. It was bloody awful. As well as scratching like there was no tomorrow, big blotches appeared on my 'how's your father'. I was actually worried I'd caught the clap."

"So you went to the hospital. Where? In Bath?"

"No fear. I'm too well known. I came back here, and found the biggest hospital I could, which happened to be St Mary's in Paddington. And having given a false name to a woman at the desk, I waited in the emergency department for someone to see me. Finally, it was my turn, and I went into a consulting room and showed my penis to a very nice looking Irish doctor."

"And he told you, you had scabies."

"No. He said what an impressive instrument I had and asked to meet me for a drink."

Mervyn fell backwards onto a cushion in shrieks of laughter.

"I'm joking, of course," I shouted. "He gave me a prescription for something called quelada lotion and sent me to the pharmacy counter."

"You almost convinced me, you bugger!" Mervyn yelled.

At that moment, there was a knock on the door and we composed ourselves as a waiter laid the table.

Still savouring a delicious supper, I asked the waiter for port and cigars. I wished to mark the moment, considering on the morrow Mervyn and I would be setting out on a rescue mission, as well as an exciting adventure. The evening had been splendid, and both of us were at one with the world, so much in fact that when I suggested we retire to bed, instead of climbing into his own bed after we undressed and put on our pyjamas, Mervyn decided to clamber into mine, causing it to be a little cramped to say the least.

"Where else did you go to find sex?" he said snuggling up against me.

"Do you mind dear boy! I call it a brief moment of comradeship and mutual satisfaction."

"Alright, if you say so. Then where?"

"Lyon's Corner House in Coventry Street was popular. Also the one in the Strand. You could sit there as long as you liked, providing the Nippys served you tea. I remember the way to tell a man was out for a bit of fun, was to watch him. If he disregarded the Nippys, then you might be lucky."

"What's Nippys?"

"What are Nippys, you mean. The Lyons Nippys were famous all over England for their looks. Everywhere you went you couldn't help seeing their pictures on advertisements and billboards. Mr Jo Lyons himself handpicked them. Seven years ago, there was even a musical at The Prince Edward Theatre called 'Nippy', starring Binnie Hale."

Mervyn turned on his side, and began leaning his head on my shoulder, one arm against my chest the other draped across my belly. My earlier observations in the taxi were potentially becoming reality.

"So what you're saying, if a bloke you're eyeing shows little interest in a shapely ankle, he's queer."

"I might have put it another way. But yes."

"I've never needed to look for it." Mervyn said, haughtily. "It's more often looks for me."

"Then you're very lucky. You're fortunate to be young and attractive, and confident in your appearance. I don't think I've ever really appealed to a man or a women."

"Don't be so hard on yourself Ron. I certainly know of one thing that keeps me interested."

His hand moved up the bed and under the blankets.

"You know what I'm talking about. Now where is it?"

He soon found what he was looking for, and I made no attempt to stop him.

"How did you know someone's looking at you for a reason?" he said.

"Sometimes with difficulty. I've never gone for the feminine type. I mean the ones you can tell at a glance. Mine had to be masculine. So at times, it was necessary to take risks to let your intentions known. But usually, a look, or a turn of the head was enough to relay your meaning."

As I recalled my past, I remembered the day in Naples when Conner and I visited the Aquarium. How timid and innocent I had been, and how I had changed since.

"What makes us do it?" Mervyn asked, suddenly relinquishing his hold, and rolling on to his back, while putting his hands behind his head.

"Hormones my dear chap," I said. "Why does the male animal behave as he does? The urge to procreate, that's why. Except, for the likes of us, our instincts are reversed. Not perversed, reversed. The emotion I feel towards my own sex seems as natural to me as preferring one cheese from another or the scent of one flower from the next. You and I, and millions like us, have no say as to how we are. To us, it's as normal as being left or right handed."

Mervyn yawned. "I agree."

The third glass of port we drank before coming to bed was

causing us to become philosophical.

"No one would choose to live as we do. Always keeping our true self a secret. To lie, or risk disclosure and prison. All the while leading a clandestine life, and never able to tell the truth about oneself."

"Alright Mervyn," I said. "How do you see your life panning out?"

"Spending it with you I suppose. If you'll have me that is."

"But of course dear boy."

"Then I promise to love, honour and obey," he said, his hand returning to its previous location.

However, knowing Mervyn as I do, I suspect there might be a condition to the promise, but I refrained from mentioning the fact. Instead, I suggested we switch off the bedside light and get some sleep since a busy day lay ahead of us. However, Mervyn had other ideas.

Part Two
Cairo: The Mother of the World

Chapter One
Bon voyage - Rough seas - The Captain's table

"This is the BBC from London, and here is the weather for today, January 16th and I am Alvar Lidel, reading it."

The radio in the corner of the hotel room crackled and hissed as Mervyn and I finished our breakfast.

"Fresh southerly winds will veer southwest or westerly later. Cloudy, or dull. Occasional rain or showers. Average temperature. Provisional forecast for tomorrow: renewed rain, probably spreading from the west, with stormy conditions developing. Rain or hail in the channel, sea rather rough. Sunrise 8.01am; sets 4.20pm."

"Oh dear," I said, "It doesn't look good for us. I'd better buy some seasick pills at the station."

Since the Midland Grand Hotel has been purpose built to encompass the terminus, we could hardly have been closer to St Pancras Station. Therefore, following the occasional sign through the ground floor lobby, Mervyn and I eventually found our way onto the concourse and down to the underground. Having arrived at Fenchurch Station, my watch said nine o'clock and the train ride to Tilbury would take just under an hour. So with the ship scheduled to sail at midday, there was no need to worry about being late.

With our luggage on its way to the train, Mervyn went to WH Smith's bookstall to purchase a newspaper and comics, while I bought cigarettes, pipe tobacco, and a bottle of seasick pills from the tobacconist's kiosk under the clock.

It is rather an uneventful journey from London to Tilbury Docks, and since I have made the trip several times, I always find it rather disheartening. As the train winds its way through northeast London, it passes through cuttings fringed by innumerable terraces of ochre and red brick houses, their skimpy gardens backing onto the railway line. It depresses me to see them appearing so drab and pokey. Nonetheless, the inhabitants are indifferent to any other way of life. To them, the little front parlour, two bedrooms upstairs, a toilet in the yard, and the scullery, is a palace.

The pub on the corner and the picture house in the high street are their places of entertainment. The greengrocer, the butcher shop and market at the end of the street are where they buy their groceries. Why then have I the right to feel sorry for them? They are straightforward people, happy with their lot and contented to be whom and where they are. This populace is the backbone of the nation and might one day be tested to the limit, but will face the trial with fortitude.

The announcer was correct in his weather prediction, because, as we drew out from under the protection of the cast iron and glass roof of the station, long shafts of rain slashed the carriage window, while blustery gusts buffeted the door.

When we finally encountered the marshes, a broad expanse of leaden sky greeted us, the river turned tortuous by a brisk southerly breeze.

"When do we take the pills?" Mervyn asked gloomily, peering through the bleary window.

"It says on the label, an hour before we sail. You know, in the past, we've been lucky. When we went through rough weather on the way back from Norway, it didn't affect us one bit."

"Because by then we were used to the sea. But that was over a year ago."

"There she is," I said, as the train pulled into Tilbury Docks. "See the ship with the yellow funnels with black tops; that's the Orontes."

Mervyn and I expected to get wet, so before leaving the carriage we pulled on our overcoats and put on our trilbies. But we need not have bothered, as the canopy over the platform was excellent protection from the rain. People were queuing at a desk inside the customs hall, an officer checking their tickets and passports.

"What does Orontes mean?" asked Mervyn as we joined the line.

"It's a river in the Levant, and very famous in classical history. Its deep valleys and gorges were means great armies could pass from north to south. Recently, some Belgian archaeologists have unearthed Apamea, a Greco Roman city that stood on the Plain of Ghab, above a bend in the river. The name of every ship in the Orient Line begins with the letter O. For instance Osterley, Orion, and Orcades."

"You know such a lot Ron. You should have been a teacher."

"Perhaps you're right. I took Ancient History the second time at Trinity. Maybe I missed my vocation. The war has a lot to answer for. Plus I had responsibilities, ensuring Eric received his education, which also may have been an obstacle."

At this point, I will briefly pause my narrative to praise the efficiency of the Orient Line. From the moment Mervyn and I left the hotel, our every need was catered. The luggage was swiftly spirited away to the luggage van, and equally speedily transported to the nets and craned aboard the ship. Outside the rain fell in torrents, although, as we climbed leisurely up the gangway, Mervyn and I remained dry, since a canvas awning, attached to the terminus building, covered it.

Once aboard, and with the formalities complete, a steward on F Deck, escorted us to our suite of cabins, C78 and B77, on C Deck, where we discovered our trunks had preceded us.

"You'll find the veranda café on B deck is open for coffee, tea and beverages, gentlemen," the steward said, using his passkey to unlock the door between Mervyn's cabin and mine. "However, the dining saloon on F Deck will remain closed until an hour after we sail. My name is Lewis, and I'll be your steward for the next ten days. I understand you're disembarking at Port Said."

We thanked him, and he left us alone to unpack.

"Have you seen the folder on your desk?" called Mervyn from his cabin. "The red booklet gives a list of every passenger travelling in first class. I can't believe it! You and I are mentioned. So far, I've counted one Lord, six Ladys, and one Dowager Lady, six army types, including you, one Vice Admiral and the Bishop of Gibraltar."

"Of course," I laughed. "Egypt's very popular right now. Not just for the climate either. The archaeological sites draw the crowds. And now Tutankhamen's in the Museum of Cairo, he's a huge attraction. Also, it's a bit of a political hot potato too. That's why a great many army fellows are backwards and forwards."

"Look at the P&O folder! It's excellent," Mervyn continued. "The blue booklets tell you all about each port of call. Gibraltar, Toulon, Naples, and Port Said, including maps and descriptions. Where's Toulon?"

"South of France. It has a fantastic harbour. You packed your camera I hope."

"Of course. I'll be the one to take pictures this time."

"When does it say we reach Port Said?"

"27th of this month."

"Then they're confident we'll keep to the schedule."

Mervyn came to the connecting door wearing the white jersey slacks and cream silk shirt I bought for him at Jolly's only the week before. I must say he really did look the part.

"The book I borrowed from the library lists all the sites worth visiting," he said. "Of course, we'll see the Pyramids and the Sphinx. Do you think we'll visit Luxor and Memphis? The statue of Pharaoh Rameses the second looks incredible."

"Luxor is quite a way up the Nile, meaning a boat trip. Although, Memphis can be reached easily in an hour. Hang on though. We mustn't forget why we're going. We've to think of your poor brother."

"Of course. In all the excitement I'd put him to the back of my mind."

"When we've made contact with my cousin, and set the ball in motion, then we'll think about a holiday. Here! Take your sea sick pill."

With our articles of clothing stowed in wardrobes, cupboards and drawers, as well as our shaving and bathing gear arranged in the bathroom cabinets, Mervyn and I went up to watch proceedings from the promenade deck, since it was under cover.

Another boat train was disgorging onto the platform. But unlike Mervyn and I when we arrived an hour earlier, the people were in a hurry, as the boat was to sail in half an hour. We were drawn to the top of the gangway, curious to see the progression of passengers coming aboard.

"How can we tell the ladys from the ladies?" asked Mervyn.

"The ladys will be wearing fur coats, whether it's raining or not," I said. "And more than likely the odd bit of visible jewellery."

"Welcome aboard, Lord and Lady Butler," an officer said, standing beside the gangway ticking names on a passenger list. "A steward will see you to your cabin."

"We know who they are at least," said Mervyn quite audibly.

"The noted and the notorious always aspire to arrive late, so as to be noticed," I said, "Look how crowded the rail has become."

Having finished unpacking, other first class passengers were scrutinising arrivals, two young women near us, beginning to comment on the variety of fashions coming on board.

"Doesn't she look lovely," one said. "Who is she?" asked the other.

"Lady De L'Isle and Dudley of course. She always spends the winter abroad. Last year it was Cape Town, so mother told me. If she's bound for Cairo, then I dare say she'll be staying at Shepheard's, so we'll be bumping into her all the time."

Becoming rather bored watching the elite arrive, I suggested we adjourn to the smoking room. In all the activity, I still had not found an opportunity to read my newspaper. Therefore, while Mervyn joined a group for an organised tour of the ship, I settled down on a sofa, beneath a window to read The Times.

Leafing through, as is my habit, endeavouring to find the choicest piece of news, I casually glanced at an account telling of Goering's visit to Italy. He and Mussolini attended a demonstration of fencing at a fencing school, Benito putting on an impromptu display of his own. There was also an item telling of the fighting at Estepona and the British Government imposing a yearlong prison sentence in an attempt to stem the tide of young men volunteering to fight the fascists in Spain. But these stories were hardly riveting. Coronation fever was beginning to grip the country, so there were several columns devoted to the plans and speculation of the intended date. Even grim reports of the gradual Nazi aryanisation occurring in Germany, with Jews forced to sell their businesses and banned from working in offices, failed to hold my attention.

However, one headline sent a chill through me akin to an icicle stabbing my heart. It read, 'Court Martial on Captain. Acquittal on two charges'.

Four boys, all scouts, or former boy scouts, from a north London scout troop, were making accusations towards two army officers, Captain Loftus Tottenham, and Captain Jocelyn Chase, of the Royal Engineers. But given both men had distinguished army records, and were accomplished sportsmen prior to their arrest, Loftus Tottenham in hockey and water polo, and Chase, appropriately, in athletics, it appeared the police were willing to hush up the allegations and encourage the officers to escape abroad until the whole thing blew over. Proceedings were reinstated nonetheless, after Captain Chase contacted his commanding officer, explaining his and Loftus Tottenham's absence from duty. Arriving back in the country from Belgium, they were arrested at Victoria Station and prepared to face a Court Martial, accused of committing forty-four acts of gross indecency and disgraceful conduct towards civilian boys while acting as scout masters at the Hendon scout troop.

The previous week, at the Royal Engineers Headquarters in Chatham, Captain Loftus Tottenham, son of Vice Admiral, Henry Loftus Tottenham, stood before a panel of high-ranking army officers to face the charges.

The first boy to enter the witness box admitted to being just fourteen when Loftus Tottenham invited him to stay in his flat at Makepeace Gardens, Highbury, the night before the troop were about to leave for their annual summer camp in Cumberland.

Here apparently, various acts of an indecent nature took place.

The other lads testified, but there seemed to be some confusion regarding their statements, the boys denying they had said the words that were read out in court. This inferred the police were putting words into their mouths, resulting in several counts being dismissed.

Frustratingly, the case was adjourned, so I would have to be content to read the report of Captain Chase's trial, later. On Monday morning, 'Orontes' will be embarking passengers at Plymouth, so I resolved to purchase a copy of The Times as soon as we docked.

Folding the newspaper, I laid it aside and lit my pipe.

Here then was another scandalous case involving the scout movement. Not only Bath scoutmaster, Lawrence Bullied, down at heel engineering draughtsman and son of a noted portrait painter, was making headlines. Now, two Captains in the Royal Engineers, Chase, thirty-six, and Loftus Tottenham, thirty-four, were caught using their position of trust to usurp sexual favours from young boys.

A great blast from the ship's foghorn drew my attention, and I realised we were about to sail. However, the weather conditions were such that it was preferable to watch our departure through the smoking room window. As a result, on Mervyn's return, we took up our positions and eagerly waited for 'Orontes' to be underway.

***

"What a great ship," Mervyn said. "There's an open air swimming bath in the stern at the end of the deck, a massive ballroom, I've lost count of the number of bars, and I saw a huge dining room. Also, you won't believe it! Near the shop and the barbers, there's a door marked 'dark room'. What a great idea! You can develop your photos as you go along."

The veranda café was accessed through glazed doors at the far end of the smoking room, so we wandered to its rain slashed windows. Through them, we watched four, smoke billowing tugs, nudging the ship away from the dock, and then propel her out into the open river. Suddenly, Lewis our steward appeared beside us.

"Excuse me sir," he said, passing me a sealed envelope on a silver dish. "First Officer Petit Dann asked me to give you this sir."

"It's an invitation," I said, opening the envelope. "Captain Sullivan is inviting us to his table for dinner this evening. Thank you Lewis. Could you thank the first officer and say Mr Watson and Captain Fry would be delighted to accept."

"There you are Ron," laughed Mervyn. "Just shows where being a millionaire can get you. We'll be surrounded by all the Lords and Ladys. That's one way to find out who they are."

"Surely, I'm not the only millionaire on the ship. There must be some other reason for the invite."

Although it was mid-January, the southerly wind felt almost warm, causing a dank fog to fall once we reached the estuary, making it hardly worth a glance out of the windows. A thick grey pall immersed the ship, while the foghorn bellowed mournfully into the morass.

After lunch, most first class passengers moved to the lounge on B Deck to take either tea or early cocktails, Mervyn and I opting to play a game of rummy. All the while Mervyn was scrutinising the company, convincing me he was fast becoming a dreadful snob.

"According to the booklet," he said, as I won yet another hand. "There're one hundred and ninety seven in first class. Do you think they're all here?"

"I've no idea," I replied, shuffling the pack. "I imagine the oldies are taking a nap. And after that enormous lunch, I feel I might also do the same."

"Who do you think will dine with us tonight?"

"The upper echelons, I shouldn't wonder," I teased. "Captain Sullivan would have decided who's the most important amongst us."

As expected, Mervyn's reaction made me smile and confirmed my earlier suspicions.

Once we left the protection of the Thames Estuary, the fog dispersed. Entering the channel, beyond the North Foreland, RMS Orontes steered southwest into the Straights of Dover, a notorious stretch of water and predictably, here a powerful southerly wind whipped the sea into a frenzy, causing the ship to pitch wildly.

As we continued our game of cards, Mervyn and I noticed the number of people around us rapidly diminish. Almost certainly feeling ill, the men had either retired to their cabins, the ship's rail, or else the gentleman's lavatory, situated between the smoking room and the café. The unfortunate lady passengers are not provided for on B Deck. Therefore, it is necessary they take the stairs or the elevator down to C Deck, where amidships there is a large powder room and ladies' convenience.

"Those pills are working a treat," Mervyn said. "I feel absolutely fine."

The rough weather persisted throughout the remainder of the afternoon and into the evening, which made dressing for dinner quite hair raising. When we finally entered the dining saloon, it was practically empty.

"Step this way gentlemen," the headwaiter said, seeing us standing at the entrance. "The Captain will be with you shortly. Miss Plunkett Dillon, Monsieur de Fontarce, and the Bishop are already seated."

He led us to a splendidly laid, large round table in an alcove under a window, where crystal, silver, starched linen and floral decorations abounded.

"Good evening everyone," I said, once Mervyn and I had sat down. "My name's Captain Fry and this is my nephew, Mervyn Watson."

"How do you do Captain," said the young woman sitting beside Mervyn. "Miss Plunkett Dillon. How do you do Mr Watson. Are you both going far?"

"How do you do," Mervyn said, shooting me a glance, while shaking her hand. "Egypt."

"On business," I added. "Business first. Pleasure later."

Doreen smiled. "May I present Monsieur de Fontarce?"

"Maurice de Fontarce," said the young man sitting on her left. "Egypt, also."

"For the archaeology?" I asked.

"No Captain. My father has business in Cairo. He's asked me to see to something while he's away in Argentina."

By Mervyn's expression, it was clear he was already taken with the young man, since to describe Mr Fontarce, as bearing a strong resemblance to the bust of Antinous in the Paris Louvre, would be no exaggeration. His features were perfect, the same appealing mouth, arched eyebrows, and gracious nose. Seeing this Roman deity represented in the flesh and not in cold marble, I could perfectly understand why Emperor Hadrian became enamoured with him and mourned his loss so deeply. However, my aesthetic differed somewhat from Mervyn's, because I could literally see drool appearing at the corners of his mouth, derived no doubt, from something other than hunger.

Speaking of which, the headwaiter returned to our table with the news that Lord and Lady Castlemaine, Lord and Lady Butler and Lady Robb, had declined the Captain's invitation due to the weather conditions.

"Which leaves Mrs Casdagli," he said. "In addition, the Captain begs his pardon and implores you to begin without him."

"I completely understand," said the Bishop. "He must be terribly busy."

Due to our stunned and mesmerised state caused by the vision of Monsieur de Fontarce, Mervyn and I had completely forgotten the Bishop of Gibraltar sitting on the far side of the table.

"I do beg your pardon your eminence," I said. "How rude of us. Captain Fry and Mervyn Watson."

The headwaiter appeared again, this time with a slim elegant young woman, dressed exquisitely in the latest fashion and of vaguely eastern appearance.

"May I present Mrs Casdagli," he said

As she sat down beside Monsieur de Fontarce, Mrs Casdagli greeted him in French.

"Quel plaisir de vous revoir, Maurice."

"Pardon Eugene," he said. "Il serait etter si nous pillions en anglais."

"Of course. How silly of me," Mrs Casdagli said. "Are you in Egypt for the season?"

"Yes. But not of my own choice. Father wants to sell the island to fund more horses, and you know how he distrusts the Egyptians."

"Then you're there to see it go through without a hitch."

"Exactly. And yourself?"

"Emanuel sent for David and I. David's had such a dreadful cough. It's been so damp in Manchester. He's consulted his doctors in Cairo and they've said the little one should be in dry air. We're so worried. There's been such a lot of tuberculosis in northwest England."

"Will you stay at the Villa?" De Fontarce said, glancing at the menu.

"For a couple of days. Emanuel has a suite at the Cataract Hotel, so we'll be steaming to Aswan. I hope David and I might see you at Villa Casdagli before we go."

Sitting across the table from the couple, I could hardly ignore their conversation. In addition, the glances passing between them hinted at an association a little closer than just a chance shipboard encounter. My judgement of a woman's age is quite reliable. Therefore, I would put Mrs Casdagli at twenty-seven, since she also has a little boy. Moreover, since Maurice de Fontarce is older than Mervyn was by a couple of years, there would be seven years difference in his age and that of Mrs Casdagli. Sharing graceful aristocratic bearing, as well as stunning good looks, were she not already married, she and Maurice de Fontarce would make a striking couple.

Mervyn had struck up a rather one-sided exchange with Miss Plunkett Dillon, so it was up to the Bishop and I to begin a conversation. And typically, when one instinctively feels one has nothing in common with the other party, the primary subject invariably becomes the weather.

'It had been an unusually mild winter.' 'Precisely. Except Egypt can be cold this time of year.' 'It would be wise to take along an overcoat.' 'The desert can be a pleasant kind of climate.' 'Dry heat is always preferable to wet.' 'Recently, Gibraltar had its coldest day in ninety years.'

Mercifully, the waiter appeared and the subject changed to the menu.

The soup course was a choice between green pea and turtle, myself being the only person to choose the latter. Roast duckling with applesauce, boiled corned ox tongue, or roast prime rib of beef, comprised the meat course, served with broccoli hollandaise, string beans and mashed or boiled potatoes. The beef seemed to be the most popular, while the dessert was either fruit salad, Peach Melba, or Neapolitan ice cream. Mrs Casdagli and Fontarce decided on the Peach Melba, Miss Plunkett Dillon and the Bishop, the fruit, and Mervyn and I the ice cream.

Soup was a hazardous affair, as the ship refused to abandon its erratic motion. However, we amused each other as we endeavoured to find solutions to keep the soup inside the bowl, or on the spoon. As the ribs of beef arrived, so did Captain Sullivan.

"I'm terribly sorry," he said, quickly sitting down beside the Bishop. "I've been preoccupied as you can imagine. The channel is the busiest waterway in the world. Even busier than the Suez Canal. In this weather, who knows what's around and about?"

"At least the fog's lifted," said Miss Plunkett Dillon. "That dreadful foghorn fills me with the shivers."

"Will there be much more of this Captain?" I asked, as my soup bowl decided to set a course towards him.

"We expect not Captain Fry. My radio officer contacted the Lafayette. She's due at Plymouth tomorrow from New York. Her man reports the weather's clear over Biscay."

"That's a relief to say the least," said the Bishop.

The Lafayette's radioman was correct, so even as we brushed our teeth and folded back the sheets and blankets on our beds, the storm outside abated. And with the light from the lighthouse on the island of Ouessant piercing the cabin window, Mervyn and I looked forward to a peaceful night's sleep.

Chapter Two
Gibraltar - Toulon - Lewis' story

For the following three days, we enjoyed perfect weather, with clear bright days and calm seas, the temperature climbing gradually as we cruised the coast of France, Portugal and Spain.

At Gibraltar, Mervyn and I said goodbye to our friend the Bishop, who in fact proved to be quite a card, as well as an excellent chess partner for Mervyn.

As you might remember, I visited Gibraltar on my way to India with the Prince Albert's. So, while RMS Orontes' decks swarmed with dark skinned, voluble gesticulating men, selling tobacco, cigars, Florida water, Spanish lace, fans, and fruit, I took Mervyn on a brief sightseeing tour of the Rock. He was particularly keen to see the Barbary Apes that inhabit the upper reaches. Also, he enjoyed the gun galleries, burrowed out of solid limestone, with openings wide enough to take a powerful gun, as well as commanding a magnificent view all the way across the straights to North Africa.

Remembering the Alameda Gardens and their attractions, I took Mervyn on a wire rope elevator, leaving behind the repair shops, coal supplies and victualling yards of the Dockyard. Once we reached the interior, I showed him the bust of General Elliot, the defender of the Rock during the Great Siege, as well as a statue of the Duke of Wellington, defended by several cast iron cannons. Here too we encountered the other side of life on the Rock, since we became aware of shadowy figures lurking in the sub-tropical shrubbery.

After lunch at the Rock Hotel, we returned to the ship, which later raised her anchor. Leaving Gibraltar Harbour, we were treated to a splendid view of the British war fleet at anchor. Then, passing the Europa Point Lighthouse, we eventually entered the Balearic Sea.

The Spanish coast slipped by while we took tea in the veranda café, Mervyn and I sighting the soaring snow-capped Sierra Nevada, including its white towns nestling in the valleys and along the coast. On one occasion, the ship encountered a fleet of Spanish fishing boats, their swallow winged sails bulging in the stiff breeze.

SS Saturnia, the ship that transported my unit of the 4th Somerset Light Infantry to India, had called for coal at Marseilles and not Toulon, so all I ever saw of the great port were its distant lights. Therefore, I was keen to see this so called 'Jewel of the Mediterranean'. Hence, during dinner, the evening before our arrival, Miss Plunkett Dillon, Mrs Casdagli, Maurice de Fontarce, Mervyn and I, arranged to take a shore excursion.

At around nine o'clock the following morning, the ship dropped anchor, and after waiting in the smoking room to collect our passports, our party proceeded to the after gangway on E Deck, where the quarter to ten tender waited to take us ashore.

"Did you see the notice board at the top of the gangway?" Mervyn said, as we settled into our seats. "The last tender from the quay is at midnight, which means we can see the sights, have a meal, and maybe do a nightclub."

"It doesn't say anything about nightclubs here," I said, referring to the Orient Line booklet. "I wouldn't know where to find one."

"Come on Ron. From what you told me back in London. It strikes me you could smell out a queer bar in a thunderstorm."

"Should I take that as a compliment?" I answered. "Very well. We'll see how the day progresses."

After weaving our way between gigantic French warships bristling with guns, our tender finally dropped us at Quai Cronstadt where, by the overpowering odour of garlic, we immediately recognised we were in France. Beyond the quay is The Old Town, which is dominated by lofty crumbling warehouses, where decaying, rust laden pulleys, as well as other lifting apparatus jut from the walls and above large shuttered openings. Here, the busy trade of an important French port occurs, and by appearances, things had not changed for many centuries. At Maurice de Fontarce's suggestion, we split up. He and Mrs Casdagli said they wished to search of a good cup of coffee. Nonetheless, I was reluctant to see Miss Plunkett Dillon walking the back streets alone, so suggested she join Mervyn and I on our exploration.

We said our goodbyes and ducked into the labyrinth of narrow side streets, which, like rustic ravines, border the quay. It struck us that almost all the houses possessed a shop at ground level. Boulangeries, butcheries, charcuteries, confiseries and fromageries, whose smell in particular we found both intoxicating and evocative. Looking up at the houses, and at the tiers of windows, we saw most had balconies and pretty iron balcony rails, some displaying colourful geraniums, a rarity for English people to see in January. Yet, it hardly felt like January, since the midday sun was penetrating the narrow walkways, warming us at every turn

Peeling wooden shutters, closed over some windows, while others were open, allowing us to see strings of washing hanging on makeshift washing lines. In addition, here and there, across the streets and dangling at random, large black lamps swayed in what little breeze permeated the boundaries of the lanes.

Since it was Friday, these narrow thoroughfares thronged with people purchasing provisions. Occasionally, Miss Plunkett Dillon, Mervyn, and I would stumble upon a small, quiet square, at its centre an ancient fountain, the echo of gently trickling water resounding off the adjoining houses. In the corner of one square, we came upon a tiny café, where, to our surprise, we saw Mrs Casdagli and De Fontarce, sitting at an outside table. They were holding hands and completely unaware of everything around them. We chose not to make ourselves known. After a while, and the further from the quay we went, a significant change in the architecture began to occur, as we entered the Upper Town, being the creation of Baron Haussman, civic planner and responsible for remodelling the centre of Paris. As in the French capital city, here in Toulon, the boulevards are wide and lined with trees, as well as the decorative facades of apartment buildings.

The Opera House was easy to find, which our booklets said was opened in 1862, thirteen years before the Paris Opera. The group of sculptured figures on the top, and the arched portico and pink marble columns, I thought most impressive.

Next on the itinerary was La Place de la Liberte, and we happened upon it easily by following the Boulevard de Strasbourg, which crosses the square on its southern side. Not as large as the Place de la Concorde in Paris, nonetheless it is striking in comparison, with imposing buildings on all four sides. Plus a magnificent fountain at its heart, dominated by a statue of Liberty holding a flaming torch. Miss Plunkett Dillon suggested we search for the Cathedral of Sainte Marie, since she said it was eight hundred years old and therefore the oldest building in Toulon. It was necessary we return to the old town, where we found it snuggled amongst the canyons of houses, the ornamental frontage looking incongruous beside the plain faces of its neighbours.

The interior was equally staggering. The nave appeared Gothic, with crystal chandeliers hanging from each transept arch. A delightful rose window above the altar was ablaze with coloured glass. With a retable in a side chapel, a homage to everything Baroque, displaying a towering group of sculpted angels, archangels, and prophets, surmounted by God himself.

A mass was being said, so Mervyn and I quickly saw as much as we could, while Miss Plunkett Dillon lit a candle. At this point, we decided to stop for lunch, discovering a quiet café in one of the nearby streets. Sitting at an outside table, resting our weary feet, we waited for a garcon to bring the menu. Our lunch began with feuillete, a small savoury pastry stuffed with a mixture of ham, and mushrooms. This was followed by petit quiches filled with a cheesy egg mixture of bacon and vegetables. Next came Croque Madame. Cheese again, topped with a fried egg. Then Steak Tartare, a combination of lean raw steak, onions, herbs, and the yolk of an egg. Thus sustained by this culinary romance we continue our excursion.

Miss Plunkett Dillon decided she was tired and chose to return to the quay to wait for the tender, and naturally, Mervyn and I accompanied her to ensure she reached it safely.

Once Miss Plunkett Dillon had embarked without harm, Mervyn and I turned towards the quay and the many shops crowded there. One was particularly interesting since it specialised in colourful coral, shells, and sponges. Also, there were postcards to purchase.

By my watch, it was almost four o'clock, so I suggested we find a bar. Subsequently, as we wandered back along the quay we came upon a large bronze statue, representing a naked young man, pointing out to sea; standing beside an anchor, holding a rudder, his appendage regrettably hidden by a scanty piece of fabric. Apparently, the statue is called 'The Genius of Navigation', and a location for local men to congregate. This was obvious by the number leaning on the railings surrounding the base, everyone talking, smoking, or reading newspapers. It intrigued me to see that most were young French sailors, wearing blue berets, with the characteristic red pompom, white and blue vests and white uniforms, including exceptionally tight bell-bottom trousers.

Mervyn and I sat down on a bench in order to watch this captivating parade.

"It looks like they're coming and going from that café over there," said Mervyn.

He was pointing beyond the statue to a wide, open façade, where beneath a red canvas awning, men, and women sat at tables, smoking, and drinking.

"How about we take a look."

It was cool and dark inside the café and reeked of strong tobacco, a heavy pall of smoke filling the cavernous depths. Mervyn and I stood in the doorway uncertain whether to venture further. Nevertheless, the vision of dozens of sailors, leaning or sitting at the bar, overcame our trepidation. The men were drinking either cognac, Pernod, or simply wine and were animated and gesticulating, as do the French. Whatever they were consuming, everyone from man to youth were smoking cigarettes. Of course, I was aware of the brand from drinking occasionally in the French Bar in Dean Street Soho. They are called Gauloises, made from a combination of Syrian and

Turkish tobacco, and are the strongest cigarettes in the world. During the war, French soldiers smoked Gauloises in the trenches, and nowadays every Frenchman considers it patriotic to do the same.

While we searched around for a table, Mervyn suddenly nudged me.

"Look who's over there!" he shouted, over the babble of incomprehensible conversation.

"Goodness!" I exclaimed. "Lewis! Our steward. Well I never!"

"Shall we make ourselves known?"

"We'll have to. He's seen us."

Sitting at a table near the door, Lewis waved to us sheepishly. Personally, I would rather have found a table of our own, but Mervyn made a beeline towards him, so I was forced to follow. By no means am I a snob. But there must be some kind of status quo when one is travelling at sea, or any kind of conveyance for that matter. I believe it is hardly appropriate to dine with the waiter who served you, or drink with the bus conductor who clipped your ticket. It is necessary for people who serve to keep their place. By the look on Lewis' face as we approached, I believe he felt the same. Though unfortunately, Mervyn, being the working class lad that he is, did not see things the same way.

Because we had chosen to sit at a table, and not stand at the bar, it was the French way that we be waited upon, and therefore required to tip the waiter.

Mervyn and I sat down opposite Lewis and for the first time I noticed how severely his nose was twisted, also the scars around his eyes, causing me to wonder how he was able to keep the position of a first class steward.

Although we smiled and nodded at each other, there was an awkward silence, with each of us unable to begin a conversation. Even so, since Mervyn created the situation, I let him be the first to speak.

"Would you like another Lewis? Was it a beer?"

"Thank you Mr Watson," Lewis answered. "Kronenberg please."

Mervyn signalled a waiter, and we waited while he languidly approached our table.

"How about you Ron? What's your poison?"

"I'll join Lewis."

"Then so will I. Three Kronenbergs garcon," Mervyn said to the waiter, who flared his nostrils and walked away.

"Have you been with the Orient Line for long Lewis?" I asked.

"Seven years Captain Fry. I was seventeen when I joined as a galley boy in 1930."

"You've done a bit of boxing in your time I see," Mervyn said, in his usual ingenuous manner.

"You mean this?" Lewis said, laughing and touching his nose. "No Mr Watson. Two blokes did this. We were in the back of a taxi. They beat me up and stole my money."

"I hope they were justly punished," I put in, immediately realising how pompous I sounded.

"Yes Captain. The cabbie identified one, but the other got away."

Suddenly, the Kronenbergs arrived, three towering glasses of topaz liquid, topped with a thick layer of froth. Silently, we drank the first mouthful, feeling the tang of bitter beer in our throats.

"Then the case went to court?" I said.

"It did Captain. Even made the papers. They said I was drunk and didn't remember a thing. But I wasn't that pie eyed. I knew if I made out I was, then the men would take the whole lot."

"What happened?" Mervyn asked, offering Lewis a cigarette.

"Thanks. Don't mind if I do."

Lighting Lewis' cigarette with my lighter, I lit Mervyn's, then my own.

"You're men of the world," Lewis said, a little too informally for my liking. "I've a notion you'd be a sympathetic ear. Because my sixth sense never lets me down."

What Lewis was driving at I could hardly guess. Might Mervyn and I be about to hear some kind of confession?

"We'd been cruising in Norway for three weeks and just arrived back in Tilbury. They'd paid us off and I had twenty-five quid in my wallet. My pal on the ship was a radio operator and once we birthed, he went home to Kent to see his mother, but with only a couple of days turn around, it was pointless me going all the way to Cardiff. So

I stayed on the ship feeling lonely, as you do when your pal's not around."

At this point, Lewis paused to take a drink, clearly allowing Mervyn and myself time to take in his words, as well as their obvious inference.

"It was so quiet on the ship that one afternoon I took the train to Fenchurch Street and jumped on the Piccadilly Line."

Lewis had lowered his voice, making it necessary for Mervyn and me to lean towards him in order to hear. In the process, we glanced at each other and Mervyn winked at me.

"When I was first up from Wales," Lewis continued. "Some bloke took me to a pub in Knightsbridge opposite Hyde Park, and with the barracks just across the road there were always heaps of guardsmen. It was a gay old place."

Although I had a sneaking suspicion where the story was leading, I began feeling rather embarrassed by Lewis' sudden frankness, induced no doubt by Kronenbergs imbibed before our arrival.

"In those days," Lewis went on. "I was young and timid, and daren't say boo to a goose. But the fellow who took me to the pub introduced me to a captain in the Life Guards, and ever after, I'd telephone when I was in London and we'd meet at his flat in Albert Hall Mansions. We became great pals."

"How exciting," Mervyn added. "Sounds like you were quid's in."

"You'd have thought so wouldn't you? But no. Three months at sea is no good for such friendships. The captain took up with another friend and lost interest in me. Anyway, that's by the by. Whenever in London, The Paxton's Head became my local, so of course, that's where I headed that night. It was early and quiet, so I got myself a pint and perched on a stool at the bar. A couple of blokes were sitting in the corner and I could feel them staring at me. I knew their game. I was nineteen, but no bloody fool. They were rough types. Looked like labourers, just off the job."

Rapidly, I was becoming rather uncomfortable listening to this young man's guilelessness. After all, he was our steward. I wondered how he had gotten the idea we were interested in his escapades, despite the fact that we were.

"I tried to ignore them," Lewis continued. "But the pub was empty, so there was nothing to take my attention. The next minute, one of them was beside me, asking if he could buy me a drink."

"Did you say yes?" said Mervyn keenly.

"I said no. But he was insistent."

'Two pints of Trumans,' the bloke said to the publican. 'And one for the lad here.'

'Why not join us,' he said. 'My mate reckons he knows you.'

"That old trick. We all knew what was going on. Even Bert behind the bar. He's been the publican for years. I sat down with the blokes, and the one who'd bought me the drink told me he was Jack. I never knew the other bloke's name. They said they were working on the underground extension at Paddington, and I said I was a steward on RMS Orontes. At one point, I took out my wallet to buy a round of drinks, which was a big mistake. There was nearly twenty-five quid in it. I should have left it with the purser, but you don't think do you. Hey! You don't mind me telling you this, do you? You're the first gentlemen, I feel I can trust and would understand. I've never been able to tell ma and pa. I told them I got my nose broken larking around."

To Lewis, the disguise of normality and conventionality Mervyn and I created, guarding so carefully, was invisible to him. Clearly, there is an unseen energy between men like us, a glance, a turn of the head, a word. It happens in a moment. But is enough to establish we are like-minded and share kindred spirits.

"Drinks flowed," Lewis, continued, "I must admit I was getting drunk. But the blokes seemed all right. I was young. Their years of drinking, maybe ten ahead of me, had hardened their resistance to alcohol. A few times, one or the other would visit the gent's and ask me why I didn't want a Jimmy Riddle? I was clever and said I was all right. After a while, the bloke whose name was Jack suggested we go for a walk."

'It's a lovely evening,' he said. 'It might clear our heads.'

"Like the silly bugger I was I went along with it. As we crossed the road, I could barely see the park on the other side. It was then I realised there'd been something else in the last drink they bought me."

'Hey!' said the one whose name I didn't know, 'I'm bursting for a piddle. There's a lav over there.' 'Me too,' Jack said, 'Come on lad.'

"I must admit, I was desperate by this time and was forced to follow them to a lavatory, half-hidden in a clump of bushes. Eventually, all three of us were standing at the urinal."

At this point, I was becoming so uneasy listening to Lewis' story I almost made an excuse to relieve myself. But it was impossible to see where the lavatory was through the crowd of sailors. As a result, I controlled my desire.

Once more, I was astounded by the candid way the younger generation speak of such activities. In my day, one never breathed a word about such events. They were private memories, laden with a perplexing mixture of guilt, touched with a twinge of excitement. Mervyn of course was captivated by what might happen next, eagerly oblivious, and caring little that, in a few hours, Lewis might be turning down our beds, serving us breakfast, or replenishing the soap and towels in our bathroom.

In my distracted moment searching for the gents, I must have neglected to notice Mervyn signal the waiter, because further glasses of beer appeared on the table. Heaven knows how many Lewis must have consumed by this time, as he was clearly showing the effects.

"As I emptied my bladder," Lewis continued. "I could see out of the corner of my eye, the two of them waving their gear at me."

Mervyn snorted, and began to snigger.

"I'm sorry Captain," Lewis said, seeing my stern expression.

"No Lewis," I said. "Please continue. I'm intrigued to discover what happened."

"If you're sure. Anyway, just then, a couple of blokes came into the lav, and stood each side of us. Who knows! They might have been coppers for all I knew, but they got their 'what sits' out all the same."

'Come on lad,' Jack says. 'It's getting dark. This is no place for you. You're a bit the worse for wear, my lad. Me and his nibs will see you home.'

"They bundled me outside and frog marched me to the gate,

where they hailed a taxi. I sat between them in the cab, all the while feeling I was about to be sick. As we headed towards Piccadilly, the nameless one undid my flies, while Jack reached inside my jacket and began to tickle me. I tried to holler, but the bloke feeling me up, put his hand over my mouth. At one point, I remember looking out of the window, seeing the crowds in Piccadilly Circus, and Eros shining in the lights from the Troc. I don't remember anything after that, until I came too in St Thomas Hospital. A detective told me I'd been assaulted. He said, the cabbie had let two men off in Regent Street and switched on his light to ask me where I wanted to go. It was then he saw I'd been beaten up and got me to hospital. It seems I was able to tell him that I'd been robbed. A detective asked me lots of questions, but I only told him what I thought he needed to know."

"How exciting," Mervyn gasped. "Oh! I'm sorry Lewis. Not very nice for you. Were you badly hurt?"

"Pretty much. Two black eyes. A broken nose in two places and a fractured jaw. I was in St Thomas' for a fortnight. As soon as I was able, I went back to Cardiff, but I didn't go back on the ship until three months later."

"And you explained to your mother and father all that was caused from larking about," I said.

"I did Captain. And thankfully they believed me."

"Did the police catch the men?" asked Mervyn.

"They did Mr Watson, thanks to the cabby. The man calling himself Jack was John Bousfield. He got eighteen months and twelve strokes of the cat, also the judge gave a reward to the two cabbies who helped bring him to justice."

"But you never saw your money."

"Ten quid of it. The two fivers the coppers found on Bousfield. I reckon the other bloke got the rest. The bastard! If you'll excuse my French, Captain."

"The Orient Line was good to give you your job back," I said.

"I think I'm popular sir. The paymaster's a special friend of mine."

Mervyn and I laughed. It was a good story, and well worth the telling, even if a little close to the mark. We drank the last mouthfuls of Kronenberg and prepared to pay at the desk.

"I've to be back at the ship by five," Lewis said. "But I dare say you'll be wanting to see more of Toulon."

"Is there anything else?" I asked, as we pushed our way to the bar.

"You can't leave Toulon without visiting 'The Dancing Dubois'. It's right up your street, if you know what I mean."

"Dancing Dubois! Who's that?" asked Mervyn.

"Not who's that? But what's that? Les Dancing Dubois is a cabaret. Friday's the big night. You shouldn't miss it."

"Come on Ron," begged Mervyn. "It's exactly what I suggested this morning. The last tender leaves the quay at midnight. That gives us plenty of time. Please!"

"Where do we find this Dancing Dubois, Lewis?" I asked rather reluctantly.

"Number eight, Rue de Lorques. Just ring the bottom bell."

"Would you be able to show us it on our map?" asked Mervyn, taking it out of his pocket, and unfolding it.

"Just there," Lewis said, pointing to the labyrinth of laneways between the quay and the Boulevard de Strasbourg.

It all sounded rather clandestine, but how could I refuse, after all, Mervyn and I were supposed to be enjoying a holiday, as well as rescuing his brother Harry. As a result, we said goodbye to Lewis, and sauntered into the old town to see what else we might discover.

Chapter Three
Poularde, bisque and lapin - Les Dancing Dubois

Passing an impressive café further along the quayside, I suggested we might have a bite to eat. After all, it was nearly five o'clock, and it promised to be a long and possibly an eventful evening. The afternoon was balmy, accompanied by the smell of baked bread, the ever-present odour of garlic, also bacon, or some other kind of smoked meat.

A sad tune was playing on a gramophone as we entered the café. A woman singing about lost love no doubt, a common theme in French songs. Almost immediately a waiter was on hand to show us to a table, where we had not only a view of the quay and the harbour, but also the exotic array of passers-by. Toulon really surprised me that day. Up until then I had no idea it was so cosmopolitan and enlightened. In fact, I felt a sense of liberation I had never before experienced.

"Messieurs. Bonjour," the waiter said, putting a bottle of water and two glasses on our table. "Welcom au, Café Baroque. Voulez-vous prendre soin d'un aperitif?"

"No thank you garcon," I said, the last word giving me a clue as to his question. "We are already a little too full of beer."

"Tres bien. Je vous apporterai le menu."

"Yes please. But tell us. The song on the gramophone. Who's the singer?"

"Piaf Monsieur. Edith Piaf."

Mervyn shrugged, and I had to admit I had never heard of the woman. All the same, as the waiter walked away, we sat back, lit cigarettes, and listened.

"Do you know Mervyn," I said. "I believe you and I could live here quite freely without the dread of being discovered or put in prison. Being the way we are seems hardly important here. Even in the few hours we've been ashore, I've seen men obviously like us, bravely walking together with no embarrassment."

"Not only men," Mervyn agreed. "Did you see those two lads a few seconds ago, walking so close their hands were touching?"

The menu arrived and we delved into its complexity like a couple of intrepid explorers.

"I understand that," Mervyn said, pointing to the entrées. "Half a dozen oysters. But what's Bisque et Marmite?"

"I believe bisque is soup made from stock derived from shrimps. But as for marmite. I thought that's what we have on toast or in a sandwich. My scouts love it."

"Sole Marquery," Mervyn said. "That's easy. I can see what that is too. Except, the marquery's a bit doubtful. I've no idea what the Selle Lapin avec Cepes et Tomates. Something with tomatoes. Why don't they have it in English?"

"Because we're in France," I laughed. "The French are very particular. They expect everyone to know their language and tough luck if they don't. Poulet are young chickens, I think. That's the meat course."

"Pullets! That's right. And Pate de Fois Gras we had on the Viceroy. But not the 'en gelee' bit."

"Don't you remember? It comes with jelly around it. There are asparagus tips with butter, and for dessert waffles, cheese, fruit, ice cream, and wafers. What'll we have?"

Before we could decide, we were distracted by the arrival of a woman and an elderly gentleman at an adjoining table, and watched as the waiter held the chair for the woman to sit down, while the gentleman seated himself. They nodded in our direction and we did the same in kind. The waiter gave the couple a bottle of water, glasses, and the menu. Then returned to our table to take our order.

"I'll have the bisque," I said, snatching something from off the top of my head. "Although, what is marmite may I ask?"

"Marmite, Monsieur, is a cooking pot."

"Ah! I see," I said, still quite confused. "Very well. Yes. I'd like the bisque and the poularde."

"What's Selle Lapin, please?" interrupted Mervyn.

"Saddle of rabbit Monsieur. Served with capers and tomatoes."

"Can I have oysters Ron?"

"Of course."

"And the rabbit sounds nice."

"Then have it."

"I'll have oysters please garcon," Mervyn said. "And the Lapin. Thank you."

In the ensuing silence, we heard the repeated clicks of a cigarette lighter, and noticed the gentleman at the next table was having difficulties lighting his cigarette.

"If I may." I said, leaning across and offering him mine.

"Obliged sir," he said. "Damn thing's given me trouble since it got wet at Tilbury."

"Indeed. Dreadful weather when we left wasn't it. May I introduce myself? Captain Fry. And this is my nephew, Mervyn Watson."

"Pleased to make your acquaintance," the old man said. "My wife. Lady Castlemaine."

She nodded graciously.

"Lord Castlemaine," he said, gently touching his gold tiepin. "You're on the Orontes?"

"Just as far as Port Said. Yourselves?"

"Port Said. Cairo. Then Khartoum. My wife seems to think the Nile will do me good. I've other ideas. Damn flies and mosquitoes."

"I'm sorry," I said. "Are you unwell?"

"The doctors seem to think so."

"They've prescribed complete rest Captain Fry," interjected Lady Castlemaine. "A month on the Nile will be just the ticket. The air you know. It's so beneficial."

Our conversation was temporarily interrupted as the waiter arrived at the table to take Lord and Lady Castlemaine's order.

"What do you know about them?" whispered Mervyn.

"They're the old Irish aristocracy. He's older than she is. Inherited the title just after I was born. A few years ago his younger brother was up in court charged for manslaughter, since he killed his wife in a motoring accident."

My bisque and Mervyn's oysters arrived, so the peerage lesson was curtailed while we savoured the delicious fresh flavours of the various dishes.

"How far up the Nile will we go?" asked Mervyn, squeezing lemon on the shiny grey contents of six huge oyster shells.

"Probably just to Luxor or Aswan," I said. "We won't really have time to go further. The Nile's over four thousand miles long. It's the longest river in the world."

"What's at Luxor?

"The temples of Luxor and Karnak on the east bank. The Valley of the Kings and the Colossi of Memnon on the west. We'll stay at the Winter Palace Hotel."

"Will we catch a steamer?"

"There's a choice. Either steamer or train. The road's not very comfortable."

"Train! Let's go by train."

As always, amongst the British when abroad, conversation became minimal while we consumed the unfamiliar dishes and tasted strange, as yet, untried flavours.

"It would be nice if you were able to introduce me as your friend rather than your nephew," said Mervyn, taking me off guard.

"I'm sorry. It was Eric who put the bee in my bonnet," I replied. "He set me worrying how people would regard a middle aged man and a youth, travelling together."

"Just as it is most likely. Most folk in England haven't a clue we exist. It's only the likes of psychiatrists and the police who know we're around."

"That's pretty astute. I can see you're beginning to have an opinion of your own. My influence must be rubbing off."

"Of course. That's what it's all about isn't it? The benefit of the more mature intellect effecting the juvenile mind."

"That's what Plato says. My word!" I exclaimed. "Is this the lad from Swinbourne's Buildings sitting across the table?"

"It's been two years. You must have had some effect."

Perhaps these sensible words reassured me, since, from that moment on, I promised to refrain from introducing Mervyn as my nephew.

By the time we finished our meal, it was seven o'clock and almost dark, the lights of the French fleet at anchor reflected in the harbour, resembling a million fireflies dancing on the water.

"What was the address?" I asked, once I had paid the bill.

"Eight, Rue de Lorques," Mervyn answered. "The map says it's towards the upper town. Near the Cathedral."

Ever since Roman times, the streets of old Toulon have retained a grid pattern typical of those days. So, by taking a zigzag route, we found Rue de Lorques quite easily. As in most cities all around the world, Friday evening is always the busiest, with everyone wishing to celebrate the end of the working week. This was equally so in Toulon, since the streets thronged with young people, eagerly anticipating a meal and a night on the town. Mervyn and I acquiesced this mood, buoyed along by a wave of high spirits, until we came down to earth on the doorstep of, 'Les Dancing Dubois'. We knew it to be so by the illuminated sign above the darkened doorway. Tentatively, I put my finger on the doorbell and pushed the button.

We waited, vaguely aware of the faint sound of a sad accordion coming from somewhere close by. Then suddenly a set of bolts shot back and the door slowly opened.

"Qui vous envoie?" A woman said gruffly, her painted face filling the gap between the door and the doorframe.

When in Egypt during the war I picked up a little French, mostly at the Kit Kat Club and the restaurants. As a result, I hoped I had understood her.

"Lewis," I replied.

"Lewis! Der schone mann," she said, suddenly switching into German. "Come in bitte. Ich bin Mimi. English ya?"

She seemed to understand English perfectly, but clearly wished to speak in another language.

"Pleased to meet you Mimi. Yes. Lewis told us about 'Les Dancing Dubois'. He said it mustn't be missed."

"Dann hat er Recht. Lewis kennt uns gut. Er ist hier drei oder vier Mal im Jahr."

Sometimes, I find it strange that, although a person speaks a foreign language, the odd word here and there can convey the entire meaning of the phrase. Here was a case in point, because it was only necessary to hear the words, jahr, drie, and vier to understand that Lewis was a frequent visitor to the club several times a year. Her last question was obvious.

"Warum ist er nicht bei dir?"

"He couldn't," I answered. "He had to return to the ship. We sail at midnight."

As Mimi led us down a narrow passage, lit only by a guttering gaslight, there was an odour of stale sweat that one rarely encounters exuding from a female. This, plus the broadness of her shoulders, confirmed to me that, in truth, Mimi was a he rather than a she. I wondered if Mervyn held the same opinion.

"Watch how you go ducky," said Mimi, as she led us down a steep staircase and suddenly switching to perfect English.

While the whining accordion grew louder at every step, I was aware that Mervyn was close behind me because, time and again, he coughed, a sure sign he was nervous. I must admit to feeling a little the same, especially when we reached the bottom of the stairs and faced a sparkling, glass bead curtain, hanging across an open doorway. Suddenly memories of the Caravan Club in Covent Garden came flooding back and I felt my heart flutter with excitement and anticipation.

As Mimi pushed the curtain apart and beckoned us inside, a heavy aroma of strong tobacco smoke, brandy and human sweat, suddenly overwhelmed us

"It's so exotic," whispered Mervyn. "This is amazing."

Naturally, I had to agree, since we were standing in a cellar, perhaps fifty foot long by twenty feet wide. A cavern of a place, entirely painted black from the floor to the dark beamed ceiling.

Candlelight from maybe a dozen night-lights, flickered on tables ranged either side of a red carpet running down the centre, the tables cloaked in red and white check tablecloths.

In the half-light, young men sat talking and laughing, smoking and drinking, the majority wearing naval uniforms, a few close to us obviously Germans, noticeable by the style of their caps. French sailors predominated, wearing the typical dark blue jackets, striped open necked shirts, and blue caps with red pom-poms.

"Asseyez-vous s'il vous plait," prompted our hostess. "Ze cabaret vill begin in fifteen minutes. Schoo Schoo will get your drinks."

Out of the darkness appeared a young girl, or should I say youth, dressed in nothing but a tight black lace corset, a slash of ruby lipstick around his mouth, his eyebrows plucked within an inch of their lives.

"Follow me," the young man said in an accent roughly discernible as Eastern European.

Doing so, we wound through the sea of tables and sailors, until our guide gestured limply towards two empty seats at a table already occupied by four Frenchmen. At this point, may I say in all honesty, that the Gallic good looks of our table companions rendered me speechless to such a degree it required a nudge from Mervyn to alert me that Schoo Schoo was poised to take our order.

"What should we drink Mervyn?" I asked.

"Beer seems the thing," he said, looking at the tables around us.

"I don't think I've room for beer."

"Have a scotch."

"I'll have one beer please," I said to Schoo Schoo, who gave me a withering smile.

"A beer, and a single whiskey," I said, slowly and deliberately.

"Ve av no viskey. You av brandy?"

"Very well. One beer. And a brandy."

While we waited for Schoo Schoo's return, we lit cigarettes and glanced around, taking in the atmosphere, as well as marvelling at the attractiveness of our drinking companions. They were a crowd of the most handsome men I had ever seen, and evidently like-minded by the way they associated with each other. By his expression, as he leaned across the table in order to be heard over the babble of animated conversation, clearly Mervyn thought the same

"Most have black moustaches," he shouted. "How do you think mine compares?"

"A little more luxuriant than yours?" I said, laughing. "Yours is fair and makes you look like a totter."

Evidently, my whimsical reply had gone unheard, because Mervyn smiled and leaned closer, however drew back, as Schoo Schoo returned with our drinks.

"You know last summer you took me to the art gallery!" he shouted, once I had given Schoo Schoo a few Francs.

"Yes. The Burlington? The Surrealist exhibition?"

"Remember the artist we liked whose pictures were full of sailors, prostitutes, and Negroes?"

"His name's Burra. Edward Burra."

"This place reminds me of one of his paintings."

"Not surprising. Because the catalogue said Burra drew his subjects from Harlem in New York, also the bars of Toulon."

Just then, a light appeared at the end of the room, and I realised, what I previously imagined to be a wall was in fact a pair of black curtains. At the same moment, as the crowd grew quiet, red light from a dozen footlights at the front of the stage began to glow. While at the rear of the stage, a small group of musicians appeared and began to play a woeful tune, which Mervyn and I immediately recognised.

"It's the song we heard earlier," whispered Mervyn.

Saxophones played several chords of the melody, and a bugle, blowing a theme, something akin to a reveille, quickly joined these. Next, a voice joined the instruments, unattached, as if coming from thin air. A woman was singing, or rather speaking, her quivering voice emphasising the letter R whenever it appeared in the song. Then came a chorus, and as if by magic and previously hidden amongst the musicians, the owner of the voice appeared and approached the footlights. She, or rather he, was barely eighteen.

A handsome youth, dressed in an elaborate, gold and lapis patterned headdress, the kind an Egyptian Pharaoh might wear, and the motif on the headdress appearing on his outfit, resembling a man's swimming costume. A scarf wrapped around his chest and knotted in the middle, discreetly covering his nipples, completed this outlandish ensemble. His pouting ruby lips and sultry eyes, covered in thick black makeup, apparently represented him as female, except the youth was strapping and well built. In addition, judging by the cheers and whistles from the throng of young sailors, the youth possessed tremendous appeal.

After another verse there was a further chorus, which everyone sung, except Mervyn and I, because neither of us had an inkling as to what she might be singing about, although the mention of, 'Mon Legionnaire', may have given us a clue.

"It's not her singing," Mervyn said. "She's making out by mouthing the words to a record. It's the same voice we heard in the café."

"Do you think so?" I said. "I was only thinking how good he was. If it is her, then he's a very good interpreter."

As the last verse concluded, abruptly, the stage was filled with a horde of boys dressed as Foreign Legionnaires, although they had forgotten to put on their jackets, only wearing khaki jodhpurs, brown leather boots, and the typical legionnaire's hat. The sight of the half-naked young men brought an enormous cheer from the audience. Furthermore, as the band increased the tempo, the young men formed a line across the stage, threw down their hats, and goose-stepped towards the footlights, causing a standing ovation from the crowd. I wondered whether Mimi, our German hostess, had anything to do with the choreography.

Clapping and singing in a language all his own, Mervyn was in another world and having a splendid time. Nonetheless, his reverie turned to frenzy as each lad, having arrived at the footlights, sat on the edge of the stage and began to undo his bootlaces.

"I don't believe it!" he yelled. "They're not, are they?"

"I think so!" I shouted.

With their boots now on the floor, when the jodhpurs came off the whole gathering cheered, stamped and whistled, the reason being the lads were entirely naked, something that took me completely by surprise. Sadly, there was little time to appreciate the tableaux, since the stage was suddenly plunged into darkness and the show was over.

"We'd better get moving," I said, looking at my watch.

"Really!" whined Mervyn. "Do we have to? I bet there'll be another show in half an hour. Everyone's buying more drinks."

"It's almost nine o'clock. It's been an incredible day, and I'm tired. I'd like a drink when we get back to the ship, and the smoking room closes at eleven."

Reluctantly, Mervyn conceded, and after going to the bar to thank Mimi for a delightful evening, we climbed the stairs and stepped into the night. Even so, the evening was not quite over, as I was keen to keep a memory of our extraordinary time at 'Les Dancing Dubois'. So, arriving at the quay, I purposely sort out Café Baroque, where we dined earlier. As it so happened, our waiter was still on duty and he welcomed us as we entered.

"Bonsoir Monsieur,"

"Good evening once again garcon," I said. "I wonder if you might help us. The shops are now closed, which is a pity because I would like to have purchased the record you were playing this evening. As we sail tonight and will not have another opportunity, perhaps you might sell it to me."

"Certainemant Monsieur," the waiter said smiling. "It's my pleasure. You like Piaf yes? I will get it for you."

He returned, holding the gramophone record, sliding it into its paper sleeve.

"You may have it Monsieur. A present from Toulon. Bon voyage."

We thanked him profusely and carefully carried our precious gift back to the ship, determined in the morning to ask Lewis to find us a gramophone.

With Mervyn snoring like a steam engine, and clearly audible beside me, I lay in bed listening to the series of bells, whistles, and hooters, announcing our imminent departure from Toulon, and subsequent passage to Naples.

Chapter Four
Smell Naples and Die! - Court martial - Lupanar and Pompeii

RMS Orontes hauled up her anchor almost on schedule. However, since we left Toulon at night, as we navigated the Straits of Boniface, we were deprived of a glimpse of the cliffs of Cape Corso, and Elba, the island prison of Napoleon. Instead, as Corsica slipped by to port and Sardinia to starboard, I had to be content to catch up with the news, before switching off the bedside light.

On our return to the stateroom, after a late drink and cigarettes in the smoking saloon, I discovered our steward, Lewis, had been most attentive. Because while ashore, although it was Saturday, I found a copy of Tuesday's Times lying on my desk. Therefore, as Mervyn slept, dreaming no doubt of legionnaires, I searched the law notices for any account of the court martial of the army officers accused of indecency, which I read about a week after our departure from Tilbury. Immediately, I found the report on page nine. This time, the second man accused was named as Captain Jocelyn Leathley Heber Chase. And, as in the case of Captain Loftus Tottenham, the court martial was conducted at Chatham, where the men were officers in the Royal Engineers. Heber Chase, aged thirty six, was called to answer twenty-two alleged offences against civilian boys.

Lieutenant Colonel H Shapcott, acting for the prosecution, began by detailing Captain Heber Chase's military career, beginning in the summer of 1920, and up until his promotion to Captain in 1931. In addition, Shapcott mentioned that Heber Chase had been interested and involved in the Boy Scout movement since 1922, until the date the recent charges were laid. Shapcott went on to tell the court that, in October the previous year, Captain Chase communicated by letter with his commanding officer, Colonel Dove, of the 19th London Regiment at St Pancras, from Belgium, requesting to resign his commission. The letter went on to explain that Heber Chase had become involved in a scandal, which, if it became public property, would be most unpleasant. Chase's solicitor told him that should the case come to court he had fair prospects of success, although there would be much mud thrown about. However, provided the military agreed, and Chase remained abroad, the whole thing could probably be kept quiet. Heber Chase also resigned his position as assistant District Scout Commissioner for Hendon.

What prompted, Chase and Loftus Tottenham to endanger themselves by returning to England would probably never be revealed. Nonetheless, in late November, the Assistant Provost Marshal arrested the couple in a taxi at Victoria Station.

At this point, I must admit my reaction to the story, as well as my attitude to the accused, is mixed. Being as closely involved with the scouts as I am, part of me sympathises with the officers. Boys can be chatterboxes at the best of times and can easily misconstrue a harmless action, or make up stories based on nothing at all.

Of course, the report was restricted. There would never be a time when one might read the actual statements made by the boys. As a result, it is difficult to form a true opinion of who did what to whom, and who was innocent, or who was not.

It did appear, as the boys were cross-examined by Mr St John Hutchinson representing the defence, they may have been prompted and rehearsed into making their statements prior to reading them later in the presence of Captain Heber Chase. Hutchinson also made it known that one boy was told by the police to hold back his allegation of indecency, as nothing would come of it. Then it all came to light at the end, which I found quite puzzling. Could it be the establishment was endeavouring to protect the officers, but a higher power had intervened?

Reading the evidence of the detective inspector, he stated that twelve or fourteen statements were taken from twenty to thirty boys, from three different scout troops. Furthermore, the detective said, that in early November it was the decision of the Director of Prosecutions to discontinue the case. The Judge Advocate asked the detective if he knew of any evidence that might have brought about such a decision. The detective said he was unaware of any. The question was then asked whether the court should act on evidence the Director of Prosecutions might have, or any other. The detective answered no, since new evidence had come to light. This, he thought may have been ascertained in December from a statement made by a boy from Chertsey. The Judge Advocate asked if there was any confirmation the Director of Prosecutions had reached a decision not to go ahead, because the police had been unable to corroborate the boys' stories. The detective answered no.

Mr St John Hutchinson addressed the court, saying that the case for the prosecution had failed to prove the more serious charges against Captain Heber Chase. The Judge Advocate agreed, and informed the panel that they could not possibly pronounce a guilty verdict on the strength of the evidence provided, and advised to acquit Captain Heber Chase. Hutchinson went on to produce character witnesses to speak on Heber Chase's behalf. In addition, he reminded the court of Captain Chase's exemplary military record, plus his ability and great success as an athlete, representing the army in numerous running races in which he invariably finished in first place. The case was to continue, so it appeared I needed to be patient and await the outcome.

***

'Smell Naples and die'! That was appropriate when I first saw Naples back in 1914, thirteen years ago, and still applied the day Mervyn and I sailed into the picturesque Bay of Naples, the great peak of Vesuvius in the distance appearing ominously lively. I remembered all too well the detritus piled in the streets, impoverished and pestering people, as well as the overall stench of the city.

The morning was sunny and warm as chugging tugs nudged us towards the Molo Luigi Razza, the Orient Line berth. However, I was a little under the weather, and feeling the effects of the night before, a result of the excitement of, 'Les Dancing Dubois', as well as staying up far too late reading the newspaper. Moreover, with Mervyn's interminable snoring, this resulted in me having an extremely poor night's sleep, the remainder spent tossing and turning, visions of naked legionnaires, judges, scoutmasters, detectives and royal engineer captains, frolicking before my eyes, all the while accompanied by Edith Piaf, singing soulfully about 'Mon Legionnaire'. So, at breakfast I suggested Mervyn might go ashore alone. There was a tour of the city beginning from the Via Piliero. In addition, I suggested he put his name down for the Pompeii excursion.

"You've to hand your passport to the Italian police in the smoking room," I said. "They'll stamp your receipt which you'll need to show at the museums and galleries."

Judging by Mervyn's expression as he buttered another slice of toast, I waited for objections.

"You said we'd do it together."

"I told you all along I had no desire to see Naples again. The first time was bad enough. But you'll enjoy it. The tour takes you to all the best places. When I was here last, the man who showed me around was only looking for one thing. But that's another story."

"You promised we'd see Pompeii together."

"I know I did. Very well. You see some of the city. Then I'll meet you at eleven. The ship leaves at three, so we'll not have much time."

"Then if you're coming you'd better come with me and get your passport receipt. Where shall I see you?"

"The map in the folder says the station Circum Vesuviana, on Corso Garibaldi, is where we catch the train. Shall I write it down?"

"Yes please."

I took out my fountain pen and wrote the name and address on the back of the menu.

"Don't let the boys bother you. Just shoo them away and shout,

No! Almost certainly, Miss Plunkett Dillon will book the tour. Stick with her and you'll be fine."

"Thanks a lot. What will you do?"

"Relax. Find a good book in the library, a deck chair beside the swimming bath, and lie in the sun. It'll do us both good to be on our own for once."

That's exactly what I did after seeing Mervyn on his way, amused to watch him follow Miss Plunkett Dillon to the end of the gangway, then turn and wave miserably.

The following few hours passed pleasantly. I had a wealth of choice in the library, since it was stocked with the very latest novels, meaning I was hard pressed to decide which to borrow. Agatha Christie's 'ABC Murders' was hot off the press, along with Margaret Mitchell's 'Gone with the Wind'. 'Eyeless in Gaza' by Aldous Huxley, might prove too heavy reading, and I was tempted by Daphne du Maurier's 'Jamaica Inn', which I heard was a gripping yarn. I eventually chose 'Drums Along the Mohawk' by Walter D Edmonds, mainly because the dust jacket illustration appealed to me.

I have always been a keen settlers and indians type of chap, and interested in early North American history. After all, sugar is cultivated in America, and naturally, where would I be without sugar. Before leaving the library, I chose a book for Mervyn. The next few days would be spent entirely at sea, so it was important to have something to pass the time. I picked 'Tarzan and the Leopard Men' by Edgar Rice Burroughs, once more deciding upon it on the strength of the cover.

Much to my delight, Maurice de Fontarce appeared alongside the swimming bath, and glancing in my direction, smiled and took off his towelling dressing gown, to reveal the scantiest of costumes, obviously the latest beachwear from Nice or St. Tropez. I wished I had thought to bring my camera, because a picture of him lying on the canvas lounger might have been the one I might have treasured forever. I was hardly surprised when none other than Mrs Casdagli and her son David appeared, and was amused to observe, as they lay side by side, the unspoken language passing between them. You would be correct in presuming there was very little reading done for the remainder of the morning.

Mervyn was waiting at the station as planned, and with the money I exchanged on the ship, I purchased two return train tickets to Pompeii.

It was only sixteen miles to the ruined city. Nonetheless, the journey was tedious, as the train made a stop at every station. It was Saturday, and one whole week since we departed England on that cold damp morning. Yet there we were, gazing out of the carriage window at the palm trees, vineyards, sleepy terracotta roofed villages, azure sea, and an all-encompassing cobalt blue sky.

The train was narrower than we were used to, but well equipped in first class, with upholstered leather seats and a clever ventilation system in the ceiling. Our guidebook said we should prepare to leave the train when we reach Torre, a small town backed by the Mediterranean Sea and surrounded by volcanic hills.

Sadly, the lengthy train journey meant we were pressed for time. Furthermore, considering the trip back to Naples would take the same amount of time, Mervyn and I saw little of the ruins. However, at the entrance, we attached ourselves to a guided tour, advertised to include only the main features.

Our guide, an old whiskered custodian, informed us, in very broken English, that only a few days before, fourteen skeletons had been unearthed during excavations of a recently discovered gymnasium and swimming bath complex, two of them appearing to be adolescents. He went on to tell us that, scattered around the bodies were the objects they were hurriedly carrying away. Various kitchen utensils, plus one hundred gold, silver and bronze, Roman coins, as well as various items of gold and silver jewellery.

The guide led us along a series of paved streets, bordered by the ruinous walls of houses, some apparently once shops, and private dwellings.

He pointed out tiny pieces of white marble, fitting tightly between the paving stones under our feet, saying they reflected moonlight and therefore illuminated the way for people out late at night; a little like the recently invented Cats Eyes along our roads at home. Some roads exhibited evidence of chariot wheels, by the deep ruts, caused by hundreds of years of wear. Pedestrian pavements were also an inclusion in Roman street design, allowing folks to walk them in safety. There were even crossing places constructed of stepping stones, so people's feet might remain dry should the weather be wet. At various points, we came across a hapless victim, frozen in stone, in the dreadful agony of his or her dying seconds. Even the twisted writhing of an expiring dog was captured in pumice.

Our route took us into the Forum, where the beautiful Temple of Jupiter once stood, the massive stone base, all of which remained, while steps led up to a row of fluted columns, some erect, others fallen. This location was the oldest part of the city and obviously the hub of urban life. Made clear by the presence of public buildings such as the Basilica, the Temples of Apollo and Vespansian, as well as various market halls called Macellum. Even such edifices as these however were dwarfed by towering Mount Vesuvius, only five miles distant. What is more, in the Forum, a citizen of Pompeii would have seen statues of laudable or notorious Emperors, such as Augustus, Claudius, Caligula, and Nero, the bases of the statues still visible today.

The corner of a street called Vico de Lupanare, several streets east of the Forum, was our penultimate destination and an attraction our guide warned might offend the ladies in our group. Here was the Lupanar, or brothel, our guide explaining that Lupanar is Latin for brothel and literally means, 'den of she wolves', Lupa being the Roman slang for prostitute.

Some of our lady companions declined to enter, while others, particularly the younger females, were more inquisitive. Mervyn and I were eager to see inside and were the first gentlemen to pass through the doorway, following the ladies.

We arrived in a chamber perhaps fifteen feet long, with a brick screen at one end and smaller chambers leading off to the left and right. These belonged to the 'Lupa', the guide explained, and here she would perform her duties for the clients. Mervyn and I poked our heads inside and saw a plastered windowless room, plus a large brick platform constructed into the walls at the far end.

This we were told was the bed on which was thrown a straw filled mattress.

Upstairs was the same, except behind the screen at the end, was a latrine for the use of clients and prostitutes alike. Downstairs, I had been unaware of any decorations, because perhaps they were rather more damaged, seeing they were on the ground floor. However, on the upper level, the frescoes over each door were plain to see.

The young ladies on our tour would never have seen, or even grasped the meaning of such lewd images, considering they were almost certainly virgins.

Their significance, nonetheless, was obvious to the more mature amongst the party. Even I caught Mervyn twisting and turning his head to try to make out the various positions the couples were taking. Were these possibly advertisements for the variety of postures on offer? The client simply pointing to the picture over a particular door, where his wish would be provided. Otherwise, merely humorous decorations, aimed to titivate and arouse potential punters. Even so, as we travelled back to Naples later that afternoon, they certainly gave Mervyn and I food for thought.

Chapter Five
Distant volcanoes - Mon Legionnaire - Port Said

RMS Orontes sailed at three o'clock as planned, having taken on coal and fresh supplies for the next leg of the voyage.

"Well Mervyn. Did you enjoy Naples? I asked.

We had ordered tea in the smoking room, as we watched the colourful towns of the Amalfi Coast slipping beyond a window off the port bow.

"Not much," Mervyn said, lighting a cigarette. "The people are horrid. They spoil it. All you see are beggars and touts. Everyone wants to sell you something, or take you places you've never heard of. I didn't trust anyone. Even the horses were a sorry sight. We didn't see any galleries or museums. All Miss Plunkett Dillon wanted to do was shopping. Would you believe! We trailed up and down the Galleria Umberto searching for a scarf. By the time she'd found what she wanted I had to be at the station to meet you."

"People are terribly poor," I said. "The city's been devastated by earthquakes and dreadful cholera epidemics."

Of course, I completely sympathised with Mervyn, since I formed the same opinion about Naples on my first visit.

For the remainder of the afternoon, until we dressed for dinner, Mervyn and I rested in our cabins, reading our books and talking about the events of the day. Except, since he chose to sit beneath my porthole, Mervyn gave me updates regarding our position by referring to the Orontes booklet.

"That must have been Sorrento back there. We'll be sailing between the mainland and Capri. We would see it, if we were on the other side of the ship."

***

That evening, once again, Mervyn and I dined with Captain Sullivan, and he pointed out a large island on the horizon ahead of us."

"Stromboli," he said. "It erupted seven years ago killing four people, one of whom was washed away by the tidal wave it caused,"

For me, what happened in Pompeii, forty-six years after the death of Christ, suddenly became a reality. Volcanos like Vesuvius and Stromboli can erupt without warning, as in Pompeii in 79AD. If, or more likely, when this happens again, all the hard work of excavating might easily be buried once more. A chilling thought, although I kept it to myself.

Later that evening, while enjoying a nightcap back in our cabins, Mervyn continued to reconnoitre from his bed beneath the porthole.

"Those must be the lights of Scilla," he said. "If it is, then we're entering the Strait of Messina. At dinner, didn't the Captain mention we should expect strong tides?"

"He did," I said, climbing into bed. "That means Sicily is off our starboard bow."

"I wish it wasn't dark. We'd be able to see Mount Etna."

Mervyn turned off his bedside light, and I did the same. Thus, both suites were in darkness, all except for the small emergency devices over the doors. Perhaps the fact that it was dark, and we were in separate cabins, with just the open connecting door between us, possibly initiated a sudden intimate moment between Mervyn and I.

"Look at the stars," he sighed. "They're so bright you can see even the smallest."

"I think you're enjoying this voyage more than the Norway cruise," I said.

"I am Ron. And do you know why? Because it's just you and me. No Mickey, Teddy, or to contend with Gilbert Fry. Mickey and

Teddy are my friends. But you're more than that. If a chap can have a best friend, then I'm lucky I have you. Do you reckon our friendship is a kind of love?"

There is nothing like a sky full of stars and a couple of large brandies to turn a chap into a philosopher.

"It's possible," I answered. "Once, when I was a few years younger than you are now, I fell in love with a boy at school. I think he loved me. I know I loved him. I told him so. But he refused to accept that men could feel the emotion of love for one another. He was never able to come to terms with himself."

"What happened? Did he marry and have a family?"

"No. He did himself harm."

"How do you mean?"

"Anthony drowned himself."

Strangely, that was the first time I had mentioned his name for almost thirty years. I must have locked away the dreadful incident in my subconscious, perhaps in a bid to forget it ever happened. All the same, I felt relieved to have spoken of it after so many years.

"That was silly," said Mervyn in his usual matter of fact way. "He still may have found happiness with a wife and children, while keeping his other life a secret."

"Easier said than done old chap. I don't think Anthony had the inclination to father children, if you know what I mean."

"Heavens!" Mervyn chuckled. "You won't ever catch me doing that! But I'll marry all the same. My brothers and sisters will marry. It's what we do. I wouldn't want to be an object of curiosity."

"So you're not going to be the eternal bachelor and man of mystery like me? 'What's wrong with Ronald?'" I said, changing my voice to sound like my mother. "'A man his age should be married.' Of course it wouldn't enter mother's head that I had no liking for women in that way."

Mervyn laughed. "But it's all right for you. You've money, and can come and go as you please."

"Fair enough. But that too can be lonely. I'm just glad I have you to share my life."

"And I have you. My life would be very different had we not met.

I certainly wouldn't be gallivanting around the world. I'm a bit of a duffer really. I still don't know how I'll earn my living."

"You might never need to."

"What do you mean?"

"If I adopt you, and anything happens to me, you'll inherit half my fortune. On condition of course that you remain single."

For a moment, even in the darkness, I could sense the effect my statement had on Mervyn. He was suddenly faced with an enormous dilemma, to sacrifice a life of normality for one of leisure, an existence of which he had already sampled. I waited for a reaction.

"Eric will get the other half?" he said.

"Perhaps. But Eric is already doing quite nicely. I would rather my money go to a good cause."

"What me?"

"Yes. And a bit to a couple of hospitals, the scouts, and the boys club."

"That would mean I'd be your son. But what would people say, especially mother and father? They'd think it rather odd a bachelor having a son."

"I've done it before. Many of my single relations have adopted children. Just think about it."

Out of the darkness, I heard a noise that could only mean one thing. Mervyn had left his bed and was standing at the connecting door, the beautiful whiteness of his nakedness illuminated by the single emergency light above my cabin door.

"When you say such things to me, you usually want something in return," he whispered. "Is there any room over there for me?"

"I can always make room my boy, you know that."

I watched his shadowy figure slide the connecting door shut and move towards my bed, allowing me to glimpse what has intoxicated me from the very beginning. So, lifting my blanket and shifting to the far side of the bed to allow him room, I felt him crawl in beside me, suddenly experiencing the warmth of his body against mine.

I have always found it rather a cliché, when, in the best of Hollywood motion pictures, the moon inevitably pops out from behind a cloud at the precise moment the leading couple are in the throes of a kiss. Well, I swear to you, that the self same thing actually occurred, moon light, all of a sudden, bursting through the porthole beside my bed, allowing me a wonderful close up of what happened subsequently. Needless to say, twenty or so minutes later, had there really been a man in the moon, he would have heard Mervyn and I snoring away happily.

***

Several hours later, and unbeknown to us, RMS Orontes made a sweeping course variation to the northeast, and entering by the channel between Cape San Vito and the island of San Paulo, she arrived at Taranto. As well as being the base for the Italian Navy, the town of Taranto is positioned deep inside the instep of Italy's boot. In addition, and while Mervyn and I slumbered, a mail train steamed along the jetty where we were moored. Then, under the glare of arc lights, sailors and officers, commanded by the second officer, began to unload the mail wagons, and then label the bags for the various ports along our route.

Before the bags were loaded onto the ship, they passed by an officer who called out each destination, which was subsequently recorded by the mail officer in the mail papers. Once the entire operation was complete, Orontes quietly slipped away into the night.

By morning, we were in the Ionian Sea and out of sight of land. Then came two days of endless sky and open water, with only the lights of Crete, seen on the first night off the port bow.

Mervyn spent his time playing tennis with his opponent, Keith Steel-Maitland, the younger son of Sir Arthur and Dowager Lady Steel-Maitland. The Dowager and her son were also disembarking at Port Said.

Except when he was batting a ball to and fro, Mervyn swam in the swimming bath, or read the book I found for him in the library, 'Tarzan and the Leopard Men'.

Other than eat our meals together, one particular activity Mervyn and I did as a pair, was listen to music. On my request, Lewis, our steward, found us a gramophone. Playing records in the cabin was not allowed as it could easily disturb the other passengers. As a result, and after consulting the information card, we discovered we could play them in various locations on the ship, the smoking room being one, along with the veranda café. The latter appeared to be the best choice, as the former was usually the habitat of elderly gentlemen who might not appreciate some of our choices of music.

Ever since Toulon, I had been far from idle, since I summoned the translating skills of Maurice de Fontarce, who kindly set about interpreting the words of Edith Piaf's, 'Mon Legionnaire', so Mervyn and I could finally appreciate her song in English.

'Il avait de grand yeux tres clairs,' Edith sang, or rather spoke. *'Ou parfais passaient de éclairs. Comme au ciel passent des orages.'*

"What's she saying Ron?" asked Mervyn.

He and I had placed the gramophone on a table beside the window in a quiet corner of the veranda café.

"He had big bright eyes," I said, reading from Fontarce's translation. "Where you might see lightning reflected from a passing storm."

'Il etait plein tatouages,' Edith continued. *'Que j'ai jamais tres bien compris.'*

"He had many tattoos, although I never really understood what they meant."

'Son cou portait,'

"On his neck."

'Pas vu pas pris.'

"Not seen. Not taken."

'Sur son cour on lisait.'

"On his heart," I read.

'Personne.'

"No one."

'Sur son bras droit un mot.'

"On his right arm, one word."

'Raisonne.'

"Reason. Now we come to the chorus."

'Jais pas son nom.'

"I don't know his name."

'Je n'sais rien d'lui.'

"I don't know anything about him."

'Il m'a aimee toute la nuit.'

"He loved me all night, Mon Legionnaire."

"Does she really sing that?" gasped Mervyn, looking around the café to see if anyone was listening.

"The French have a different way of regarding things like love," I said.

'Et me laissant a mon destin,' Edith warbled on. *'Il est parti dans la matin.'*

"Leaving me to my destiny, he left me in the morning."

"The rotten devil," Mervyn said, under his breath.

'Plein de lumiere! Il etait minc. Il etait beau. Il sentait bon le sable chaud. Mon Legionnaire.'

"Full of light. He was thin. He was handsome. He smelled good. Like warm sand. My Legionnaire."

'Y avait du soleil sur son front.'

"The sun on his forehead."

'Qui mettait dans ses cheveux blonds.'

"Put light into his blond hair."

With Edith continuing to sing, I broke off translating, as Mervyn and I settled back in our chairs to listen, while memories of 'Les Dancing Dubois', the smell of Gauloises cigarettes, brandy, and the handsome faces of the young sailors filled our minds.

"What happens in the rest of the story?" Mervyn asked, as he wound up the gramophone for the second time, "It doesn't sound very cheerful."

"It's not. She sings of lost happiness and how she always thinks of him at night."

"He must have been pretty good," sniggered Mervyn.

"She lusts for his skin, which eats her up."

This time it was my turn to glance around, although people were preoccupied with either making conversation, or drinking tea. Anyway, since Maurice de Fontarce was the only French person on the ship, and knowing the British as I do, it was unlikely anyone understood French, let alone spoke the language.

"She says," I continued. "That she wished she'd expressed her happiness when he was making love to her. But she didn't dare in case he saw her smile."

"That's odd."

"Not really. It's very French. Rather than give him the impression he was something special, or held sway over her, she remained strong and impartial. Then comes the sad finish. He's found dead in the desert, naked, with his eyes open, showing his tattoos for all to see. She says she forgives him for not knowing how she felt, but then dreams she'll see him again and they'll live in some wonderful country, full of light."

"It's a kind of happy ending, if still a little sad."

With the gramophone fully wound, we listen to the song for the third time.

***

At nine o'clock on the morning of January 27[th,] RMS Orontes steamed into Port Said and our eleven-day voyage came to an end. With the trunks packed and labelled for the train, as well as Lewis' assurance that once they arrived on the quay they would be safe in the hands of the Arab porters, Mervyn and I waited in a queue in the smoking room to receive our passports. Once they were stamped, we stood in another queue while Egyptian customs officials inspected our documents, also taking fifteen piastres each for quarantine tax, which amounted to about three shillings and sixpence. In addition, because Mervyn and I had a trunk each, we were required to pay two piastres per item for porterage and quay dues.

Lastly, after standing in a further line at the port gangway, we crowded onto a launch that would convey us to the Customs Quay.

Even before coaling had begun, all the while around the launch and ship, the turgid water swarmed with dozens of little boats, each crawling with dark skinned, Egyptians, endeavouring to sell peanuts, oranges, tangerines, handbags, watches and bracelets, everything at five times the actual value.

"Don't buy anything," said Maurice de Fontarce standing beside us at the rail. "The watches are stolen and have no insides. Also, wash any fruit you buy before you eat it. You never know where their hands have been."

Suddenly I realised this was a different Egypt from which I left eighteen years earlier. The British were once treated with respect. We had fought and won a great war, saving Egypt from certain incursion by the Ottoman Sultans, and inevitably by the Prussians. Despite this, in the succeeding years, Egyptian esteem for Great Britain seemed to have radically altered.

"Another thing," Fontarce continued, as the launch powered us away from the ship. "If you're riding in a tram or a taxi, don't lean your arm out of the window. Some wog will be sure to slash your watch strap and grab your watch."

Once we reach Cairo, it is my intention that Mervyn and I stay at Shepheard's. It is by far the best hotel in the city, commanding wonderful views towards the Citadel and the Mosque of Mohamed Ali. Except there remained a four-hour train journey before we could completely relax.

I had no desire to see Port Said again, being certain it had changed little since Fritz Barnhoff and I made our tour of its delights back in 1914.

When I asked Mervyn if he was interested to see the town, he said he would rather begin for Cairo immediately. So, having successfully navigated customs, where an Egyptian officer took exceptional interest in my camera, even making a note of it in my passport, Mervyn and I made the short walk to Gare Maritime. There, at a quarter past twelve in the afternoon, our train would depart for Cairo.

With enormous relief, I now saw the reason why Lewis had strongly advised us to have our luggage forwarded to the train. The jetty in front of the customhouse was swarming with men and boys, wearing the traditional Egyptian garb of black, white, or striped robes, as well as sporting red tarbushes with black tassels. Gabbling in Arabic or broken English, they hassled the tourists by eagerly offering to carry luggage here, there and everywhere. Mervyn and I saw one man, whom we recognised as a passenger from the Orontes, have his suitcase almost pulled savagely from his hand by one aggressive nuisance. Boys continually waved shoddy jewellery, canes and candy, watches, cigarettes and postcards, in our faces, some postcards clearly French and no doubt contraband. In addition, they were so belligerent and insistent, it was necessary to become equally violent, both verbally and physically, in order they realised we were not potential customers.

Even at the station the pestering continued, with little boys teeming around us begging for piastres. At one point, Mervyn became so annoyed with the bunch that followed us from the jetty; he dug into his pockets, pulled out an English three-penny piece and gave it to a boy. The kid looked at it, made a face, and threw it along the platform in disgust. With that, Mervyn rolled up his sleeves and made a rush at him, fists raised. At the sight of this red faced, sandy haired Englishman sprinting towards him, the lad and his friends turned tail and ran away towards the concourse, jeering as they went.

In no time, we found the State Railway Office and purchased two first class tickets for the Pullman train to Cairo. After being told it would depart from platform one, it pleased us to see it standing there, the carriage doors open, with people we recognised from the ship about to climb aboard. Away from the babble of unintelligible conversation and the shouts of food vendors, it was satisfying to finally locate our compartment and relax into our seats.

Chapter Six
First class to Cairo on the Train de Lux - Introducing Miss Annie Schletter

"Don't you think one pound three and eleven's a bit expensive?" Mervyn said. "After all, it's only four hours. Does it cost that much from Bath to London?"

"Not at all. But most Egyptians are far too poor to travel first class. I suppose the railway thinks foreigners can afford it. The money's probably subsidising something else. Perhaps another big dam construction somewhere."

At the time, I remembered thinking that Mervyn had a kind of shrewdness where money was concerned that I never had. As a child, I was fortunate, my father and mother never concerned themselves over finances. Unlike Mervyn's parents, who scrimped and saved for every scrap of food and stitch of clothing. He would have seen this at first hand and had never completely forgotten the experience.

The train was particularly comfortable, entirely living up to its status as Egypt's 'Train de Lux'. Then again, it was important that it did, because it was the first impression virtually every traveller had of the country. We seemed to have the compartment to ourselves, therefore, following a delicious lunch in the dining car and an exquisite bottle of French champagne, it was hardly surprising, that in no time, Mervyn and I were snoring happily, while beyond the carriage window the Suez Canal slipped quietly by.

Waking an hour later, I was surprised to find we were no longer alone, since while we slept an elderly female travelling companion had joined us.

"I'm sorry dear," she said. "I woke you. I've this terrible cough come on me. It must be all the dust. It is awfully dusty, don't you think."

Looking out of the window, I saw we were hurtling along in the midst of a dust storm obliterating the landscape. Believing Mervyn should see this phenomenon I leaned forward and touched him on the knee in order to wake him.

"My word!" I exclaimed. "I see what you mean."

"Allow me to introduce myself," the old lady said. "Miss Annie Schletter. I do believe I saw you on the ship."

"Captain Fry," I said. "Very pleased to meet you Miss Schletter. I recognise you too. Didn't you play the piano in the lounge on several occasions? Songs from the musicals as I remember."

"That's correct Captain. Captain Sullivan kindly allowed me to put my poster in the café. I had a lovely attendance."

"Let me introduce my young friend Mervyn Watson. He and I are here for the season."

Although not quite awake, Mervyn shook the old lady's hand.

"Pleased to meet you I'm sure," he said.

"Mervyn has a fine voice," I said. "If I'd thought of it I would have had him join you. He's up on all the London shows."

"Not quite Ron," Mervyn said blushing. "Only the ones I hear on the radio."

"It's all pantomimes at the moment," Miss Schletter said. "But at least we've a couple of hits for people to see when they come up to town. Have you seen 'Anything Goes'?"

We shook our heads.

"Not yet," Mervyn answered. "Do you recommend it?"

"Of course dear. But it's not as marvellous as when Leslie was the star."

"Leslie?" I asked, naively.

"Leslie Henson, Captain Fry.

By her confidence in calling this famous matinee idol by his

Christian name, I suspected Miss Schletter was more closely involved in the theatre than a mere audience member.

"But Ivor's new one at The Lane is the one to see."

"Ivor?" I said.

"Novello Captain. 'Careless Rapture'. It's wonderful."

Assuming Miss Schletter was in her seventies, she possessed a commanding presence and would have played Lady Bracknell, or Mrs Higgins with immense aplomb. Although a little shorter than the former, the towering figure of Edith Evans having become everyone's stereotype. Bravely, I dared to ask the obvious question.

"Are you a thespian Miss Schletter?"

Mervyn snorted and covered his mouth with his hand. I do believe the word was new to him, but realised he may have mistaken it for one to which he was more familiar. Naturally, Miss Schletter knew its meaning completely.

"Yes dear. I'm proud to say I am. But not as active as I used to be. Purposely so, don't you know. At seventy nine it becomes increasingly difficult to remember the moves."

Almost gluing his face to the window, Mervyn endeavoured, unsuccessfully, to stifle a fit of the giggles. That is, until the toe of my shoe hit his shin, unseen by Miss Schletter I might add.

"Could we have seen you in something?" I asked.

"Possibly dear. Although it's been nearly four years since the Adelphi, so I doubt if your young friend would have."

"Singing, of course?"

"Deary me, no Captain. I wouldn't presume to have a voice for the musical play. These days I'm known as a character actress. A little thing in Wimbledon Park, nearly fifty years ago, started me off. After that, it was Lady Simpleton Simon, a funny little part in the 'Guards Burlesque' at Chelsea Barracks in 1905. I was at the Court in the 'Lonely Millionairess' in 1905, and His Majesty's in 1906 in 'Colonel Newcombe'. The year before war was declared I auditioned for Gerald and landed the part of Marquise de Rio Zares in his revival at Wyndham's of 'Diplomacy'. My Marquise was 'capitally done', so said The Times, although I've still to discover the meaning of 'Polyglot humour', or 'Rastaquouere'."

"Gerald?" I asked.

"Gerald du Maurier dear. After the dreadful war was over, I appeared at the Queens with Owen Nares in 'House of Peril'. Then in 1924 came the revival of 'Diplomacy' at the Adelphi, dear Gerald doing me the great honour to think of me once more."

"Then I'll have seen you," I exclaimed. "I was up from Cambridge in the spring of that year, with a pal. You were funny as the Spanish countess from South America."

"How clever of you to remember," Miss Schletter said, laughing. "Did you enjoy it?"

"Indeed! You were tremendous."

"Thank you dear. And Gladys. What did you think of her?"

"Gladys?" I asked.

"Cooper dear. Wasn't she marvellous?"

"I agree. The last scene was riveting. My friend and I were transfixed when she hammered on the door as the curtain came down."

"Yes dear. I saw that over two hundred times. We had to. Waiting for the call, dear."

"Call?"

"Curtain call, Captain Fry. 'Diplomacy', discovered Gladys. She's doing terribly well in America. She writes to me from Hollywood quite often."

Miss Schletter opened her reticule, took out a lacy handkerchief, and blew her nose a little too loudly for polite company.

"Dreadful dust!" she said, tucking the handkerchief into her sleeve. "Honestly, I'm surprised I'm here at all. I'd be in Italy if it wasn't for Hilton and Michael."

"What brings you to Egypt?" I asked.

"A new girl named Rutherford was set to play Prism in Cairo next month. But she fell off a camel and broke her ankle, poor thing. Hilton wired me to ask if I'd step into her shoes, the only condition being that I pay my own fare. Bit of a cheek if you ask me. Of course, I know the part like the back of my hand. But the girl was playing Emilia in 'Othello', Maria in 'Twelfth Night', and Lady Sneerswell in 'School for Scandal'. So I've jolly well got my work cut out learning three new parts."

"Who's the theatre company?"

"Dublin Gate dear. We're rehearsing for a month. Then four weeks in Cairo and a week in Alexandria."

"We'll come to see you. Won't we Mervyn."

He smiled, although rather half-heartedly.

"Obviously Michael's playing Algy," continued Miss Schletter, "Iago, Malvolio and Sir Oliver Surface."

"That's Michael MacLiammoir of course."

"Yes dear. How clever. You've heard of him and his friend, Hilton Edwards."

Miss Schletter loaded the word 'friend' heavily, as if I would understand her intimation, to which of course I remained unresponsive. Women have ways of recognising men such as us, and whether or not she had come to the same conclusion about Mervyn and myself, I was not going to give her the benefit of the doubt.

"I saw his 'Hamlet' at the Westminster a couple of years ago," I said instead. "Most impressive."

"Yes. And his costumes and sets are lovely, don't you agree? He does it all himself, don't you know. Of course, Hilton's the producer, or director as the word is today. How they work together so well is quite a mystery. Usually 'friends' quarrel so, don't you think?"

Once again, I continued to remain indifferent to her intimation, changing the subject.

"Where will you stay?"

"Do you know Cairo?"

"I was there in the war."

"I think the boys have booked me into the Continental. Nice and handy for the Opera House."

"Then we'll practically be neighbours, won't we Mervyn. We plan to stay at Shepheard's."

All the while, during my conversation with Miss Schletter, Mervyn had been staring petulantly out of the window, the way a child does when adults are talking. Now and again, Mervyn gives me the impression he has grown into a mature young man, but then behaviour like this convinces me he is still a child. Except, that is the way adolescents are I suppose, neither one nor the other.

"I must say," said Miss Schletter, taking a gold compact from her reticule. "I've always liked Cairo. But it's been a while since I was last there."

She carefully inspected her reflection, dabbing her forehead with a tiny powder puff, while pursing her lips.

"My sister Pauline and I loved it here before the war. In those days, the season was huge. The clubs were so gay. We'd see Agatha at all the parties and dances. She was coming out at the time."

"Agatha?"

"Christie dear. Who would have believed it? Just look at her now. Would you like one of my snaps Captain? I always have a few handy to give out, don't you know."

"That would be lovely Miss Schletter. Thank you. Mervyn and I will treasure it."

Reaching into her reticule once more, Miss Schletter produced a picture postcard, which I saw was a photograph of her taken, judging by the fashion, a decade or so earlier.

"Here you are Captain. I'll sign it on my return. All this chatter, as well as the wretched dust, has made me quite thirsty, so if you don't mind I'll potter along to the dining car and have a spot of afternoon tea."

Putting her photo into my inside jacket pocket, I smiled. By this time, I had lost count of the names Miss Schletter had dropped. Nevertheless, it was an endearing side of her character and I could hardly reproach her for such a foible.

Mervyn was deep in his Rice Burroughs story, 'Tarzan and the Leopard Men', so I took the opportunity, in the tranquillity of Miss Schletter's absence, to pick up The Times, which I hurriedly purchased before we left the station, and idly turning the pages, my attention was drawn to a small article headlined, 'The Troops in Egypt'.

"Do you know Mervyn," I said. "You've never told me your brother's unit. It might help us find him a great deal quicker if I knew."

"The 7th Queen's Own Hussars," he answered without looking up from his book.

"By George! Here they are. It says they're based at Abdul Moniem Barracks, in Abbassia. That's where the X Aircraft Factory was at the end of the war. It'll be good to see the old place again."

"Harry's cards were always addressed Main Barracks, Abbassia," Mervyn said. "Do you think they might be one and the same?"

"We'll soon find out, won't we."

Chapter Seven
Shepheard's Hotel, Cairo - Cocktails in the Long Bar - Ezbekiya Gardens by moonlight

Reaching Ismailia, and with the landscape beyond the window, changing significantly, we said goodbye to the Suez Canal. To the left of the train, sweeping tracts of the Arabian Desert sped by, interrupted by the occasional lonely date palm. While, to the right, lush green terrain could be seen, clearly showing signs of husbandry. We passed villages of mud and straw, where we might glimpse a man and his camel, the animal laden with goods, or else a boy riding a donkey, all the while tapping its rump with a long thin stick.

As the train drew closer to Cairo, the distance between each hamlet became less, the signs of agriculture gradually disappearing, until we were wending our way through the outskirts and into the heart of the city.

Mervyn and I saw nothing more of Miss Schletter that afternoon, that is, not until we were standing beside the train waiting for a porter to collect our trunks from the luggage van. She was busy in conversation with Miss Plunket Dillon, I dare say acquainting the girl with some theatrical story or other.

With a good deal of baggage to unload, Mervyn and I had plenty of time to appreciate our surroundings. Rameses Station, as it is known to the citizens of Cairo, is a delight to the eye, resembling any number of counterparts throughout central and Eastern Europe.

Constructed at the end of the last century from pale honey coloured limestone. The three-story building possesses at one corner an imposing clock tower, as well as two large arched entrances to the south and east. However, the interior of the edifice is what impresses anyone who might see it. Inside clearly suggests Moorish architecture, but also reflects the influence of the Egyptian style of today calling itself Art Deco.

In true Hollywood fashion, massive arches resemble the entrances of ancient temples. In addition, frieze motifs taken from Karnak or Luxor decorate the walls, doors, and windows. In contrast, huge elaborate fretted lamps, intricate ironwork, and dazzling patterns of blue mosaics recall the interiors of mosques of long ago.

High above us, an enveloping canopy of iron and glass seems to suspend invisibly, encompassing the chaotic activity and mayhem far below, where the incessant babble of unintelligible language, the hissing of steam and blowing of whistles, is the order of the day. In fact, so intense was this sudden confrontation with the orient, Mervyn and I were relieved to see the porter at last, and hurry after him along the platform and out into the hot and dusty square.

It is just a short distance from the station to the hotel, but our porter insisted we take a taxi. And as Mervyn and I climbed inside, in truth, I was glad to be out of the clawing dust and the scorching sun.

Shepheard's Hotel appeared civilised and inviting as the taxi drew up alongside the steps, where a tall, tarbushed, concierge waited to open the door. I gave Mervyn three piastre to pay the taxi driver, and then together we walked into the lobby, while two hall porters ran down to collect our luggage.

Suddenly I was propelled back almost two decades to 1919 and the end of the war, since the hotel had hardly altered. The same cool lobby, its design harking back to Egyptian temples of long ago, the gigantic columns resembling those of Karnak or Luxor. Palms in decorative urns, as well as a pair of statues portraying ancient Egyptian serving girls carrying lamps, flanking the marble staircase. While beneath our feet, extravagant tiles and luxurious carpets cushioned our progress to the reception desk. Behind us, the famous terrace overlooking bustling Ibrahim Pasha Street, its canopy screening the European occupants from the hot Egyptian sun. Nubian waiters swished back and forth, serving cold drinks and cocktails, appearing rather comical in immense baggy pantaloons, crimson bolero jackets, and red felt tarbushes with black silk tassels. How many times had I sipped Turkish coffee on the terrace with my fellow officers, the conversation inevitably focusing on the latest reports on General Allenby and his push to Jerusalem? Also, how it might be when we finally arrive home? And of course, the girls we met at the dance the night before.

"May my friend and I have a room for two," I asked the young Greek, male receptionist behind the desk.

"Certainly sir," he said, smiling, while running a finely tapered finger down a column of names written in a large ledger. "We've staterooms on the third floor at the front, with a bathroom and sitting room. Would that suit?"

"Perfectly. Thank you."

"I'll see the porters take up your luggage sir. Room 317. Your key sir."

Naturally, the rooms were sumptuous. Therefore, it is unnecessary to describe them, except the bedroom possessed two large double beds. In addition, a wide balcony allowed us extensive views of the city. Plus with the balcony doors wide open, a delicious breeze filled the suite, scented with the fragrances of spice, acacia blossom, and Nile water. Also, unfortunately, animal dung which doubtless belonged to camel or donkey.

"I'm having a bath," Mervyn said, collapsing onto his bed. "I'm covered in dust. Is it always this dusty?"

"I'm afraid so. It's necessary to change your clothes once, or even twice a day."

A sound of wailing suddenly issued across the rooftops, as countless Muezzin called their brethren to prayer. So evocative was it that Mervyn and I went out on to the balcony to listen, becoming mesmerised for a moment. Although it was eighteen years since I last gazed upon the city, Cairo remained unaltered. Even now, a thousand minarets pierced the sky, the domes of numerous mosques, resembling turquoise mushrooms, punctuating the pink limestone of the surrounding dwellings.

"Now I know we're not in Europe," I said.

"Exactly," said Mervyn. "It's certainly not like hearing the bells of Bath Abbey on a Sunday morning, which I find reassuring. This gives me the shivers."

"Because it's foreign. Once you've heard it enough you'll begin to like it as I do."

"What do you mean?"

"You can't avoid it. The call happens six times a day. From half past five in the morning until seven o'clock at night."

We took turns in the bathroom, after which we began to unpack. Our stay would be lengthy, therefore, to avoid hefty laundry and ironing bills, I advised Mervyn to bring four of everything. As a result, there was a considerable amount of clothing to stow in drawers and wardrobes. By the time we were finished, we were both in need of a drink.

Even when I was last in Cairo, the five thirty call to prayer was always regarded as cocktail hour. When we arrived at the terrace, however, we found it crowded and clearly impossible to get a table. Mervyn and I finally resorted to the Long Bar, which we found beyond the lobby and occupied by European businessmen and two middle-aged army officers. As we sat down the officers nodded in our direction. Here I thought was an excellent opportunity to discover the whereabouts of Harry's regiment.

"Good afternoon gentlemen," I said. "Allow me to introduce my companion Mr Watson. And I'm Captain Fry."

"Pleased to make your acquaintance," said one of the officers. "Major Fielden."

"Major Shepherd," said the other. "Pleased to meet you. Just arrived?"

"This afternoon. It's good to be back in Cairo."

"Here in the war?" asked Major Fielden.

"Royal Flying Corp. Left in 1919. You fellows?"

"Mesopotamia, Bagdad, don't you know," Major Fielden said. "Shepherd, also."

A waiter carrying a tray of drinks approached the officers, and placed them on their table. Then, seeing Mervyn and I, he crossed the room to take our order, Mervyn preferring lemonade, though I requested a dry Martini.

"Have you been in Cairo long Major Shepherd?" I asked.

"Left Aldershot in thirty five," he answered. "Came out on SS Nevasa. Can't see the regiment getting back for a while either, by the way things are with the Italians making a bid for Abyssinia."

"I remember around the time I left, things were going a bit skew whiff," I continued. "There's been an immense change since. Egypt's still a British protectorate, but we seem to have lost control."

"I'll try to explain," Major Fielden, said. "In 1919 the men leading WAFD, the Nationalist Party, were pushing for independence, saying Britain was domineering Egypt's cotton trade and diminishing its power to rule itself. We resisted however, and arrested the leaders, deporting them to Malta. This resulted in mass demonstrations by government officials, students, and workers. Even women took to the streets. Britain tried to suppress the riots, but there were many deaths. As a result, the following year it was recommended a 'Treaty of Alliance', replace the protectorate. Two years later, the British Government declared Egypt independent, but kept control of the Canal Zone, remaining Egypt's external protector."

"However," Major Shepherd interjected. "With the Italians now in Libya, as well as East Africa, and Mussolini threatening to take Egypt, last year an agreement was signed with Great Britain that we withdraw our troops, all except those in the Canal Zone, which we're supposed to give up in twelve years' time."

"Though we shouldn't complain," Fielden put in. "The weather's always pleasant; the women amenable, and the polo, racing, golf and squash keep us fit."

"What brings you to Cairo Captain?" asked Shepherd. "Antiquities and the weather? We read it's not too good in Blighty at the moment."

"That's true," I replied. "Yesterday's Times said it was snowing in London. In fact, you might say Major, Mr Watson, and I are on a mission, and extraordinarily you both might be able to help us. We were wondering where we'd find the 7th Queens Own Hussars."

Both officers seemed to find my question amusing.

"You're joking of course," Shepherd said.

"I'm in complete earnest Major."

"That's our unit!" exclaimed Major Fielden. "Who were you after?"

"Your commanding officer to be precise."

"Lieutenant Colonel Weatherall. You'll find him an amiable sort of chap, although he's had a lot on his plate lately."

"How do you mean?"

"You must have heard. We've been mechanised. It was officially announced at Christmas last year. We're all pretty devastated by the news. The Saucy Seventh charged at Waterloo, don't you know. When you've been around horses as much as we have, it's shocking news to hear we're to exchange them for Mark II tanks and armoured cars."

"What'll happen to the horses?" asked Mervyn.

"You might well ask lad," Shepherd said. "It was a sad day when we said goodbye. Officers and troopers alike saw their old pals loaded on a train that took them to Ismalia and the Remount Depot at Moascar."

"Did they end up with another brigade?"

"All the cavalry regiments in Egypt have been ordered to mechanise, so horses are redundant."

"You don't mean Major that they were slaughtered?"

"Hope so lad. I wouldn't want my old charger trudging the streets of Cairo with a gyppie on his back, or pulling a carriage load of tourists out to the pyramids."

"Granted," Major Shepherd put in. "Colonel Weatherall gave us an option to remain with the regiment, or transfer to a unit still using horses, like the Household Cavalry, or the Yorkshire Dragoons. It says a lot for the spirit of the corps that out of five hundred and thirty officers and troopers, just sixteen elected to transfer."

"Where would I find Lieutenant Colonel Weatherall?" I asked.

"At the General Headquarters in the Semiramis Hotel. Next to the Kasre El Nil Bridge. Tell his adjutant you spoke to us."

As our conversation continued, from the way Shepherd and

Fielden talked of dances, parties and the odd parade, despite everything sounding gay and exciting, I formed the impression they were rather jaded with life in Cairo. Both harked on about England, recalling with great enthusiasm, polo triumphs, and show jumping successes. The waiter also seemed to arrive at their table a little more often than I thought appropriate. Our chat continued unremarkably, during which I ordered another Martini, and Mervyn a further lemonade, until the Majors made their apologies, wished us luck in our venture and left the bar.

In truth, I was glad they left when they did, because my additional Martini would have certainly induced me to ask them what the odds were these days, in buying a man out of the army. To which my question would certainly have received a curt and extremely negative response.

"How about a stroll before dinner?" I suggested, finishing my drink. "We could sit in the Ezbekiya Gardens."

With the sun dipping low over the city, accompanied by the droning of yet another call to prayer, Mervyn and I ventured into Ibrahim Pasha Street. Here, government officials from nearby office buildings, having finished work for the day join tourists and businessmen crowding the pavement, packing trams, or propping up the bars of numerous drinking establishments along its length.

Motorcars and taxicabs honking gaily, jostling backwards and forwards, dodging persons crossing the street; while horse drawn carriages called caleches, together with donkeys and camels, take little regard as to which side of the street they should be travelling.

Situated in Ezbekiya, an area of the city south of the main station, Shepheard's Hotel joins others calling the district home, including the Windsor, Victoria, and Bristol. Should you continue south towards Shari Abdin, you would discover Cairo's Opera House, plus the Post Office, an American Mission, and the Continental-Savoy Hotel. Actually, Ezbekiya is more European in appearance than any other part of the city, reminding many of the sixteenth Arrondisement in Paris. Yet, just a few blocks away to the west, the eternal River Nile, an immense turquoise ribbon, surges under the bridges of the El Gezira Island, then on towards Alexandria, the Delta, and the

Mediterranean Sea.

To our consternation, a pack of donkey boys and dragomen were gathered at the foot of the hotel steps. The concierge obviously accustomed to dealing with such situations, hurriedly driving them away with a whisk of his hand and a few harsh words in Egyptian.

The Ezbekiya Gardens are almost opposite the hotel, so Mervyn and I needed simply to cross the road, to reach the gate located in the iron railings acting as the garden's defence against loiterers and delinquents. Although, being almost sunset and closing time, we were required to pay a couple of piastres to gain entry.

Like a pair of intrepid explorers, we plunged into the lush interior, passing groves of date palms, huge Aloe Vera plants and even a giant Baobab tree. We reached a watercourse where unexpectedly several swans were swimming on its olive green surface. Then, as electric lamps began to transform the shadowy gardens into a kind of fairyland, we crossed a small iron bridge across the lake and sat down on a seat.

"It's been such a marvellous day," Mervyn said. "So much has happened. I can hardly believe we only left the ship this morning."

"What'll we do tomorrow?" I asked.

"We'd better find Harry."

"I can't help remembering that the Majors said sixteen troopers elected to transfer. Do you think your brother was one of them? He might have thought the offer was a way to get out of here."

"But wouldn't he have told mum and dad? He's been in trouble for over a year. His last letter sounded so desperate."

"You remembered to bring it?"

"Of course. It's in my trunk at the hotel

"Good! We've some plausible evidence to show Colonel Weatherall."

The light was rapidly fading, as it does in Egypt, and in the dusk, a swan was preening, no doubt preparing to nest for the night. Back in Bath, Mervyn and I could see swans on the Avon any day of the week. Although, it was rather remarkable to see one in Cairo, at the top of the African continent, where one might normally expect to see egrets and sacred ibis. A swan might appear incongruous had the park not been at the centre of the European quarter. On the other hand, if a swan showed up a few miles south in the native quarter, it would look entirely out of place. I pondered how they remained in the gardens. The Avon swans fly at will. It would be difficult to clip a swan's wing.

From somewhere nearby a bell rang, breaking my speculative mood.

"I think we'd better get back," I said. "They're closing the gates."

Before we left however, I pointed out the Cairo Opera House through the trees, already lit by a dazzle of floodlights. Built almost entirely of wood, yet taking the appearance of stone, it resembles a giant pink wedding cake, as tier after tier of fluted columns and arched windows ascend to a parapet surrounding the roof. A Khedive ordered its construction towards the end of the last century to celebrate the opening of the Suez Canal. Also, the world premiere of Verdi's grand opera 'Aida' was almost staged here. I wondered how Miss Schletter's Miss Prism would go down with the eight hundred and fifty strong audiences.

Following a customarily excellent dinner, Mervyn and I took the elevator up to our room, and after soaking in long hot baths, climbed into our beds to sleep the sleep of the dead.

Chapter Eight
Hotel on the Nile - Negotiations begin

"Mervyn, I think I'd better see Weatherall's adjutant alone," I said, as we waited for the concierge to hail us a caleche. "I'm going to see if I can arrange a meeting with Weatherall in the next few days. The Colonel is almost certainly a busy man and won't be able to see me immediately."

Surprisingly, there was no objection from Mervyn, and we enjoyed a pleasant ride along Shari Abdin Street past the Abdin Palace, the home of young King Farouk. It was a pleasant sensation riding in a carriage and I failed to remember when I last experienced anything similar. Reaching the end of Kasre El Nil Street, I realised Mervyn was not as conciliatory as I had first thought.

"What am I supposed to do while you're inside the hotel?" he grumbled.

"Visit the Museum," I suggested. "It's just around the corner. I'll ask the driver to drop you off and meet you outside when I'm finished."

At Midan Ismalia, the caleche made a detour to the right, pulling up a few seconds later beneath the enormous red walls and arched entrance of the Egyptian Museum.

Gloomily, Mervyn climbed out of the caleche.

"Enjoy yourself," I said. "You'll find it fascinating. Be sure not to miss the Tutankhamen exhibits. I've not seen them yet, so there'll need to be another visit."

Semiramis Hotel had been yet another immense fanciful edifice, built at the beginning of the century, as were most of the hotels in the centre of Cairo. However, most were found in Ezbekiya District, close by the Opera House and Ezbekiya Gardens, while the glistening white Semiramis was the first to stand alongside the River Nile. If a person made sure of a room at the front and on the fifth floor, they would have the best views of the Nile and able to watch the happenings on the river. Heavily laden feluccas, their white sails swollen with a breeze straight off the Arabian Desert, paddle steamers crowded with tourists, together with lonely fishermen standing in their boats, silently casting nets.

Another of Semiramis' novelties was the roof garden, also a first for arid Egypt. Some say it resembles one of the Seven Wonders of the World, akin to the Hanging Gardens of Babylon, where the Assyrian Queen, Semiramis, was said to have had so much pleasure. During the war, I remember attending glamorous parties on the roof, where one could sip cocktails and watch the sun set over the Pyramids.

The interior of the hotel was once the most sumptuous Cairo had yet seen. Baroque, and in the style of Louis the fourteenth, the salons, dining room, bars and billiard rooms were decorated with marble columns, lavish tapestries, classical statues and elaborate furniture.

Thirty years later, the mirrors, tapestries and ornaments are now stored in the cellars, because the British Army occupy the public rooms. They are now using them as offices and wardrooms, the public no longer overly welcome in the bar or billiard room.

Climbing the steps and approaching the revolving door, I passed two armed infantrymen standing at ease in the entrance. Inside the lobby, an officer sat at a desk, absorbed in a newspaper. He looked up as I walked in.

"Yes sir. May I help you?" he asked.

"Good morning lieutenant," I said, noticing the pips on his shoulders. "I wonder if I might have a quick word with Lieutenant Colonel Weatherall's adjutant."

"May I ask the nature of your business sir?"

"It's a rather delicate matter lieutenant. I'd rather the adjutant heard it first-hand."

"Very well."

The officer lifted the telephone.

"Whom may I say wishes to see him?"

"Captain Fry. Also you might mention that I've already spoken with Major Shepherd and Major Fielden?"

I walked away from the desk in order the young man might feel free to speak candidly, allowing my attention to be drawn to an impressive marble statue of a naked Greek or Roman youth, unfortunately wearing a fig leaf.

"He's sending a man down sir," said the lieutenant, replacing the phone. "Please take a seat."

Thanking him, I sat down on a leather sofa beneath the statue. Almost twenty years had passed since my time in the Army, and as I sat waiting, I reflected on my previous spell in Cairo. Then, as now, the British Army made use of a hotel as headquarters. During the four years of the war, they requisitioned the Savoy Hotel, down the street from Shepheard's. It was there, in June 1917, Sir Archibald Murray relinquished command of the Egyptian Expeditionary Force to General Edmund Allenby. This became the turning point of the war. Allenby rebuilt the shambolic Egyptian Expeditionary Force into a strong XX and XXI Corp, combining both infantry and the Australian Desert Light Horse. The months after Allenby took command and transferred his headquarters nearer the battle lines were jolly exciting for us chaps based in Cairo, since daily we heard or read about Allenby's advances towards Jerusalem, pushing the Ottomans back in the process.

In addition, because of his extensive knowledge of the Middle East and command of Arabic along with other languages, young Lieutenant T. E. Lawrence was posted to Cairo to join the Intelligence Staff. Subsequently, and on the orders of the Arab Bureau, he began to search the Sinai for King Faisal.

It was at the Savoy, in 1917, and after the fall of Aqaba, I had the great honour to meet Major Lawrence.

The war ended in October 1918, and six years later the glorious

Savoy Hotel was a pile of rubble, pulled down to make way for an even more glamorous venue, The Metropolitan, or later, the renamed Continental-Savoy Hotel.

Eventually, a handsome junior subaltern showed me into an office on the first floor, wearing khaki shorts and long woollen socks, causing me to suddenly recollect and hanker for my boy scout troop back home.

"How do you do Captain Fry. Please sit down," said the officer, getting up and shaking my hand. "I'm Captain Haig, adjutant to Lieutenant Colonel Weatherall. I understand you wish to speak with the Colonel."

By his accent, the young Captain definitely hailed from north of the border.

"I do Captain Haig. On a matter of great importance. It might save a young man's life so to speak."

"Dear me. That sounds rather drastic and worrying. Could you acquaint me with a few details?"

"May I smoke?" I asked, pulling a packet of Woodbines from my pocket.

"Of course Captain. But have one of mine."

He took out a packet of Gold Flake.

Having practised what I would say in my head a number of times, I remained daunted as to how my explanation would sound.

"Recently," I began. "The parents of a young acquaintance of mine have received communications from their eldest son which have greatly disturbed them. He joined the 7th Hussars in 1934 at the age of 18 and sailed to Egypt on the SS Nevasa in September, 35."

"I was on that ship!" exclaimed Captain Haig.

"As you can imagine his mother and father are most distressed by what they've read. So much in fact, they urged his younger brother, who is in Cairo with me by the way, to ask if I could do something to aid their son's predicament. We arrived in Cairo yesterday, and last evening at our hotel, met Major Fielden and Major Shepherd who advised me to contact you."

"Ah yes. Our two best Polo chappies. What's the matter with the lad?"

"That's the strange thing. No one seems to know. All he says is he's unwell, and pleads for them to do something to get him out and back home."

"Unfortunately Captain, that's hardly a reason for discharge. I imagine many men could say they felt likewise. Nevertheless, they must knuckle down and get on with it. The day they sign up, they do so for the duration."

"Of course Captain Haig. I completely understand. But if there were some underlying circumstances affecting the individual, either physically or mentally surely there's justification in implementing a solution to his problem."

Captain Haig got up and crossed to a filing cabinet under the window.

"Do you know his troop?" he asked, pulling open the top drawer.

"Regrettably not. His letters and cards just say Abbassia Barracks, Cairo."

"What's his surname?"

"Watson."

The Captain shut the top drawer and pulled out the second drawer from the bottom.

"Here he is. Trooper Harry Watson; C Troop; Main Barracks. I don't think we need bother Colonel Weatherall just yet Captain. All I can do for the moment is to have a word with Lieutenant Chapman, the regimental MO. Quite possibly, he may be able to shed some light on the matter. I'm sure you're aware how slowly things happen around here, so at present I can't promise a speedy solution. In the meantime, I suggest you enjoy your stay in Egypt. Relax and see the sights. If I have any information I'll contact you at your hotel."

"We're at Shepheard's," I said, as we shook hands. "Thank you Captain. I look forward to hearing from you."

Chapter Nine
Ali Rashid - Khan El Khalili - Al Fishawy's - Sheesha

Shunning fervent cab drivers, I decided to walk the short distance to the museum, where I had arranged to meet Mervyn. In doing so, I marvelled at the hot dry air and strong sunlight, even at that early hour. Egypt certainly lives up to its reputation as being the favourite destination of sun seeking tourists avoiding the rigours of the English winter.

When I reached the entrance to the museum Mervyn was sitting on the steps waiting for me, although he was not alone but talking with a young Egyptian man.

"Hello Ron," Mervyn said cheerfully, "I'd like you to meet Ali. We met inside. He knows such a lot about King Tut. Ali's offered to be our guide while we're in Cairo."

Ali smiled, his black moustache highlighting a set of brilliant white teeth. At first glance, he appeared older than Mervyn by a couple of years, making him around twenty-one. Of medium height, and dusky in complexion typical of Egyptians; his eyes were as dark as umber and clearly his best feature.

"Pleased to meet you Ali," I said. "My name is Fry. Captain Fry. Thank you for your offer, but Mervyn and I will manage on our own. I know something of Cairo. I was here during the war."

"Cairo's very different now," said Ali. "It can be dangerous for gentlemen. Nowadays, there are many beggars, drug dealers, and donkey boys. You'll be safe if I show you the city, pyramids, camel rides, Nile, mosques."

"Hold on," I said. "Our hotel runs tours to those places. What makes you any different?"

"I'm a dragoman effendi. I'll look after you. Protect you. There is much I know and can tell you about The Mother of the World. I am extremely qualified."

From my previous experience, I was aware that, for hundreds of years, the dragoman held an exalted position over the entire Middle East. Being multilingual, initially they were used as translators by the Ottomans and Muslim officials during political negotiations. Even Napoleon used a dragoman as mediator between himself and those nations he occupied.

Originally Greek, by modern times their standing had diminished to something more akin to a tour guide, where the ability to speak numerous languages remained their greatest talent.

If Ali were truly a member of this elite echelon, then perhaps he was no ordinary tout and simply out for baksheesh.

"Very well Ali," I said. "We'll accept your offer for one day. What's the going rate for a dragoman these days?"

"Six piastres an hour effendi, not including food and drink."

"So we feed you too."

"Certainly effendi. Where the gentlemen eat, dragoman will eat."

"That seems fair," Mervyn said. "If we stop off somewhere we can't expect Ali to eat on the street."

"Does effendi have plans for today?" Ali asked.

"I was thinking we'd do the Native Quarter. That is after a bite of lunch."

"Then effendi will definitely need Ali. I also take the young man and effendi to a special café. You will like it."

As he spoke, he laughed and tapped his tummy, at the same time boldly making a movement with his other hand towards my corpulent abdomen.

"Hey!" exclaimed Mervyn. "Not so much of the young gentleman. My name's Mervyn and effendi is Ron. Now come on! Let's get moving. The sun's beginning to burn my face."

The Native, or Islamic Quarter, in the El Gamaliya district of Cairo, is perhaps a mile southeast of Ezbekiya Gardens and just within the old north wall. The name derives from an ancient camel road, Sharia Gamaliya, from which run the narrow alleys of Khan El Khalili, the native bazaar. During the war, I was a frequent visitor, enjoying the sights and scents of the souk. However, while the atmosphere seemed unaltered, Khan El Khalili's exterior had significantly altered. The streets were always dust tracts and had hardly changed, but the dwellings appeared to have crumbled, as if a kind of conflict or earthquake had occurred, although I knew of neither in Cairo's recent history.

When I asked Ali why this should be, he explained that, in the last twenty years, the Egyptian Government was more concerned with building dams and new irrigation projects than releasing funds for social redevelopments. The reason being, since the end of the war, the decay of the Islamic quarter had proceeded at a rapid pace.

Even so, the shady passages and alleyways of Khan El Khalili still smelt the same.

Together with dodging donkey carts, as well as camels laden with straw, or huge mounds of alfalfa, we took moments here and there to stop and admire the intricate carving of the shutters covering the overhanging balconies and windows. At the same time, marvelling at the occasional minaret pointing, dagger like, into the azure sky. The alleyways teemed with people. Women, their faces uncovered, gliding barefoot through the dust, wearing a small gold ring in a nostril and thin chains around their ankles. Some carried metal jugs containing water, otherwise a bundle, no doubt holding the ingredients for the evening meal, everything balanced effortlessly on their heads. A turbaned water seller, with a pouch of skin slung across his back, his fist clenched over the spout, eagerly searching for the next thirsty customer. Mysterious women sidling by shrouded from head to toe in black robes, with nothing but a slit to see through.

"What's the smell Ali?" asked Mervyn, as a delectable concoction assaulted our nostrils

"Musk," he said sniffing the air. "Spice, grilled lamb, fried Tamiya and rose petals."

Other than these delicious scents, enticing as they were, there were also more unpleasant odours. For example, rotting vegetables and urine, human or animal, hard to distinguish which.

As we dove deeper into the warren of dusty streets, by the babble of language around us, it was immediately obvious to Mervyn and I that we were the only Europeans, yet we remained unimpeded, clearly due to the presence of our dragoman. The young men, old men, donkey boys, unveiled women, and itinerant children were distinctively Arabian, their faces the colour of burnt sienna one might see in a box of watercolours. Conversely, the faces we saw of the occasional Nubian were as black as blue-black ink.

Since they were built from the same limestone the Ancient Egyptians used to construct the temples and tombs millenniums ago, each house, shop, café and mosque, took on the shade of the dusty streets. Even stone pillaged from the Great Pyramid made up the construction of countless mosques, including the great Citadel itself.

Mervyn and I learned all this from Ali as he led us down ally after ally and street after street, and further into the labyrinth of the Souk.

Obviously, our guide's reputation was preceding him, because the people passing by appeared unaware of our presence. Nonetheless, at one point, close by the Mosque of Sayyidna Al Hussein, on Shari Gamaliya, we lost Ali in the crowd, abruptly finding ourselves vulnerable and suddenly entirely at the mercy of the populous.

"You want beads sir? Very good sir. Cheap."

They appeared from inside the entrance, bead sellers, postcard vendors, sellers of plaster scarabs, a couple of donkey boys and some detached, yet expectant juveniles.

"Gentleman want scarab? Look! Great queen! Very lucky."

"No thank you," I said, hearing myself sounding awfully English. "Will you please go away!"

"Bugger off!" cursed Mervyn.

"You look sir!" said a bearded old man, ignoring him and smiling, revealing his cracked and stained teeth. "Real lapis. Very good. Very cheap."

"You want donkey ride sir?" said a boy. "This donkey jolly good donkey. Gin and Tonic donkey sir."

"My donkey better," another said, pushing the first boy aside. "That donkey bad sir. He fall down."

As one would do if attacked by a swarm of angry bees, I gestured wildly, but nothing deterred them.

"Baksheesh! Baksheesh!" whimpered the grimy infants in the dust at our feet. "Baksheesh. Baksheesh."

"Ladies, sirs. Pretty ladies. You Englishman like."

A man held up a tattered postcard that could only have originated on the streets of Paris, since I was horrified to see it depicted a prostitute astride a gentleman, his penis visibly entering her vagina.

"Just pretend you're deaf," I shouted. "They'll give up if we keep walking."

Never had I been so wrong, since the horde continued to pester us relentlessly, until all of a sudden, a sharp retort split the air, and as quickly as they appeared, our tormentors melted away resembling cowering wolves caught in the glare of searchlights.

"Thank heaven Ali!" I exclaimed. "Now I see what you mean. A dragoman is very important in Cairo."

He smiled triumphantly.

"Come on," Mervyn urged. "I'm hungry. Where's this café?"

Ali led us down a laneway lined with Coppersmith shops, outside of each, hanging in great profusion, pots, plates, salvers, jugs, lamps, and urns, of every size and shape. While on racks beneath them, dozens more were piled in abundance. At the same time, under a tattered awning, old men, wearing long robes and soiled white turbans, beat out tattoos on metal shapes, transforming the once plain surface into traceries of florid glistening designs. At one such shop, a rather large tea urn struck me as familiar, perhaps because of its peculiar Persian form. It was then I remembered seeing the exact type on my previous visit to the Khan, almost twenty years ago. As I recall, I wanted to buy it, however, I sensibly resisted, since it would have been a cumbersome object to fit into my kit bag.

"Keep moving effendi," Ali shouted, turning to see me pausing to take a closer look. "If you don't they'll try to sell you something and we'll never get away."

"Very well," I said unhappily, "But can we look later?"

"Of course."

Finally, we stopped outside a narrow shop front where tables and chairs spilled over into the alleyway, every seat occupied by men young, and old, either huddled over hookah pipes, or drinking dark liquid from extremely small glasses.

"You like Turkish coffee?" Ali asked. "Very strong. Very good. Cok Guzel."

Ali had given up looking for a table outside, so Mervyn and I followed him into the interior of the café.

"I remember the coffee well Ali," I said, once we had found a table. "Although, Mervyn's never tried the Turkish kind, have you Mervyn."

"We never have coffee at home. Father says coffee's for nobs. It's expensive you see Ali. Only when I'm at Ron's do I have the real thing. But I don't really like it. I prefer a cup of tea, a glass of beer, or cider."

"Then perhaps Mr Mervyn might like mint tea," Ali suggested.

"At home, my mother makes mint sauce when we have lamb chops, but I never realised you could make tea with mint."

"Try it Mervyn," I said. "You might like it. We've a rather nasty essence called Camp Coffee, Ali, but nothing like this."

The aroma of roasting coffee beans was heady. In addition, the smell of skewered lamb grilling over hot charcoal, possibly coming from the back of the café, was intoxicating.

"I'll introduce you to Akram," said Ali. "You'll enjoy meeting him."

While he left Mervyn and I to look for the proprietor, we were free to speak candidly.

"He's rather exotic, don't you think?" Mervyn said. "I've never spoken to a person with brown skin. You really don't get much opportunity in Bath."

Mervyn comes out with some funny remarks at times. Then again, I failed to recall if I had ever seen a black person walking through Bath. The first time Mervyn left the shores of England, he was with his friends and me on our cruise to Norway, and Norwegians are more like us than we care to think, considering they were once our

Viking invaders. Now, however, here in Cairo, and on the cusp of the Occident and the Orient, the combination of east and west must appear contradictory and unusual to a young man from Swinbourne's Buildings.

"He's very pleasant and smart," I answered, attempting to ignore the inference. "Most polite and intelligent. We were lucky to find him."

"You mean, I found him," Mervyn corrected cynically.

Ali returned to our table accompanied by a large moustached Egyptian, dressed in a European suit, appearing quite inappropriate amongst his fellows, since they were wearing robes, turbans, and tarbushes.

"Effendi's," Ali said. "May I introduce Mr Fishawy? This is his coffee shop. Akram al Fishawy, meet my new friends from England, Mr Ron and Mr Mervyn."

Akram Fishawy made the Arab sign of greeting by bowing, while touching his chest, his mouth, and lastly his forehead with the fingertips of his right hand.

"Most pleased to meet you gentlemen. You do me much honour to visit my humble coffee shop."

"Don't be so modest Akram," Ali said. "Your humble coffee shop is probably more famous than Shepheard's Hotel. It's been in your family for a hundred and seventy seven years."

"As always, Ali is correct gentlemen," Akram replied. "My great-great-grandfather was a busy coppersmith and enjoyed entertaining his friends with mint and anise tea inside his shop. But meeting at Al Fishawy's became so popular he gave up being a coppersmith and turned the place into a coffee shop."

"When was this?" asked, Mervyn.

"Seventeen hundred and sixty."

"My word!" I exclaimed. "That's astonishing. Whose idea were the mirrors, Akram?"

From one end of the shop to the other, the walls were lined with mirrors of every shape, size, and age, from those from the time of Louis the fourteenth to present day 'Art Deco'.

"Each generation contributed to the interior," replied Akram.

"Always respecting the generation before."

This then explained the varying lamps hanging from the ceiling, or perching on cabinets and tables, from the traditional copper and brass, to sparkling crystal chandeliers, ablaze with electric light bulbs. The whole haphazard affair also occurred in the array of furniture. Buttoned leather armchairs stood alongside wicker stools, black ebony dining chairs drawn up to card tables, while deep plush velvet armchairs, stood beside cane tables. Informality was everywhere, a jumble of this and that with knick-knacks abounding.

Even so, all this contributed to an agreeable atmosphere that caused one to smile, just the place to linger over strong coffee and stimulating conversation.

"Would the gentlemen care for sheesha?" Akram asked.

"Hookah," Ali translated. "In Egypt we say sheesha. The English say, Hubble Bubble."

"Thank you Akram. We would," I answered. "Can I also have a coffee? Mervyn, are you going to try a mint tea, or would you rather fruit juice?"

"I'll try a mint tea, thank you Akram."

"What flavour would you like your sheesha, gentlemen?"

At this point, I was completely stumped.

"You've a choice effendi," Ali said. "Either apple, apricot, mango and tangerine. If you're smoking a double, then you'll have to choose the same."

"Apple sounds nice," Mervyn said.

"Then apple it is," I said. "A double sheesha for Mervyn and I, Akram, and of course, one for our friend Ali, as well as whatever he wishes to drink."

As we waited for our drinks and the mysterious and extraordinary sheesha, and while Ali explained to us the history of the Khan, I took a moment to study our surroundings and its occupants.

Consisting of a series of Arabic arches, combined with numerous mirrors, Akram's coffee shop was long, narrow, and crowded with customers from the front to the rear. Most were men, middle aged, or younger and obviously affluent, since at this hour of the day, if they were not, they would surely be about their trade.

The majority wore traditional robes, either black, white, or striped, as well as turbans, or else red felt tarbushes. There were however, several men wearing suits and ties, appearing quite European except for their tanned faces and dark moustaches. Here, I must admit to a predilection for the Arab countenance. Their dark, ambiguous eyes hold a mystery, as if they might oblige a man such as me, even if they were not of my persuasion. In addition, lately I discovered my taste for smooth fair skin had altered, finding the occasional glimpse of chest hair between Ali's open collars, quite attractive.

I was also surprised to see women amongst the gathering, grouped around tables, although not mixing with the men.

Wearing black from head to toe, with no trace of hair emerging from under their headdresses, they seemed extremely independent and self-possessed, bringing to mind Major Shepherd's description of the riots after the war, when women took to the streets to demonstrate against British oppression.

All things considered, El Fishawy's impressed me enormously. The atmosphere was cultured, with a strong sense of tradition, as well as progress. Endeavouring to think of such a café in London, I failed.

"How do you smoke this thing Ali?" Mervyn asked, as two sheesha pipes arrived at the table.

"You and Mr Ron smoke the double one," he said. "Mine's a different flavour. I prefer apricot. It's sweeter than apple. But have your coffee and tea first, while the tobacco catches."

When last in Egypt, I recall men smoking sheesha pipes, though had no opportunity or inclination to do so myself. The reason being, in my naivety, I am ashamed to confess, I believed the sheesha or hookah pipe, to be an instrument for imbibing hashish, a drug commonly found in the Middle East. Innocently, I had no idea one could use it to smoke ordinary tobacco. I suddenly realised the great disservice I did to the men I saw smoking them back then, categorising them as drug addicts.

Wisps of pale grey smoke began to emerge from the wind guards of both sheeshas, Ali saying they were ready.

"Take the end of the hose in your mouth and suck," he said, doing so with his.

Following his instructions, Mervyn and I immediately heard the familiar bubbling as we dragged the tobacco smoke down the body of the sheesha, through the water jar, up the hose, eventually filling our mouths, and subsequently our lungs, with strong cool smoke, which tasted of ripe Worcester apples. It was truly an extremely pleasant experience and we agreed with Ali when he explained how popular a social activity smoking sheesha was in Egypt.

"Why not buy one?" suggested Mervyn. "We could smoke it at Hyde House."

"Can you imagine what Wilfred and mother would say if they saw us. They hold the same conviction as I once had. They'd think our travels had turned us into a couple of opium addicts."

Still, after much debate, we decided we would purchase one anyhow. Even though the kind of tobacco used, along with the flavoured essence in the water, might be difficult to buy on the streets of Bath. We also considered a sheesha might look particularly fine on an occasional table at the foot of the stairs at Hyde House, serving as a fond reminder of our day at El Fishawy's.

Chapter Ten
Wikala al Ghouri - Delicious delights

"I'm hungry," Mervyn, said. "Can we order food Ali?"

"Not here," he answered. "This is a coffee shop. I'll take you somewhere where they have good kebab and kofta."

Finishing our drinks, and taking the last puff from the sheesha, we paid the bill. Then saying thank you and goodbye to Akram, we returned to the street, for my part, feeling somewhat light headed from the effects of strong coffee and tobacco.

Ali hurried us along passages and down narrow alleyways, past captivating perfume sellers, a gleaming goldsmith and brass bazaar, pungent fruit stalls, vegetable and spice markets, noisy tin smiths, not counting shops selling sheeshas of every imaginable size and description. There were also the inevitable shops where one is able to purchase authentic Egyptian artefacts fresh from the tomb of a recently exhumed Pharaoh, hieroglyphics painted on loose sheets of papyrus, or mounted under glass in ebony frames. We even encountered a tent bazaar, a more colourful exhibition of fabrics and embroidery I have yet to see.

Arriving beneath the twin towers of the massive fortress gate, Bab el Nasre, we paused in its shadow. Then, off again, along Shari Nasre, crossing the busy thoroughfare of Shari Mouski, glimpsing the twin minarets and gate of Bab Zuweila, subsequently diving headlong towards the Azhar Mosque.

Considering it was almost twenty years since I last visited Cairo, it surprised me how well I remembered the names of streets and places of interest. Clearly, the city had made a huge impression on me.

Finally, in a narrow street behind the mosque, Ali brought us to a halt beneath the immense walls of a great crumbling edifice.

"This is the Wikala al Ghouri," he said, as Mervyn and I gathered our breath. "Five hundred years ago this was a Caravanserai their caravans began and finished its journey. Here agents bargained with wealthy merchants and conducted deals with traders, either from the city or the rest of the known world. It was an inn and also where locals, as well as foreign dealers, were accommodated and found refreshment, while purchasing goods for their countries far away."

"How did the camel caravans get here?" Mervyn asked.

"Mostly along the Silk Road from Persia. But also from all over North Africa."

"What things did they carry?" I asked.

"A huge variety of luxury goods from China, like silk, satin and tea, hemp and musk, plus spices, tea and ivory from India; also jewellery, glassware and even medicine. But several hundred years ago the arrival of sea travel brought an end to the camel caravan trade."

We were standing in front of the massive limestone entrance to the building, beneath two elaborately sculpted arches, one inside the other, adjoining a pair of huge wooden doors, appearing so ancient I was sure Noah himself had fashioned them. The walls towered to a staggering height of perhaps eighty feet, encompassing four floors of windows, some covered by decorative ironwork grills. At the top, just below what I imagined to be the roof, lattice covered oriole windows projected over the street. These, Ali explained, were Mashrabiyas, a characteristic style of window found all over the Arab world. Projecting out of a room, they give anyone sitting inside a protracted view of the street below, yet the occupant remains unseen to passers-by.

However, the most interesting feature of the building was its colour, since the stone walls were layered alternately, one yellow, the other red, reaching the top successively, reminding me of one of Mrs Lanesome's chocolate sponge cakes.

"Inside Wikala," continued Ali. "The camels were loaded or unloaded, rested, fed and watered. There were shops where the camel drivers could purchase provisions for their journey, as well as kitchens and refectories where they took food, along with chambers where they could lay their heads.

"Most civilised," I said. "What's its use today Ali?"

"Wikala is now a historic monument and preserved for all Cairo citizens to enjoy. There are exhibitions of art and cultural shows. Here you can see the Dervishes. They perform every Saturday evening. But for our purposes today, and why I have brought you here, is the restaurant, perhaps the best in all Cairo."

"Come on Ali," Mervyn said. "I'm starving. Let's go in."

We ducked through a Judas gate within the door to find ourselves surrounded on four sides by an enormous rectangular courtyard, completely open to the sky and a duplicate of the outside in style. Except on ground level, and one floor above, were a series of large arched recesses. Ali told us these openings were once shops, refectories, storerooms, bakeries, and kitchens. It was truly fascinating to imagine the busy daily life in this most romantic of places. I could almost see the hustle and bustle. The courtyard crowded with camels, some resting, idly chewing the cud, others lugubriously rising to their feet, feeling the weight of their new burdens. All the while, a babble of haggling and banter, as men beat down prices, or boasted gains.

Ali pointed across the courtyard to a cluster of people sitting at tables and shaded by a yellow awning

"You see the restaurant in the corner," he said. "It's very famous. Most famous in all Cairo. Owned by a well-known Cairo actor. A very funny man."

Crossing the square, we passed a magnificent mosaic fountain, the sound of drizzling water reminding me of a holiday Eric and I took in Spain, and a visit to the gardens of the Alhambra Palace in Cordoba.

"Welcome to Naguib's," Ali said proudly, as the Maître D stepped forward to greet us. "A table for three please Ahmed."

"Certainly Ali," he said. "Gentlemen. This way."

At the table, three waiters held out our chairs while we sat down, and another gave us menus once we were seated. At this point, I must mention the waiters, since they were dressed in voluminous white pantaloons, a cream silk shirt, red and gold brocade bolero, and scarlet tarbushes. They were also extremely handsome and obviously the choice of someone with an eye for masculine beauty. Mervyn and I looked at each other across the table and raised our eyebrows. Of course, Ali was unaware or our preference and therefore unconscious of the gesture.

Our surroundings were sumptuous, barely out doing the Abdin Palace itself. Portraits of Mameluk rulers hung in gilded frames on the ancient walls, while numerous copper and brass lamps dangled on chains from a brilliantly decorated dome overhead. Everything, from the intricate lattice of the wooden screens, the elaborate designs on the tiled floor and the luxurious couches and divans, reminded me of mosques I had visited. I was familiar with the interior of many, but never thought I would eat in one. Positioned beside each table was a low occasional table, the now recognizable sheesha placed on a pristine linen tablecloth beside a bowl of rose petals. With this delicate perfume, along with the aroma of spice scenting the air, the experience was entirely theatrical and mysterious, as if Mervyn, Ali, and I had truly entered the world of Ali Baba and a Thousand and One Nights.

The restaurant's clientele were equally glamorous. Most of the thirty or so tables were occupied by both well-dressed Egyptian businessmen and fashionable European women, more than likely, wives of diplomats or financiers. In addition, tourists like ourselves abounded, sampling the delights of Naquib's for the first time, or making a return visit after a long overdue leave of absence. Several Arab women were sitting at a table, wearing the familiar headdress and black robes. However, a glimpse of gold on the wrist or ankle, and a ring on a finger, betrayed their elevated status.

The menu was in English as well as in Egyptian, so there was a moment of silence as we scanned the delicacies on offer. Furtively, I glanced around at the dishes other diners were consuming.

"I like the look of that over there Ali," I whispered. "What is it?"

"Kebab Captain. With a bean and eggplant stew."

"What's the meat?" asked Mervyn.

"Anything you wish Mr Mervyn. Beef, lamb, or chicken. I like lamb."

"Mahshi Warak Enab sounds nice," I said. "I've eaten stuffed vine leaves before at a Greek restaurant in Soho."

"Egyptian cuisine is similar to Greece in many ways," Ali continued. "Our bread is almost the same as Greek pitta, while in Turkey, Syria, Lebanon, and Palestine. You can buy Shawama any day of the week, just as you can on a street corner in the Khan. Shish kebab and koftas are eaten all over the Middle East. Shish translates in Turkish as a sword and Kofta as mince. In the case of shish kebab, because meat is grilled on metal skewers, it's said that shish kebab originated hundreds of years ago when Persian soldiers spiked meat on their swords and cooked it over an open fire."

"You're exciting my taste buds Ali," I said. "It's shish kebab for me."

"And kofta for me," said Mervyn.

"Lamb, beef, or chicken?"

Mervyn chose beef and I decided upon lamb. Ali also asked the waiter to bring us mezze and kusharie, enough for three, explaining that kusharie was a rice and lentil dish, which I secretly thought sounded boring. Nonetheless, no one was more surprised than I when it arrived looking quite splendid, delicately coloured beans and rice, topped with a vibrant tomato sauce and crispy brown onion rings.

Mervyn's kofta came with khiar be lebaan, which Ali informed us was yoghurt, a kind of curdled milk yet to be heard of in England. This being combined with chopped cucumber, garlic, spices, and mint.

Tasting the yoghurt, Mervyn turned up his nose saying it was off. I hardly thought it would be the case, so tried some myself, finding it bitter, tangy, and minty, all at the same time; perfectly complimenting the taste of the lamb.

While we ate the mezze, we chatted about our different lives, the contents of the platter in the middle of the table gradually diminishing.

"I would like to see your Tower of London," Ali said. "I read in British history books about your Kings and Queens. Kings have many wives and chop off their heads when they stop liking them. Many caliphs and khedives would have wished to do the same."

Ali must find our history fascinating, since his own is much older. Yet, we British know a great deal more about the lives of our royalty than the Egyptians do of Pharaoh Rameses the second or young Tutankhamen, their records surviving as hieroglyphics on the walls of ancient temples and tombs. Ali would regard our more recent history and the scandalous machinations of Henry the eighth, Anne Boleyn, Charles the first and George the fourth, as a person might reading a penny dreadful novel.

"Why not pay us a visit Ali," said Mervyn, cutting a stuffed vine leaf, and then dipping a piece into a sauce, which Ali said was Tahini.

"I'd dearly wish to," he answered. "It's so green and everywhere there are streams and rivers, not sand, sand, sand, and sun, sun, sun."

"But we have rain, rain, rain, and snow, snow, snow," I put in. "Lots of it sometimes."

"Last winter, Cairo had one inch of rain, from November to January. Everyone goes crazy when it happens and run around getting wet. As for snow. I have never seen it."

"I'll talk to Ron Ali," Mervyn whispered, although loud enough for me to hear. "He's a knack of making things happen that's quite miraculous."

Soon, the koftas, kebabs, rice, stuffed vine leaves, yoghurt, salad and pitta bread were simply a memory. Then we sat back, lit cigarettes, while Mervyn and I drank the last of a bottle of chardonnay.

"May I take it upon myself to order dessert," Ali asked. "As a surprise, you might say?"

"Of course," Mervyn and I answered.

He called a waiter and whispered a word in his ear.

"Tell us a little about the owner Ali," I said. "He sounds interesting."

"In Egypt, Naquib Al Rihani is known as the Father of Comedy.

He's been an actor on the Cairo stage for many years and appeared in numerous films. He not only acts, but also has his own ensemble, writing and directing his own plays and films. His wife is the famous Lebanese actress and dancer, Badia Masabni. It is her cabaret place, Casino Badia in Shari Emad El Din, the street behind Shepheard's Hotel. Naquib's latest film, 'Salamah Fe Kheer', is showing at the Metropole at the moment."

Once again, it is necessary for me to express my amazement at Ali's depth of knowledge, every question answered succinctly and intelligently. Mervyn and I were seeing the real Cairo and learning more than ever we could, going around on our own, or tagging on to a tour organised by the hotel. How else would we have visited the fascinating El Fishawy's or Naquib's, the very best restaurant in all Cairo all in a day? These were places to stumble upon if fortunate, or miss altogether, never to have the pleasure of experiencing them. Ali was well worth his six piastres an hour.

The waiter appeared, this time carrying a platter arrayed with a collection of mouth-watering Egyptian sweets and pastries, which Ali introduced individually.

"These are Baklavas," he said, pointing to a group of small glistening treats appearing to be swathed in puff pastry. "A mixture of ground pistachio nuts and honey, wrapped in filo. The small diamond shaped cakes are Basbousa, semolina soaked in sugar water and topped with an almond. Then we have the square white cakes, Asbusa, creamed wheat mixed with butter, yoghurt, sugar and slivered almonds."

"What are these?" Mervyn asked. "They look like birds' nests."

"Exactly Mr Mervyn. They're Pistachio Birds' Nests, very popular with children, sweet and crunchy, a nutty mixture in a round of vermicelli pasta and soaked in honey. Also, you'll see there are dates stuffed with shelled almonds, hazelnuts, and honey."

"Stop Ali!" I exclaimed. "Do you wish me to drop dead on the spot? They're probably fine for Mervyn. But I don't think my waistline can cope with them."

"Mr Ron," he said. "Try a Baklava. They're very small."

"If you insist Ali."

Of course, it tasted exquisite. How could such a tiny morsel burst with such flavour? Delicate nuttiness rolling around my tongue. A treat fit for sultans, pashas, caliphs, and kings. Mervyn tried one of everything, his expression changing from nonchalance to bliss as each taste exploded in his mouth.

***

It was after three in the afternoon when we finally left Naquib's, with the easy sensation one has after experiencing a wonderful meal in the pleasant company of friends. Out in the street, Ali hailed a caleche, the Cairo version of a hackney cab.

"I don't know about you chaps," I said. "But I'm exhausted. I think a long soak in a cool bath is in order this evening. How about you Mervyn?"

"Definitely," he agreed.

"Ali. Can we drop you somewhere on our way back to Shepheard's?"

"I live in Imbaba, across the Nile, on the other side of Gezira. It's too far out of your way."

"No, please. It'll be our pleasure. Mervyn's not yet seen the Nile, and it'll be good to get some fresh air."

With the hood down, the breeze was indeed delicious, and with Ali pointing out places of interest along the way, our caleche clattered along the busy streets, the roll of the wheels and ring of horse's hooves resounding off the elegant frontage of the Sphinx Bar and other restaurants that we passed.

Once past the Opera House and Ezbekiya Gardens, the driver turned left onto Fuad El Awal Avenue, a beautiful wide thoroughfare bounded by tall impressive buildings. This led us through Bulaq, towards the twin pillars topped with lamps of the Abdul Ela, or Bulaq Bridge, and the River Nile itself.

"The bridge used to open for water traffic," explained Ali, as we bowled along, the criss cross ironwork making us giddy for a moment. "Every day, except Sundays, from twelve noon until quarter to one. Then three in the afternoon, until quarter to four."

"Which means it's closed to road traffic at the moment," I said, looking at my wristwatch. "But we're still heading across?"

"Because several years ago the machinery broke down, and no one's bothered to mend it."

"How then do boats go up the Nile?" asked Mervyn.

"Around the other side of El Gezira, up El Bahr el Ama, or the Blind Nile as some call it."

Still travelling along Fuad Avenue, we were now on Gezira Island, a lush paradise during the war, entirely devoted to leisure, remaining so to this day. Almost every afternoon, one can visit the racecourse and gamble ones hard-earned pay on a horse. See a chukka of Polo between rival British cavalry brigades, and either play cricket, hockey, tennis, a round of golf, or roller skate.

If you so wish, you can visit the Nile Aquarium Grotto and see more than just fishes, if you are lucky. Have a drink with pals at the exulted Gezira Sporting Club, the YMCA club, or National Sports Club. Alternatively, relax in the shade of a tree and read a newspaper, or book in the El Zuhriya or El Kubri Gardens. Also, you could visit an exhibition at the Royal Agriculture Exhibition Ground. I remember being impressed with the island on my first visit, and I was keen to show it off to Mervyn, although, that would need to wait.

The northern section of the island, the part we were driving through, is known as El Zamalek, an extremely affluent district of Cairo, lived in by the Egyptian elite. It was once the location of Royal Palaces, villas and apartment complexes, and it interested me to see it unaltered.

It was that glorious part of the afternoon when the sun has lost its heat and the land begins to cool. Therefore, by the time we crossed the island, I anticipated a balmy evening and yet another glorious sunset.

Since Mervyn and I were facing forward in the carriage, and opposite Ali, after crossing the Zamalek Bridge, he turned and said a few words to the driver. As a result, a short while later we made a right turn and began following the west bank of the Nile.

Imbaba is a more recent quarter than Gamaliya or the Khan el Khalili, the buildings reminding me of the back streets of Paris. In particular, Montmartre, where similarly crumbling tenements, iron balconies, shuttered windows prevail. With forlorn attempts to beautify with dismal pot plants. Suddenly I recognised the area, since I had visited Imbaba twenty years earlier when my army pals and I would drink at a club, and watch the belly dancers.

"I know where we are Ali!" I exclaimed. "Near here, during the war, there was a club called the Kit Kat."

"It's still here effendi."

Ali pointed across the road to a large courtyard, open to the sky, with dozens of tables and chairs, set out around a large stage.

"My word!" I cried. "In all those years, it hasn't changed."

"Yes effendi. And it remains the best club in Cairo."

"I'm glad Ali. We three must go one night. I used to enjoy watching the dancing girls. Where shall we drop you?"

"Just here will be fine. I share a houseboat with a couple of chaps. I'd ask you both on board, but it's rather disorganised. Maybe another day. My room has a veranda. Perhaps we could take lunch there."

"Certainly," I said. "That's a splendid idea."

Ali explained that, since the next day was Friday, and the Muslim holy day, he would be unable to act as our guide, although he made himself available over the weekend. So we arranged to collect him from the same place early on Saturday morning.

Once Mervyn and I saw him disappear through a gate in a high hedge, I told the driver to take us back to Shepheard's.

Chapter Eleven
Camels – Keffiyehs - Abbassia Barracks

Over the following days, our lives became a whirlwind of sights, sounds, smells and flavours, as Ali sped us around Cairo, from one place of historical or cultural interest to another. Mervyn and I saw the Tombs of the Caliphs, a gigantic complex east of the old city walls, where we marvelled at Qaitbai Mosque and its beautiful ceiling.

We visited the Citadel and the magnificent, Mosque of Mohammed Ali, otherwise referred to as the Alabaster Mosque and for good reason due to its astounding interior, only challenged by The Blue Mosque in old Constantinople. The views of Cairo from the walls of the fortifications were incredible. I used a substantial amount of film photographing the panorama across the city and the unique close proximity of the Mosques of El Rifai and El Hassan at the foot of the ramparts.

All the while, Ali acquainted us with facts and statistics regarding the age of the building, along with the sultan, caliph, or khedive responsible for its construction. He was a mine of information, Mervyn and I incredulous as to how he retained such knowledge, while wondering whether there was ever a question he was unable to answer.

The day at the Citadel presented a doubt in my mind, since the sight of the British soldiers quartered in the barracks at the rear of the fortification, caused me to remember that Mervyn and I had unfinished business, before we could properly enjoy our holiday.

From the time we arrived, I enquired at the hotel reception if there was a message for me from Captain Haig, but each time the answer was in the negative. Therefore, after a week of hearing nothing I decided to take the initiative. After all, Harry was at Main Barracks in Abbassia, that much we knew. So I asked Ali if we might take a trip to the district.

As I was stationed at the X Aero Factory during the war, I knew the tram to catch, but having grown accustomed to Ali's company, I invited him along.

"Mr Ron," he said, as we waited at Rameses Station for our tram. "I know a man in Abbassia who owns camels. Would you like to hire three?"

"Please Ron," begged Mervyn. "We've been here nearly a week, and you promised I'd ride a camel when we see the Pyramids."

Seeing a visit to one of the seven wonders of the ancient world was such a splendid excursion, I purposely delayed our trip until we had exhausted the sites of Cairo. I wished the experience to be memorable for Mervyn, planning to stay overnight at the Mena House Hotel. Rising before dawn, seeing the sunrise over the monument, and then viewing it at sunset, both events spectacular beyond doubt.

The tram rattled northeast, exchanging the banks, hotels and recreation clubs of El Ezbekiya, for the book-publishing district of El Faggala, also El Zahir. The former, Ali explained, being the centre of the Coptic Christian church in Egypt, the latter named after Sultan Al Zahir, the first Egyptian ruler to build a cruciform mosque.

Bowling along, I was surprised at how many landmarks I remembered. As we trundled around Midan El Zahir, the familiar Sultan El Zahir Mosque appeared in the centre. Whereas, the new Shalom Synagogue coming into view, impressed me as the tram turned into Shari el Abbassia.

Ali was sitting opposite Mervyn and I, so I divided my time between gazing out of the window, scrutinising him.

In most Arab countries, on any form of public transport, women have the option to sit together, away from male passengers.

Occasionally, less orthodox females sit amongst the men, usually those who wear only the veil over their head and not completely hiding their faces.

Several less traditional women were sitting near to us, and watching Ali, I wondered if he would show an interest? Of course, the teachings of Mohammed say it is strictly forbidden to look at a female, male, or youth, with any kind of lust in mind. Therefore, it interested me to see his reaction when, at a stop near the French Hospital, a woman sat down beside me, and directly opposite Ali. As I mentioned a while ago when we were smoking sheesha at El Fishawy's, the abstruseness of Arab men intrigues me. Once again, I am mystified. Visible familiarity occurs between men, even openly holding hands, something unheard of in northern Europe. On the other hand, if this familiarity was happening in public, what then went on in private? As with Catholic men and youths, who, starved of sexual encounters with the opposite sex, liaise with each other. Were these young Arab men similarly experimenting in order to gain experience before they eventually marry? I understood the practice was regarded as quite normal in either culture, as long as one man played an active role, while the other remained passive.

Sitting opposite Mervyn and I, so embedded was his religion and culture, Ali made no attempt to look at the woman sitting beside me and continued to gaze, abstractedly, out of the window. To Ali, leering was a sin before Allah and therefore punishable. As a result, Ali's enigmatic personality and romantic preference was to remain a mystery to me for a while longer.

Before we reached the military complex, Ali rang the bell and the tram stopped under an avenue of jacarandas and acacia trees, which fortunately provided shade during the short walk to his friend's house.

Arriving at the entrance to a courtyard, Mervyn and I were daunted to see it crowded with camels; so many in fact, we were reluctant to enter, being aware of the aggressive nature of the creatures. Ali forged ahead into the multitude, however, with Mervyn and me following, unenthusiastically.

The camels were either sitting in that particular folded posture so typical of them, or standing gazing at us as we passed, while idly chewing the remains of their breakfast of alfalfa. I was pleased I had eaten my breakfast at an early hour, since the smell of their breath, urine, and faeces, was quite revolting, and might have easily caused me to give up the contents of my stomach.

Ali found the owner and began to barter the price of hire, a great deal of waving of arms and hands accompanying the deal. It was obvious the man could see Mervyn and I were English, and thought to double his rate. Ali would have none of it nonetheless, and finally, after smiles and handshakes, he beckoned us into the melee.

"Before you choose your camel," he said. "I am worried you have no hats effendi. The sun is very hot. Your faces will burn. My friend can lend us three keffiyehs. One for each of us. The Arab headdress will protect you effendi."

"What a good idea," I said. "May as well look the part. Don't you think Mervyn?"

Ali and his friend went inside the house, leaving Mervyn and me to face the camels alone. Nevertheless, they soon returned, holding a couple of linen sheets and the traditional agal, or cord, which fastens around the keffiyeh to hold it in place.

"How do you wear this thing," Mervyn said, looking at it curiously.

"Fold it into a triangle," Ali explained. "Place the folded side across your forehead, a little over your eyes, and then make a figure eight with your agal and push it onto your head."

We did as he instructed, and soon began to realise the benefit of the headgear, as it entirely shaded our face, head, and neck.

Once dressed, next came the task of choosing our camel. I decided upon a white, smooth creature, its eyes and eyelashes its best feature and reminding me of a photograph I once saw of the film actress, Marlene Dietrich. Mervyn picked a dark brown camel, much woollier than mine. Since they were sitting it was difficult to distinguish whether they were male or female, but I gambled upon mine being female and Mervyn's male.

Ali's friend had gathered a couple of boys, more than likely his sons, and they approached, wending their way through the sea of seated camels, carrying embroidered rugs, saddles and halters. From a respectful distance, we watched the boys attach the halters and reins to each animal, then throw the saddle and rugs across the camel's backs.

"What keeps us from sliding off Ali?" I asked. "There's no girth around the middle."

"The hump," he replied, visibly amused by my question. "A wooden frame with a stuffed leather pad fits over it. The rugs then cover the saddle, leaving the pommels front and back, to hang on to."

"Do you think it'll take my weight? I'm a lot heavier than when I last rode a camel."

"Camels can carry anything up to nine hundred pounds effendi."

"That's reassuring at least."

I could see my questions were making Ali giggle.

"My friend Mamoud says yours is his favourite," he said. "She's middle aged and called Nizeh."

"Isn't that the name of King Fuad's wife? I don't think King Farouk's mother would approve of having a camel named after her."

"No! No! Effendi," Ali laughed. "Our Queen is Nazli."

Nonetheless, as he spoke, he touched his hand on his heart as a gesture of respect.

"How old's middle aged?" Mervyn asked.

"Twenty five Mr Mervyn. Camels can live for fifty years or more."

"Camels are wonderful creatures. The ships of the desert," I said, avoiding the gaze of Nizeh. "But I understand they can be bad tempered with a tendency to spit."

Ali shook his head.

"Not so effendi. Europeans see their sneery expression and the growling sound they make as menacing. But most camels are docile and even friendly. They can get quite attached to their owner and fret if they are parted from him for any length of time."

Positioned beside our camel's heads, the boys held the halters as a signal they were ready. Nonchalantly, trying hard not to let them sense the fear we were experiencing, Mervyn and I sidled up to our camels.

Reaching the side of his, Mervyn suddenly panicked.

"What shall I do Ali? I've never ridden a camel. Not even at Bristol Zoo."

"Use the stirrup hanging from the saddle Mr Mervyn," Ali said, mounting his own animal. "Then swing your leg over. He'll get up, back legs first, so lean back when you feel him begin to rise."

I was also listening to Ali's instructions, as it was nearly twenty years since I had ridden a camel. But, like riding a bicycle, as Nizeh rose to her feet I automatically leaned back as I catapulted into the air, then forward as she straightened her front legs. Looking around, I saw Mervyn's camel had also risen to his feet without mishap.

"Sit in the middle Mr Mervyn and hold onto the pommels, back and front," Ali continued as the boys passed the halters up to us. "You won't need to kick him. He'll follow Mr Ron and me."

We moved off across the courtyard at an easy pace, passing through the gates and out onto the hot and dusty road, where I was immediately thankful I was wearing my keffiyeh.

Leading our little caravan, Ali appeared completely relaxed, his legs wrapped around the front pommel in a most calm fashion. On the other hand, Mervyn and I were rigid with anticipation of falling and landing in the dirt. Further, along the road, Ali turned to us and pointed to a tall tower up ahead.

"That's the observatory. The Main Barracks are just behind."

"I can see why they're called ships of the desert," Mervyn shouted from the rear. "I believe I'm feeling seasick."

"Just go with the motion," I called. "Don't fight it. You'll soon get used to it."

To the left, beyond a large mosque, appeared a block of austere official buildings. The sound of drilling soldiers, along with the bark of a regimental sergeant major, echoed across a parade ground; very reminiscent of my day's square bashing in India.

In a little while, Ali turned his camel towards another dusty road, this time lined with date palms, and here at last I saw a formidable gate in the distance, marking the entrance to the Main Barracks at Abbassia. It was then that I realised how ridiculous we must look and began having misgivings as to whether I was doing the right thing.

Reaching the gate, a guard challenged us.

"Who goes there?" he yelled, just his tanned nose and chin appearing under the peak of his cap.

"Captain Fry," I said. "To see the medical officer, Lieutenant Chapman."

"Wait there!" ordered the guard.

He marched to the guardhouse, and after saying a few words to the soldier inside, returned to his post. We waited in the hot sun while flies buzzed around our camels, causing them to flap their ears and shake their heads. After a moment, a soldier leaned out of the guardhouse window.

"The M.O's not here," he shouted. "He's at the hospital."

"Where's that?" I asked.

"Down the road."

Thanking him, we continued.

"They must be cavalry stables," Mervyn said, when a group of low, narrow buildings came into view. "Maybe someone there knows Harry."

Three young troopers were forking straw onto a cart. So being resourceful souls, we directed our camels through the gates and into the yard.

"Oi! Oi!" one trooper said. "Who've we here? Bloody Lawrence of Arabia, and Rudolph Valentino?"

The others laughed, leaning on their forks, welcoming a break from work.

"What can we do for you gents?" asked the first trooper.

"I hope you can help us," I replied. "We're looking for a trooper,"

"Aren't we all," he said, nudging the young chap standing beside him, causing much merriment from the other, "What might his name be?"

"Trooper Harry Watson."

"Harry! We know Harry. He's in our mob. What's your business with him?"

"I'd rather not say. Although, we're rather concerned regarding his health."

"Us as well mate. They've got him locked up."

Mervyn was suddenly beside me, and seeing him, I realised how ridiculous we must look to the three young cavalrymen. However, I threw doubt and embarrassment to the wind.

"Why?" I continued.

"Hey!" the trooper said. "Before we give away a mate's private business, might we know who we're addressing?"

"I'm Captain Fry, retired, Somerset Light Infantry and late of the Royal Flying Corp. And this is Mervyn Watson, Harry's younger brother. The young man over there is our guide, Ali."

"Pleased to meet you Captain. Harry's brother! Delighted to make your acquaintance Mervyn. I'm Trooper Peter Harding, and this is Trooper J B Shaw, and Trooper Burns. We're all in the 7th Queens Own Hussars."

From my lofty position, I could see along the entire length of the stable block, and the piles of straw outside every open door.

"I dare say you're wondering what happened to the horses?" Trooper Harding continued. "The last went yesterday."

"This is the final time we'll ever muck out," Trooper Shaw added. "We're being mechanised. They're knocking down the stables and putting up tank sheds."

"We know," I said, "Your Major Fielden told us a few days ago. I must say. I'm sorry. It's the end of an era. But progress is progress I suppose. We can't halt that."

"I agree Captain," Harding said. "But I can't see us getting attached to a tank or an armoured car like we were to our old chargers."

"Tell us though Trooper Harding," I said. "What's the matter with Harry? You say he's locked up. Is he in trouble?"

"If you've spoken with the major," Harding said. "Then I shouldn't think it'll do any harm to tell you. Harry's not really locked up. He's in the hospital. In there for his own good, you might say."

"Is my brother ill?" Mervyn mumbled, clearly embarrassed to be speaking for the first time.

"Far from it lad," Burns said. "Never seen him fitter. He's always enjoyed sports. In the hospital, there's a gymnasium. He told us on our last visit how he's there every day swinging clubs, chucking about medicine balls, climbing ropes and leaping vaults."

"My word!" I exclaimed.

"We reckon it's the only thing keeping him going."

"But if he's not ill, then what's the problem?"

Trooper Harding lowered his voice. "It's mental Captain. Harry had a queer turn Christmas before last. They said it was a nervous breakdown."

"That's when the letters to mum began to arrive. Remember Ron?" put in Mervyn.

"We helped him send them," said Shaw. "We sneaked them out of the hospital. They wouldn't have wanted anyone on the outside to know what was going on."

"Who's they?" I asked. "You make it sound like a prison Trooper Shaw."

"Because it's a mental hospital Captain," Harding said. "They've told Harry he's going to have electricity put through his head."

"But that's shocking," I said, immediately realising my inappropriate choice of words.

"It began the year before last, when Harry was kicked in the lower regions by a horse."

"How painful."

"Yes Captain. Ever after, you couldn't get him near one."

"Not especially good when you're a trooper in the Hussars."

"For a long while he kept it a secret. Just made excuses for not attending parades or mucking out duty."

"All the while though," Trooper Shaw said, taking up the story. "Harry was slowly getting worse. Until one night, towards Christmas before last, he finally snapped. We were in the Services Club. He had one or two and just went crazy, telling us he wanted to leave the regiment. Of course, we were staggered. We'd never heard of anyone having a mortal fear of horses.

"I looked it up in the barracks library," Harding said. "It's called Equinophobia; a recognised psychological condition. I reckon that's why they say if a horse throws you then climb back on immediately."

"In the end, Harding and I persuaded Harry to see the doctors," Shaw said. "That's when they put him in the there."

Shaw pointed ahead to a large squat building at the end of the road.

"You mean he's been in there nearly eighteen months!" I exclaimed. "But haven't you told him he needn't worry now, as all the horses have gone?"

"We have Captain. But it's not made a scrap of difference. He still wants out. Harding and I think it's all down to him being homesick. He's always talking about his family, especially his mum."

"Are they giving him tablets? Perhaps he doesn't know his own mind."

"He seemed all there on our last visit," Harding put in. "Just a bit strung up. With all the exercise he puts in he's lost heaps of weight."

"Weren't you all given the option to transfer? Harry could have put himself on the list."

"Although Captain, that would mean a move to a cavalry regiment with horses.

"Of course. I see the problem."

Harding, Shaw, and Burns, seemed good intentioned chaps, keen to help Harry and see an end to his plight.

"Is there a way I might see the medical officer? The guard at the barracks said Lieutenant Chapman was here."

"If you'll forgive me Captain," Harding said, moving closer to the side of my camel. "Lieutenant Chapman's a pretty serious sort. If you wish to get anywhere with this I advise you get rid of the garb and leave the gyppie here, if you know what I mean."

"Thanks Trooper Harding. I quite understand. Then you think there's a chance?"

"Wait until I've cleaned up Captain, and I'll take you and Mervyn to the gate."

While Harding rolled down his shirtsleeves and put on his tunic and cap, Mervyn and I passed our headgear to Ali.

"Cush! Cush!" Ali ordered. Accordingly, our camels descended to the ground and the three of us dismounted.

"It's not far. You can see it from here," Harding said as we set off. "I've asked Shaw to give your dragoman a drink of water and some hay for your camels."

Chapter Twelve
A stumbling block at Abbassia Lunatic Asylum

Ahead, down an avenue of acacias, I saw a stone entrance gate, the cement render painted an attractive pale blue, intended I imagine to encourage confidence in the mind of a potential new patient. I must admit to feeling a strong wave of anxiety, as we approached a pair of daunting iron doors. In addition, Mervyn began coughing, a sure sign that he was nervous.

We let Peter Harding ring the bell, and then waited for a reaction.

After a while, a bolt shot back on the other side of the Judas Gate and it opened to reveal a small Egyptian man dressed in white, and wearing a white turban.

"These gentlemen are from England," Harding said. "They wish to see Lieutenant Chapman."

"Do they have an appointment?" the man said, staring at Mervyn and I intently.

"Sorry. No we don't," I said. "We have a question regarding one of the patients. This lad's his brother, and we were wondering whether he could visit him."

"It's a little out of the ordinary. But come inside and I'll take you to the Lieutenant's office. More than likely his secretary will know where the Lieutenant is."

"Do you wish me to come with you Captain?" Harding asked.

"Of course trooper. We wouldn't be here without your help, and if we get in to see Harry, I'm sure he'd be pleased to see you."

We followed the little Egyptian fellow across a leafy courtyard and into the main block. Then down a corridor smelling strongly of carbolic soap, while passing on the way many ominous iron doors, seeing closed food hatches and covered spy holes. Thankfully, everything was silent, with none of the expected sounds one imagines issuing from such places of confinement. So quiet in fact, I wondered whether the institution was still functioning.

Stopping in front of a door, the nameplate reading 'Lieutenant Chapman', we heard the sound of a typewriter. Knocking on the door the little Egyptian allowed us inside, where a young soldier, sitting at a desk under the window, was busy typing. He looked up as we entered, then continued with his task.

"Two gentleman to see the lieutenant," the Egyptian said. "Do you know where he is Private Watts?"

The young man stopped typing and consulted an open book on his desk.

"Lieutenant Chapman signed in at ten thirty, and this says he began his rounds in C Ward. That was two hours ago, so it could mean he's in the canteen having his lunch. Right where I should be. If it wasn't for this damn report."

"Fill in the relevant blanks if you please gentlemen," he said, passing me the book. "I'll have Mohammad look for the M.O. Meanwhile, please take a seat."

The young soldier indicated two plain wooden chairs against the wall, and once we had written our names, addresses and the date and time of our arrival, Mervyn and I sat down, while Harding remained standing. No one spoke, and the young soldier resumed his typing.

Abruptly, the door opened and a tall, lean officer strode in, slamming it behind him, clearly unaware that we were sitting beside it.

"Private Watts!" he yelled. "This better be important! I was just deciding whether to have another bowl of treacle pudding when that bloody gyppie, Mohammad, kowtowed up to my table and told me you wanted to see me."

"Yes Lieutenant Chapman," Private Watts said, nodding in our direction.

Realising he and the private were not alone, Chapman turned on his heels and faced us, causing Mervyn and me to jump to attention.

"Gentlemen," said Lieutenant Chapman. "What is it you want?"

His abruptness was quite alarming. Nonetheless, I took a deep breath and introduced everyone.

"My names Fry. Captain Fry, second of the fourth, Somerset Light Infantry, and late of the Royal Flying Corp, retired. In addition, may I introduce Mervyn Watson and Trooper Harding?"

"Pleased to meet you gentlemen," snapped Chapman. "What can I do for you?"

Chapman was the type I remembered from my days at Farmborough, bombastic and intimidating to a degree. Nevertheless, clearing my throat and swallowing hard, I pushed my misgivings to the rear and plunged forward.

"Last week, at the Semiramis Hotel, I was introduced to Captain Haig, Lieutenant Colonel Weatherall's adjutant, and I put to him a delicate matter regarding a trooper who has lately served in his cavalry regiment the 7th Queens Own Hussars. Captain Haig said he would bring the matter to the attention of the regimental medical officer. He said he would contact me again when it might be possible to see him. He mentioned your name. Consequently, because I've heard nothing since, I've taken it upon myself to move things along a bit."

"You have, have you? And what things may they be?"

"A little matter of my friend's brother. He's in a bit of a predicament, and we're given to understand he's a patient at this hospital."

As I faced the full brunt of this abrasive fellow, Mervyn and Trooper Harding stood motionless, since the tension in the room was thick enough to cut with a knife.

"The trooper's name?" retorted Chapman.

"Harry Watson."

"Do we have a Watson, Watts?"

"I'll see, sir."

Private Watts went to the filing cabinet and pulled out the bottom drawer.

"Wadded. Wagstaff. Wakim. Yes sir. Here he is. Watson. H."

"Are they the notes?"

"Sir!"

"Let's see what the professor's been up to."

Private Watts handed the lieutenant the file, then returned to his desk.

"Resume your seats gentlemen," said Lieutenant Chapman. "I'll be with you in a moment."

As we waited, the clock on the wall and the ceaseless rat-tat-tat of the typewriter, kept pace with the minutes.

"I see," Chapman said at last. "It seems the man in question is receiving treatment for anxiety. Cause unknown."

"Excuse me lieutenant," I said. "Would you know what the treatment might be?"

"ECT I should imagine Captain. It's the latest way we treat our most difficult patients. Two Italians discovered its uses only last year, and our Professor Hussein's been experimenting with it for about six months."

"Are you able to explain, in laymen's terms, exactly the nature of ECT?"

"Electroconvulsive Therapy. Electrodes are placed on the temple of the unconscious patient, and an electric current passes through his head. The results are quite astonishing."

"We've got to get Harry out of here," murmured Mervyn through his teeth.

"In the case of this young man," I said. "I'm given to understand that he's otherwise physically quite healthy. Surely that would indicate he's on the mend."

"I'm unable to answer that Captain. I've not seen the man. He's under the Professor's care. My role here is merely managerial. I have no say in the treatment of patients."

As initially anticipated, our mission to save Harry was not going to be easy. It was obvious he was enmeshed in bureaucracy and the manoeuvring of the medical profession, all the while serving as a guinea pig for experimentation. I joined Mervyn in the opinion that it was imperative we find a way to extract Harry from the situation. But how?

"Where would I find Professor Hussein?"

"Private Watts. Do you know?" Lieutenant Chapman asked.

"His rooms are in the city sir. The address is on the report."

Chapman turned to the front page.

"Ah yes. Here it is. Suite 12. Third floor. 64 Shari Imad el Din. Telephone, Taufiqiya 284."

Watts wrote the address down on a sheet of paper, handing it to me.

"Thank you Private Watts," I said, "Shari Imad el Din is behind our hotel, Mervyn. You were able to see Harry, Trooper Harding. How did he seem?"

"Yes Captain, a fortnight ago," said Harding. "Harry was on the up and up when Trooper Shaw and I saw him."

Lieutenant Chapman glanced once more at the file. "It seems the treatments began on the 20th January."

"That's just before we were allowed to see him sir. Harry mentioned he was about to start some new treatment. He seemed okay to us."

"That's no indication of his mental state, trooper," Chapman said. "I'm sure Professor Hussein knows what he's doing."

"Are we able to see Harry, Lieutenant Chapman?" I asked.

"I'm afraid not Captain. Since his treatment has begun, you'll need the professor's permission. He's the boss here."

Realising there was nothing more we could do for the present, Mervyn, Harding and I prepared to leave.

"Thank you lieutenant," I said, as we shook hands. "It seems our next step is to meet the professor. Perhaps we'll get some answers from him."

Gloomily, we followed Mohammad back to the sunlit courtyard, waiting while he let us out through the Judas gate.

"Once you're in a place like that," Mervyn said. "You're in for good."

"Don't say that, Mervyn," I said. "I'll move mountains to see Harry out of there."

"Abbassia Asylum's got a rotten reputation Captain Fry," Trooper Harding said as we began the walk back to the stables. "It's true. The people in there believe in locking up the insane and throwing away the key."

"But going on what I've heard, I honestly think there's nothing wrong with Harry. We need to have him properly assessed, and think of a strong reason to persuade them to release him."

Ali was waiting for us when we arrived, and insisted we put on our headgear once more.

"You'll be ill otherwise," he said, "The sun's at its strongest this time of day."

Feeling decidedly miserable and realising Mervyn felt the same; I asked Ali if we might return to the hotel.

"Mervyn and I would prefer not to do any more today, Ali. We're afraid we've lost the spirit for adventure."

Therefore, after saying goodbye to Trooper Harding, as well as Troopers Shaw and Burns, Mervyn, Ali, and I mounted our camels and returned them to their owner, catching the tram back to Ezbekiya.

Chapter Thirteen
Professor Hussein

Half an hour later, it was a relief to lay in a cool bath, also, just the place to mull over the events of the morning. Understandably, we were in a quandary. Never before had I felt so powerless to think of a strategy to secure Harry's release. Until that is I was bathed, dressed and sitting with Mervyn on the hotel terrace, watching the world go by, while sipping a long glass of ice cold Pimms.

Earlier, I had thought to buy The Times at the desk, and it lay unopened on the table. Glancing at it, a small caption caught my eye: 'Officers Cashiered'.

"My two Royal Engineer Captains!" I exclaimed. "They've reached a sentence."

"Which Captains?" Mervyn asked.

"I've been following the court martial since we left. Captain Chase and Captain Loftus Tottenham. They've been cashiered and Chase is to serve three years, hard labour."

"What for?"

"Messing around with boys. Both were district commissioners in the boy scouts."

Mervyn shook his head, and judging by his expression, it was unnecessary for me to ask his thoughts on the matter. Rather, he summoned a waiter and ordered us another round of Pimms.

"What did the other chap get?" he asked, stirring his drink with a swizzle stick, drowning a couple of mint leaves in the process.

"Eighteen months hard labour. Guilty on nine counts of indecency with boys under sixteen."

"Men like him give the boy scouts a bad name."

Opting to ignore this comment, I continued to read the newspaper.

"Hey! Look at this!" I said.

"Sir Victor Warrender announced in a Parliamentary reply," I read aloud, "that in the recent experiment to bring recruits, previously declared unfit, up to military physical standards, the extra cost, over and above, that of a normal recruit, was 3s 2d a week for each man. He moved on to state, that if the experiment were to be used on a bigger scale, the overall expense would be considerable. That's interesting and gives me an idea."

"What's that?"

"Nothing. I haven't thought it through yet. Tomorrow, I'll call the professor as soon as we've had breakfast."

***

Surprising even myself, and feeling quite the worse for several additional Pimms, plus cocktails and two bottles of Château Mouton, after my telephone call the following morning, in no time, Mervyn and I were sitting in Professor Hussein's rooms.

"You wouldn't think it was a letter written by a man half out of his mind would you professor," I said. "It's succinct and lucid. The fellow is begging someone to release him from purgatory."

"And I presume that someone is you Captain Fry," said the professor, laying Harry's letter on his desk.

"Yes professor. Trooper Watson is the brother of young Mervyn here, and we've come to Cairo from England to discover his whereabouts, only to discover he's locked away in your dreadful asylum."

"I thank you to keep your opinions to yourself Captain Fry. Asylums are not supposed to be spa hotels."

"Neither are they prisons. Surely, the inmates have the right to be treated with respect, whatever their mental condition?"

"Admittedly, the building is old and the amenities somewhat outdated and inadequate, but in the current political climate we do the best with what we have."

"Here Professor Hussein, I may be of assistance. If you could see yourself to personally assess Mervyn's brother, I could be of great assistance in improving your facility."

Saying this I could feel Mervyn's eyes suddenly upon me as I switched into my benefactor mode.

"Do I take that to mean, that if I pull a few strings regarding this young man's brother, you are offering me a bribe?"

"I regard it more as an incentive. Nevertheless, if you like to see it that way, then yes professor, that is precisely what I mean."

Normally, I discover that when money enters the equation people invariably have second thoughts, and are eventually won over. Therefore, I saw an immediate change in the old man's expression.

"What form of sum are we talking about Captain?"

Plainly, Hussein was oblivious of my status, as well as my family connections.

"Name your price professor."

Hussein raised his bristled grey eyebrows behind his horn-rimmed spectacles.

"Really! We're urgently in need of a modern operating theatre, let alone a swimming and therapy pool."

"Exactly professor. Now maybe we're getting somewhere. If you can guarantee Watson gets a fair assessment, conducted by yourself, with the benefit of a positive outcome, then these acquisitions are entirely possible."

Mervyn and I left Hussein's rooms, half an hour later in a totally different mood than when we went in. We were inspired by the encouraging response we experienced and fortified by the resolve of the professor's handshake at the doorway.

"Money talks again," said Mervyn as we climbed the hotel steps.

"Correct Mervyn," I said. "Money is only worth something when it's put to good use. Here everyone will benefit. Not only Harry, but also the poor devils locked up in that dreadful place."

Feeling decidedly more confident and cheerful than earlier that morning, Mervyn, and I took coffee on the terrace, while anticipating another day of discoveries with Ali.

Chapter Fourteen
Tutankhamen - Hall of Mummies - Groppi's

"No more mosques Ali," protested Mervyn, as we walked to the tram stop.

Actually, I see little use always travelling everywhere by taxi, or caleche. When visiting a new location, I believe in sampling the excitement of the city at the roots, not riding about like a pasha in an open carriage. How else can one see the faces of the people, especially the men, the women being mostly veiled.

"Very well Mr Mervyn," Ali said.

"How about the museum," I suggested. "I've still to see Tutankhamen."

"Ron!" Mervyn exclaimed. "I've seen him. Don't you remember?"

"But Mr Mervyn," Ali interrupted. "Did you see the hall of mummies? Some of them are unwrapped."

"All right. I missed it! But we better do it before lunch, because the sight of those shrivelled up dead people might turn my stomach."

The Tutankhamen exhibit was spectacular. His gold funerary mask, more fabulous than any photograph could ever depict. How breathtaking it must have been for Howard Carter, when he finally opened the burial chamber and lifted the lid of the red granite sarcophagus to discover the first of three gold coffins. The horde of treasure found in the tomb is more magnificent than I have ever seen, and I found it difficult to drag myself away from the display cases.

Mervyn was nonetheless anxious to see the mummies, at the same time getting hungrier by the minute.

Indeed, the leather like bodies in the Royal Hall of Mummies are lurid. Sunken eyes, their eyelids with eyelashes remaining, hands, and feet even now with nails, as well as stark white teeth between stretched lips, fixed in either a smile or a snarl.

We were immensely impressed by the mummies of Rameses the second and his father Sethi. It is always presumed Rameses was the Egyptian Pharaoh who finally released Moses and the Israelites from bondage, although this is a popular myth. While studying ancient history at Trinity during my few years at Cambridge, I discovered that scholars prefer to think the liberator to be Pharaoh Thutmosis the third, since he was on the throne of Egypt at the time of the Exodus. We know this from the date recorded in the Bible.

Satiated by all things ancient and antique, Mervyn, Ali, and I returned to the museum entrance where we hailed a caleche to return us to the hotel. But after leaving Qasr el Nil Street and clattering across Suleiman Pasha Square, I saw a familiar entrance, surrounded by colourful gilded, Art Deco mosaics.

"Stop driver!" I called. "Come on you two! I'll treat you to Groppi's."

"What's Groppi's?" asked Mervyn.

"Probably one of the most famous coffee shops and patisseries in the world," I answered. "Rivalling London's Ritz Hotel and Stohrer's of Paris."

Surprisingly, I knew something about the teashop's past, therefore after paying the driver, and as we strolled across the square, I explained to Ali and Mervyn a little of its history.

Groppi's has delighted Carienes for almost thirty years. Swiss born, Giacomo Groppi, arrived in Cairo in 1880 to take up employment as a pastry chef at Maison Gianola, a popular Swiss pastry and teashop on Bawaki Street. Ten years later, the clever and talented young Giacomo bought one of Gianola's premises in Alexandria and opened a shop of his own.

In 1905, Giacomo retired, selling his business to a Frenchman,

Auguste Baudrot, the owner of Alexandria's most famous tearoom.

In the economic crash of 1907, however, Giacomo lost his savings, so was forced to return to work, opening an establishment, the Aldi Tea Rooms in Cairo two years later. In the mid nineteen twenties, Giacomo's son, Achilles was responsible for opening the Groppi's we all know, on Midan Suleiman Pasha, where it was soon to become the hub of Cairo society.

Groppi's brought Paris to Cairo with its delectable pastries, crème glacè, petit Suisse, crème chantilly, cream flavoured with vanilla and then whipped within an inch of its life. Quite delicious, and extremely naughty for someone of my proportions.

Furthermore, Groppi's confectionery is renowned throughout the world and is always the particular choice of every crown head of Europe, including all the Arab royal families. It is said that young King Farouk has a penchant for marron glacè, a sweet chestnut, candied in sugar syrup and then glazed. There are rumours the young king also eats so much Groppi chocolate that his once youthful schoolboy waistline is rapidly expanding.

Midan is an Egyptian word meaning square. But in truth, Midan Suleiman Pasha is a Parisian style junction, off which six streets radiate. Here, one might find the best boutiques, hairdressers, men's tailors, restaurants, and teahouses in Cairo. However, it is to Groppi's the elite gravitate, to read a newspaper, join friends for social gossip, or simply appreciate the famous clientele, over a long cup of frothy, rich coffee and several cigarettes.

As I sat at a table by the famous window during my army days, it was possible to glance out and see a Rolls Royce drive up, the chauffeur opening the door to allow a member of a particular European aristocracy to step onto the pavement. Of course their arrival caused little stir amongst the esteemed Groppi clientele, so secure were they in their own status and lineage.

Groppi's was hardly small, easily able to accommodate the usual gathering of artists, writers, sportsmen and women, explorers, archaeologists, statesmen and army officers. Newspaper correspondents searched for gossip, spies sought or exchanged information, spinster debutants hunted for prospective officer husbands. Although it was at night when Groppi's became the hot spot of Cairo, flashing lights over the door advertising, 'Full Dinners with Dancing'.

With the women dressed in the latest Paris fashions, and men in uniform, or dinner suits, my friend Sheila, an Australian nurse and dance partner, and I would dance the foxtrot and sometimes the tango, which apparently appeared funny, since it always amused everyone.

"It must have been with your long legs," said Mervyn, as we made ourselves comfortable at a table beside the window. "You had a pretty good war Ron."

"Looking back," I said, while lighting everyone's cigarette, "I suppose I did. Although at the time, most of us would have preferred to be in France in the thick of it. Easy to say now, because none of us were aware of what the lads in France were going through. At least there were no mud and trenches here, just sand and flies."

Groppi's was unusually quiet considering it was almost Tiffin Time. So a waiter appeared to take our order, more or less, immediately.

"I'm having an ice cream soda," Mervyn said. "If this place is anything like it's cracked up to be, by what you say Ron, my ice cream soda will be better than those we have at Fortes."

"How about you Ali?" I asked.

"When I was a boy, my father and mother would bring my sisters and I here. But now, not so often. I hear the coffee is still good."

"Very well. One ice cream soda and one coffee. Cream or milk Ali?"

"Neither, effendi."

"One café noir. And I'll have white tea."

"India or China sir?" the waiter asked.

"India please. Also, a selection of your pastries."

Mervyn laughed. "Ron! We've still not had lunch."

"We're not in Groppi's every day. We can spoil ourselves once in a while."

As we waited for our order, I refreshed my memory of the interior, and reassured to see it unchanged. Like Shepheard's and other long established Cairo hotels, Groppi's had resisted the urge to modernise. Art Deco in design, when Groppi's first opened in 1926 the interior must have been regarded as enormously innovative and the height of fashion. Nowadays, it possessed a dignified air of comfort and coolness, and I was pleased to see again the delicate wrought metal lamps, along with the columns of cream marble supporting the lofty ceiling.

Looking through the window, and across the square to the corner of Qasr el Nil Street and Shari Suleiman Pasha, I noticed a beautiful new building.

"What's the name of the place over there Ali?" I asked, while the waiter set our table.

"It's the Baehler Building effendi. It was commissioned six years ago by Mr Charles Baehler, the owner of Shepheard's Hotel."

"It appears to be a mansion house. Am I right?"

"Yes effendi. It's now one of the smartest places to live in Cairo."

"Is the Mohammad Ali Club still on the corner of Shari El Bustan? I had some high times there. Less stuffy and restrictive than the Gezira Sporting Club.

"It is effendi, and still popular with Cairo society."

Once our order arrived and as I poured myself a cup of tea, I noticed the headline on the front page of the Egyptian Gazette a gentleman was reading at the next table. It read, 'The Kings Birthday', followed by, 'A day at the Races'.

Had I seen the last phrase five months later it would have caused me to smile, as the Marx Brothers released an extremely funny film of the same title last July.

"Ali!" I exclaimed. "It appears your young King Farouk is celebrating his birthday tomorrow by going to the races. How about we join him?"

At this juncture, I should make it clear that I have never been either a race goer, or a gambling man. Rather, I have more respect for my pocket than to throw money away on a risk. If I gamble at all, then it is with people. I set great store by them and hope they come up trumps. Sometimes I am lucky, sometimes not.

"Please Ron," Mervyn said. "I love the races. Dad took mum and us kids to Bath races once. It was great fun. Although he was the only one to put a bet on, just because Prince Monolulu said the horse was a dead cert."

"And did it win?" I asked.

"No. It came second. But dad lost his money, because he put it to win."

"Ali. Would you care to join us?"

"I'm an Arab effendi. Arabs and horses are inseparable. We're addicted to horse racing. It's in our blood. I'd very much enjoy accompanying you and Mr Mervyn."

"Then we'll go. Anyway, I'd like to get a look at this boy King, seeing he's Egypt's chief scout."

"How old is he?" Mervyn asked.

"Seventeen, this birthday," answered Ali.

"Two years younger than me."

"His father, King Fuad, died last year while Crown Prince Farouk was in England."

"Indeed," I said. "I remember reading that he's been studying for the army at Woolwich, and apparently enjoys old books, as well as possessing a good eye for antiquity. In which case, I'm sure he and I would get on."

"Don't be silly Ron!" Mervyn said. "You're hardly going to meet him, are you."

"It's true effendi," added Ali. "The Royal Family is closely watched day and night, in case of assassination attempts by political extremists who wish to see an end to the monarchy."

Of late, the young King had been in the public eye, and consequently much publicity surrounded him.

"He won't officially take the throne until next year. Is that correct Ali?"

"Yes Mr Ron. At present, we are ruled by his uncle, Prince Mohammad Ali Tewfik. It is called a regency."

It pleased me to hear Ali begin to call me Mr Ron, as I was becoming rather tired of the very formal title, 'effendi'.

"Is he the dapper gentleman we see all the time in the newspapers?" I asked. "I must say, his beard and moustache are most fetching. Also, he wears his tarbush at such a jaunty angle."

Ali refrained from joining the ensuing laughter that my statement caused, taking this to mean he considered the Egyptian royal family beyond joviality.

"Our King has just returned from a royal tour of upper Egypt," Ali continued. "He wished to see the ancient monuments, as well as introduce himself to his subjects. They say, while the royal yacht 'El Horria' steamed up the Nile, with the royal family aboard, our King's many Rolls Royce's and sports cars followed by road. I also read in Al Ahram, the King was most generous to the poor people of the villages he visited, giving them gifts of money."

"Different to his father," I said cautiously. "I hear King Fuad was quite the opposite, which is the reason the family is so rich. Fuad amassed a fortune in Swiss banks."

Once more, Ali abstained from making a comment.

"The Prince Monolulu, Mr Ron," he said instead. "Is he a race horse owner?"

Mervyn laughed. "Hardly Ali! He's a Negro."

"That's not quite true Mervyn," I interrupted. "Apparently, he was born on a Caribbean island, and I think you'll find his family raised horses."

"Well there you are," Mervyn said, sounding crushed. "I got it wrong Ali. Sorry."

"No Ali," I continued. "In England, Prince Monolulu is called a tipster. He's famous for giving betting tips and turns up at race meetings all over the country shouting his catchphrase: 'I gotta horse!' Monolulu's always at Epsom on Derby Day and at Aintree for the Grand National. You can't miss him. He's very colourful."

Ali laughed and was clearly amused to have been so mistaken in his initial assumption.

"He says he's an Abyssinian prince," I continued. "Dressing accordingly. With tall red and white feathers attached to a band around his head."

Our lunch at Groppi's continued merrily, with idle chatter, small talk, and repartee, which strangely Groppi's induces. If only the walls could speak, since they would tell a thousand stories, and we would benefit from thirty years of scandal, gossip, and intrigue.

An hour later, outside on the pavement, happily Mervyn and I said goodbye to Ali, promising to meet him Thursday lunchtime for our keenly anticipated, 'Day at the Races'.

As soon as we returned to the hotel, and before I could wallow in a cool bath, I telephoned Professor Hussein and arranged a meeting for Friday morning.

Chapter Fifteen
The Gezira Sporting Club - A day at the races

With the Gezira Sporting Club up ahead, the caleche clattered along the avenue of acacia trees, passing the croquet lawns on the way, although I could feel Ali's apprehension as we drove onto the forecourt. Naturally, I was aware it would be impossible to arrange for him to be admitted. It was difficult enough for an Egyptian man of any status to become a member, whether a Cairene, an Egyptian, or a temporary resident. Even though the current president, Seifullah Youssri Pasha, is an Egyptian, the reason for his election being that in 1922 he played polo on the club's polo ground with Edward, Prince of Wales.

Before Mervyn and I left England, and realising we were to visit Cairo, I dug through the bottom drawer of the tall boy in my bedroom at Hyde House. There I found my old wallet containing my rail pass, a few old tram tickets, some Egyptian pounds, and my Gezira Club life membership card, dated 1918. Thus armed, I would be able to get Mervyn and I past the doorman and into the bar.

Regrettably, it was necessary we leave Ali sitting on a bench beside the cricket ground, although he said he was quite happy to do so. But to assure myself that he would not go hungry, I bought him a tamiya from a street vendor in Midan Ismalia.

I was keen for Mervyn to see inside the clubhouse. However, it surprised me to find it quite altered since my previous visit.

"This is new," I exclaimed. "Here used to be the secretary's office, and over there was the ladies room. The old squash courts have gone too, because I can see they've built a new cricket pavilion."

The windows of the dining room now commanded a wonderful vista across the veranda to the cricket pitch. The room now had an added function by the addition of an oak parquet floor, transforming it into an ideal location for dancing. Plus, with a gallery above, a perfect place to view the proceedings below.

It is well known, that before the war; when it was winter back in England, Cairo swarmed with what was affectionately called the Imperial Flotilla, or Fishing Fleet. This took the form of a horde of debutantes who poured off the ships at Port Said, or Alexandria, heading hotfoot to Cairo in the frenzied pursuit of unattached infantry, or cavalry officers. Regarded back in Britain as wallflowers, they hovered around the dance floors of Shepheard's and the Semiramis, smiling demurely or uncomfortably, since no young man had yet shown an interest in them. The gallery at the Gezira would be an ideal, as well as a discreet place to scrutinize their prospective prizes.

Since it was race day, the bar was crowded with army officers and their wives, along with Egyptian businessmen and government officials. However, before we sat down, I led Mervyn across the room and out onto the rear terrace.

"I want you to see this," I said. "A couple of years ago there was an article and photographs in the Illustrated London News. I've been dying to see it in reality. What do you think?"

"It's the most beautiful swimming pool, I've ever seen," gasped Mervyn. "Can we come back when I've got my costume? I'd love a swim."

It was indeed stunning, and lived up to everything I had seen in the photograph. When last in Cairo, swimming and sunbathing were not regarded as fashionable. But since the late twenties and early thirties, with the advent of movie magazines, in which bronzed film stars soaked up the sun beside their swimming pools, suddenly the craze has taken off.

The pool is large, with a rectangular section in the front, divided into five lanes, where one might swim laps should one feel the necessity. On the right, is an area set aside for more leisurely wallowing, an elegant curve of steps leading into the water. At various intervals, steps and rails are provided for easy access and a bridge enables people to cross to the terrace without returning to the water.

A dozen or so men and women, stretched on cane loungers, were taking advantage of the bright winter sunshine to sun bathe, while others played catching games, or slavishly swam back and forth in the lane ways.

"Just look at the fountain over there!" Mervyn exclaimed, pointing across the pool. "It would be lovely to get under on a hot day."

Other than the new additions to the dining building and swimming pool, the club remained unchanged. Nubian waiters still padded about amongst the wicker tables and chairs, wearing long white robes, red tasselled tarbushes, and scarlet belts.

After an excellent lunch, Mervyn and I met with Ali, and we joined other European or Egyptian race goers and strolled through the gardens towards the racecourse entrance, where I bought tickets. Then we made our way past the paddock and the member's enclosure to the front of the grandstand.

Having recently been engulfed in souks and mosques, surrounded as it were by brown faced Egyptians wearing tarbushes and turbans, all of a sudden it was bizarre to be somewhere abounding with pink, sweaty faces, shaded by hats of every description. Military caps, utilitarian Panamas, stylish sun hats decked with bows and ribbons flourished. In addition, there were the occasional red tarbushes of the Nubian waiters as they passed through the crowd, carrying silver trays of champagne, Pimms or Campbell's whisky. The air was full of chatter, the high trill of women's laughter, the sound of the inevitable fly swish, plus the whiff of cigarette and cigar smoke. During the war, and my time in India, the Andaman Islands, and Egypt, I must have witnessed a similar scene a dozen times, remaining unaltered for a hundred years, and continuing throughout the Empire. I must admit to wondering how long it will endure.

Cavalry officers, their horses and their wives, and in that order, predominated. Hence the addition in the race card of several regimental races, including The Green Howard Sweepstakes and the Polo Race, a favourite of the Indians. Also, a couple of equestrian displays were included, plus Horseback Musical Chairs and The Lloyd Lindsay. It promised to be a jolly afternoon. I thought this with my tongue firmly in my cheek.

From our vantage point at the front of the grandstand, Mervyn, Ali, and I had a splendid panoramic view of the racecourse, also into the unsaddling and members enclosures below. Here, people thronged around numerous tables containing dainty edible delights, all quite fitting for such an occasion. Mervyn was lapping up the atmosphere and keen to be amid the elite of Cairo. Ali on the other hand was studying the race card intently.

"There are some very good horses running today effendi," he said. "Perhaps it's because it's our King's birthday."

"Certainly," I said. "Also I read in Al Ahram yesterday that the authorities have jiggled around with King Farouk's birth date. According to the Islamic calendar, it seems today he's officially eighteen and able to legitimately take the throne."

"Then there'll be a coronation," Mervyn said. "Will it be soon? We should go if it is."

"Al Ahram says sometime in the summer. It'll be far too hot for us Mervyn. Anyway, I hope we get Harry's situation sorted out at least by the end of the season. We've our own coronation in May don't forget."

"We are very honoured today effendi," Ali said, drawing my attention to the race card. "We are in the presence of the best Arabian stallion in Egypt."

"Which is that?"

"Nazeer, effendi. He is the top stallion at the royal stud and has already sired several foals to top Arabian mares."

"Once again Ali I'm impressed. Is there anything you don't know?"

"I am a dragoman effendi. I am proud of Egypt, and proud to be Egyptian. I wish my tourists to leave knowing a little more about my country than when they arrived.

"We'll certainly do that Ali," said Mervyn.

"I must admit to knowing very little about horse breeding," I said. "What makes the Arabian so special?"

Ali's eyes lit up, clearly pleased to have a chance to speak on his favourite topic.

"The Arabian is hot blooded and fast effendi. Very agile and light of foot. He is loyal to his master and noble to his master's family. He is a good stayer, meaning he can run a long race and still win. But most of all effendi, the Arabian is beautiful. His neck arched, his head well boned and dished in shape, eyes large and dark, long level croup, and his tail carried high."

Mervyn laughed. "Ali! I can't wait to see one."

"You'll see many Mr Mervyn. The first race is the Newmarket Stakes, for three year olds and over. Nazeer's up against his half-brothers, Sheik El Arab and Shahloul. He's the oldest, so my money would go on either of the others."

"But you'll bet on Nazeer of course," I said.

"He'll be the favourite effendi, so the odds won't be great."

"What are the others?"

"Sheik El Arab and Sid Abouh. They're three year olds. Makata. She's six.

"So colts race against fillies."

"Yes effendi."

"Isn't that a bit unfair?"

"Not at all effendi. The mares are as strong as the stallions and sometimes have a bigger heart for racing. Egypt must be thankful to an English lady for my country having such special animals."

"Really! Who's she?"

"Lady Anne Blunt effendi. She and her husband travelled a great deal in Arabia, where they purchased many fine horses from the Bedouin. These horses were the beginning of her studs, Crabbet Park, in England and Sheykh Obeyd Gardens in Egypt. But a long time before Lady Blunt, two Egyptian khedives were instrumental in breeding Arabians. First was Muhammad Ali Pasha."

"Isn't he the man who built the mosque in the Citadel?" said Mervyn.

"Correct Mr Mervyn. We call Muhammad Ali Pasha the father of modern Egypt because he made great reforms in the way the country was run. He also believed people should be educated and even sent a mission of Egyptian students to Europe to acquire a cultural education. Muhammad Pasha loved Arabian horses and horse breeding. He was particularly keen on the horses bred by the desert Bedouin and spent large sums acquiring many horses. The khedive also kept extensive records and knew the bloodlines of every one of his purchases. When Muhammad died, his son Ibrahim became his successor, although he had little interest in horses. Thankfully, the Pasha's grandson, Abbas Pasha, shared his grandfather's passion and bought the stock for his own stable."

"I've just remembered," I said. "I knew the name was familiar. Wasn't Lady Anne Blunt Lord Byron's granddaughter?"

"Of that effendi, I'm really not sure."

"I'm sorry Ali. I interrupted you. Please continue."

"Unhappily, Abbas the first was murdered by two of his slaves and his horses inherited by his eighteen year old son, El Hami Pasha. With little interest in horse breeding, Hami Pasha gave many away and put the rest to auction. Thirty horses were purchased by a distant relative, Ali Pasha Sherif, and the breeding programme began again. As time went by, Ali Pasha began experiencing difficulties financially, also politically, so was forced to sell his horses. Here Lady Anne Blunt appears on the scene. She was able to purchase many of his best animals for her stud in Egypt, while exporting several to England."

Hearing the name Crabbet Park brought back another memory from when I was in Egypt previously.

"I think I recall her dying just before the end of the war, and when I got home. I remember there was a terrific hoo-har about who should have Crabbet Park, her husband Wilfred, or their daughter Judith. I'm sure the daughter won."

"Then she must be Lady Wentworth," Ali said. "Prince Muhammad, Prince Kamal and Khedive Abbas Pasha the second, were all keen to restore the Arabian stud of Ali Pasha Sherif. So with their backing the Royal Agricultural Society went to Lady Wentworth to purchase some of the horses Lady Anne had exported to England."

"My word Ali!" I cried. "You're a positive history book of the Egyptian horse. How do you come to know all this?"

"Every Egyptian who loves his horses knows the story effendi. It's passed down from father to son."

"Well, I think it's admirable. I never believed I'd find the history of a breed of horse so fascinating."

Mervyn however, seemed unable to agree. Because for the entire time Ali had been speaking, his binoculars were trained on the member's enclosure, and the trays of delicacies carried by the Nubian waiters.

"Are there others running?" he murmured, abstractly. "I haven't heard a name I like yet."

"Dynamite," Ali explained, reading from the race card. "Kuhakan Abu, Urkub, Pompeian, Darug and Pigskin. The last three are owned by an American lady."

"Mrs Chester Bennett," I said, leaning over Ali's shoulder and seeing the name on the card. "I've heard of her. She's the wife of Sir Alfred Chester Bennett, the American mining millionaire. You say she owns a horse named Pigskin?"

Ali nodded.

"Surely Ali, not a popular horse amongst Muslim Cairenes."

"You are correct effendi," he said, shaking his head. "I read in Al Ahram, Mrs Chester Bennett is exporting Pigskin to England where she has high hopes for him."

"Then I wish her the best of luck. Despite Nazeer being the favourite, I'm rather drawn to him. Tell me more about him."

Strangely, I was beginning to find bloodlines and horse business rather fascinating, although Mervyn still had his eyes on game pies, roast beef, lamb cutlets, and cucumber sandwiches.

"He's a three year old grey," continued Ali. "But he's already the head stallion at the royal stud. His bloodline goes back to the horses Lady Anne bought from Ali Pasha Sherif. He was the get of another famous horse, Mansour, out of a dam, Bint Samiha."

"Who owns him?"

"The R.A.S effendi. The Royal Agricultural Society. They own most of the top Arabians in the country."

"Are you going to tell me who you fancy in the first race?"

"Certainly Mr Ron. I'm going for a long shot, and put my money on Kuhakan Abu. He's yet untried, so you never can tell."

"Your religion is very strict. I'm surprised you're allowed to gamble."

"We can effendi. The Prophet says it is allowed. It is said he gambled many times on his best horses winning a race. Muhammad, the Prophet says next to his wives, the horse is a man's most prized possession. It is written in the Koran that every man should love his horse. The expression in a horse's eye is like a blessing on a good man's house."

"That's very profound Ali."

"Not my words Mr Ron, but the Prophet's himself."

"Do you want us to give you some money to bet with?" Mervyn asked, suddenly entering the conversation.

"No thank you Mr Mervyn. I have my own. I knew we were coming today, so had put some aside. Since meeting you and Mr Ron, you've been more than generous. I give my mother money every week, but I've also saved a little."

Since Ali failed to mention his father, I assumed his mother was a widow. However, I refrained from saying as much.

"Do you have brothers and sisters?" I asked instead.

"One brother and two sisters."

"Hey!" Mervyn exclaimed. "I've three more than you Ali."

Our conversation was unexpectedly interrupted as a piercing fanfare of trumpets echoed around the grandstand bringing everyone to attention. A ripple of applause caused us to look towards the far end of the finishing strait, where a procession of open carriages and mounted cavalry had appeared.

Chapter Sixteen
Horse flesh - A good win all round

"Is it the King, Mr Mervyn?" Ali shouted. "Can you see him through your binoculars?"

"I'll need to adjust the magnification," Mervyn said, twiddling the knob. "It's him alright. He's in the first carriage, wearing a black tarbush, riding beside a gent with a white beard and moustache.

"That's Prince Muhammad Ali Tewfik. The Regent."

The cheers of the crowd growing louder with the carriages getting nearer, it was possible for Mervyn, Ali and I to see the occupants with the naked eye. Quickly covering the ground, the cortege arrived at the grandstand, stopping at the gates of the unsaddling enclosure. A groom left his place beside the driver and opened a small door in the side of the first carriage to allow the King to step down.

"Farouk looks very smart in his gold braid and medals," I said.

Actually, this was the first time Mervyn and I had seen the King in person, and I remember thinking at the time that he was rather more handsome than he appears in photographs or on the Pathe News.

"I wonder where his mother and sisters are." Ali said. "They usually go everywhere together."

"Ron told me he has four sisters," said Mervyn. "Is that right Ali?"

"Yes Mr Mervyn. Fawzia, Faiza, Faika, and Fathiya."

"All those F's must make it extremely confusing," I said. "What with their brother being Farouk and their father Fuad."

"The old King was very superstitious effendi. They say he believed F was the luckiest letter in the alphabet."

Members of the Gezira Club Committee, including officials from the Egyptian Jockey Club and the Royal Agricultural Society, were in line to greet the King, the Regent and the cabinet. Therefore, after many handshakes and good wishes, the royal party, flanked by the Royal Guard, continued through the member's enclosure to the entrance to the grandstand, where a section had been set aside for them.

Suddenly, a flash of colour and movement drew our eyes to the parade ring, around which the horses for the first race were being led. Having listened to Ali praising the Arabian I could now see clearly the reason for his passion. With all ten horses circling the ring, they were indeed splendid creatures in every respect.

"There's Nazeer," Ali said, with hushed reverence. "He's the grey, wearing number one."

Scrutinising the saddlecloths, I picked Nazeer out of the group, a dazzling white horse, not grey at all, although I was aware that this is the correct term for a horse of his colour.

"What do they call the brown ones?" I asked.

"Bays effendi. Arabs think him the strongest, and can endure hunger and thirst the longest. The grey is most esteemed, but has to be perfect. The muzzle, eyes and membrane, must be black. Dark Chestnuts must have black legs, with a deeper chestnut line from the withers to the tail. These are highly prized. But above all, the Arab reveres the black horse, as they are rare and full-blooded. More than often, the chief of the tribe will possess a black. The chestnuts are said to be the fastest, as in the past they always brought news of victories. The grey horse is useful in hot countries, where the glare of the desert makes its detection more difficult."

"Why are they such good racehorses?"

"The Arabian has two extra ribs than other breeds, which means he has room for larger lungs. He also possesses bigger nostrils to allow him to breathe in more oxygen."

"I now know more about the Arabian horse, Ali than anyone else

I know. You're a mine of information. Come along! Let's place some bets. You're going for Kuhakan Abu. Any reason why?"

"The Frenchman, Charles Semblat, rides him, the horse owned by Mr Baehler."

"Shepheard's Hotel owner, Mr Baehler?"

"Yes effendi. It's a good combination. Also, it's Kuhakan Abu's first time out, so he's untried. I always like to back the underdog, plus the odds will be good."

"Alright. I'll go for Nazeer. What about you Mervyn? That is if you can tear yourself away from those binoculars."

"I'm checking the field," he said. "There're some mighty fine animals down there. Ali, which one's Dynamite?"

"Number ten Mr Mervyn. George Woolf is riding him, so he stands a good chance."

Nazeer's handler had stopped walking and was holding the horse's head while the jockey climbed into the saddle.

"Who's riding Nazeer?"

"Red Pollard. Both he and Woolf are Canadian and brought to Egypt for the season by Mr Baehler."

"We've a lot to thank Mr Baehler for."

"Indeed effendi. All the best hotels in Cairo, Luxor, and Aswan are owned by him. That's Mr Baehler over there, talking to the King and his uncle."

Out of politeness, Ali refrained from pointing, indicating instead by a turn of the head in the direction of the Royal Box, where the cabinet men were already seated. All excepting the King and Muhammad Ali Pasha. They were standing talking to a tall, distinguished European gentleman, dressed in a dark grey morning suit, while sporting a mass of curly iron-grey hair, in addition to a large neatly shaped moustache.

"How interesting," I said. "I knew of him of course, but up until now have never seen him. It's a well-known fact that Charles Baehler has a fascinating past."

"How do you mean?" Mervyn said, no doubt expecting me to reveal some lurid and scandalous gossip about the gentleman.

"At the beginning of the war the Egyptian Government deported hundreds of German and Austro Hungarians, and I'm afraid Mr Baehler was one of them, although he managed to remain in Egypt for two years."

"Is that correct effendi? Now it is your turn to tell Ali something new."

"Everyone at Shepheard's was aware of it," I continued, "since it was the talk of the terrace you might say. Before the war, there was an influx of Germans into Cairo. All three hundred and fifty singers from the Berliner Lieder Tafel, plus the Berlin Philharmonic Orchestra, toured Egypt giving many concerts. They had to stay somewhere and Charles Baehler put them up. Also, one of the guests at Shepheard's was Herr Harry von Gwinner, the managing director of Deutche Bank, which was directly linked to the Ottoman Bank. Von Gwinner and Baehler made no secret of their friendship and were often seen conversing at parties and balls. This intimacy came to the notice of the Judicial Advisor to the Egyptian Government, Sir Malcolm McIlwraith, who passed on his thoughts to Kitchener. Ever after, Baehler was obviously watched, and in 1916 he was finally deported on suspicion of having German sympathies."

"But I thought he was Swiss," Ali said. "They couldn't do that."

"At the time everyone sympathised with Baehler and were of the same opinion. Whoever was involved clearly were out to get Baehler. Personally, I believe it was jealousy brought about his deportation. By this time, Baehler was an extremely influential man. He arrived in Egypt at the age of seventeen, as a humble clerk with a genius for accounting. The then owner of the hotel, Samuel Shepheard, got into a terrible muddle with the books and Baehler sorted it out. When Shepheard died, Baehler took over the reins, eventually becoming chairman and managing director of the firm."

"But he was able to return from exile," Mervyn said.

"Obviously Mervyn. Rumours about what had happened to him were rife. However, life at the hotels went on as before. After all it was war, and although the tourist business was dead, Shepheard's, The Semiramis, the Savoy, and the Heliopolis, were full of military personnel, the only difference being that Baehler was no longer at the helm."

"Did you discover where Mr Baehler went?" Ali asked.

"It was only after the war that the story came to light. It seems Baehler ended up in England, where he was confined in Brixton Prison."

"Was it true that he sympathised with Germany?"

"Who knows? But the charges were dropped and he was allowed to live out the rest of the war in Switzerland."

"It takes a brave man to come back to Cairo after the finger's been pointed at him," said Mervyn.

"He's well liked by everyone in Cairo society," I continued. "Baehler still has a huge share in the Cairo Hotel business. It's fortunate he did return, because, with the war over, it was the roaring twenties and Egypt was booming, his hotel chain making an absolute fortune. If you ask me, his story is a testament to hard work and perseverance."

By now the horses were mounted and making their way to the start on the opposite side of the racecourse.

"Are you going to the tote Ron?" Mervyn asked.

"Very well," I said, realising there was about to be an ulterior motive for Mervyn's question.

"Then can you bring us back something to eat. I'm getting hungry, and so is Ali I'm sure. I saw a kebab seller as we came in."

Given my orders, I looked for and found, firstly the totaliser shed, then the kebab stand, exchanging my money for three betting slips, and collecting three kebabs, in that order. Returning to my seat, I was just in time to hear the crack of the starting pistol.

"Nazeer's made a great start," cried Mervyn. "He's white, so is easy to spot."

"It's grey Mervyn," I corrected.

"Alright," Mervyn grumbled. "Know it all. Take the glasses Ron. I want to eat my Kebab."

"Give them to Ali. He can be the commentator."

But there was no need, as a terribly English sounding gentleman began speaking over the loudspeakers.

"And it's Nazeer in the lead, followed by Sheik El Arab and Pigskin; Makata sitting on the rail in fourth place."

The crowd began to cheer wildly as each person's chosen horse was mentioned.

"Sid Aboub is moving up on the outside; making ground is Kuhakan Abu."

"Your horse Ali!" shouted Mervyn. "Where's Dynamite? My jockey's wearing red and green."

"The rear marker I'm afraid Mr Mervyn."

"Some name then!" he complained. "Next race I'll back an Arab name."

"And it's still Nazeer from Pigskin!" blared the voice above our heads. "Sheik El Arab is dropping back. Makata's being challenged by Kuhakan Abu."

"Come on Kuhakan Abou!" all of us shouted.

It appeared more than likely that Nazeer would win, so there was no reason why I should not root for Ali's outsider.

"What were your jockey's colours again Ali?"

"Blue and green hoops effendi," he said, without taking his eyes from the glasses. "He's taken Pigskin! He's second."

Ali certainly knew his horseflesh. If Kuhakan Abu could hold his own, he would win a considerable amount, as secretly I upped his one-pound bet by four more Egyptian pounds.

"Come on Kuhakan Abu!"

In a bunch, the horses galloped past the grandstand, the crowd rising to its feet, even young King Farouk standing spontaneously in order to get a better view.

Red Pollard was using his whip on Nazeer, which I thought at the time to be a little excessive as they were only half way around the course. Obviously, the Canadian saw Semblat's horse breathing down his neck to be a threat. Meanwhile, Mervyn was still unhappy because his horse was still last.

"Ali! I thought you said I'd do well because George Woolf was riding Dynamite. Where is he now?"

"He's making ground. They've strung out around the bend. He's moved up to fourth."

"Did you do him each way Ron?"

"Yes Mervyn. But he has to come in the first three."

Mervyn made a face as the loudspeaker crackled into life once more.

"And it's Nazeer and Kuhakan Abu, neck and neck, down the back strait. Makata holding fast, challenged by Dynamite."

"Come on, Dynamite!" shouted Mervyn.

The pack had split, the four leaders pulling away from the rest of the field. Kuhakan Abu seemed to be the choice of others, because elements of the crowd also cheered each time his name was called. Perhaps the odds had changed since I placed Ali's bet.

"And its Kuhakan Abu by a nose, from Nazeer, Makata and Dynamite!" the announcer yelled so fast that we could barely make out the names.

"All our horses are there!" I shouted.

"Dynamite's taken Makata!" screamed Mervyn. "We all stand a chance to win. What a race!"

With the post in sight, Semblat urged on Kuhakan Abu with a tickle of his whip, which seemed to be sufficient to send the horse forward by a head, Red Pollard beside him, beating Nazeer for all he was worth.

"Dynamite's going to take him!" Mervyn shouted.

However, to the roar of the crowd, they were past the post, with Kuhakan Abu winning the race.

"That was one for the books," I said. "Well done Ali!"

"Yes. Well done Ali," Mervyn echoed. "That Kuhakan Abu's going to be one to watch."

For a moment, Ali was speechless with joy.

"How much has he won Ron?"

"I don't know. I think the odds may have changed since I placed our bets. The last I knew Kuhakan Abu was a hundred to one, rank outsider."

"You bet a pound Ali," Mervyn said. "That means you've won a hundred and one pounds. How about that!"

I resisted saying anything, suggesting instead that I collect our winnings. Therefore, with my heart in my mouth, I queued at the tote shed. And getting close, I was soon able to see the tote board beside the window, the horses' names written in chalk on a blackboard, beside them the starting prices. Nazeer was eventually three to one. Dynamite, ten-to one. But Kuhakan Abu finished at thirty-to one, meaning Ali would collect one hundred and fifty five Egyptian Pounds. A fortune to a dragoman.

Overall, considering there were still six more races on the card, we three had begun the afternoon extremely well. Consequently, I appropriated a Nubian from the member's enclosure and ordered a bottle of champagne and three glasses, not forgetting a cordial for Ali.

"I hope you're not going to be stubborn or offended Ali," I said, on my return. "But I upped your stake to five. So you've won one hundred and fifty five pounds."

"Effendi! You are a very naughty man," he said, laughing. "Ali is most grateful. Ali's mother is most grateful. That's such a lot of money. It'll change our lives."

"Don't worry Ali," Mervyn said. "Ron has a habit of changing people's lives. He does it all the time back home."

"That's the reason I did it Ali," I said. "Your mother should be the one to benefit; she and your sisters and brother. If you like we could go to the bank next week and I'll open an account for you and your family. That way the money will be safe and earn some interest."

"Thank you kindly effendi. Please keep the money until then. I'm afraid I have no safe place to hide such a sum where I live."

All the while, I could feel Mervyn glaring at me, his version of charity clearly different to mine.

"How much did I win Ron?" he asked.

"I put five on for you Mervyn. Dynamite came in at ten to one, so fifty five pounds."

He took the wad of scruffy pound notes and stuffed it into his inside jacket pocket.

"Wow! That's my monthly allowance. Not bad to be getting on with. What about you?"

"Twenty."

The waiter arrived with champagne and cordial.

"Come on boys! Let's toast our victories."

***

Mervyn and I were not as successful for the remainder of the afternoon. Beginner's luck you might say.

However, Ali's chosen horse appeared in the first three in every race, convincing me he had the Midas touch.

All too soon, the last race was run, the loudspeakers echoed with the Egyptian National Anthem, the King, Regent and cabinet, departed and the afternoon was over.

"Tomorrow is Friday effendi. Mosque day. So I'll be unable to see you."

"Understandable Ali." I said. "I've an appointment to see Professor Hussein in the morning. And there's a ball at Shepheard's in the evening. So Mervyn and I would rather we didn't do anything in the afternoon."

That is how we left the arrangements. Our caleche deposited Ali at his houseboat in Imbaba and then drove Mervyn and I back across the Bulaq Bridge to Shepheard's, later to luxuriate in cool baths, having enjoyed the best of days in a very long time.

Chapter Seventeen
A done deal - Abbassia again - A boorish ball in the Moorish Room

The following morning, leaving Mervyn in bed asleep, I took breakfast alone in the splendid Moorish dining room; afterwards, by way of being fresh and alert for my meeting with Professor Hussein, I paid a visit to the hotel barber for a well-needed haircut. Thus prepared nutritionally and tonsorially, I walked through the hotel and into the garden, letting myself out of the back gate into Shari Imad el Din, where it was simply a short walk to the building and Professor Hussein's rooms.

"Good morning Captain Fry," said the professor, showing me into his office. "Please take a seat. Can I get you anything? Tea? Coffee?"

"Thank you professor. But no. I've just this moment taken breakfast."

Considering the delicate subject of our meeting, both the professor and I were reluctant to be the first to speak. However, I finally summoned the courage.

"So professor, have you been able to examine the man in question since we last met?"

"Yes Captain. I visited the hospital on Wednesday."

"How did you find Mr Watson?"

"Surprisingly well and lucid. The treatment seems to have been extremely successful. I see no reason to continue E.C.T."

"Then you'll authorise his release."

"I remember there was a certain stipulation to my doing so Captain."

Hussein was cunning. Obviously, the carrot I dangled the other day was still at the forefront of his mind. So I did not hesitate to go right to the heart of the matter.

"What would be the cost of a new operating theatre, professor?" I asked.

He coughed nervously, his fingers playing with the ashtray on his desk.

"Forgive me Captain, but since our last meeting I've made some discreet inquiries and the knowledge I have acquired has convinced me you're a man of your word and can be completely trusted.

"Thank you professor." I said, offering him a cigarette. "I'm glad I've your confidence."

"Captain, you're most generous. Naturally, you would be greatly remembered at the asylum. How about we call the new theatre block the 'Fry Memorial Wing'?"

"Most fitting professor. I already have a 'Fry Memorial Maternity Ward' back home. Please name your price."

Clearly, the professor was embarrassed even to speak the words, because taking a fountain pen from his top pocket he wrote the figure on a scrap of paper, passing it to me across the desk.

"Certainly professor," I said. "This morning I'll wire my solicitors in England and request they transfer the sum into an account which I'll open at The Bank of Egypt. Why don't we call it the 'Abbassia Hospital Account' that way the money will not be accidently misappropriated?"

"Of course Captain. You're most munificent. The Egyptian Government is justly grateful."

"Thank you professor. But please keep the word of my donation quiet for the time being? When making philanthropic gestures, it's a tradition in my family that we do so clandestinely."

"Of course Captain. I'll telephone the hospital the moment you leave and advise the charge sister to prepare Mr Watson for his release."

"When do you think that'll be professor?"

"This afternoon Captain."

"Then I'll trouble you no further. Good day. And thank you for being so understanding."

"No. Thank you, Captain. Egypt is acknowledging you a million times."

My sense of elation, as I returned to the hotel, was boundless. Sunshine filled the garden; my conscience was as clear as the air I breathed; I was walking on a cloud and riding along on the crest of a wave, as they sing in the Gang Show. Once again, my money was being put to good use instead of languishing away in some dusty vault. That week, not only had Ali profited, but also the poor inmates of the dreadful asylum. However, I decided not to tell Mervyn the news just yet, because I began to hatch a plan to surprise the brothers.

It was also important Troopers Peter Harding and J B Shaw kept it secret they had met Mervyn and I, otherwise there would be no surprise for Harry. Consequently, rather than return to the room, I hailed a caleche and ordered the driver to take me to Abbassia Main Barracks by way of the Bank of Egypt, where I opened two accounts, the first in the name, Abbassia Hospital Account and the second for Ali Rashid.

The corporal at the gate said I might find Harding and Shaw in the canteen, so a handsome young British infantryman escorted me across the parade ground.

***

"You see lads," I said, sitting opposite them at the table. "It's imperative that you don't mention to Harry that Mervyn and I are in Egypt. I'd like it to be a surprise. I've also something else up my sleeve. A way perhaps to cure Harry's home sickness for good."

"But you're not going to tell us Captain," Trooper Harding said. "I can see that."

"Correct Trooper. But you'll know soon enough."

"Would you like a cuppa, Captain?" asked Trooper Shaw. "We've

Typhoo. I bet you don't get that at Shepheard's."

"You're right Jim. It's all Pickwick, Empire, and Harrods. I wouldn't mind a drop of Typhoo. Also, biscuits? Might you perhaps have McVities and Price's Home Wheat Chocolate Digestive?"

"We certainly do Captain. Tea and biscuits coming up."

"You've got it pretty good here Trooper Harding," I said, looking around the dining hall.

"Not bad Captain. They do us proud. You should see in here on Christmas Day. All decked out with decorations. Every man's place set for Christmas dinner, with an orange, a bread roll, a napkin in a glass and a bottle of beer."

It was enjoyable chatting to the lads. They were like a breath of fresh air, extremely honest and down to earth. Harding came from Middlesbrough and Shaw, Bristol, so it was comforting to hear their accents intermingling. In addition, the taste of the chocolate digestive and strong tea took me straight back to Mrs Lanesome's kitchen table at Hyde House.

"If Harry's on the parade ground on Monday morning, at around ten o'clock," I said, as we shook hands. "I promise Mervyn will be here on time."

***

That night, the costume ball in the Moorish Room was as glittering and dreary as I anticipated. Sad dowdy debutantes, and suspicious spinster chaperones. As well as galloping, moustached, single, middle-aged cavalry officers, together with gyppie social climbers, hefty dowagers, titled minor aristocracy and the occasional discreet homosexual. Mervyn was in his element, seemingly undaunted by the string of young ladies, all eager to dance with him, one of them our own Miss Plunkett Dillon, the young women we befriended in Toulon.

Sitting on my sofa, in a quiet corner, smoking cigarettes and drinking scotch and soda, I felt relatively safe from confrontation or interference.

The smooth creamy Clan Campbell was a new whisky to me. Introduced by S. Campbell and Son earlier in the year, and obviously recommended to Mr Baehler by Joe, the head barman of The Long Bar. After two large ones, I began to assume a contemplative state of mind.

The goings-on happening around me must be repeating themselves, ad infinitum, in hotels all around the globe. The famous tea dances at Raffles in Singapore. Hong Kong's dazzling balls at the Peninsular Hotel. The receptions at Taj Mahal Hotel in Bombay. The Eastern and Oriental Palm Court Orchestra in Penang. Not to mention high tea in Colombo's Bristol Hotel. Would this way of life continue forever? The worn-out mundaneness gave me an eerie feeling. Was this existence about to disappear? The participants becoming mere shadowy images on cinema screens, or in faded photographs. With this somewhat gloomy thought, I left Mervyn to fox trot the night away, and took myself to bed.

Chapter Eighteen
Egyptian Gazette - Vital I jump a few fences and bypass red tape

What time Mervyn finally came to bed I had no idea, but he was deeply asleep when I woke. As a result, for a second morning running, I breakfasted alone. Afterwards purchasing an Egyptian Gazette at the desk, adjourning to the terrace, choosing a chair against the railing in order the sun might revive my unusually low spirits. They do say that too much excitement can bring about an attack of the blues, and quite honestly, it had been a succession of invigorating and thought-provoking days. I put my mood down to this and flicked through the newspaper, looking for a piece that would draw attention away from myself.

The Times parliamentary correspondent reported, yet again, the issue raised in the House of Commons concerning the experiment to increase the fitness of recruits. It seems they remained below the levels required for fighting men of the line. Surely, here was a means by which I might encourage Harry's commanding officer to release him from the Hussars so he can return to England and transfer to the Army Physical Training Corp.

'The Army in Egypt'. A caption above the article caught my eye, which once more quoted last Friday's Times. It seems all British units, at present serving in Egypt and residing in Cairo, are to prepare to move to new barracks at Ismalia and the Canal Zone. Suddenly, I realised how imperative it was that I put my plan in motion immediately. It was vital I arrange to meet Lieutenant Colonel Weatherall as soon as possible. Even now, I still had no word from his adjutant Captain Haig. Clearly, it would be necessary to jump a few fences and bypass red tape to gain final satisfaction.

***

"What are we doing today?" Mervyn asked, slumping into a chair beside me. "Aren't we going to the Pyramids? We've been here over two weeks. Everyone I spoke to last night has seen them except me. I felt quite embarrassed."

Folding the newspaper, I knocked out my pipe in the ashtray.

"Of course we are! I didn't spend nearly one hundred and sixty piastres on passes for both of us for nothing. That's about two pounds five and sixpence. But we'll do that sort of thing once we settle the Harry issue. Don't be selfish. Think about other people for a change."

I expected Mervyn to retaliate, but he sullenly took out his pipe and filled it from my tobacco pouch.

"There's a dance at the Semiramis Hotel tonight," he said. "Miss Plunkett Dillon wants to go, and wishes me to take her."

He looked so miserable I could hardly keep from laughing. Instead, I methodically filled my pipe and lit it, watching Mervyn do the same.

"Of course! You must go," I said, watching our smoke drift into the street below and subsequently blown away by a passing tram. "You can't let a lady down. She's an attractive young thing. She's bound to interest a few good looking British officers. You never know, you might get a surprise you're not expecting."

"Honestly! Mervyn exclaimed. "And what if I did cop off with someone. I don't think you'd care. I've seen the way you're getting friendly with Ali. I think you've got your eye on him."

"Don't be ridiculous Mervyn! I find Ali most interesting. But not in the way you think. He's bright and intelligent. Can't you see how much he's teaching us about Egypt?"

"You know me Ron. In one ear and out the other."

"How about we find a good steam bath," I said, deciding to change the subject. "I've a desire to be pampered this morning."

"Okay. Afterwards, can we go to the sporting club for a swim?"

"That sounds a good idea. But remember, we arranged to meet Ali in front of the Opera at noon."

"Ali, Ali, Ali! Can't we have a day by ourselves?"

"You're not jealous are you?" I said, trying not to laugh. "I do believe you are. That's why you're so quiet when he's with us."

"You only talk to Ali when he's around and ignore me most of the time."

"Only because you never contribute to the conversation."

"I'm not usually that interested. I just see things. I don't think about them and talk about them like you and Ali."

"Then that's what makes us different. I've an enquiring mind, which Ali satisfies. We really can't leave him waiting. We have to make a show at least. Also, he's bound to know of a good steam bath."

"Ah! I get it. Naturally, we'll invite Ali to join us. That way you'll get a closer look at him."

"Honestly Mervyn! You have such a dirty mind sometimes. You'll be the one leering, I don't doubt."

It was clear there would never be an end to the argument, so instead, I returned to my newspaper, while Mervyn faced his chair to the railing so he could get a better view of the busy street.

Chapter Nineteen
Hammam Bishtak

Cairo Opera House sparkled in the midday sunshine, appearing all the more like a giant wedding cake than it did in the moonlight on our first night in Cairo. We found Ali as arranged, in the middle of Midan Opera, sitting on a seat under the statue of Ibrahim Pasha.

"Mervyn and I fancy a steam bath Ali. Do you have one you can recommend?"

"I'm told Hammam Bishtak is good effendi. They say Sahid the masseur is most vigorous."

"That's just what we need, isn't it Mervyn. A good pummelling."

Mervyn smiled archly, but remained silent.

"Then it's Hammam Bishtak. How do we get there?"

"By tram effendi. It's below the Citadel. At the end of Sharia Suq Al Silah. Do you wish me to join you?"

Instinctively, I felt Mervyn staring at me, waiting for my answer.

"Of course Ali. Do you not care for this particular bath?"

"Yes effendi. But on Fridays, before prayers, I visit the hammam beside my family mosque in Bulaq."

"Come along then," I said. "Let's catch a tram. What number Ali?"

"Number thirteen effendi. The cemetery tram."

"Unlucky for some," said Mervyn sardonically.

The three of us jumped on the tram outside the post office and it rattled us around Midan El Ataba, past the vegetable market, and into Sharia Mohammad Ali, a wide street lined with impressive apartment buildings.

"That's Gamil George's," Ali said, pointing to a small brick arch, enclosing windows and a shop doorway. "He's the famous oud maker."

"What's an oud?" asked Mervyn.

"A wooden stringed musical instrument Mr Mervyn. Like a Mandolin, or a Balalaika, but shaped like half a watermelon. Its unique feature is that it has no frets. The neck tapers and the peg box is bent backwards."

"There you are Mervyn!" I exclaimed. "Now you know what an oud is. See how useful Ali is."

Ali frowned, suddenly aware of the tension existing between Mervyn and myself. However, he continued undeterred.

"From one end to the other, this street's always been famous for instrument makers. Once, there was a shop for every kind imaginable."

"Should we have brought our swimming costumes?" asked Mervyn, looking at me sideways, "Or do we go as nature intended?"

Ali laughed nervously. "I'm sorry Mr Mervyn. It's strictly forbidden to show your body between your knees and your navel. The Ma'allim will give us towels and a cloth to wear around our waist."

Trundling merrily on, the tram entered the square backing on the gardens and massive rear walls of Sultan Hassan Mosque, along with the lesser, Mosque of El Rifai, Ali indicating that we should get off at this point, saying it was only a short walk to the hammam.

Mervyn and I were completely taken aback when we arrived at the door, or should I say a hole in the wall. For that is what it was. Just a small arched entrance elaborately sculpted out of pink and fawn stone. A heavy iron door was open wide enough for us to glimpse a man leaning against the wall, dressed in a white gallibaya and a skullcap.

"Come in Messieurs," he entreated, smiling broadly, revealing his cracked and missing teeth. "Welcome to Hammam Bishtak."

Seeing I was the first to duck inside, my eyes had lately been dazzled by the sunshine outside, so they took several seconds to discern the crumbling stone passage ahead, where orange light flashed through an arch.

"Go inside gentlemen," continued the man. "Sahid will look after you."

"How old's this place?" Mervyn whispered from somewhere behind. "It looks about to fall down around our ears."

"Over six hundred years Mr Mervyn," said Ali, following us along the passage. "I think Hammam Bishtak was commissioned by Bishtak, a wealthy Amir, as a gift to Sultan Nasir Mohammad for the honour of marrying his daughter. It's been in the family ever since.

"My word!" I exclaimed. "Now that's what I call inheritance. The entrance is very ornamental. But why is it so small?"

Ali touched his nose. "To stop curious persons seeing inside effendi. When the Mameluks ruled Egypt, whose tombs we saw a few days ago, there were many hammams in Cairo. Some say as many as the days of the year. Everyone visits the hammam at least once or twice a week, women in the morning and men in the afternoon. Our Prophet says we are to wash our hands, face, and ears each time we pray. This, we do at home during the week. But on Fridays, when we go to mosque, we must be thoroughly clean. So it is our habit to visit the hammam before the call to prayer."

The three of us stooped through the second arch to discover a reception room lit by a rusting skylight and various flickering gas brackets. However, I quickly realised we were not alone, as several, semi naked, men were sitting or lying on large stone divans, draped with ancient Bedouin rugs. The men appeared to be asleep. In fact, I distinctly heard the sound of snoring.

Gathered around and about was a haphazard collection of furniture, as well as a profusion of mirrors hanging from the crumbling walls, some appearing to derive from ages past, while others were more contemporary, although shabby.

This strange fascination with mirrors reminded me of Fishawy's coffee shop. Perhaps they too were the contribution of a previous relative, left in place as a mark of respect to a lamented ancestor. On one side of the chamber, against a lurid green wall, stood an ancient dressing table, clearly once a woman's pride and joy. Now, it was almost an antique, leaning against the wall covered in a thick layer of grime, the shining mirror merely a memory in an empty frame. Ancient electric fans clung to the walls, or stood on cupboards and dressers. These shared space with photo frames, the glass now yellowed with nicotine, covering photographs of stern men, dressed in suits and tarbushes, staring impassively into the room.

China jugs, buckets, mops and brooms, surrounded a cracked enamel sink, the once shining taps now green with verdigris, giving evidence the hammam was cleaned occasionally. For entertainment as well as refreshment, sheesha pipes stood beside the stone platforms. Also copper coffee pots on a wooden draining board beside a sink indicated some type of sustenance was provided. Pervading all this was an overwhelming smell. A blend of steam, water, scented soap and boiled towels. It reminded me of washing day at Royal Crescent, when a similar odour seeped through the house, its source the washhouse in the basement, where Emma our scullery maid, scrubbed, boiled and wrung the washing, eventually to hang on the line at the bottom of the garden. Nevertheless, as Mervyn and I were soon about to discover, it was not just washing that would be scrubbed, boiled, and wrung out that afternoon.

"Did you not visit the hammam when you were last in Cairo effendi?" asked Ali, as we waited for Sahid to bring towels.

"Surprisingly Ali, I did not. To be honest, the only steam baths I've ever visited are the Roman Baths in my home city of Bath in England. Only the Great Bath and the Kings Bath are functional these days. But we're advised not to bathe as they're contaminated. The hot spring that feeds them still supplies the therapy hospitals nearby. The waters of Bath are famous for treating and curing many ailments, rheumatism being the most common."

"The same can be said for the hammam, effendi. Any skin problem disappears. Aches and pains in the joints vanish, and influenza is immediately cured."

At this moment Sahid appeared, holding a pile of red and yellow chequered cotton cloths. And bowing, he passed one to each of us.

"They do say it helps fertility," Ali continued. "Women stay for many hours."

"Then I suppose we can put all this down to the Romans," Mervyn said. "Are you sure the place wasn't built by them? It sure resembles the baths Ron's talking about."

Sahid gestured to us to follow him to a stone platform covered with rugs and cushions.

"Here we undress," Ali said.

"You mean there're no cubicles!" exclaimed Mervyn.

"No one will look Mr Mervyn. My religion teaches that to regard another man in any way other than a brother is sinful. To look at the area between the legs is forbidden lest it bring on lustful thoughts and feelings."

While untying my shoelaces, I quickly glanced at Mervyn to see him smirking roguishly. As a result, the three of us continued to undress in silence, each keeping their eyes on the task, finally covering our various modesties with Sahid's chequered cloth.

"Sahid will look after our clothes effendi," said Ali, once we were suitably attired. "Your watches and wallets he will give to the Mu'izz for safe keeping."

After disappearing with our belongings Sahid appeared again, this time carrying three pairs of wooden clogs, which he bade us put on. Then, smiling broadly, he signalled us to follow him through another low stone archway in the wall. Considering I am over six feet tall, with the height of the clogs, this took me to almost seven. Therefore, ducking through archways was beginning to give me a pain in the neck, which I hoped Sahid would shortly remedy.

We entered a large vaulted chamber where the fragmenting aged walls and numerous marble columns supported a cupola pierced by oculi. In other words, a dome with small circular glazed openings. (Please accept my apologies. I thought you might be impressed by my newly acquired knowledge of Ottoman architecture.) The floor of this ancient room reminded me of the crazy paving, a fad for garden paths quickly catching on back home.

Here, was no modern trend. The floor on which we stood was hundreds of years old and consisted of a chaotic collection of coloured marble pieces, grouted with rough cement. Furthermore, it appeared stained and ingrained with grime, hence betraying its age. An exact arrangement of marble encased an octagonal platform in the centre of the chamber, on which several men lay, their privates covered by chequered loincloths similar to our own. Against the wall, and at several points around the room, hot and cold water gushed from brass taps into marble troughs, thus filling the room with steam. This caused the chamber to feel extremely warm, to such a degree that, even though we were standing in the entrance, I began to sweat from every pore.

"I think Sahid wants us to climb on the slab," Ali said.

Ali appeared the more confident out of the three of us and quickly found a place among the men. Mervyn and I however, approached the podium with foreboding, and although there was plenty of room, the prone occupants shifted positions, thus enabling us room to lie down on the marble.

Already I considered myself hotter than I had ever been in my life, yet the temperature of the marble on which we lay was greater, causing me to perspire even more, until I was thoroughly drenched and sliding about like a giant dead fish. In comparison to Ali and the other Arab men, Mervyn and I were the colour of porcelain, all except our forearms and foreheads, which, during the fortnight in Egypt, had become quite tanned. Growing accustomed to the heated marble, I furtively glanced at the prone figures lying around me.

Ali was on his back beside Mervyn, and in contrast appeared as brown as a conker in October. Also, Mervyn's skin was smooth, whereas Ali was hirsute, as were the other Arab men, thick copious black hair sprouting from legs, arms, chests, and backs. I have heard it said that hairiness denotes virility. If this is the case, then that afternoon I was surrounded by more masculinity than I had yet to encounter. Mervyn was lying on his stomach beside me and I heard him sigh.

"This is wonderful Ron," he whispered. "I think I'm falling asleep."

"Try to stay awake Mr Mervyn," Ali mumbled. "Soon Sahid will be along to give us a massage."

Almost on cue, Sahid appeared and climbed onto the slab.

"You go first Mervyn," I said. "You're the youngest."

"No Ron," he said. "As you're the oldest; how about you go first. I'd like to see what happens."

"Very well," I said, sitting up and adjusting my loincloth.

Up until now, I have refrained from describing Sahid. Mainly, because he was so breathtakingly handsome I was afraid it would be necessary to devote several paragraphs to him. Nonetheless, I will endeavour to keep the description as brief as possible.

Despite being close in age and appearance to Ali, Sahid possessed features that signified finer breeding. If one can imagine the funeral mask of the boy Pharaoh, Tutankhamen, this then is close to the beauty god granted Sahid. However, his face was not his only attribute, since, as he knelt down beside me, dressed in nothing but a skimpy loincloth, it was his powerful chest, arms, and legs, which entirely thrilled me.

Remaining on his stomach, and now the colour of a boiled lobster, Mervyn turned his head in order to see what was about to happen.

Taking my left hand, Sahid began bending back each finger until it cracked. This hardly concerned me as I am occasionally in the habit of doing so myself. Although, when Sahid proceeded to crack my wrist, something I had previously thought to be impossible, I began to worry. Next, taking my arm, he extended it across his biceps, and as he pulled it backwards, my elbow made a sound similar to a child firing a pop gun. After indicating that I lay back, Sahid took my arm once more, and placing it across his thigh, lent his chest hard against my shoulder, and I heard a deep thump as the ball and socket of my left shoulder dislocated and promptly relocated again.

"Are you alright Ron?" Mervyn whispered.

"Fine," I answered. "It's not painful. Just a little disconcerting. Although it does have its benefits."

"I can see that. It makes me wish I'd gone first."

"Don't worry Mervyn. Sahid has plenty saved for you."

With my left arm feeling detached from the rest of me, Sahid turned his attention to my right, beginning as before with my fingers, completing the erotic procedure with my shoulder. Next, he motioned me to roll onto my belly, and there, with my eyes shut and my cheek pressed against the warm marble, I waited to see what would happen next.

Taking hold of my left ankle, Sahid pressed his chest across my buttocks, at the same time placing his forearm behind my knee. Still clutching my ankle, he bent my leg backwards towards my head, until I could almost feel my heel on my shoulder blade. Then, to my horror, my knee made a sound like a whip across a horse's back.

Were there any more joints Sahid could disjoint, I wondered? It seemed so, because he bade me roll over and slither across the marble until he had my head in his vast hands, his palms covering my ears. It was then I heard my pulse pounding and felt the throbbing arteries in my neck. Clearly, the combination of heat and manipulation was causing my blood pressure to rise. Nonetheless, I felt too stimulated to ask Sahid to stop.

He rocked my head several times, while his fingers plied the muscles in my shoulders, which I took to mean I should relax. Then suddenly he placed one hand on the back of my head, the other on my chin, and twisted my head so violently a resounding crack echoed inside my skull. Almost immediately, Sahid resumed the gentle rocking and massage, quickly repeating the process on the other side.

"I heard that!" Mervyn exclaimed. "Did it hurt?"

"Surprisingly not," I said, blinking the sweat out of my eyes. "My neck feels so loose I'm afraid my head might fall off."

Then the massage began, and a more delectable experience I have yet to encounter. Straddling my thighs Sahid rubbed my arms from the tip of my shoulder to my fingertips, a rippling squeezing motion; his fingers darting over my skin like butterflies. Next, he moved to my chest and belly, which I must admit both tickled and slightly aroused me; something I hoped would go unnoticed. Sahid climbed over me and knelt by my side, this time his hands concentrating on my thighs, manipulating my leg muscles from the knee almost to the groin, all the while, carefully avoiding the edge of my loincloth by millimetres.

At this point, I began to embarrass myself. Sahid gave no

impression anything was out of the ordinary. After all, he must have seen the same reaction a thousand times.

My feet were last on the list, and this was so erotic I almost moaned with ecstasy. Once every toe was pulled and cracked, the balls and heels of my feet were scoured with a metal scraper similar to an engineer's file, until every callus was worn away and the soles of my feet were as smooth as silk.

During this operation, I chanced to look up into the cupola above my head, where the sun streamed through several oculi, causing dagger like shafts to pierce the thick steam. Then suddenly, through a blur of stinging sweat, something caught my eye. Black creatures jostling around the glazed openings. Cockroaches. Huge cockroaches, crowding for position, reminding me of bats quarrelling in a tree.

During my previous period in Egypt, I became acquainted with the dirty creatures and remembered being appalled to see how big and menacing they were. Even after twenty years, they still fill me with horror. How can they survive in this steamy, soapy environment? Then I realised. Skin. They fed on human skin. Exfoliated dermis was the secret of their success and enormous size.

Picture the scene at night, when the hammam shuts its doors and the fires beneath the slab are extinguished. Down the insects crawl, only to scurry about the floor, drains, basins, and divans, in search of the thick white slime that is their food.

My disgust turned to anticipation however, as Sahid disappeared into the vapour, only to return holding a brass bucket filled with soapy water and several webbing cloths.

"Sit up effendi," Ali prompted. "It's time for your bath."

Using the soapy water from the bucket, Sahid began to scour my skin with a mitt, which Ali told me later was called a Keseh. Sahid then held my right hand and began rubbing my arm vigorously, except this time the experience was quite unlike the massage, since it felt akin to being scraped by the coarsest of sandpaper. In spite of this, as Sahid worked his magic, I grew accustomed to the scratching, eventually succumbing to its hypnotic effect, as my skin began to tingle from the stinging heat and forceful exfoliation.

"It's almost over effendi," Ali said, interrupting my reverie. "You can sit up."

"Really Ali," I murmured. "Are you sure? Isn't there somewhere else Sahid might rub?"

Mervyn snorted with laughter, and had he been able to see beneath my foaming face, he would have seen me smiling. I can always count on him to appreciate my sense of humour. I was also tempted to see if Ali had got the joke, but realised in doing so I might fill my eyes with soap.

Using the remaining soap, Sahid made additional lather in the bucket. So much in fact, it spewed over the top and onto the marble slab. Then, picking up a piece of webbing he filled it with soap suds and swathed my chest, moving to my back, head, legs, and finally my arms, until I was covered from head to toe. Commenting afterwards, Mervyn said I resembled a snowman, since all he could see of me were my eyes, nose, and mouth.

Seeing my eyes were tightly shut, I was completely oblivious to what was about to happen, because, all of a sudden, icy cold water engulfed me as Sahid poured bucket after bucket over my head. This happened so suddenly that my breath was snatched from me and I thought I would faint. As I took the force of the freezing water, all I could hear was Mervyn's merciless laughter, although not from Ali. Obviously, he knew the procedure and had more respect for his effendi.

"That's all very well Mervyn," I spluttered. "But you're next."

Now fully awake, I saw Sahid beckon me to follow him under a low archway, only to find we were standing inside another chamber, this time containing a swimming bath.

"Get in effendi," Sahid said. "Stay for half an hour. Then go there."

He pointed to yet another archway in the wall, and then returned to the slab where Mervyn waited nervously. Without removing my loincloth, which I knew would be frowned upon; I tiptoed down a set of submerged steps and into the water, which was hot enough to boil an egg.

For a while, I was convinced I would be unable to endure it, because my skin was still smarting from the heat of the slab and the freezing water doused over me. However, eventually, I grew accustomed to the temperature and began to luxuriate in the soft water.

It seemed an extreme luxury to waste so much water on simply washing, and I previously asked Ali the source of such copious amounts, since Egypt may only have a few inches of rain a year. He explained that each day thousands of gallons are taken from the Nile and delivered to the hammams of Cairo in skins. Therefore, like Claudette Colbert, bathing in Ass's milk in Cecil B DeMille's film, there I was bathing in Cleopatra's eternal Nile.

Several men sharing the bath with me were gathered in the corner, deep in conversation. But seeing me climb down into the water they stopped and acknowledged me, which I thought enormously polite.

Being deep enough in which to swim, by leaning my arms on the side and lifting my hips to the surface I was able to take my feet off the bottom and float. At that moment, with the murmurs of the Arab men, the gentle lapping of water and sunlight streaming through the oculi in the cupola above me, I realised I was more relaxed than I had ever been in my entire life. It was a totally blissful experience. This then was the reason Ali and his friends visited the hammam before attending prayers. Just as the prophet advised them to do, they perspired, massaged, exfoliated, shaved, and bathed. Thus, in a state of grace and cleansed of their sins, they were ready to greet their god. Now, I saw the reason for the hammam. It was not a place of indulgence, where one satisfied one's vanity. The hammam was an essential part of Muslim culture, with an indispensable place in the religious faith of Islam. My musings were interrupted by Mervyn leaping into the pool.

"Yow!" he screamed. "It's boiling!"

"Not really," I said. "It's just that you're cold from the dousing. You'll get used to it. How was your massage?"

"Smashing. Although, I got rather excited when Sahid sat on me. At one point I swear I felt his balls on my leg."

"You're lucky. My belly must have got in the way. Is Ali having his massage?"

"Yes. Sahid is giving him a shave and cutting his hair. Also, he's having the hair removed from his legs and chest. Sahid spread paste stuff on him and it just melted away."

"Well I never! What on earth is it? If Sahid gives us the recipe, we could make a fortune back home. I believe Veet Cream has the monopoly over there."

Mervyn and I remained in the bath until an extremely smooth Ali joined us. Then, after a further quarter of an hour, we made our way through to yet another domed chamber, where we sat on warm marble divans and began to sweat. By this time, my pores had opened and shut so often they needed no encouragement to give out copious amounts, which dripped from my forehead onto the marble tiles.

In a while, I began to feel quite chilly, and mentioning this to Ali, he suggested we take a shower and return to the reception area. Here we found the ever-present Sahid, ready to envelope us in thick warm towels. Then, once thoroughly wrapped, he urged us to lie down on the carpeted divans.

"Now we sleep," Ali said.

And sleep we did. A deep heavy dreamless sleep. The kind one has on Sunday afternoons, after consuming a dinner of braised beef, Yorkshire pudding and roast potatoes.

Since the manager possessed my watch, when Sahid woke me with a cup of coffee, I had no idea how long I had slept. The battered antique clock on the wall said almost half past four, meaning, we had been in the hammam for almost five hours. I had risen that morning despondent and out of sorts, putting my mood down to over stimulation and excitement. Nonetheless, hours later, I felt completely the opposite, all thanks to Hammam Bishtak. Now I understood how addictive the hammam can be, and resolved to have at least two a week, until our time in Cairo was over.

Chapter Twenty
Khan El Khalili - Cafe Riche

Unlike in Great Britain, where the Sabbath remains a holy day, with shops shut and cinemas and theatres closed, in Cairo there is little difference between Sunday and any other day of the week. Khan Al Khalili is busy as always and Mervyn and I took the opportunity, along with Ali's help, to spend the next morning shopping. The first item on our list was a sheesha pipe and there was hardly a problem finding a sheesha shop, since they were numerous as the sands of the desert, boasting such a variety Mervyn and I were stuck for choice. Finally, we decided upon a sheesha made of brass and glass, with exquisite etching into the crystal and metal. We agreed it would look outstanding stood on the brass-topped table we subsequently purchased in the Brass Bazaar.

It was also Mervyn's wish to buy presents for his family, I too, realising I must do the same for Eric, Amy and little Emily, along with Wilfred and my mother. The day we met Ali, the morning we first visited the Khan, he had taken us to a shop selling wooden camels wearing traditional Arabian saddles and leather bridles, so it was there we headed next.

From beneath a red and yellow awning, the shop not only sold camels, but also numerous varieties of souvenirs displayed in disarray on shelves and tables that tumbled into the street.

"How about the Sphinx," I suggested.

"Yes!" Mervyn snapped. "How about the Sphinx! When are we going to see it?"

"Soon," I replied. "Just be patient. Why not buy them each a little Sphinx."

There was an array of small polished ornaments, some in the shape of pyramids, others representing sarcophagi, lions, horses, Tutankhamen's funeral mask, and Sphinxes.

"What are they made of Ali?" Mervyn asked.

"Egyptian red granite Mr Mervyn. Same stone as the sarcophagus in the Great Pyramid."

"Alright. I'll have six. One of each. Well I may as well buy myself something. How about you Ron? What are you going to buy?"

"There's so much to choose from. That Aladdin's lamp up there looks nice. Do you think Amy would like it?"

"What about the scarabs mounted in gold?"

"I doubt if it's gold Mervyn. But I agree. They're very nice, although I'm drawn to the little onyx cat. Emily might find it fun."

Eventually Emily got her cat. Mervyn bought his camel and a green scarab for his mother. I purchased a framed and decorated papyrus for Wilfred, a red scarab for mother, the head of Queen Nefertiti for Amy, and for Eric, a small black stone statue of Horus the falcon god.

Time flies when you're spending money, or rather someone else is spending your money, consequently, before we knew it, it was lunchtime. Since we were in the bazaar, the obvious place to eat would have been Naguib's in the Caravanserai. But Ali suggested we sample a café close to his mother's apartment, so we hailed a caleche, telling the driver to take us to Maaruf.

By now, we knew the route well. Around Ezbekiya Gardens and along Fouad Avenue, where the wide boulevards reminded me of Paris, saying as much to Ali.

"Which is not surprising effendi. Khedive Ismail Pasha, the man who built the Opera House in time for the opening of the Suez Canal, commissioned French architects to design this entire area."

"So that's why the squares, streets, and buildings have a consistent appearance."

"Yes effendi. Although, the development put Egypt into terrible debt, and is partly the reason the Sultan of Turkey ordered Ismail to abdicate and hand the title of Khedive to his son Twefik."

Our caleche clattered down Suleiman Pasha Street, crossed Suleiman Pasha Square, passing the statue of the grand old man himself. And once beyond Groppi's Restaurant, stopped on the corner of Sheikh Hamza Street outside a coffee shop, with Café Riche emblazoned across the fanlight above the door. Having given Ali piastres to pay the driver, I asked him to instruct the driver to wait, since the carriage was loaded with the results of our shopping excursion.

"This café is famous effendi," Ali said, as we stood admiring the façade. "It's been here for nearly thirty years. My father, when he was alive, never took our family anywhere else. So as children, my brother, sisters and I, thought Café Riche was the only café in Cairo."

By then, it was lunchtime and Café Riche was full of customers, so we waited inside for a waiter to show us to a table.

"What was your father's profession Ali?" I asked.

"A violinist effendi. A very fine one. He played in Umm Kulthum's orchestra. You've heard of Umm Kulthum of course."

"I'm sorry Ali. I haven't."

"You hear her everywhere effendi. Umm is the most famous singer Cairo has ever known, or ever will I think. She is the voice of the Middle East"

"When we were in the bazaar," Mervyn said. "Most shops had a wireless playing, and it always seemed to be the same woman singing."

"That's her Mr Mervyn. Umm is everywhere."

"It sounds complicated music. Lots of ups and downs."

"We like it that way Mr Mervyn. Arab music is very different to European. Umm sings for the people of Cairo on the first Thursday evening of every month. She broadcasts her concert from the Opera House. On such nights the streets of the city are very empty."

"Then we'll be back in England by that time," I said. "What a shame."

The headwaiter found us a table in the corner. Thus, a favourable position to observe the clientele, which I saw instantly were the intelligentsia of Cairo, as the atmosphere was overflowing with quotes, theories, opinions and concepts, a little akin to my once frequented Cave of the Golden Calf, off Regent Street, or the Ivy in London's West End.

A pair of European women dressed like men, in dark suits, shirts, and ties, were smoking Turkish cigarettes through long tortoise-shell holders. With short Brylcreamed hair and faces devoid of makeup, they leaned towards each other intimately.

Might Café Riche be the hub of Cairo's alternative set? It was most avant-garde.

Slightly resembling Groppi's, Café Riche certainly was quite different to the simplicity of Fishawy's, also far less sophisticated than Naquib's. Ali must have seen me scrutinising the patrons.

"Most people are intellectual effendi," he said. "Poets, writers, artists and politicians. But the café is also popular with actors, singers, and musicians. It's been so since the nineteen twenties. Once a medical student ran out of here and threw a bomb at the Prime Minister as he rode by in his car."

"Really!" exclaimed Mervyn. "Was he killed?"

"There were no casualties Mr Mervyn. After the war, the revolutionary party became quite strong, secretly publishing and distributing a newspaper from this very café. Their printing press is still in the basement."

"You mean it wasn't confiscated," I said.

"Café Riche has become something of a shrine to political activists. I think subversives still meet here. Mother lives close by, so I often come for coffee with my younger brother. When we see men huddled in a corner, deep in conversation, we make wagers as to who's who, or whether they are or not."

While Ali acquainted us with the history of Café Riche, my attention was drawn to the main eating space, which struck me as surprisingly narrow, although possessing an intimate, yet light and airy atmosphere. Since our table was in the corner at the back and facing the door, to our right, the wall was panelled wood, having once been painted white, although now quite yellowed from years of tobacco smoke. On our left, ran a long line of windows, beneath which the panelling was repeated. Had these windows not been half covered by white muslin curtains, we would have seen into Suleiman Pasha Street.

Surely, the proprietor would wish passers-by to see inside, and be attracted by the cosy ambience. Alternatively, were the curtains a device to allow the occupants some sense of privacy, away from the prying eyes of men whose thoughts dwelt on something other than liquid refreshment? Small vestibules allowing additional space for tables, led from the main dining area, transforming what I initially thought to be a small establishment, into one more sizeable. Furthermore, because of the intimacy of these alcoves, the natural colour of the panelling was retained.

Whether in the main area, or the alcoves, each table was set for four, six, eight, or even a dozen, depending on the demands of the patrons. Every table was covered with a red and blue tablecloth and surrounded by brown, wooden chairs with the motif 'Café Riche', etched into the backrest.

To my immense fascination, handsome, enigmatic waiters padded about, wearing white turbans and blue gallibaya, discreetly embroidered with gold thread. Serving coffee, trays of Mezze and tureens of meat or beans, their flamboyant costume appeared entirely out of keeping with the unpretentious interior.

"Do you know Mervyn," I said, looking at the menu. "I feel quite at home. It's a little like the Oak Room at Fortts in Bath, don't you think."

"Kind of. But Fortts doesn't have pictures of Arabs hanging on the wall. Who are they Ali?"

"The man in the photo behind you Mr Mervyn is Ahmad Shawqi, the prince of poets. He died five years ago and a special dinner was held here to honour him, attended by all his friends."

"How about the man over Ron's shoulder?"

"I believe that's Abd Al Rahman Al Rafai, an Egyptian nationalist party politician and historian. He's still alive."

"Are they mostly writers, poets, and politicians?" I asked.

"Not all effendi. See the photo of a woman on the wall beside the bar. That's Layla Murad. She acted with Naguib el Rihani, the man whose restaurant we visited. And next to her is Ismail Yasin, the actor and comedian. The men you see on the wall would meet here, take breakfast, and drink coffee, or something stronger. Yes Mr Mervyn. Alcohol is served at Café Riche. They would exchange ideas and discuss important issues. At Café Riche seeds of revolution are sown."

"Then it's a great honour to have your photo on the wall."

"Indeed effendi. One day I'll ask if my father might join the collection."

"So everyone we see has made some contribution to Egyptian culture."

"Certainly effendi. Although, some men have since died or disappeared."

"How do you mean, disappeared?"

"Around the time you last left Cairo, because Café Riche was a known meeting place for members of the Waft party, the police raided it regularly, taking away for questioning anyone they supposed might be plotting to overthrow the British. If you'll excuse me saying so effendi."

"Of course Ali. Please go on."

"During those days the owner was rumoured to be Mr Baehler."

"Shepheard's Baehler?"

"Yes. It was Mr Baehler who first asked the intellectuals for their photographs, the tradition lasting to this day."

"Maybe that's the reason Baehler was exiled. Perhaps he had too close an association with Egyptian political factions."

"Very possible."

For once Mervyn asked an intelligent question.

"In which way was your father linked to Café Riche, Ali?"

"It's also a meeting place for musicians Mr Mervyn, where they can be with friends, at the same time tell each other about future engagements. Musically, Cairo is an extremely busy city. With the Opera, nightclubs, radio broadcasts, hotel tea dances and balls, there's never a shortage of work for a good musician."

"And your father was one of them," I said.

"I am very proud of my father. Especially because he played in Umm's orchestra. Whenever I hear her records on the wireless, I know my father's playing his violin."

"Is Umm on the wall?" I asked.

"She takes pride of place in a vestibule, alongside Ahmad Rami, the poet and the man who writes her songs."

"Hey! Look over there," exclaimed Mervyn. "That poster says Umm Kulthum. The rest's in Arabic. What's it say Ali?"

"It says she'll sing two songs here tomorrow night."

"That's a coincidence!" Mervyn chuckled. "If she's that famous, wouldn't you think she'd sing in a theatre or concert hall?"

"She does Mr Mervyn. But fifteen years ago, Umm was unknown. When she arrived in Cairo, Café Riche was the first venue to engage her. Umm has a spot in her heart for the place and as a gesture of thanks, performs here at least twice a year. Also, it's a well-known fact that she sings for free."

"Then we're lucky we caught her," I said. "Why don't we come here tomorrow night?"

"We'll need to be early effendi. It'll get crowded by ten o'clock."

"Ten o'clock! That's late."

"Umm never sings earlier than ten. It's her practice."

"The poster said she'll sing two songs. Then, it's going to be a short show."

"Not so effendi. Umm's songs are usually two hours long."

"My word! I've never heard the like."

"That's how Arab songs are. We like them that way."

"Well, it won't stop us will it Mervyn."

"Excuse me, both of you," mumbled Mervyn. "I need to use the toilet."

With Mervyn otherwise engaged, I took the opportunity to speak to Ali confidentially.

"I'd like to visit the barracks tomorrow morning. Do you think your fellow might supply camels and garments for us again?"

"Certainly effendi. I'll meet you both at Mamoud's house. Will you be able to get there on your own?"

"I think so. It's the last stop but one on the number twenty-six tram to Heliopolis. Am I right?"

"You are effendi."

Mervyn appeared again, and so did our glamorous waiter. Consequently, I let Ali set about ordering our lunch.

Chapter Twenty One
A nice surprise for Harry

After keeping his promise to escort Miss Plunkett Dillon to the dance at the Semiramis, Mervyn partnered her again at the Valentine's Ball at Shepheard's. On the other hand, I spent the evening relaxing, chatting to Joe, the nice Canadian barman in the Long Bar.

However, before switching out my bedside light, I read a few more chapters of, 'Drums Along the Mohawk', which Mervyn inadvertently, or intentionally, packed when we left the ship, along with his Tarzan book. Then, catching up with my diary, I fell asleep.

***

The next morning, I managed to rouse Mervyn early and we breakfasted together.

"What's the plan for today?" he asked, crunching on a slice of buttered toast.

"I thought we'd play it by ear. Just jump on a tram and see where it takes us."

"With no Ali?"

I nodded, since my mouth was full of poached egg.

"How amazing. A day on our own for once. No lesson about Cairo's glamorous past."

"Don't be nasty Mervyn. We've had this argument before. We're lucky to have Ali. We'd hardly have done as much without him."

Breakfast over, and after collecting our hats from the cloakroom, we stepped into the sunshine, relishing its warmth despite the early hour.

"Do you know," said Mervyn, as we waited at the tram stop opposite Ezbekiya Gardens. "I still can't quite believe it's winter. It's the 15th February. Just think what the weather's like in England. Probably snowing."

"That's the benefit of spending the season in Egypt my dear chap," I said. "By the time we get back we'll be over the worst."

A tram appeared around the corner of Fuad Al Auwal Avenue, number thirteen on the front.

"Come on," Mervyn said. "Aren't we jumping on the first that comes along?"

"Let's see what comes next. I'm superstitious. We caught the same tram to the hammam on Saturday. Don't you remember? Ali called it the cemetery tram, and that's where it ends up. I don't think that'll be a very agreeable destination."

Luckily, the next tram was a number twenty-six and bound for Heliopolis, so we climbed aboard and sat down on one of the seats at the front.

"We've been on this one before," Mervyn said, as we took off up Shari Al Amir Faruq. "I recognise the restaurant over there. The name over the door made me laugh, but I couldn't say anything because Ali was with us."

We stopped at a set of traffic lights, just long enough for me to see the restaurant to which Mervyn referred, and immediately saw the reason for his jollity. It was called Al Khok, with a painted sign portraying a colourful fighting cock. However, I refrained from drawing attention to it, or commenting because a group of Coptic nuns were travelling with us, escorting a party of adolescent schoolgirls. But I hardly think that the nuns would have seen the significance of the word.

"I know where we're going," Mervyn said, as we left the network of streets behind, exchanging them for the open spaces of the suburbs. "We're going to Heliopolis. You see. You can't get one over on me Ronald Fry. You think I go around with my eyes shut. Well this proves that I don't."

"You may be right, but you may be wrong. Just wait and see."

Enjoying the daily panoply of Cairo life beyond the tram windows, we continued the ride in silence. I too began to recognise various buildings along the way; the French Hospital, for instance, although, when we passed the New Shalom Synagogue I knew it was time to get off.

"But there's nothing here," Mervyn said, as we watched the tram trundle away. "I imagined we were going to Heliopolis. I've read there's a fantastic place there called Luna Park, with merry go rounds, a big dipper and even a skating rink."

"Where did you see that?" I asked. "Luna Park was an Army Hospital by the time I arrived in Egypt in 1917. It was closed when I left two years later. Maybe it's open again. As we're near to the house of Ali's friend Mamoud would you like another camel ride?"

We stood in the road as the tram trundled away.

"Isn't that the way to his house?" I said, pointing across the street.

"Yes!" Mervyn exclaimed. "The camel man is half way down on the left. Where are we going on a camel for heaven's sake? Also, I don't think I can do it without Ali being here."

At last Mervyn admitted Ali was useful, although rather selfishly.

"Mervyn! It's just like riding a bicycle. Once you've ridden a camel you never forget."

Walking into the yard, we were greeted by the familiar scene of forty or so camels sitting or standing, all of them either eating or chewing the cud, while in their midst, Mamoud was spreading Lucerne grass about the enclosure. He saw us standing at the entrance and waved.

"There's Ali," Mervyn cried. "What's he doing here?"

Ali was helping his friend, but hurried out of the multitude when he saw us, dodging camels as he went.

"What a coincidence you're here Ali," gasped Mervyn. "But I'm glad all the same. Ron has a crazy idea to take a camel ride. I said I was reluctant to climb on a camel without you being with us."

"You honour me Mr Mervyn. I'm pleased you feel that way. But you did very well last time, so I'm sure you don't need me. If you wish me to join you though, I'd be pleased to."

"Of course Ali," I said. "It'll be our pleasure."

Mamoud arrived carrying our clothing, and he and Ali helped us into our gallibayas and keffiyehs. Suitable attired, and after giving him money to pay Mamoud, Ali led us to our respective camels and instructed them to sit, while we climbed aboard.

I was beginning to feel apprehensive and a little excited at the thought of what was about to occur. Yet, I made no sign to my young friends that anything was out of the ordinary.

"Why not go by the barracks," I shouted, from my position at the rear of our caravan. "I'd like to find Trooper Harding and Trooper Shaw."

"That's a good idea," Mervyn replied. "Maybe they've news of Harry."

We were about to turn our camels onto the main road, when surprisingly, the traffic speeding along sending up clouds of dust, pulled up and graciously let us cross, as if our way had suddenly been marked by a pair of Belisha beacons. Ali explained the phenomenon as we continued.

"In Egypt effendi, camels and horses go first. It has been so for centuries and will be for centuries to come."

"How civilised Ali. I'm most impressed. I wish this were so along the country lanes where Mervyn and I come from."

Soon, through the heat haze, the barracks loomed ahead, a forbidding collection of limestone buildings, the three tiers of pillared walkways and ablution blocks, appearing vacant and unwelcoming. As we approached, an armed sentry at the gate challenged us.

"Who goes there," he barked, in typical British fashion.

"Captain Fry retired. 4th of the 2nd Somerset Light Infantry and the Royal Flying Corp," I said, looking down at him from my camel. "My companions are Mr Mervyn Watson and our guide, Ali Rashid. May we have permission to enter the barracks?"

"My word Captain!" said the sentry. "For a minute I thought you were a couple of natives. Can't be too careful. The Brits aren't liked much nowadays. What's your business may I ask?"

"Mr Watson's brother is a trooper in the Queen's Own Hussars.

We're here to enquire after his health."

"Watson! I thought the name rang a bell. My unit's the Saucy Seventh. His brother's not Harry is he?"

"That's him," Mervyn interrupted. "I haven't seen him for two years. We've travelled all the way from England."

"Ordinarily I'd need to get the okay with my superior. But seeing it's you Captain, and that the lad here is Harry's brother, I'll turn a blind eye."

Our camels bore us leisurely across the scorching parade ground towards the shaded colonnades, where, through the shimmering heat I saw a group of troopers sitting on a couple of benches in the shade. They seemed to be cleaning their rifles. Mervyn had also seen them. However, as the feet of camels hardly make a sound, the men were oblivious to our approach.

"There's Trooper Harding," yelled Mervyn. "The man sitting in the middle? Look at the man on the end smoking a pipe, the bloke in front of Trooper Shaw. Ron! That's Harry. It's my brother!"

Mervyn shouted so loud the men stopped cleaning their guns and looked up.

"You've come prepared again Captain," Trooper Harding called, seeing us approach

"Yes trooper. When in Rome, as they say."

"Harry!" Mervyn shouted again. "Harry! It's me! Mervyn!"

Standing abruptly, the man to whom Mervyn referred, broke from the group, and shading his eyes from the sun, strode purposefully towards us.

"Mervyn!" he yelled. Is it you? I don't believe it. What are you doing here?"

"Are you alright?" asked Mervyn. "We've all been so worried since mum and dad got your letters."

At this point, I suddenly wished I had my camera to capture the moment, since the photo would have been worthy of publication in the London Illustrated News. Mervyn sitting astride his camel, dressed in gallibaya and keffiyeh, the facade of the barracks looming behind him, Harry looking up at his younger brother in astonishment.

"This must be quite a surprise," Mervyn said. "Well let me assure you, it's just as surprising for me."

Harry nodded, as a cheer went up from his mates on the benches.

"Is it really you Mervyn?" stammered Harry. "You look like a Gyppie."

"It's me alright," Mervyn, said, pulling off his headgear. "The Captain must have arranged this. He's responsible for dressing me up. It's his little joke."

"Ah! The Captain. Mum mentioned the Captain."

"I'm he," I said, revealing my face from under the keffiyeh. "Captain Ronald Fry. I'm pleased to meet you Harry, also glad to see you looking so well. We've been here nearly three weeks trying to bring about your release from the hospital."

"It was Ron who got you out of that terrible place," Mervyn continued.

Ali ordered our camels to kush, so Mervyn and I were able to greet Harry properly, although I noticed he was rather reluctant to approach the animals.

"How are you old chap?" said Mervyn, shaking his brother's hand.

"Okay. And it seems, thanks to the Captain, I can breathe fresh air once more. I really believed I'd never see the light of day again."

"Why on earth were you there?" I asked. "Your friends told us you had a bit of a spell."

"You might say that Captain. Did they tell you I was kicked by a horse?"

"Yes. Quite badly we understand."

"After that, I couldn't go near one without a terrible wave of panic taking over. Not very good when you're a trooper in the hussars. I was so ashamed. But daren't tell anyone. Who would have listened anyway? They'd have thought I'd gone crazy. So I kept it to myself. Bottled it up for months. Until one day, I fell apart. You ask the lads. I was a mess. I had bad thoughts Captain. Did they tell you I tried to top myself? Jim Shaw found me with the gun. That's when they put me in that place."

"Trooper Harding said you were given some sort of new treatment."

"They stuck a needle in me that made everything go numb, then fixed wires to my head and gave me electric shocks, though I find it hard to remember how it felt."

"How many times?"

"Maybe three."

"Are you alright?" Mervyn asked.

"I think so Merv. I don't feel afraid anymore and the sick feeling in my stomach's disappeared. But I really miss home, and mum, dad and the kids."

It hardly took a psychiatrist to guess that homesickness was the reason for the panic attacks and not equinophobia. I have heard this form of longing can be almost akin to physical sickness and bring on symptoms such as Harry described.

"They all send their love," Mervyn said.

"How's my little Eric? Still getting into mischief."

"Of course. He wouldn't be Eric if he didn't."

The brothers laughed, obviously sharing fond memories of their baby sibling.

"Harry," I said. "Your friends told us you used the hospital gymnasium."

"It's true Captain. I think the exercise helped me get better. It also got me away from those lunatics. There're some real bad head-cases in there."

For the first time, Harry smiled and I searched his face for a family resemblance. He and Mervyn were quite dissimilar. Mervyn possessed fair hair and a fair complexion, which was prone to freckle. Whereas, Harry's hair was dark and wavy, his face, chest, and arms deeply tanned from two years under the Egyptian sun. Moreover, Harry was taller than Mervyn by at least nine inches. His countenance was comely as well as healthy, with smiling blue eyes and brilliant white teeth. However, the family resemblance was to neither Mervyn, nor his brother Richard, or their sister Sarah. Harry likened to his younger sisters, Ruby and Doris, all three strongly resembling their father.

Although he was wearing his uniform breeches, held up by a wide leather belt, Harry was stripped down to a tight white singlet, which accentuated his brawny arms and chest, no doubt created by months of vaulting the horse, swinging on parallel bars and vigorous work on the rings.

"How did you get in here with those bloody things?" he asked, referring to our camels.

"Oh! Sorry Ali," I said. "Let me introduce our dragoman, Ali Rashid. He's been indispensable while we've been in Cairo, as well as instrumental in helping with your cause."

Ali stepped forward and bowed, making the Arab gesture of greeting.

"Most honoured to meet you effendi. I am extremely glad Allah has seen fit to set you free."

"I must admit Ali," Harry said, shaking Ali by the hand. "I said a few prayers while I was in the loony bin. I might now begin to believe in him."

Mervyn and I laughed, hoping Ali would understand Harry's joke, and were pleased to see him smile.

"The guard on duty was very obliging," I said. "Things seem very relaxed around here."

"We're getting ready to up stakes and leave for the Canal Zone, that's why. The army's been ordered out of every barracks in Cairo. Hey! Talk about mad dogs. What are we doing standing out here in the sun? Come on! I'll introduce you to the boys."

Throwing an arm over Mervyn's shoulder, Harry marched him away towards the shade of the colonnade, while Ali and I followed.

"You kept this secret very well effendi," Ali said. "Mervyn is very pleased. He has a lot to be grateful for having you as his companion."

"Never a truer word was spoken Ali my friend. But thank you all the same. But my task is not quite over. There's still some more I must do."

Someone suggested we move to the canteen, where we enjoyed a jolly time sitting around a table, drinking tea and demolishing a tin of Huntley and Palmer's Family Assorted Biscuits, a present to Trooper Shaw from his mother. Then Trooper Burns appeared with a packet of Crawford's Custard Creams, Mervyn's, absolute favourite and mine also. Next, he produced a tin of Ginger Snaps, which disappeared equally as fast.

We discovered this was the first time Ali had savoured such delicacies, therefore it amused us to see his expression, as he tasted each biscuit in turn.

Life in the barracks seemed pleasant, to such a degree, I found it difficult to imagine why anyone should feel homesick for England. However, there is no accounting for other folks' feelings. How life would change for the men in the Saucy Seventh over the following months, with their transfer to the Canal Zone and the months of intensive training with tanks and armoured cars?

"Tonight Harry," Mervyn said, "Ron, Ali, and I are going to a concert given by Umm Kulthum."

"We've a bunch of gyppie lancers billeted upstairs," Trooper Harding said. "I reckon she's the one they listen to all the time."

"Could you blokes get passes tonight and come with us?"

Harry looked at Ali, seeing him enjoying a fig roll, since the Egyptians invented the delicacy it was something familiar to him.

"Not our cup of tea Mervyn," he whispered. "Now if it were Hekmet Fahmy, the belly dancer, we'd be there like a shot. The lads and I saw her at the Kit Kat Club, before my trouble began."

By now, due to the amount of tea I had swallowed, my bladder was feeling as if it was about the burst. As a result, I excused myself and headed towards the door marked lavatory.

"Don't mind me Captain," Harry said, also leaving the table. "But I'll join you if I may."

At this point, I am going to confess something I have never told a living soul. I find it impossible to pass water standing at a urinal, should a man be standing beside me. Even if I concentrate extremely hard on the task in hand, nothing happens. I have often wondered whether the person next to me ever notices.

Harry was behind me as I pushed open the lavatory door, joining me at the stall beside mine.

While unbuttoning my fly, out of the corner of my eye, I saw him do the same.

"You and my brother are pretty close I think Captain."

Remembering the abruptness of his father all those years ago, even so, Harry's statement took me completely off guard.

"In her letters, mum's told me what you've done for us," he continued. "I wondered what had happened when one arrived addressed Camden Place."

All the while, I stared persistently ahead at the white tiles on the wall, willing the contents of my bladder to break free. Nonetheless, whatever valve we men have at the top of our penis, it refused to relax to allow the waters to flow.

"I couldn't see your family continue to live in that terrible slum," I said. "I had to get them out of there."

"You've done the Watson's proud Captain."

"There's one thing more though Harry," I said, forcing myself to look at him, while catching the briefest glimpse of what he held in his right hand. "I want to get you away from here, and home. That's your wish isn't it?"

"Dearly Captain. I made the biggest mistake joining the army. Father pushed me into it. More than likely to make one less mouth to feed. For two years, I've longed to be back. I love Bath. Cairo's all right. I've made good mates in Trooper Harding, Shaw, and Burns. I should be happy. But all the time I feel sad, and can't stop thinking about Mum, Dad and the kids."

"Don't worry. I've a plan. Tomorrow I'll try to see your C O, at the Semiramis Hotel. There's just a chance I might convince him of your usefulness back in England."

"I can't thank you enough Captain," Harry said, buttoning his fly. "And let me tell you, since we're talking confidentially. Whatever's going on between you and Mervyn is no concern of mine. If you know what I mean."

Suddenly, he looked over the urinal and quite blatantly stared at my slightly excited, yet still, redundant member.

"I've known about Mervyn for ages," he continued. "Brothers do you know. Up until I left for Aldershot, Merv and I slept in the same bed. He'd cop a feel when he thought I was asleep. I never made a fuss. What was the point?"

If it was difficult to urinate previously, then now it was completely impossible. What was I supposed to say to this admission? I was hardly in a position to deny everything and appear outraged at his suggestion. Therefore, I simply capitulated.

"That's very kind of you Harry. Your brother and I were close once, and in a way you've implied. However, these days we're merely friends."

"Understood, Captain," Harry said, crossing to the washbasin and running the tap. "But I can see our Merv's very fond of you."

"And me of him," I said, finally able to relax, the sound of the water aiding me to empty my bladder.

***

"You were a while in the gents with Harry," Mervyn said, as we returned to our camels. "What were you up to?"

Harry and his friends were walking ahead, talking to Ali. It seemed Troopers Harding, Shaw, and Burns were keen to organise a camel ride and Ali was describing how to find Mamoud's house. I was surprised to see Harry was also interested. Maybe he had decided to face up to his greatest fear.

"Nothing. Silly boy!" I said. "He took the opportunity to thank me, that's all. Also, I told him my plan. Well, a bit of it."

"What plan? Haven't we done what we needed to do? Can't we see the Pyramids now?"

"We'll see the Pyramids. But I must get Harry home for good. Otherwise I'm almost positive he'll become depressed again."

"He really misses home, but how on earth are you going to get him transferred?"

"Pull a few strings. Talk to the right people. You know me. I'm going to be busy tomorrow morning. What will you do?"

"Catch a tram to Gezira. Have a swim in the club pool. Then lie in the sun and get a tan."

"How can you? You're not a member."

"I'll say I'm staying at Shepheard's. Won't they give me a temporary membership?"

"Yes. But it'll cost you a couple of pounds."

"That's okay. I've still a bit left from my winnings last Thursday."

"Then you'd better make sure you take the Perla Sun Cream we bought at Sinclair's. You know how quickly you burn."

"Also," Mervyn continued, "it says in the guide book, at the south end of the island there are grottos and an aquarium. I wouldn't mind having a look."

"You'd better be careful. Even when I was here twenty years ago, there were some nasty characters found skulking around. Take it from me, I know all about the goings on in aquariums."

"Really!" Mervyn laughed. "I feel a bedtime story coming on."

"That's all very well. But we've Umm to see tonight at ten o'clock. I don't think we'll be keen to do anything by the time we get to bed."

Having said goodbye to Harry and his friends, after arranging to meet them at the hotel on Sunday evening, Mervyn, Ali, and I, returned our garments and camels to Mamoud, and caught the tram back to the city.

Chapter Twenty Two
A call to prayer - Umm Kulthum

Later that afternoon, considering our evening appointment at Café Riche; also, since it was almost five o'clock when we arrived back at Shepheard's, there seemed little point in Ali returning to Imbaba. Therefore, I invited him to our rooms, ignoring the stares and frowns from the Europeans in the lift. The reason for this hostility is due to the hotel rule stating that dragomen are not allowed to stand in front of the hotel, let alone enter. They must remain on the opposite side of Ibrahim Pasha Street until a tourist requires their services. Subsequently, the concierge calls the dragoman to cross the street and wait at the bottom of the steps for his client to appear. Sensible I suppose, but rather xenophobic and typically British. You might well ask how I managed to get Ali into the hotel and here again a few piastres quickly palmed, worked wonders.

All of us were considerably dusty, even though Mervyn and I had worn Mamoud's gallibaya and keffiyehs over our European clothes. Of course, this was Ali's normal dress, except ordinarily he would wear a red tarbush. Today, nonetheless, he looked most handsome in white robes and turban, except currently, he was the dustiest of us all.

"It will soon be maghrib effendi, the quarter to six prayers. I must perform wudu."

"What's that?" Mervyn asked irreverently.

"I must be clean Mr Mervyn."

"Then go and take a bath," I said. "Mervyn and I'll have one later. Also, pass out your robe and I'll see if I can get it washed and ironed."

"Don't you think that's going a bit far?" whispered Mervyn as Ali closed the bathroom door. "You'll be scrubbing his back next."

"Shut up!" I said, going to the desk and picking up the telephone. "You heard him. He has to pray. If he doesn't, it's a terrible sin, and he can't pray unless he's performed his ablutions. Unlike you, I think of others before myself. I look after people I like. I'm surprised you don't know that by now."

"That is, when you get something back in return. All you want to see is a bit more of him than you did in the hammam. When I play with you, like you like me to do before we get up in the morning, or go to bed at night, I bet you're thinking of him these days and not me. I've noticed you keep your eyes shut, when you used to look at it all the time. You always say the sight of it makes you happy every time."

"That's ridiculous Mervyn. You know how I feel about you. You're the apple of my eye. Nothing or no one will ever change that."

"But knowing you the way I do, and your love of all things big, we know these Egyptians have nothing to be ashamed of, that's why you're dying to get a look at it."

"Of course I'm not. You know that won't happen. Ali told us himself. It's forbidden to be seen naked in front of another man."

"But if I was out of the room you'd be spying through the keyhole."

Ignoring Mervyn's comment, I telephoned the desk and arranged for a waiter to pick up Ali's clothes and have them washed, dried, and ironed. As I put down the receiver, Ali appeared at the bathroom door, a towel wrapped around his middle.

"You are so thoughtful effendi," he said, handing me his robe and turban. "It was indeed a lucky day when I met you and Mr Mervyn."

"And we reciprocate in kind Ali. Café Riche will be crowded this evening, so I'll order something for us to eat in the room. Anything you'd particularly like?"

"I'll have whatever you decide," Ali replied. "Except pork of course."

Not wishing to offend, I refrained from explaining to Ali my real motive for us dining in private. Instead, I urged him to return to the bathroom and resume his ablutions.

"If there's anything you require Ali," I said, as he closed the door. "Don't hesitate to ask."

Mervyn shook his head and flopped down in an easy chair beside the balcony door.

"I'm exhausted," he gasped, taking out a packet of Woodbines. "It's been a really exciting day. Thanks for getting Harry out, and arranging the surprise. I'm sure he'll never forget it. I certainly won't."

"You've changed your tune from a moment ago."

Lighting his cigarette, and then my pipe, I relaxed in the chair opposite his.

"Thanks Ron. Hey! Isn't that the call to prayer? Didn't Ali say it was a quarter to six? By my watch, it's only ten past five."

"No," I said. "It's Ali. He's singing."

"Okay. Then, it's not just us Brits that sing in the bath. It sounds like a song we heard coming from the radios in the bazaar."

"I bet it's one of Umm's."

"If it is, I hope it's not going to last two hours."

"Do you think we'll survive?" I sighed. "It's rather different from the kind of thing we're used to."

"Umm's no Gracie Fields, that's for sure."

"By what Ali says she's revered throughout the Middle East. I'll feel embarrassed if at some point we get up and leave. I'm sure Ali would be upset."

"We mustn't offend the dragoman," mocked Mervyn. "We'll stay to the bitter end. We've no choice."

Presently, the singing from the bathroom altered, as the hypnotic words of prayer began to issue through the door.

"Allahu Akbar. Allahu Akbar. Allahu Akbar. Bismillahi r-rahmani r-rahim Al hamdu lillahi Rabbi l-alamin."

With the spellbinding chant beginning to numb my senses, I gazed through the open balcony doors towards the rooftops, minarets, and domes of the city, every building glowing pink in the setting sun. Mervyn, languidly blowing smoke rings, was also listening.

Hearing our friend reciting the age-old words of the Qur'an made me realise the stupidity of the exchange that had just occurred between Mervyn and I. Ali was a man, and not an object to leer at or yearn for. This response is typical of men of Mervyn and my persuasion, who see nothing in a person except the apprehension of what might lie between his legs. How shallow and immature. There must be more to a friendship than simply sex. After all, an intellectual companionship is a great deal more lasting than an orgasm.

***

Every day at Shepheard's, the Nubian who makes our beds and changes the towels, kindly leaves a menu for the day on the writing desk. Subsequently, after some consultation, I ordered two Lange de Boef al'Italienne for Ali and I, and Canard Sausages for Mervyn, the dishes duly arriving with great ceremony, along with Ali's sparkling clean robe and turban.

Although it was almost eight o'clock when Ali, Mervyn, and I arrived at Café Riche, we discovered it virtually full and were lucky to find a table, helped by a little baksheesh on my part to the Maître D. Mervyn and I ordered scotch and sodas, Ali preferring Turkish coffee. Then we settled back to enjoy the atmosphere, since we were clearly in the presence of many of Cairo's cultural and privileged elite by the number of dinner jackets, diamond necklaces, sequinned gowns, and pearl earrings. Were they here to see and hear Umm, or merely here to be seen?

A platform had been placed in one of the vestibules off the main eating area, transforming it into a stage, where already several musicians were tuning up. Ali pointed out the oud, a mandolin type instrument, which he described a few days earlier. We also noticed something Mervyn and I could only compare to a zither, which Ali explained, was a qanun, saying it was very prominent in Arabian music. Several violinists appeared, taking up positions in the middle seats. One of whom Ali recognised, since he suddenly stood up and waved, and the man waved back.

"He was my father's best friend," Ali said. "They played together in Umm's orchestra from the very beginning. Almost fifteen years."

"If you don't mind me asking Ali, did your father pass away recently?"

"Yes effendi. Very suddenly. He'd always had bad veins and ulcers in his legs. Every day my mother would bandage them. One morning, around Ramadan last year, he woke, coughing so badly mother wanted to take him to the hospital. But father was due to play at an Umm concert at the Opera House that night and refused to go. Later that afternoon he died."

"Dear me! What happened?"

"It seemed a blood clot in father's leg moved through his heart and lodged in his lung. Don't be sad effendi. My father was a good man. He prayed every day. Never missed. He will see Allah in paradise."

After another hour, and several more scotch and sodas, I was beginning to wish I had chosen Ali's beverage, as the noise of the crowd, in addition to the pall of cigarette smoke, was beginning to take effect. Similarly, I could see Mervyn becoming rather the worse for wear.

At one point, I asked a waiter to pull back the curtain behind us and open the window, thus revealing a mass of people standing on the pavement. Obviously, not a single person was going to miss the opportunity to see Umm in the flesh.

With the orchestra filling every seat on the stage, I realised the instruments were chiefly of the string variety. Along with the oud, qanun and violins, there were double basses, cellos, and guitars, the other instruments being two accordions and a thin reed flute. With the absence of horns and percussion, this was the reason for the unique sound of Arab music

A chair remained vacant in the centre of the stage. And, as the hour hand of the clock on the wall hit ten, the lights in Café Riche turned to full, and a wave of rapturous applause accompanied Umm as she walked towards it and sat down, a sparkling vision in shimmering white satin.

"She's so glamorous," I shouted over the cheering crowd.

To be honest, I imagined we were about to see a kind of singing belly dancer, except how wrong could I have been. Although, still in her thirties, Umm was tall and stately, a little dowager like in stature, with smooth, shining black hair, parted keenly down the centre. Possessing a rather plump, oval face, her beautiful eyes made even more striking by an application of black eye shadow and mascara. I saw at once, why the bewitching mystery of Umm Kulthum had captivated an entire nation.

As the orchestra began to play a haunting rhythmic discordant melody, the audience cheered, plainly the tune a familiar favourite. Umm however remained seated, her head slightly bowed, hands in her lap, the left holding a white chiffon scarf. Was the orchestra playing an introduction, or a piece of its own? Mervyn and I glanced at each other in apprehension, except at that moment, to the cheers from the patrons of Café Riche as well as the people on the pavement outside, Umm stood up and walked to the front of the stage.

Umm began to sing, and from that instant I was transported, and although I had no idea what she was singing about, the series of vocal ornaments, scales and trills both enchanted and elated me. This then was Umm's magic and the reason for her complete adulation. With a voice as smooth as honey, she could heal the soul. The music seemed almost religious, and unlike a similar concert in England, the atmosphere was quite informal. People continued to smoke and drink, swaying in their seats, clapping and laughing. Umm's vocal acrobatics, which she repeated a second or third time, each with a slight variation, had the audience increasingly ecstatic at her vocal dexterity.

"What's she singing about? I asked Ali at one point.

"Love effendi. Love unrequited. Love exultant. Love eternal. Riad Al Sunbat composed this song for Umm, from a poem written by one of our most famous poets, Ahmad Rami. It's entitled after the first line, 'I Fra ya Qalbi'."

"How does that translate?"

"Effendi, it is difficult to put into words. The closest I can get is

'A Branch of my Heart'. Soon this song will finish and there'll be a short break. Then Umm will sing a second song, which is also composed by Riad Al Sunbat, from another poem by Rami. The title is 'I like the Nile' or, 'Song of the University'. It's an Anthem, and regarded as a song of revolution that encompasses the spirit of Cairo and all of Egypt."

As Umm came to the end of her song, surreptitiously, I glanced at my watch.

"My word Ali. It's nearly midnight. I can't believe it."

"That's what happens when you listen to Tarab. You lose all sense of time and place."

In fact, I had been so mesmerised, I had entirely forgotten that Mervyn was sitting beside me, and turning, saw his head resting on my shoulder, and that he was fast asleep. I nudged him, but he refused to wake.

"I'm sorry Ali," I said. "It seems Umm has had an intoxicating effect on Mervyn."

"That's fine. It happens sometimes. After all, Mr Mervyn can be forgiven. He's had a most exciting day."

Umm returned to the stage, to rapturous applause, this time wearing a black satin gown, which glittered with jet, her diamond necklace, and earrings, sparkling in the light.

Once again, the format remained the same. At the start, the orchestra struck up the tune, this time strident and rhythmic, something akin to a call to arms. Then, after a quarter of an hour, Umm stood and sang the first phrase of the University Song to joyous cheers.

My explanation of this song, which Ali describes, as an anthem to revolution, can hardly be sufficient to give you an idea of the expansive power of Umm's rendition. All I can say is, should you ever come across a gramophone record of Umm singing her Tarab songs, my only hope 'Nachid El Gamia' is included in the repertoire. If so, then you will hear what I heard that night and be able to appreciate the magic of that moment.

The night concluded at two in the morning, and although the audience stamped the floor and hit the tables, Umm left the stage, smiling radiantly, without returning to sing an encore.

The culminating noise finally roused Mervyn, and with an arm through each of ours, Ali and I ushered him into the street, where we hailed a caleche.

Chapter Twenty Three
Planting a seed and watching it grow - The Pyramids, at last

The dawn call to prayer woke me, and quietly so as not to disturb Mervyn. Not that anything would, considering how drunk he was when I finally put him to bed. Going to the telephone, I rang down for a pot of coffee, and then walked onto the balcony to watch the sunrise.

Most days in Cairo begin the same, with the sky turning golden behind the rooftops, blending upwards into orange, then blood red, and finally indigo. In due course, as the call to prayer issues from countless mosques, the gold conquers the red and blue, as the sun suddenly flashes above the buildings, striking like a blazing sword into the heart of the city. Despite having seen the spectacle a hundred times, it continues to inspire me.

With everything almost settled in Harry's case, it was time to fulfil my promise to Mervyn, that we visit the Pyramids. Therefore, on my way to breakfast, which predictably I took on my own due to Mervyn nursing an enormous hangover, I asked the desk clerk to phone the Mena House Hotel to reserve us a room.

The previous evening, after leaving Café Riche, since Mervyn was completely unfit to remember any of Ali and my conversation during the caleche ride to Ali's houseboat at Imbaba, I was able to tell Ali my plans.

"You don't mind us going without you?" I asked.

"Of course not effendi."

"We'll be back in a couple of days. Let's meet next Monday morning. We can visit the hammam again."

I was now able to arrange a visit to the Sphinx and the Great Pyramids, although there remained one person yet to see.

Nowadays, what I did after breakfast, I believe is called, arriving unannounced.

Captain Haig welcomed me rather guiltily, which was hardly surprising considering his laxity in attending to Harry's plight, except he seemed pleased the trooper's dilemma was partially resolved. When I insisted on speaking to his superior he realised I was in earnest and snapped to attention.

"I'll tell him you're here Captain."

Lieutenant Colonel Nigel Weatherall was not as I expected. He turned out to be a rather jolly chap, and a little younger than myself. A rugged, sporty type, possessing a handsome tanned face that one would expect of an officer serving in Egypt.

His office, once the sitting room of the Royal Suite of the Semiramis Hotel, was full of morning sunlight. Except, with the windows shut tight it was extremely stuffy. To such a degree, as I sat down in a chair opposite his desk, I was forced to loosen my tie, surreptitiously unbuttoning the top button of my shirt.

"You're lucky to catch me Captain," Weatherall said. "At any minute a car's due to take me to Ismalia. Care for a cigarette?"

He shook two out of a packet of woodbines on the desk beside the telephone, offering me one. Then, after a pause while he lit them, he smiled and leaned back in his chair.

"What can I do for you?"

"Firstly," I began, "may I thank you for seeing me at such short notice. I hope my business will not detain you. It concerns a trooper in your regiment. I strongly believe his attributes would greatly benefit the new recruits back home. Lately, there've been speeches in the House of Commons, along with reports in The Times expressing concern regarding the fitness of new recruits."

"Indeed Captain. I've seen the reports. The army is aware of the situation and endeavouring to increase the number of instructors at

The School of Physical Training at Aldershot, which, you may be aware, is the home of the 7th Queen's Own Hussars."

"And this Colonel is the very reason I'm here today. The man of whom I speak has recently spent time in the hospital at Abbassia. To aid him to full recovery, he spent considerable time in the hospital gymnasium, reaching a degree of fitness to be envied. The man is a keen athlete, competing in a variety of regimental team events. I believe he would be invaluable to the army in the cause of fitness, and therefore wasted here in Egypt."

"I admire your frankness Captain, and by what you're saying I understand you to mean that I should transfer the man to the Physical Training School."

"Exactly Colonel Weatherall."

"A very interesting concept Captain Fry, although I'm intrigued to know how you're aware of him. It's most unusual for a civilian to take such an interest."

"I've become acquainted with the trooper by way of a friend. The friend is the man's brother. We're here in Cairo for a winter holiday and my friend was particularly keen to meet with him."

"Thank you Captain," Weatherall said. "This has me thinking. I'm always keen to promote my regiment. I was a second lieutenant before I was twenty. The Hussars are my life. We've been through a rough patch lately. I know they call it modernisation, but getting rid of the horse has knocked the men's self-esteem for six. If I'm seen to be taking a personal interest in the lives of my men, then this can only be good for morale."

By the manner in which he stubbed out his cigarette and began lighting another, I could see Weatherall begin to warm to my idea.

"Shortly after we arrived in 35," he continued, "the men got wind of a printing press going begging, and ever since have produced a monthly newspaper they call, 'The Charger'. Some of the wags amongst them submit funny stories, cartoons, along with bits of poetry. Through this they keep abreast of the news, entertainments, and facilities at the various clubs and military venues around Cairo."

As the Colonel continued to describe the content and concept of his regimental newspaper, I began to see the direction his thoughts were taking.

"Should an article appear in the next edition concerning your friend's brother, reporting how I've given him an opportunity to use his new skills to benefit the boys back home, I feel it would make highly interesting and useful reading."

"I see your point exactly Colonel," I said.

"Then leave it with me Captain Fry. And let me be the one to thank you. You may have saved the Saucy Seventh from sinking into the doldrums, which is the last thing we need when we're about to move to the Canal Zone."

Weatherall and I shook hands, and after giving him Harry's rank and serial number, I walked out of the hotel into the sunshine feeling extremely satisfied. However, this time it had not been necessary to use money as an incentive. All that was needed was to plant the seed and watch it grow.

***

Later that morning it was easy to spot Mervyn beside the swimming pool at the Gezira Sporting Club, since he was whiter, or should I say pinker and greasier than any other sun worshipper lying beside the swimming pool.

"I take it you've applied the sunburn lotion," I said, pulling up a lounger beside him. "You know what they say about mad dogs and Englishmen. Have you been here long?"

"A couple of hours," Mervyn murmured into his towel.

"Did you have trouble getting in?"

"It was a cinch. They gave me a temporary membership. Now I can call the club my own for the rest of the time we're here. Do you know Ron! I'm falling in love with Cairo. It'll be hard to leave."

"I wondered how long it would take. It's very agreeable, don't you think. Civilised, yet mysterious and evocative. They don't call it the Mother of the World for nothing. But hold your horses. I've a surprise for you. We're leaving for Giza as soon as we get back to the hotel."

Mervyn sat up and opened his eyes, their colour astounding me for a moment, his rosy face highlighting their blueness.

"At last we're to see the Pyramids!" he exclaimed. "That means you've finished your secret business. Come on Ron! Tell me what you've done."

"I've managed to persuade Harry's C O to send him home."

"You mean he's out of the army?"

"Not quite. But he'll be doing something he does best. He's joining the Physical Training Corp. The school's based at Aldershot."

"You're a marvel! When will this happen?"

"I'm not sure. Colonel Weatherall was impressed with my suggestion, so I've left him to make the final arrangements. It appears Harry's going to be the subject of a newspaper article.

"I can't get over how clever you are. You've managed to achieve everything we hoped for."

"Alright," I said laughing. "Enough of the flattery. Go and have a swim, you're getting redder by the minute."

The midday sun was scorching, so while Mervyn wallowed in the bright blue swimming pool and frolicked under the fountain, I found a another lounger, this one shaded by an umbrella, and flopped onto it, feeling rather ridiculous in a waistcoat, trousers, and shoes. Nevertheless, this hardly prevented me from dozing off, as my early appointment with the sunrise had caused me to feel quite drowsy.

***

"Aren't we going then?" Mervyn said, waking me with a start. "I'm just about fried. Wait while I change."

There is always a constant stream of taxis coming and going from the forecourt of the Gezira Club, so we managed to catch one with little difficulty.

"Did you look around the aquarium?" I asked, as we crossed the Kasre el Nil Bridge.

"Yes. Although it was a bit disappointing. I hoped I'd see a bit more action. There were a couple of huge sluggish Nile perch, a grizzly catfish, and a rather ferocious tiger fish."

"A Nile crocodile was there when I was last here. He must have been twelve feet long and lay in a pond of stagnant water with just his eyes poking through the surface."

"I didn't see him. Perhaps he died."

My plan was for us both to stay at the Mena House Hotel for five nights, returning to Cairo on Sunday morning, so we packed a minimal amount of shirts, underwear, and Textor socks. Naturally, our dinner suits went along, also, two pairs of slacks and a couple of lightweight jackets. Stout walking shoes and Panama hats were definitely part of our baggage, not forgetting our guidebooks and cameras.

I wished that Mervyn's first glimpse of the Pyramids at Giza to be at sundown. So, as the sun sets at around a quarter to six in February, the half hour car ride would just about get us there in time.

Chapter Twenty Four
The Road to Giza - The Great Pyramid of Khufu

The road to the pyramids took Mervyn and I on a southwest route out of the city, crossing the Kasre El Nil, where we admired once more the magnificent stone lions guarding the entrances at either end. Once on the island of El Gezira the taxi sped us across Midan El Gezira, past the gates of the National Sporting Club and onto Shari el Kubriel Ama.

Mervyn had never seen this part of the island, so I pointed out the Exhibition Grounds and the Royal Agricultural Society stables, in addition, the El Kubri Garden.

Before long, we reached the southernmost bridge linking the island with the Nile's west bank called oddly The English Bridge. The centre of the short iron structure is designed to open, allowing watercraft to navigate up and down stream. Therefore, when we arrived at the eastern approach, it pleased me to see it closed, thus enabling us to cross it unhindered.

This was hardly the case when we reached the railway level crossing on Shari El Giza, since the queue of waiting vehicles, horses, donkeys, camels and carts, stretched for almost two hundred yards.

"Where does the rail go?" Mervyn asked, as we sat sweltering in the back of the taxi.

"Luxor and Aswan," I answered. "It's the main line south."

"Then that's the direction we'll take."

"Yes. I remember you said you wished to make the journey by train. But how about we come back by steamer?"

"You bet," said Mervyn. "The ones I've seen look very smart. Not at all like I expected."

"You thought they'd be like steamers at home. Not at all. These days, Nile steamers are luxurious."

"Look!" exclaimed Mervyn, pointing over the taxi driver's shoulder. "There's the train!"

As he spoke, an immense, shining black steam locomotive, belching smoke and steam, raced across the level crossing, followed by a procession of pristine white carriages, the train travelling so fast it was impossible to count their number.

"I'd say that was the Sunshine Express," I said. "Three of them run between Cairo and Luxor each day."

"When will it arrive?"

"The journey takes twelve hours. So about five tomorrow morning.

"How romantic Ron! I've never slept on a train. Not in a bed that is."

"I once travelled on the 'Queen of Scots' Pullman to Edinburgh. I think that's the only time for me. I remember I found it very difficult to sleep."

With the train a distant memory, the gate wallah opened the gates allowing the horde of vehicles and animals through to the road on the far side of the track. Our taxi man wove his way between them, joining other vehicles heading in the same direction.

This part of Giza is comparatively modern, with apartment buildings just recently built, some reflecting the new Art Deco style for which Egypt is now famous.

Very soon, we left the pink limestone of the suburbs, as our road entered the lush green countryside, the awesome spectacle of the pyramids growing more immense with every furlong we travelled. Had the road not been rutted and bumpy, I would have taken photographs, seeing the sun was dipping rapidly towards the monuments, causing them to appear in stark silhouette, a picture seen in guidebooks a million times.

I even remember seeing a watercolour painted by the artist David Roberts depicting the same scene. Or was it by moonlight? Anyway. One or the other.

Mervyn was reading the SS. Orontes handbook.

"It says the Great Pyramid of Cheops was built nearly four thousand five hundred years ago. By the way that's his Greek name you know. His Egyptian name is Khufu. For three thousand eight hundred years, it was the tallest man-made structure in the world. But in thirteen hundred the spire of Lincoln Cathedral was completed, which is just a bit taller."

Even though in the twenties I immersed myself in ancient history at Trinity College, I still find the statistics quite overwhelming. Something so remote in time is difficult to conceive.

"The Pyramid itself covers an area of thirteen acres," Mervyn continued, "and took a hundred thousand men twenty years to build, containing two million three hundred thousand blocks of stone."

"Thousands of slaves," I said, "whipped into submission, dragging the stones into place."

"Not according to this. It seems the workers built it willingly because Khufu treated them kindly. They lived in a village close by and he supplied them with food, water, and clothing. In eight hundred and twenty an Egyptian Caliph burrowed inside to look for the mummy and buried treasure. But all he found were tunnels leading into empty chambers, plus a large vacant granite sarcophagus without a lid."

"Was it robbed before the Caliph entered?" I asked.

"This says no. At present, there's no evidence to suggest that any other persons have ever been inside."

"So what became of the mummy and all its treasure?"

Suddenly it dawned on me, and I made my thoughts known to Mervyn.

"Maybe Khufu was never buried in the Pyramid. Perhaps he decided to build another tomb?"

"All that work for nothing!" exclaimed Mervyn. "Say the burial chamber and tunnels are a trick and Khufu's buried inside, but in a different place altogether. How long after Tutankhamen did Khufu live?"

"Khufu was long before Tutankhamen. If I remember my studies correctly, Khufu was the second ruler of the fourth dynasty of the Old Kingdom, or The Age of Pyramids. Whereas, Tutankhamen was the New Kingdom, coming from the eighteenth dynasty, one thousand three hundred years later.

By Mervyn's expression, I could see he was completely incapable of understanding the enormity of the time that the Pharaohs ruled Egypt.

Our way began to elevate onto a causeway, since the fields of crops and market gardens flanking the road indicated the land was subject to the Nile's annual flood. Also, to our left, the road was now accompanied by a tram line and had become completely straight, shooting like an arrow northwest, bringing us closer by the second to the last surviving wonder of the ancient world.

"Wow!" Mervyn gasped as the enormity of the edifice became clear. "I can't believe how massive it is. How high is it again?"

"You've just said it was once the tallest man-made structure in the world. Here! Pass me the book."

Even as a child, I was never keen to read while travelling in a motor vehicle. Even following a route on a Bartholomew's Ordnance Survey Map causes me to feel queasy. As a result, I flicked through the pages until I found the statistics, occasionally keeping my eyes on the road ahead.

"Four hundred and fifty five feet high," I read aloud. "But it's lost twenty five feet over the centuries, because the smooth white limestone that originally covered the top was removed during the construction of Cairo, as a great deal can be found in the walls of the Citadel."

Eventually, we exchanged the green fields for the sands of the desert, although an avenue of date palms fringed our way, their shadows growing longer as evening rapidly approached. Then I saw the hotel, nestled in the shade of the Pyramids, occupying a luxuriant oasis of acacia trees, gracious lawns, and tall palms. A complex of buildings, ranging up a gentle westward slope, appeared in arbitrary sections, just as if they were added over the years, rather than conceived as a complete design.

For me the hotel needed no introduction. However, Mervyn was seeing it for the first time.

"That's where we're staying," I said. "At the Mena House Hotel, one of the most famous hotels in the world."

At the top of the drive, the taxi stopped beside the front steps, where a concierge waited to open the door.

"Welcome to the Mena House Hotel gentlemen," he said, as we clambered out.

"Can you look after our luggage," I asked. "We're booked in the name of Fry. I'm rather keen to get to the Pyramids before sun set."

"Of course sir. Shall I ask them to bring you horses?"

"I thought we'd carry on by car, but a horse would be more fitting, don't you agree Mervyn."

He nodded, although rather apprehensively, clearly as inexperienced a horseman as I. The doorman produced a small tin whistle and blew several short blasts, undoubtedly alerting a man in some distant stable yard. Then, as if by magic, two horses appeared, led by a couple of turbaned Arabs wearing black robes.

"Ahmad and Sairi will accompany you gentlemen," said the doorman. "They'll see you're not endangered."

Endangered! Whatever did he mean? Obviously, things had changed since I was last here. At the beginning of the war, Mena House Hotel was requisitioned by the Australians and converted into a hospital. Soldiers from down under swarmed over the Pyramids like lemmings, keeping order amongst the hordes of beggars, donkey boys, and souvenir sellers, with a strategic clip around the ear, or a blasphemous curse. With their influence now gone, it seemed this horde of degenerates had become a major threat to the security of foreigners.

More of a pony than a horse, my animal was rather small. Whereas, Mervyn remarked that his was too large. Perhaps we should have swapped, but communication between our Arab guides and us was almost nil, so we remained with what we were given.

A high white wall flanks the way from the hotel to the Pyramids. Why this should be, I cannot think, since it results in obscuring the very landmark we had come all the way to see. With the sun quickly setting, I was anxious we move faster, but the men leading our horses seemed to have other ideas and shambled laboriously up the slope. At long last, and to my relief, we broke free of the barricade and finally faced the object of our desire.

"It's amazing seeing it so close," yelled Mervyn from up ahead. "It's more massive than anything I've ever seen. I've got to take a photograph."

"Me too!" I shouted back. "Eric and Amy must see this."

Even though it was almost six o'clock, Giza Plateau thronged with people, some walking, others riding camels, donkeys, or horses. I even saw a couple of chaps pedalling bicycles. Darting about amongst the crowd were Arab males of every age, their robes billowing in the evening breeze, white turbans flashing in the sun. The entire scene was infused with chatter as they cajoled, pleaded and boasted, with every type of request one might imagine, thus spoiling my romantic notion of how Mervyn would initially see the Pyramids. He seemed unperturbed however, entering into the spirit of the occasion.

"Bugger off!" he shouted to a donkey boy attempting to sell him a postcard. "I don't want to see the lady bits. Clear off!"

Also, I was being hassled to buy scarabs from some dusky youth who refused to understand the word no.

"Hey!" I yelled to my guide. "Aren't you supposed to deal with this?"

The man turned and smiled.

"Effendi pleased to buy nice scarab for wife."

"No wife!" I said. "Keep them away."

He said a few words to the boys, and luckily, they melted into the crowd.

"This thing's pretty docile," Mervyn shouted to his man. "Give me the reins. I feel stupid you leading me about. It's like I was on a donkey at Weston Super Mare."

The Arab did as he was told, and Mervyn skilfully turned the horse and trotted back to me.

"Hey Ron! Don't you feel ridiculous?"

"I must admit I do rather. There are other tourists riding on their own, some even on camels."

"Then do the same."

Once holding the reins and feeling the horse's head between my hands, I realised I could manoeuvre the animal left and right, pull him up, or urge him on.

"Come on Ron. I'll race you."

Mervyn dug his heels into the horse's flanks and trotted away merrily. But my horse and his appeared to be stable companions, because the control I experienced only a moment earlier vanished, as he rapidly made a beeline towards his friend with me clinging helplessly to his back. All I could do was keep my feet firmly in the stirrups, my knees clenched about the animal's sides, and my hands tight on the reins.

It must have made a comical picture, all six foot of me astride a five-foot horse hurtling, pell-mell, across the sand. Mervyn won the race of course, although I did make a close second, not on my own behalf I might add.

"Where did your man go?" I asked, as we trotted towards the layer of massive stones comprising the base of the Great Pyramid.

"Same place as yours I suppose," answered Mervyn.

In fact, the two stable wallahs had entirely disappeared.

"Oh well! We can do as we please. I didn't trust mine to say the least."

Peering up at the sheer face of the Great Pyramid, suddenly the immense size of the blocks caused me to feel small, as an ant might feel staring at a sugar lump. How did human beings construct this giant edifice? Where would they start? What enormous plan did they use to conceive it? Questions that would be left unanswered until I had time to read more about its history.

"The guidebook says there're two entrances," Mervyn said, standing in his stirrups. "The original, and the one made by a Caliph hundreds of years ago. Do you want to see inside?"

Some intrepid mountaineers were scaling the blocks, which filled me with dread.

"I'd rather do that than climb it," I said. "But don't you want to see the sunset?"

"When we come out. Let's find the entrance."

People were gathered at the foot of a set of steps cut into the stone, some already ascending.

"We'd better hurry," I said. "It'll be dark soon, and don't forget to show the guide your pass. We won't get in otherwise."

In truth, the sun was turning blood red, transforming the limestone to a gorgeous pink.

Spurring on the horses, we soon arrived at the queue. Not surprisingly, in Egypt, where there are tourists, inevitably rogues and loiterers appear, begging for money or pushing cheap souvenirs.

Searching the jostling crowd, I failed to see our stable wallahs, since, if Mervyn and I were to go inside the pyramid, we could hardly leave the horses unattended. In any case, they were the property of the hotel and should they go astray, they would certainly go on the bill.

"Hey you!" I shouted, seeing a likely looking fellow amongst the crowd. "I'll give you four piastres if you hold the horses."

With one hand lifting the hem of his gallibaya and the other holding his turban, the man scuttled across the sand towards us.

"Yes indeed effendi," he panted. "Anything for you effendi."

"Are you sure Ron?" Mervyn muttered. "He looks a bit dodgy to me."

"I'm not going to give him baksheesh until we return. That way we'll be sure he won't run off with them."

"But if he sells them, he'll get a lot more than four piastres."

"We'll just have to trust him. What else can we do? They can't all be villains."

All of a sudden, I felt quite vulnerable. I wished I had asked Ali to join us. He would have complete control of the situation. But with Ali along it would have been awkward. I could hardly have booked him a room at the hotel. It would have been necessary to accommodate him elsewhere, perhaps in the servant's quarters. How unsuitable for Ali, an educated man and proud. Weighing things up I became convinced I did the right thing leaving him behind.

The steps cut into the limestone were well worn and almost as precarious as the blocks themselves. How people can climb virtually five hundred feet to the pinnacle is beyond me? Except climb it they did, and looking up at them from the base caused me to feel quite giddy, the steepness of the sloping sides seeming practically vertical.

When Mervyn and I reached the entrance, an Arab guide informed us that we must wait until the party before us had finished their tour. So we took the time to admire the view. Although, we were standing on only the eighth level, the vista was stunning, giving us some indication as to how it would appear from the summit. With the entrance on the north face, we had a marvellous view west, together with the desert disappearing into the distance. Also east, towards the green swathe of agricultural land through which we had driven. Then there was Cairo, a pink smudge on the horizon, even its thousand minarets and domes clearly visible to the naked eye.

Before long it was our turn to join the next party, and stepping through the entrance, we were immediately struck by the coolness of the interior, along with the narrowness of the passage, since it was hardly wider than a man.

"We are standing in the tunnel cut by the servants of Caliph Al Mamouh," said the guide. "When the Caliph arrived in Egypt, he was intrigued by rumours of great treasure to be found in the tombs of the Pharaohs, so ordered his men to force an entry into Khufu's Pyramid, hoping he'd find gold and precious jewels."

By the tone of his voice and his vacant expression, our guide must have said these words a million times, although I could easily imagine the men struggling to clear a way through the massive blocks of stone.

"As you can see by the irregularity of the walls," the guide continued, "the men found it difficult tunnelling though the limestone. They were just about to give up when from somewhere close by they heard a sound like a falling block. This spurred them on, and blasting their way forward, they burst into the entrance passage built by Khufu nearly four thousand years before."

The guide urged us to follow him further into the tunnel, until we reached the foot of a passage where the walls were as smooth as glass.

"This passage, ladies and gentlemen," he went on, "is at the end of the original descending entrance tunnel you see behind you. It continues down to a lower room called the Queen's Chamber, while another descends to a chamber deep inside the Pyramid's base. The ascending passage ahead is only four feet high and three and a half feet wide, rising at an angle of thirty degrees. This means I'm afraid, that the only way to get through into the Grand Gallery and the Kings Chamber is to crawl on your knees."

Since Mervyn was standing beside him, the guide indicated that he should be the first to follow him into the tunnel. Therefore, in a few seconds, all I saw of Mervyn was his rump disappearing into the hole, followed closely by a young American woman, judging by her rasping accent as she encouraged her friend.

When my turn came, I realised I would be nose to tail with a fat old German chap, so I purposely delayed going forward to give him a head start.

With the smoothness of the stone, and the steep angle of the narrow passage, had it not been for the wooden rungs embedded in the floor, and oil lamps placed at strategic points along the wall, the passage would have been almost impossible to navigate.

As I scrambled up the ramp way, I felt a draft of air, which mercifully did not originate from the man in front, but from some other mysterious source I was yet to discover.

Then it happened. From out of nowhere, a bizarre fear suddenly overwhelmed me, and although the fresh breeze wafted in my face, I began to sweat profusely as I became gripped by a sense of panic. For some silly reason I began to imagine the tons of rock above me, feel the confinement of the space, see the buttocks of the German ahead and hear the sound of heavy breathing coming up behind. I had a strong urge to stop, turn around, and go back. But how could I? It would mean squeezing past the people behind me in order they allow me out of the shaft. Thus, for the sake of others, I knew I must banish my claustrophobia. So shutting my eyes, I struggled on. Until after what seemed an eternity, from up ahead, I heard the echoing voice of our guide.

"The Grand Gallery is one hundred and fifty seven feet long, twenty eight feet high and six feet wide, tapering inwards towards the ceiling over seven courses. The hole you see to your right is a well that opens into the descending passage deep below the Great Pyramid. The shaft you see in front of you leads to the Queens Chamber, which is directly below the Gallery and in line with the centre of the pyramid."

Relieved to be out of the passageway, I saw Mervyn, the American women and the fat German, gathered around the guide.

"If you follow me, ladies and gentlemen, you will soon see the Chamber of the King."

"Is the King in his coffin, like King Tut in the museum?" asked an American woman. "Do we get to see the mummy?"

Americans abroad have an aggravating way of asking the silliest questions. If they care to read the guidebooks, which they never do, they would discover the sarcophagus they were about to see was empty, and never contained the body of King Khufu.

Walking on a planking ramp, we followed the guide through the Grand Gallery, over a three-foot step and into a low narrow passage, which eventually opened into an equally confined room, which our guide said, was the antechamber. A further passage opened from this, through which we funnelled, only to emerge inside a large impressive chamber, as the guide continued his talk.

"We're now standing in the King's Chamber, at level fifty of the Great Pyramid. The chamber is constructed of polished red granite brought by boat from quarries further up the Nile. The room is thirty-four feet long, eighteen feet high and almost twenty feet wide. There are two ventilating shafts, which connect to openings on the outside. Recently, an air pump has been installed inside one shaft to help maintain the flow of air, making it more comfortable for the visitor, with the temperature remaining at a constant sixty eight degrees."

"Where are the hieroglyphics?" asked Mervyn. "I thought all Egyptian tombs had hieroglyphics."

"Most do," answered the guide. "The other three pyramids on the plateau contain hieroglyphics. But the reason there are none here remains a mystery. Another mystery ladies and gentlemen, is contained in the great coffer you see towards the back of the chamber. It is cut and chiselled out of a single block of red granite and, as there is no tunnel large enough to allow it inside the Pyramid, it is presumed to have been placed in position during the construction."

"Then the Pyramid was built around the coffer," said the fat German.

"You're correct sir."

"When the Caliph's men found the room," I said. "Did they find Khufu in the coffer?"

"No sir. There was nothing in the coffer, or in any other chamber."

"It was the first time anyone had broken into the Pyramid," I continued. "So Khufu was never buried here."

"That is the belief of some sir. Had he been, then it is presumed there would be a granite lid, but none has ever been found."

"Perhaps the Caliphs men removed it," interrupted the German.

"Forgive me sir. The lid would have weighed over two tons, and there is no tunnel wide enough to have allowed it through."

There we have it. It seems this mystery will never be solved, unless future investigations reveal other, up until now, hidden passages and chambers, one of which contains Khufu and perhaps treasure beyond the dreams of Midas.

The conversation with the guide had so engrossed me that I failed to notice Mervyn was no longer standing beside me. However, all of a sudden, a voice coming from nowhere, echoed around the chamber.

"Ooh!" it called. "Ooh!"

One American girl screamed and clung to the other. The German laughed nervously, yet I knew exactly from where the sound was coming. Looking over the edge of the sarcophagus, I saw its owner, since Mervyn was lying inside, his arms across his chest. Eyes shut, and just about to make another eerie sound.

"Out you get!" I ordered. "Enough mucking around. You're frightening the Americans."

"I know," he laughed. "Worked a treat didn't it."

The guide nonetheless, was not amused.

"You bring great danger upon yourself young man," he said. "Very bad luck to mock the Gods of Egypt. People have mysterious accidents. Die suddenly and for no reason."

"Honestly!" scoffed Mervyn, "A lot of hocus-pocus. Come on Ron. I reckon that's all we're going to see. Let's get out of here."

Mervyn was right. The guide ushered everyone back the way we came. The narrow steep ascending passage was negotiated awkwardly, since it was required to crawl backwards, except I went after the German, meaning he had a view of my large posterior all the way to the bottom.

It was a tremendous relief to see the sky and stars above us as we emerged from the entrance, where a large crescent moon had risen in our absence.

Despite having missed the sunset, my watch told me it was close to cocktail hour. Also, we were reassured to find the man with our horses still waiting where we left him. After paying him his four piastres, we rode leisurely across the sand towards the distant lights of the Mena House Hotel.

***

"I'm going to climb it tomorrow," Mervyn, said, as we dined later in the magnificent dining room, complete with its unusual arches, quirky murals, and artificial greenery hanging in festoons from the ceiling.

"I don't think I'd make it," I said. "I'm far too heavy to be scrambling over stone blocks."

"Alright. But why not try the small pyramid? I've read Menkaure's is half the height."

"Even that would render me completely exhausted. They'd have to airlift me back to earth."

Mervyn's loud laugh caused several guests to look up from their dinner plates.

"We'll see the Sphinx tomorrow," he continued, ignoring my frown. "Why don't we hire camels? They're much more comfortable than horses. Mine's given me a sore behind."

Here, I had to agree, because as I lay in the bath an hour earlier, I noticed my legs were badly chafed, the reason I suppose experienced riders wear jodhpurs supplied with leather inserts.

Before retiring to bed, Mervyn and I opened our veranda door and walked out onto the balcony where the scent of jasmine was captivating. The moon we observed earlier as dusky red and kissing the eastern horizon, now shone silver, high in a sky as black as ebony. It joined countless shimmering stars, seeming to dance to the music emanating from the cabaret, where doubtless, a quivering belly dancer was entertaining the Europeans. Meanwhile, vast and inspiring, glimpsed above a fringe of silhouetted date palms, the Great Pyramid of Khufu, along with those of his son and grandson dominated the western sky.

"Ron," Mervyn whispered. "What could ever beat this? I've never seen anything as beautiful."

"Don't worry. There's plenty more before we go home."

Although I had to agree, nothing would surpass the magic of that night, and as I fell asleep, with my dear young friend beside me, I prayed nothing ever would.

Chapter Twenty Five
Climbing Menkaure's Pyramid - The riddle of the Great Sphinx

That night, having fallen asleep in a state of complete relaxation and bliss, I woke before dawn in a state of anxiety.

Prior to arriving, I purposely requested a view of the pyramids, meaning our room faced southwest. Therefore, it became dreadfully hot in the afternoon, despite the closed shutters on the windows and balcony doors. Despite the ceiling fan going nineteen to the dozen, the room remained stifling for the entire night. Before retiring, I threw the blanket and eiderdown off my bed, finishing with only a sheet between me and the outside world. I refuse to sleep in the nude, unlike Mervyn, who thinks pyjamas are an encumbrance.

On waking, I realised my own pyjamas were soaking wet with sweat. So much in fact, I quietly got out of bed, and taking a fresh pair from a cupboard drawer, went into the bathroom, towelled dry and put them on. Glancing in the bathroom mirror as I returned to the bedroom, I noticed I was deathly white, despite my brow having received a considerable amount of sun the previous day. The reason for my ghostly pallor was the awful nightmare that woke me.

I dreamt I was lying inside a coffin, the lid held tightly in place by six feet of earth. I was suffocating, and although in complete darkness, I could see into every corner, at the same time sensing the strong odour of damp soil. In desperation, I hammered on the lid, endeavouring to cry out, but the scream stuck in my throat. Then, all of a sudden, I was transported into the fresh air, my spirit hovering above an open grave, where people gathered around a minister, his black cassock, sadly opposing a host of gay floral tributes piled upon the mound of fresh earth beside the grave. Only then did I realise I recognised some of the people gathered there. Eric and Amy stood beside Gertrude, the widow of my friend Fritz Barnhoff. There was the lady who ran the Post Office at the end of the lane. Commander Buckmaster, my old commander, was amongst the gathering, head bowed, wearing the uniform of the 4th Somerset Light Infantry. I saw my scouts, some visibly moved, while others stood stoically to attention, fighting back the tears. Mervyn, Mickey and Teddy appeared smart in their black suits and ties, hair neatly Brylcreamed, shoes polished.

Then the vision vanished and I was alone and soaring above a church. Wildsbridge Church. I knew the tower instantly, because I recognised Fritz's monument and gravestone in the churchyard. The white stone statue of Christ, hands open wide, receiving the flowers I placed there every year on the anniversary of his death. But what was this? Another gravestone beside his. A grey slab surmounted by a tall basalt cross. My spirit plunged towards the epitaph; in fact, so close I could read the inscription. 'Here lies Ronald Willington Fry: May he rest in peace, a most kind, and generous man'. I strove to read the dates chiselled on the slab. But then I awoke; the vision still so vivid it was necessary to lie still for several minutes in order to banish it into fantasy.

Plainly, Mervyn's stunt, and the guide's ominous prediction, made such a deep impression on my mind that it created the macabre apparition. As a result, when I returned to bed, try as I may, I found it impossible to sleep. Instead, and to calm my racing brain, I planned the itinerary for the next few days.

After breakfast, it was Mervyn's wish to climb the Great Pyramid and that would certainly take all morning. On the other hand, although I had half promised to attempt the smallest of the three, I realised I was quite done with adventure for the time being. Therefore, I made the decision to spend a quiet morning relaxing beside the swimming pool. Then, after lunch, Mervyn and I would hire a couple of camels and visit the Sphinx.

Tomorrow, I thought we might take a taxi to Saqqara to see the Stepped Pyramid, then on to the ruins of Memphis, where Mervyn would see the colossal statue of Rameses the second. Thursday, we could take a trip into the Western Desert and visit some remote villages. Moreover, having never played golf, and since the Mena House boasted an extensive golf course and a resident instructor, on Friday I thought I might have a round or two. All good for the waistline at any rate.

A while later, the call to prayer from a distant mosque had its desired effect, and as I listened to the droning voice of the muezzin, I drifted into a dreamless sleep.

***

It is never advisable, or too wise to make plans independent of one's travelling companion, as I soon discovered when I mentioned them to Mervyn at the breakfast table.

"But you said you'd climb it."

"I know. But now I'm not feeling as intrepid. I had a bad dream and it's left me feeling spooky. I just don't want to put myself into a precarious predicament."

"What on earth do you mean? Climbing Menkaure's will be as safe as houses. You don't seem to be worried about me."

"You're years younger. And you're not seventeen stone."

"Whose fault is that? For months now I've been nagging you to do something about it. But you stick to the same old routine, biscuits, cakes, cream teas, eggs and bacon, and bread and cheese."

"You eat all of that too."

"I know. But I burn it off playing ping pong and swimming."

"I'm playing a round of golf on Friday."

"Good for you. I'll join you. I wouldn't miss it for the world. Meanwhile, I'm off to get my hair cut."

In the end, and just to keep the peace, I agreed to attempt the little Pyramid. Thus armed with a water bottle, cameras, binoculars, sunburn cream, hats, and walking sticks, we ventured into the sunshine and waited on the hotel steps for a taxi to take us to the camel enclosure.

It seemed odd leaving Mervyn to begin his ascent, while I continued to mine. I wondered earlier whether we might see each other when we reached the top, even suggesting we signal our arrival. However, getting to the base, and comparing the size of my Pyramid to his, I realised my idea was utterly silly.

As soon as I cushed my camel I was surrounded by donkey boys, each urging me to choose him as a guide. One doe eyed individual caught my eye, so I picked him.

"You won't regret it effendi," he said. "My friend Muhammad will look after your camel."

A boy rushed forward from out of the crowd and eagerly grabbed the harness, holding out his hand for baksheesh.

"When I get back," I said, pleased to see I was beginning to understand how to deal with these scallywags.

"And what's your name?" I asked my chosen donkey boy.

"Sharif, effendi. Have you water effendi?"

"I have Sharif. But from now on call me Mr Fry. All this effendi business is beginning to get on my nerves."

Once again, I felt strange being without Mervyn. Because including the voyage and our time in Cairo, I calculated we had been in each other's company for almost a month. I wondered whether Mervyn felt similarly.

"Come on Sharif," I said. "Let's get going. I've a bet with a friend that I won't make it. He's climbing the big one this morning and we're going to compare times."

Wearing a white gallibaya, as well as a turban, Sharif went ahead, and as he began climbing the first of the granite blocks, I caught a brief glimpse of his strong tanned, hirsute legs inside his robes. Was he wearing something else to cover his modesty I wondered? Or was his gallibaya his only garment. This question certainly gave me the incentive to follow him.

Up we went, a level at a time, the going getting slightly easier as the smooth granite became rough-hewn limestone. Sharif was as nimble as a mountain goat, bounding from block to block, while I scrambled behind, clinging to every crevice.

As we climbed higher, I was tempted to stop and catch my breath, but Sharif seemed to have other ideas and was already two courses above me.

"How many levels are there?" I asked.

"Everyone asks that," laughed Sharif. "I've tried counting, but always forget before I reach the top."

By this time, Sharif was standing almost vertically above me, so my earlier curiosity was finally rewarded when a zephyr of wind blew up his robe to reveal what I had striven to see for the previous fifty feet, a perfect and impressive view of Sharif's legs and what lay between. May I say a memory of Egypt I will cherish just as dearly as the sight of any glorious antique erection.

"Nearly halfway Mr Fry!" he shouted. "Are you alright?"

"I think so," I panted. "Just a little dazzled by the view. Do you mind if I have a drink of water?"

"Of course not Mr Fry."

Sharif crouched on his haunches a block or two above mine, giving me yet another tantalising opportunity to see what he was made of. Subsequently, swallowing the cool water, I decided the climb was becoming the most erotic encounter I had experienced in a very long while.

In his innocence, I hardly think Sharif knew what he was doing by allowing me to see so much of him. More than likely, he thought me just another man who would show little interest in a person's private parts. Presumably, he was completely unaware men such as I existed. To show himself in this way was as common and as matter a fact, as squatting on the bench beside the mosque ablution fountain.

Banishing all lecherous thoughts until later, I continued to climb and Sharif did the same, but began to ask me question after question.

"Have you just arrived in my country Mr Fry? How many children have you Mr Fry? Why do you not wear a wedding ring Mr Fry? You are a Christian Mr Fry. Are you catholic?"

It is intriguing why Arabs like to ask questions of a most personal nature. In other ways they possess a strong sense of propriety. But unlike us British they seem to have little concept of personal privacy.

We would hesitate to ask anything delicate of a person until we knew them well enough for the individual to feel safe in our confidence. But as he and I climbed higher, I ventured to satisfy Sharif's curiosity by answering each question in turn.

"No Sharif. I had business to attend to, so I've left the Pyramids until now. I've one adopted son Sharif. His name is Eric. Because Sharif I am unmarried. Yes, I'm a Christian and a Nonconformist."

"In my faith a man cannot adopt a son if he is without a wife."

"In my country also Sharif. But sometimes a little baksheesh goes a long way."

He laughed and nodded; clearly satisfied he knew a lot more about me than previously.

"Can I be your dragoman?"

I knew the question was pending and was honestly sorry that he and I were unable to become closer acquainted. However, I must remain true to our dear friend Ali.

"Sorry Sharif. I already have a dragoman."

"What is his name? I might know him."

"Ali."

"Mmm!" he shrugged. "Maybe."

Talking as well as climbing was extremely difficult, particularly when some of the blocks that required mounting were more than five feet high. It took all my breath to lift one leg after the other. As a consequence, reaching the halfway point, with my heart pounding in my throat and pulsing in my ears, I resolved to do as Mervyn urged and give up cakes and biscuits.

It was unfair to blame Mrs Lanesome's cooking, because I only had myself to blame for my overweight condition. With the sweat dripping from every pore, and driven on by perhaps another glimpse of Sharif's privates, I soldiered on.

"If you're afraid of heights Mr Fry," Sharif said when I caught up with him at last. "Don't turn around."

"That's alright Sharif. I'm only uneasy near the edge of something like a bridge, a balcony, or the roof of a tall building. In England, close to where I live, there's a city called Bristol, with a very high bridge crossing a gorge. I can't walk over it, because if I do, I have a terrible urge to jump from the parapet."

"You mean kill yourself Mr Fry? That's against the law. Allah owns our lives. It is up to him to decide when it's time to die."

"That's the rule in our religion too Sharif. The Catholic Church has a similar attitude. If you kill yourself you cannot be buried in hallowed ground, by that I mean a churchyard or a cemetery."

"But why should you wish to die Mr Fry?"

"I don't. It's just that when I'm in a situation as I've just described, I think how easy it would be should I wish to."

Naturally, we had stopped to talk. I certainly would never have been able to conduct such a philosophical conversation, struggling over four and five feet high blocks of limestone.

"Then what do you make of the view Mr Fry? Impressive is it not."

The vista was indeed spectacular. So stunning I decided it deserved to be photographed, so I sat on a ledge in order to take out my camera. Since, I was now higher than the entrance course of the Great Pyramid, what I saw through the viewfinder was a great deal more extensive than the landscape seen the day before.

Recalling my remark to Mervyn as we drove to the hotel regarding how the agricultural land ceased and suddenly turned to desert, my new vantage point emphasised this dramatically. I pointed the camera northeast where, for at least fifty miles, the immense swathe of husbandry disappeared into the distance as far as the Delta and the Mediterranean Sea. Then, turning due north, I photographed the neighbouring Pyramid of Khafre, next, taking another of the Great Pyramid of Khufu itself.

"How about I take a picture of you Sharif?" I said.

He was above me, crouching, hugging his knees, allowing me another blissful spectacle.

"Just stay like that," I said. "Smile."

The shutter clicked, capturing the moment for all time.

"My guidebook says the three monuments belong to father, son, and grandson. Khufu's grandson Menkaure built this Pyramid. He purposely made it smaller than Khafre's pyramid as a mark of respect. What a nice way to remember your father."

"Yes Mr Fry," Sharif said. "They say the King who built this Pyramid was a kind man. He died before it was finished, so they buried him inside and never bothered to carry on building."

"That's right Sharif," I said, consulting the guidebook. "Menkaure's father, Khafre, appears to have been a tyrant, changing the religion and prohibiting the people from worshipping the way they had for many centuries. When his son Menkaure came to the throne, he changed everything back, and that's why the people loved him."

"When we get down Mr Fry, would you like me to take you into the tomb?"

"No thanks Sharif. I had enough crawling along tunnels yesterday. Do you know though, reading on, it says that last century a basalt sarcophagus was found inside? They removed it, and while taking it back to England, the ship sunk in the Mediterranean Sea and it's never been recovered."

From our position, I was able to appreciate the complexity of the ancient structures across the entire Giza Plateau. A causeway ran from the mortuary temple of my little Pyramid to a lower temple, obviously the route the Pharaoh took on his last journey to immortality. Khafre's Pyramid also possessed a similar ramp connecting the temple at the base with the Sphinx Temple and adjacent to the Great Sphinx itself, which was clearly visible through my binoculars, although only from the rear.

My Pyramid also had three secondary pyramids, which I discovered once Sharif and I reached the top. Indeed, you will be pleased to know that I did reach the top and carved my name with pride into the limestone, joining hundreds of others also celebrating a similar achievement.

Going down however, I found far more difficult than the reverse. As I mentioned a while ago, some of the blocks were almost five feet tall and difficult to surmount on the upward climb. But teetering on the edge of the topmost block, with the steep side of the pyramid plunging virtually three hundred feet, I suddenly experienced an attack of vertigo.

"I can't move Sharif," I said, my stomach reeling with panic.

"You must Mr Fry. I will go before you and hold your hand."

"But if I fall I'll take you with me."

"You must start sir. If you don't you'll spend the rest of your days on top of the Pyramid."

"Don't be silly Sharif. All right. But I'll have to go very slowly."

"Of course sir. Try not to look down. Keep looking at my face, and trust me. I have done this a hundred times and never lost anyone."

With his words resonant in my mind, I sat on the edge of the uppermost course, while Sharif leapt like a Lemming onto the block below. Gazing up at me with his dark brown eyes, he held out his hands.

"Grab me and ease yourself over," he urged. "You'll soon get the hang of it."

Sharif's hands were rough and sinewy. His fingers gripping mine tightly, while I gingerly edged down the side of the block, until I was beside him and prepared for the next step. Bit by bit, stone by stone, Sharif and I descended.

However, I suddenly realised that in my joy at achieving the top, as well as my panic at the thought of going down, I had neglected to look for Mervyn through my binoculars. Khafre's Pyramid was gradually obscuring Khufu's Pyramid. However, the top remained visible.

"Sharif! Can we stop?" I called. "I must look for my friend."

"Anything you wish sir."

Pointing the binoculars in the direction of the Great Pyramid, I adjusted the focus until the jagged peak came into view, along with a dozen or so moving specks, which turned out to be people. All appeared to be men dressed either in Arab robes or European lightweight jackets, slacks and white Panama hats. In effect, exactly the costume Mervyn was wearing that morning. It might then prove difficult to pick him from the others. But Mervyn's diminutive stature was quite distinctive. As a result, my attention was drawn to a figure sitting on a block, fanning his face with his hat. Low and behold, I quickly became convinced the person was Mervyn and increased the magnification. Yes! His blonde hair, turning even blonder by time spent beside the pool at the Gezira Club, as well as the sandy moustache he was trying to grow, gave him away. I was pleased the notion we might spot each other, which Mervyn had so recently ridiculed, proved to be completely possible.

"Very well Sharif," I said, putting the binoculars back in their case. "We can go on now. We're nearly at the bottom. I'm not afraid anymore."

Once we had slithered over the last level of smooth granite, I was pleased to feel my feet on sandy soil.

"Thank you Sharif," I said, as I dipped into my pockets for a few piastres. "I can truly say I've never enjoyed a morning more. To say the least, the trip up was gratifying, even if the journey down was a little worrying. Thank you for being so patient with a silly Englishman."

Sharif took off his turban and held it out ready to receive payment.

"It was also my pleasure to be of service Mr Fry." He looked inside his turban and then gazed at me alluringly. "You are a most kind and generous man. Allah will smile upon you! I hope you enjoy the rest of your time in Egypt."

What an attractive, intelligent young man, I thought as Muhammad cushed my camel. Also, greatly endowed with god given gifts, which I was most privileged to see. A memory that would last a lifetime. As I reined the camel to the northwest, I looked back to see him standing on the causeway, waving. Yet more proof of the endearing nature of the Egyptian people.

***

By now, feeling entirely comfortable astride our camels, Mervyn and I made tracks for the hotel, but he refused to believe I reached the top of my pyramid, even scorning me when I said I had seen him at the top of his.

"You were sitting on a rock fanning yourself with your hat."

"I did do that I remember," said Mervyn. "I can't tell you how hot it was."

"It was just as hot on mine. After all, it was midday."

"So don't fib. How far did you get?"

"I've told you. Right to the very top. Although I had quite an incentive."

As I recounted my experience, Mervyn almost turned green with envy.

"You jammy bugger! Our guide was as wrinkly as are the gypsies on Wildsbridge Common. How is it you always strike it lucky?"

"I'm made that way I suppose," I said, smugly. "You'll get to see him anyway. I took his photo."

"What! With his you know what and everything?"

I nodded proudly.

"You'll be arrested when you get it developed."

"I'll do it myself, on the ship going home."

"How?"

"I know for a fact the ship we'll sail on has its own darkroom."

"How do you know which ship?"

"While you were having your haircut I noticed in the English Gazette, the good old Viceroy of India arrives at Port Said on Saturday the 27th. So I telephoned P&O and reserved a suite of cabins."

"What's today?"

"Wednesday the 17th.

"That means we've only ten days left. You promised we'd do Luxor and Aswan. We'll never have the time."

"Yes we will. But after today, don't you think we've seen all we need to see in Giza? I thought if we could check out of the hotel this afternoon, once we've seen the Sphinx, and take a taxi to Saqqara. Then see the Stepped Pyramid. Next on to Memphis, where there's a colossal statue of Rameses the second. And leave from there for Cairo by train."

"The map says we can catch a train to Luxor from Memphis."

"That's quite possible. But I want to get back to let Ali know of our change of plans. I think he should come with us. We also made a date to meet Harry and the lads on Sunday evening?"

"That leaves us five days to travel up the Nile and back. I don't think there's enough time to do it and still pick up the ship?"

"I know. So we'll meet Harry tomorrow evening instead. Tomorrow morning, you can go to the barracks and give him a message. That means we can leave on the Friday night train for Luxor. Do the sites."

"Then take the Saturday night train to Aswan. How marvellous! I get to sleep on a train, twice."

"What do you want to do after lunch," I asked, once the travel plans were settled.

"See the Sphinx of course."

"But wouldn't you rather see it now?"

"Alright. They're selling koftas over there. Why not buy a couple and eat them on the way."

***

Feeling confident enough to hold our koftas and bread in two hands, with our ships of the desert padding noiselessly beneath us across the sand, we approached The Great Sphinx from the rear.

The Great Sphinx was fascinating in its antiquity, but disappointing in its lack of charm, except it remains the largest monolithic statue in the world. And with a mouth once admired for its beauty by the ancient world, its mutilated face is now expressionless. Thought to be female, a legend based on the Greek mythological beast, with a lion's body, a human head, wings of an eagle, and the tail of a serpent; the gigantic statue is over sixty-six feet high and two hundred and forty feet long.

The Grecian Sphinx is regarded as treacherous and merciless, killing, then eating the wretch who fails to solve her riddle. However, the Egyptian Sphinx is seen as a male, benevolent guardian, often flanking the entrances of tombs.

"Once again, we have to thank the Orient Line for their fantastic guidebook," I said.

"Who built it?" asked Mervyn, as we pulled up our camels beside its giant paws.

"It wasn't built, but sculpted out of the surrounding rock."

"Alright! Clever dick! Then who was the sculptor?"

"It seems there's an element of doubt. There's never been a

reference to the Sphinx in any inscriptions, except Thutmosis the fourth referred to it in a Dream Stella found between its legs."

"How do you know all this?" Mervyn asked, suspiciously

"Because I covered the Upper and Lower Kingdoms in my studies. Even toying with the idea of becoming an archaeologist."

"Yes. I could see you as one. You're a bit of a boffin."

"Many Egyptologists say it was Khafre, the son of Khufu, who constructed the Sphinx, at the same time as building his Pyramid. But why does the causeway linking Khafre's Mortuary Temple and the Sphinx Temple, skirt around the Sphinx? Inferring the Sphinx was already here. Others say Khufu found the Sphinx buried up to its neck in sand."

"What happened to the nose?"

"Another mystery. It's believed a Mamluk Caliph ordered it to be prized off with hammers and chisels, because he discovered Egyptian people making offerings to the Sphinx with the hope of a good harvest. The wind and sandstorms have also taken their toll."

"He looks so lonely," Mervyn said. "Just staring at nothing."

"But think how many sunrises he's seen, along with those he's yet to see."

"Until the end of time. The thought makes me shudder. He'll still be here when were both dead and gone."

"As well as everyone else that is alive today."

"I can see why the Arabs call him the 'Terrifying One'. Also, the Ancient Egyptians called him Horus, the god of the sky, sun, and moon, because he's optimistic and pessimistic all at the same time."

Both of us took perhaps a dozen photographs, from the side, the front, and the back, at least one including Mervyn's camel. We were lucky, since it was lunchtime and there were few people about, increasing the sensation of the Sphinx's solitude and mystery. Solid and silent in the presence of the awful desert. A symbol of eternity and disputing time itself.

Chapter Twenty Six
Houseboat on the Nile

Entering the hotel, after depositing the camels at the door, we hurried to our room, rang down for a pot of tea, and began to pack. In hindsight, I suppose I caused a good deal of bother booking The Viceroy of India the way I did, leaving us pressed for time to see the remaining sites. But she was an old friend to both of us, and I would rather she took us home to England than another anonymous ship. I think Mervyn was secretly pleased, as she contained some private memories, along with a person to whom he once was quite attached, although Mervyn was unaware I knew of his dalliance.

Despite our rush to leave Mena House, I did take a few photographs of our delightful room, and a couple more of the hotel. Also, I saved a copy of the tariff of charges.

The taxi carried us south along the desert road, our dust obscuring any persons, animals, or vehicles we might be passing.

"So we're taking Ali with us to Luxor on Friday," said Mervyn, gazing out of the window.

"I think it's only fair. He's been a wonderful friend. I'd like to give him the chance to see his country. He's a proud and educated young man. I think he'd benefit from the experience."

As I discovered quite early on, Mervyn could be quite jealous, especially when he knows whatever he says, or however he behaves, nothing will cause me to change my mind.

"I take it he'll have his own compartment on the train," he said.

"If the sleeping cars are anything like the Train De Lux we took from Port Said, I think the cabins are shared. I thought I'd have one for myself, and you and he can share."

Obviously, I hoped this arrangement might alter Mervyn's opinion regarding Ali joining us.

"Well yes," Mervyn said airily. "That would be alright. But won't he want to pray at all hours?"

"I'd hope he'd do it in the corridor."

"But are you sure you'll be okay on your own?"

"Perfectly old chap. I'm a terribly light sleeper, as you well know. I'll more than likely spend most of the night reading. I've reached a particularly exciting place in 'Drums Along the Mohawk'."

Sitting back, I felt smug. When faced with obstinacy and childish petulance, it is always best to take the sting out of the situation, by turning the tables.

The Stepped Pyramid of Djoser needs little description as its name fully describes its shape. Built in six stages, from base to peak, and one thousand four hundred years before the Great Pyramid of Khufu, its antiquity is most impressive. Djoser's Pyramid was the first monumental tomb built in stone, causing an astounding social impact on what was to come.

We arrived in Saqqara at the middle of the afternoon, finding it dreadfully hot walking about the temple complex surrounding the Pyramid. Despite the heat and dust, we latched onto a party of Germans led by a hoary Arab dragoman. The old man spoke fluent German, so Mervyn and I were unable to understand his discourse. Therefore, we drifted away, finding some shade under a covered colonnade. After a cool drink of bottled water, we returned to the taxi and asked the driver to take us on to the ancient city of Memphis, sadly now a pile of ancient rubble.

The road continued southeast, except we left the desert behind, entering the lush surroundings of the Nile hinterland, the hot dry air replaced by the aroma of vegetation and the scent of flowering fruit trees. We drove past cotton fields; the thirsty plants supplied with Nile water from deep irrigation channels, replenished by giant water wheels called Norias. Acres of rich dark soil passed us by, ploughed and awaiting corn, barley, beans, clover, or rice, the comparison between here and the arid scenery quite staggering.

Eventually, we arrived at a shady grove of date palms, where our driver mumbled something that sounded a little like Rameses.

"I think we're here," I said. "I remember it from before."

Having asked the driver to wait, Mervyn, and I followed a well-worn path through the palms, until we reached a giant, prone statue, balanced on piles of stones, clearly there to protect the immense statue from immersion in mud during the annual Nile flood.

"At Cambridge," I said, as we stared up at the massive granite figure. "I remember coming across a book called 'The Art Treasures of England'. There was an engraved plate showing men digging this statue out of the ground. The archaeologists discovered two. The one in front of Cairo Station was restored, while the other remains here. I think this one was offered to the British Museum, but was declined because of the difficulty transporting it to England."

"Then it's been in the mud for thousands of years," said Mervyn, reaching up and running his hand over the leg. "Yet it's as smooth as if it was finished yesterday."

"I wish we could see the face," I said. "There should be a platform so we can look down on him."

In truth, no special arrangements had been made for this unique relic. For all intents and purposes, it lay on its back, a forlorn and forgotten remnant of a glorious age when it joined its pair guarding the entrance to a temple dedicated to the god Ptah, the Egyptian creator of the world. Rameses built many magnificent places of worship, leaving enormous stone images of himself all the way from Aswan to Memphis.

After taking my photograph, completely against my wishes, since I shy away from snaps of myself, seeing I am rather embarrassed as to how rotund I have become, Mervyn gazed around at the ancient rubble scattered about in the long grass.

"Is this all there is?"

"As I remember, there's the Alabaster Sphinx somewhere hereabouts. But sadly, yes, that's about it. Once Memphis was the largest city in the ancient world, the commercial and spiritual capital of Upper and Lower Egypt. In fact, Menes, the first Pharaoh of Dynasty One, is said to have purposely sited the city on the boundary, therefore uniting the once feuding kingdoms."

"There you go again," chuckled Mervyn. "Sounding like the Michelin Guide."

"I've taken the time to read up about it, that's all. At least someone's taking an interest."

"If it's that big, where's the rest of Memphis?"

"Under our feet, and around about us. Beneath the villages and fields, I suppose. When King Menes began building the city, he dug dykes to take the floodwater away. But when the Mamluks invaded Egypt, they fell into disrepair. Just think of the amount of mud the Nile has deposited since. There might be temples and palaces, still standing beneath the ground."

"Why doesn't someone start excavating?"

"Because it would amount to a huge project and cost vast sums of money. And what would become of the poor people living in the villages around here?"

"They'd make money from the tourists, that's what."

A little further on, we found the Alabaster Sphinx in a sandy area among the trees. It appeared hardly damaged, except on the left side of the base and on the haunches, obviously resulting from lying so long in the ground.

Just before the war, I remember reading about its discovery in The Times. A number of archaeologists found its tail protruding from a sand hill, so returned the following season in order to excavate. The Sphinx it seems is the last survivor of many that flanked the grand avenue approach to Rameses the Great's, Temple of Ptah.

I took a photograph of Mervyn sitting between its paws and tickling the Sphinx's beard.

"After seeing this," he said. "You can imagine how handsome the Great Sphinx must have appeared before it was damaged. How old is this one?"

"Young compared to the one at Giza. Between a thousand and fifteen hundred years before the birth of Christ."

"Time's a crazy thing. It's difficult to put a perspective on how long ago things happened. Do you think people will look at our civilisation from such a distance?"

"If man survives that is."

"Who knows? In a thousand years, a chap might be having his photo taken, just like me."

Quite a daunting thought, as well as philosophical, especially coming from Mervyn. Perhaps our holiday was making an impression on him at last.

The taxi dropped Mervyn and I at a station in a village called Turah, where we waited for a train back to Cairo.

***

In order that Ali received my request to join our trip up the Nile, I felt it best to deliver the message myself. As a result, the following morning, after seeing Mervyn off to Abbassia on a similar errand to find his brother Harry to inform him of our change of plans, I continued on to Imbaba. Once there, my caleche deposited me at Kit Kat Square, at the place where we usually dropped Ali. I crossed the busy Shari El Bahr Ama and headed towards a row of hedges and trees separating the busy street from the Nile.

Wooden gates were inserted at intervals into the greenery, Arabic numbers indicating to whom they belonged. But for the life of me, I failed to recall if I ever saw Ali enter any of them. And having never seen the houseboat, I quickly realised my difficult position. Ali was probably the most popular of all Arab names. If I asked someone at the first houseboat, would the person direct me to the correct one? I took a chance. The first gate was unlocked, so lifting the latch I ducked through, immediately exchanging the chaos of the El Bahr Ama Road for the tranquillity of a leafy garden. I was standing at the head of a timber stair, leading down to a gangway, linking the riverbank with an aged wooden houseboat, festooned with the tassels one sees on a decorated camel. Pots of red geraniums bedecked the windowsills and doorstep, while jasmine made a tangled profusion of heavily scented flowers entwining the balcony rails of the upper stories.

"Can I help you?"

The voice took me off guard for a moment, and looking up I saw a woman leaning over the rail, languidly smoking a cigarette, her long raven hair disappearing into the foliage.

"I'm sorry for the intrusion," I stuttered, nervously. "But I'm looking for someone who may be a neighbour of yours. His name's Ali."

"It is unnecessary to say sorry darling," the woman said. "I enjoy having visitors. Who told you where to find me?"

For a moment, her question confused me. Rapidly however I began to realise how close I was to getting into an extremely sticky situation.

"No! No!" I exclaimed. "I'm looking for a friend. His name's Ali. He lives in a houseboat somewhere along here. Perhaps you know him."

The woman smiled.

"What's he look like?"

She inhaled, and then exhaled a lungful of cigarette smoke.

"Maybe early twenties, dark hair, black moustache."

"Darling! You've just described every young man in Cairo."

She dropped the cigarette through the tangle of jasmine and I heard it hiss as it hit the water.

"Are you sure you don't want to come up for a drink?"

Although her origin was certainly Egyptian, her voice possessed a hint of an American accent, as did Garbo and Dietrich. In fact, in appearance, despite her hair being brunette, she could easily have been a combination of both, her seductive voice revealing the kind of life she led and the number of cigarettes she smoked.

"I'd love to," I said naively. "But it's rather early for me. Besides, I've several things I need to do this morning."

"What a pity. I'm rather partial to tall men. They always meet my expectations."

I would have enjoyed saying how much I agreed with her, but refrained.

"There are several young men living further up," she said, lighting another cigarette. "Sometimes they whistle to the tour boats at night.

You could try there."

"Thank you."

"Just follow the path until you see the blue and white boat. But do call again darling, now you know where I am."

Thanking her, I stumbled on between a maze of pot plants, empty wine, and beer bottles. Then passing a boat clearly disused and in need of repair, I arrived at a beautifully painted, blue and white houseboat. Here, a tubby Egyptian fellow was draping, what I presumed to be freshly washed vests and underwear over the first story veranda rail. He heard my approach along the gravel path, looked up, and smiled.

"Good morning sir," he said cheerfully. "Can I help you?"

"It is indeed a very fine morning," I said. "And yes. I hope you can. Would you know whether Ali lives here? If so, I'm wondering if he might be at home. He's my dragoman you see."

"He does sir," the young man said. "Also, may I say, you're a most fortunate man. For several years, Ali and I have been friends. We attended university together. Of course, that was before his father died."

"You don't say. He never mentioned he went to Cairo University."

"Ali is a modest man. More than likely he would prefer you did not know that, without his father's assistance, he was unable to pay his fees, so had to leave after the first year."

This was dumbfounding news. With his winnings at Gezira Races the week before, Ali could have bought his way back. But he insisted I keep the money and open an account for his family. There was clearly even more to this selfless man than I previously supposed.

"Then obviously I've come to the right place. Is he at home?"

"I heard him rise early sir. Ali is a most religious man. He prefers to pray at the mosque."

"Is it nearby?"

"No sir. Over the Imbaba Bridge. It is his family mosque. The Mosque of Sinan Pasha is on Shari El Khadre, in Bulaq."

"Isn't that where his family live?"

"Yes sir. After prayers, Ali goes to his mother's apartment and takes lunch."

The young man was clearly a close friend, since he knew a great deal about Ali's activities.

"How can I get a message to him? It's important he get it today. My friend and I are leaving Cairo for Luxor tomorrow evening on the Sunshine Express, and we'd like Ali to join us."

"I can see your dilemma sir. It'll be difficult to find him at prayers. The Sinan Pasha Mosque is very popular. There will be many there. But I know Ali's mother redirects his letters. Perhaps there's an envelope with her address on it? Then you could leave the message at her apartment."

"What a good idea. How clever of you. Then he'd be bound to get it."

"Wait there sir. I'll come down and let you in. Perhaps you might like coffee."

Here again I was being shown an example of Egyptian kindness and consideration it would be hard to find elsewhere on the continent.

"Please come in sir," the young man said, opening the door. "My name is Hazim. Would you care to take coffee?"

"Very much Hazim. And my name is Mr Fry."

"Do come in and sit down Mr Fry. I will begin coffee instantly."

Hazim ushered me inside, where immediately I was greeted by the most magnificent spectacle I can only describe as the kind one experiences in the cinema. That is, when the motion picture camera suddenly moves from a dark interior into a sublime landscape, bursting on the retina with colour, light and movement.

The room I entered appeared to serve as both a kitchen and sitting room. But the opposing side opened to the air, offering a superb view of the Nile. Beyond a rail skirting a veranda, the river lolled past. A great sheet of pale green water, the power of the current visible by the speed of the occasional clumps of dislodged grassy bank, or islands of detritus floating by. Feluccas, like giant winged water birds, slid past, their billowing sails radiant white in the morning sunshine. All the while, a fisherman stood in his boat casting his net over the tranquil surface. The entire scene was performed against a backdrop of greenery fringing the opposite bank, where the rooftops of opulent Zamalek were plainly visible through the trees.

"Your coffee won't be long Mr Fry," Hazim said.

"Oh yes! Sorry. I'm just amazed. You'd pay thousands for a view like this. You're lucky a hotel hasn't been built here."

"Certainly sir. But some wealthy influential men wish the houseboats to remain. Especially one in particular."

Something told me I knew to which boat Hazim referred, but I abstained from commenting.

"Even if you lived in Cairo all your life I don't think you'd ever get bored looking at the Nile," continued Hazim. "Please sit down sir."

He gestured to a comfortable leather sofa, partially draped with a colourful Bedouin tapestry.

"Thank you Hazim. But don't you find the river a distraction? I wouldn't do a thing. Just stare at it all day."

"My room faces the road sir, where you saw me hanging my washing. It is there I work."

Hazim was filling a copper coffee pot with water he poured from a jug. Then lighting a gas burner on the stove, he put the pot over the flames. Next, he spooned two tablespoons of ground coffee into the pot, along with two teaspoons of powder from a small jar he took from a shelf.

"Egyptian coffee sir? Very good with cardamom. Sugar sir?" said Hazim, taking down another jar. "There must be sugar."

Giving the liquid a stir with the spoon, he turned the burner down to medium."

"I'll go up to Ali's room and look for an envelope," Hazim said, heading for the stairs. "If you see it start to boil sir, turn it down to low."

Most trusting these Egyptians, I thought as I relaxed into the sofa, with one eye on the pot and the other on the river. There are harsh punishments under Islamic law for theft, more than likely losing a hand in the process. It appears personal property is quite safe. Therefore, it is unnecessary to put locks on doors.

As Hazim predicted, the coffee began to foam, and I heard the sound of bubbling coming from the pot. So going to the stove, I turned the gas to low, the noise suddenly ending.

"You're very lucky to live here Hazim," I called up the stairs. "I could quite easily see myself living on a houseboat. Especially one on the Nile. I feel completely relaxed already."

"Yes sir," he answered. "Sometimes it's very hard to study. There's always something happening on the river."

Keeping an ear open for the coffee, I walked onto the veranda and leaned on the rail, at the same time inhaling a pungent concoction of water, mud, vegetation and brewing coffee. I was tempted to light a cigarette, but changed my mind. Nothing was going to taint the beauty of the moment.

"So you're still at university," I said, noticing Hazim had returned to the kitchen.

"I am, sir. I'm in my final year."

"What are you studying?"

"Law sir."

Without a doubt, I could see the young man in a wig and gown. He would make a very good solicitor. Succinct, clever, yet caring. Thinking at all times of his client's best interests.

"It's important to keep the foam sir. It's foam that makes Egyptian coffee the best in the Middle East."

Hazim turned up the burner until the bubbling noise began once more. Then, lifting the pot off the stove, he set it aside to rest, while taking two small cups from a cupboard above the sink. Next, Hazim poured a little coffee into each cup, and then returned the pot to the flame in order the liquid foamed once more. Then, taking the pot off the flame for the last time, he filled our cups with black, steaming, froth, although this time to the brim.

"Egyptian coffee sir. But leave it to settle for the moment. You don't want to drink the sediment. Unless you wish to stay up all night."

Hazim had slumped into a well-worn chair, the frayed arms partially draped in an additional piece of vibrant Bedouin cloth. In fact, there was colour and gaiety throughout the room, from the glinting copper pots hanging in the kitchen, to the decorated plates, bowls, and cups on the draining board. Blue dominated the faded wooden walls, and crimson brocade curtains, bordering the windows on the shore side of the boat, as well as those drawn back along the veranda. The bohemian haphazard cosiness of everything was delightful, as well as visually stimulating. I wished I had brought my camera. On the other hand, maybe Hazim might have seen me taking photographs as an imposition.

"What did Ali study?" I asked, as we sipped the dark sweet aromatic coffee.

"History," answered Hazim.

"I thought as much," I said. "That explains his knowledge of Cairo and Egypt, which so often impresses me. What a coincidence. I studied Ancient History at Cambridge. How strange he never mentioned it."

"As I said before sir. Ali is a modest man. I've found what you need sir."

He felt in the back pocket of his trousers and took out a tattered envelope.

"Mrs Rashid lives in apartment 43/ 24, Shari El Khadre, on the same street as the mosque. I never knew Ali lived so close."

As he accompanied me to the gangway, I thanked Hazim for his kindness, and his coffee. Then I climbed the steps to the gate, where I let myself out into the street, allowing the chaos of vehicles, animals, and people to engulf me, the enchantment of Hazim and his houseboat on the Nile, now merely a memory.

Chapter Twenty Seven
Imbaba Bridge - Embarrassment in Sinan Pasha Mosque

My taxi was held up on Imbaba Bridge, as the centre section had swung open to allow a bevy of feluccas to pass downstream, giving me a moment to wonder at the miracle of its construction.

This was not the original bridge, however, but the second to span the Nile at this point. Commissioned by Khedive Mohammed Tewfik, the construction of the first bridge was begun in 1889, linking Cairo's main station and the new railway line along the west bank of the Nile, with Giza and Upper Egypt. By the beginning of the twentieth century, rail carriages were becoming larger and trains more frequent, with heavier vehicles and added pedestrian traffic. So in 1913, building commenced on a new bridge, although suspended at the outbreak of the war, then resumed in 1924.

It is unclear to whom Egypt can claim as its designer, although some say Cairo can owe the ingenious multi-functional structure to Gustav Eiffel.

"The Nile is very beautiful from the walkway above effendi," said my taxi driver, by way of making conversation as we waited for the centre section to close. "From this side you can see from the Gezira Island to the Semiramis Hotel and the Citadel. While on the other, on a clear morning, you can see all the way to the Delta."

"I'll take the time to walk across one day," I said, lighting a cigarette.

"Do not walk alone effendi. Bad boys are up there. Boys that take money for favours."

"Not in the daytime surely," I said airily, attempting to sound indifferent.

"Anytime effendi. It is well known in Imbaba. Things go on up there that cannot be seen from down here."

Imagining the scene that might be happening twenty feet above my head, I heard an increasing rumbling sound, as to the left of the queue of waiting vehicles, a train thundered into view, belching steam and smoke. The magnificent locomotive passed within feet of the taxi, so close in fact, I saw the engine driver leaning from his cab and several passengers sitting at the carriage windows.

"The Sunshine Express effendi," the driver said. "All the way to Luxor."

"Is it? Then I'm travelling on it tomorrow night."

"You are fortunate effendi. I have heard it is most luxurious."

Hearing the man calling me effendi, caused me to think of Ali, and looking at my watch, I realised we had already been waiting nearly a quarter of an hour. Nonetheless, as if on cue, the traffic began to move, and soon we were across the river, driving through the maze of streets that made up Bulaq, until finally we arrived at the mosque, made plain by the men walking through the entrance.

Having paid the driver once he dropped me outside Mrs Rashid's apartment, instead of heading for the door, and forgetting the urgency of my mission for a moment, my curiosity got the better of me and drew me to the doorway of the mosque for a peek inside.

Instantly, I saw the reason for its popularity, since, unlike urban mosques of Turkey and the Middle East, which are usually restricted for space amongst the surrounding buildings, the Mosque of Sinan Pasha is located within a large walled enclosure, set out as a garden. The mosque is modest in size and appearance in comparison to some of its grander cousins in and around Cairo. Almost certainly, this feature was the reason for its popularity with Bulaq families.

While we drank coffee, Hazim, who seemed a bit of a historian himself, acquainted me with some of the mosque's history.

It seems nearly five hundred years ago Bulaq was the great port of

Cairo, where merchant ships from all over the known world navigated the Nile. Having discharged their cargo along the river's eastern bank bordering Bulaq, they returned to their country of origin with goods traded with Egypt. Making Bulaq the commercial centre of not only Cairo, but of all of Egypt.

An Albanian, Sinan Pasha, who became Ottoman Governor of Egypt around this time, built the mosque. Sinan was a particular favourite of the Ottoman Sultan, Suleiman the Magnificent, and was brought to court as a youth to serve as the royal cupbearer. He later became Grand Vizier on five occasions to three successive Sultans. Since Bulaq's importance had waned due to the silting up of the Nile, and the rise in commercial prominence of Alexandria, in order to restore Bulaq's former glory, Sinan built a large religious complex. His building not only included a mosque, but a caravanserai, as well as a hammam, which other than the mosque, is the only building to survive the test of time.

Crossing the threshold beneath arches in a high wall, I entered a colonnade supporting three small cupolas. From here, I could see through a further archway into a garden beyond the ablution fountain. In front of me, and to the left and right, three large doorways seemed to be accesses into the prayer hall.

A stone bench ran along the closed side of the colonnade, beneath which hundreds of shoes and sandals were neatly placed, side-by-side, heels underneath, toes pointing outwards. Sitting down, I removed mine, positioning them in the same way. I must add how incongruous my shiny brown brogues appeared amongst the battered footwear of their neighbours.

As I crept across the pavement between the colonnade and the prayer hall, I passed the ablution fountain where men squatted in front of the waterspouts performing wudu.

Remarkably, and despite it being the middle of the week, the prayer hall was crowded with men, each facing the Mihrab, a semicircular niche, ornately decorated with multi coloured inlaid marble. Some knelt, while others stood, men bowing or prostrating on plush red carpets edged with an intricate pattern of gold embroidery.

The Sinan Pasha Mosque was one of the prettiest I had seen, and I could well understand why it was so popular. Both the Mosque of Sultan Hussein beneath the Citadel, and that of Muhammad Ali within the fortress, were grand, except their magnificence I found overwhelming. On the other hand, here was a building and interior that was simple and inviting. A family mosque as Hazim described it.

Moving further inside, I searched the men with a hope of finding Ali. But it was impossible, unless I went amongst them and looked into their faces, which would have been entirely inappropriate. Therefore, I was content to watch the scene, as well as enjoy the beauty of the architecture, while allowing the voice of the Imam reciting the Koran to numb and relax my brain.

Hazim says the stone dome is the largest in Cairo, and looking up, I could well believe him. It seemed incredible the prayer hall's high stone walls were able to support its immensity. Yet, the intricate patterns of stained glass in a double row of roundel windows, gave the space an ethereal quality. Behind me, and above the central entrance, I noticed a wooden balcony and most likely the place where the women prayed.

It was then I realised, that in my state of total relaxation, I had forgotten myself for a moment, and thinking I was passing wind had in fact allowed a little of the contents of my lower bowel to see the light of day. What should I do? I began to panic. Where to go in Cairo if such a thing happens? In all our meanderings, I failed to notice a public lavatory anywhere on the streets. Should the need arise, I would either wait until I was safely back at the hotel, or use the facilities at a restaurant or coffee shop. Here then, I was in a desperate situation and knew the reason why. Hazim's coffee had worked a miracle. Not only was it a stimulant of the brain, it was also a tremendously powerful laxative.

It was crucial I find somewhere close by, and private. Therefore, moving quickly and uncomfortably out of the prayer hall towards the door, I saw an old man sitting beside the ablution fountain selling soap

"Excuse me," I said desperately hoping he understood English. "Do you know if there's a lavatory close by?"

He squinted and shook his head.

"Lavatory! Latrine!" I said emphatically, at the same time making signs with my hand, which I hoped would be obvious and understood.

All of a sudden, the old man jumped to his feet and angrily waved me away, apparently deeply insulted by my gesture.

"I understood you sir," a man said, standing behind me, evidently waiting to purchase a bar of soap. "There is no such place inside the mosque. To be contaminated with bodily fluids while in the presence of Allah is forbidden. But I do know the coffee shop across the street has a lavatory."

At the mention of coffee, my bowels gave a lurch and I knew it was imperative I get across the street, or embarrass myself completely. But I still needed to find my shoes. So thanking the man, I hurried through a crowd of men heading into the mosque, making a beeline for the stone bench where I left them. They were easy to pick, so slipping them on, without even tying the laces, I ran into the street and immediately saw the café to which the man referred. Crossing the road, dodging the traffic, I reached its open doorway.

It was fortunate the café owner spoke English. However, this hardly prevented him asking me for three piastres to use his convenience, which I thought at the time to be a blasted cheek considering its condition. Having only frequented Groppi's, Fishawy's, and Café Riche, once the café owner had directed me through to the rear of his shop, I was unprepared for what I found. The toilet was filthy, foul smelling, and quite disgusting. The three establishments I just mentioned provided for Muslims, as well as Europeans, being they were popular with affluent Egyptians, foreigners, and tourists. There is at least one out of two cubicles fitted with a conventional pedestal basin, the remainder possessing the typical hole in the tiled floor one expects to see in Islamic countries. Here however, I had no choice. Each door, I opened in my dash for relief, revealed the same, and to my horror, a complete lack of toilet paper.

With little time to wait, I hurried inside the first cubicle and shut the door, only to find it was minus a lock. Subsequently, as I desperately took off my jacket and threw it over the top of the door, then unbuttoned my fly, the door obstinately swung open. There was no point trying to shut it. No time anyway, because at the point of squatting over the hole and pulling down my trousers and underpants, and at this juncture I hope you forgive my description, but I cannot think of another way to explain what happened next, my bowels released themselves to my great relief.

I remained in this position for a minute or so, my right hand keeping my trousers around my ankles and well away from the edge of the hole, while my left kept me steady by resting it against the cubicle wall.

Suddenly, something moved in the corner of my eye, and turning I saw a large green lizard clinging to the wall, scrutinising me imperiously with a cold red eye.

In my frantic rush I had failed to notice that the crumbling, weed infested lavatory walls, were open to the sky and therefore so was its interior. In addition, not only was the lizard allowed access, but the occupants of several balconies in a building above, had they been looking down at the time.

Despite this, there were more important issues to take care of, the lack of toilet paper being top of the list. Ignoring the lizard's icy stare, I looked about for a solution, but saw none, as even the pitcher of water sometimes placed to the left of the hole for the convenience of the squatter, was absent. There was however, above the rusty cistern, a type of bush dangling a branch over the wall, and I realised its leaves, although rather small, would have to suffice. The only problem remaining was the lizard since it lay between the intended branch and me. I have never been particularly squeamish regarding reptiles. Not that England is frequented by many, perhaps a sort of sand lizard and a couple of snake species. However, the creature regarding me so intently was pretty large and fat, possessing the ugliest head I had yet seen on a reptile, except perhaps the Iguanas of the Galapagos Islands.

It also appeared to be intelligent, because, when I made a movement with my hand in an effort to shoo it away, it seemed completely unafraid, and obstinately remained, flicking its tongue at me rudely.

"Bugger off!" I shouted, using Mervyn's favourite curse, which felt strange, as I rarely if ever swear.

It was then I saw an answer to the stalemate, and grabbing the door, slammed it shut, the loud crack just enough to send the lizard catapulting over the wall and out of sight. I stood to pull my trousers as high as I dare, then reaching up, grabbed a handful of leaves and squatted once more, using them for the purpose they were intended. In truth, I am sure this is what we humans used before the invention of paper. In addition, the greenery was far softer than the Izal toilet paper in common use at home, causing me to wish for a toilet paper revolution.

Feeling hugely relieved to have avoided soiling my underpants; I tucked in the tail of my shirt, buttoned my fly, and put on my jacket. Then, after washing my hands in a basin in the corridor, I beat a swift retreat through the shop and out into the street.

Chapter Twenty Eight
Lunch with the Rashid's

The door to Mrs Rashid's apartment was wedged open, so I climbed the stairs to the second floor and rang the bell of number twenty-four. When it opened, I was greatly surprised to see Ali standing on the threshold.

"I can't tell you how pleased I am to see you," I said. "Hazim gave me your mother's address. He said you'd be in the mosque. I looked inside, but didn't see you."

"I was there for the Fajr prayers effendi. My little brother is unwell, and mother required me to take him to the doctor."

"I hope he's alright."

"Just a cold. Please come in. Mother will be delighted to meet you. I've done nothing but talk of you since you and Mr Mervyn left for Giza. But why are you here? I thought you were returning on Sunday."

"There's been a change of plan," I said, as he led me along a passageway. "We've decided to sail for England on the twenty-seventh. So there's not a great deal of time to see Luxor and Aswan. That's why I'm here Ali. Mervyn and I would be pleased if you would join us."

Despite that it was almost noon, the passage would have been dark had it not been for several blazing light bulbs hanging from ceiling roses and old gas brackets in the wall. Nonetheless, the sight of the exposed wires linking them, looping across the ceiling, or tacked haphazardly along the wall, appalled me.

At the end of the corridor, Ali ushered me through a door into a room where two tall windows opened onto iron balconies, the railings reminiscent of the kind one sees around Etoile in Paris. The room was light and airy, with sounds from the street below drifting through the open windows. But once again, I could hardly help noticing the profusion of electrical wires threaded over picture frames and along curtain rails.

"Please sit down," Ali said, gesturing to a leather sofa. "I'll tell mother you're here. She's in the kitchen preparing lunch."

"I thought as much," I said. "Something smells delicious."

In addition to the buttoned leather sofa on which I was sitting, the room was plainly furnished with dark upholstered armchairs and occasional tables, one between the windows, and two flanking an ornate white, marble mantelpiece. There was an ambience of faded glory about the room, as if it had once been the handsome sitting room of a consular official, or solicitor. There was an item in the room however, which harked back to a better time, since in the corner stood a dusty, dull ebony grand piano, its lid and keyboard closed, the top now used to display several framed photographs. Behind it on the wall hung a violin and a bow, undoubtedly once belonging to Ali's father; a sad memento of a violinist's life. Leaving my place on the sofa and looking closely at the photographs, I noticed that many were family groups. Children were smiling, together with adults wearing serious expressions, conscious of the camera capturing their image. One particular photograph caught my eye.

The setting was easily recognisable since it was Café Riche. There was Ali, although much younger, perhaps fifteen. He was standing behind two girls a few years younger, and they were sitting beside a woman holding a baby. Beside Ali, a man held a violin. Clearly, this was Ali's family, and the man was his late father. Although, it was the woman seated in the middle of the group, which caused me to have a mild attack of goose pimples, as she was none other than Umm Kulthum.

"My father's proudest moment," said Ali, from the doorway.

"You startled me Ali," I said. "It must have been a tremendous honour for your family."

"We were celebrating mother's birthday. We went to Café Riche, and Umm was there having dinner. She sang for us, and father played his violin. A year later he was dead."

"How sad. And what a shock for you all. Seeing you with your brother and sisters suddenly makes your family very real to me."

"You mustn't be sad effendi. My father was a good man. I know he's in paradise with some of his friends. They can now play music forever and ever. Come along effendi, mother wishes to meet you."

Following Ali's gesture, as well as my nose, I went ahead into a room, the large family table in the middle indicating it to be a dining room, then into a kitchen, the source of the tantalising aroma.

Mrs Rashid was standing facing a sink, peeling onions under running water and wearing the traditional woman's headdress and gallibaya. She turned and smiled when she heard us enter.

"Mother, may I introduce Captain Fry," Ali said. "Captain Fry. Please meet my mother."

"Welcome Captain," Mrs Rashid said, drying her hands on a towel. "I hope Ali has asked you to stay for lunch. It is simple food. But you might enjoy it."

"It's kind of you to invite me Mrs Rashid. And I'd be delighted."

"My son speaks highly of you Captain. An invitation to lunch is the least we can do to thank you for your kindness."

Older than the woman holding the baby in the photograph, Mrs Rashid appeared less beautiful and somewhat tired, no doubt reflecting the difficulties that she has endured since being widowed. But her eyes spoke of her intelligence, honesty, and courage. Plainly, Mrs Rashid was fiercely independent and proud, the kind of woman who would fight for her rights and those of her family.

"Please Ali," she said. "Take the Captain into the sitting room. I'll ask your sister to bring you both mint tea. That is of course Captain, that you like mint tea."

"Certainly I do Mrs Rashid. Thank you."

It was pleasant being alone with Ali and without Mervyn, who tended to act rather sullenly around him, undoubtedly jealous of our developing friendship. Sitting together in the sunlit room, with the hum of the traffic passing in the street below, I dared to broach the question I had been yearning to ask Ali since he invited me into the apartment.

"Why all the electrical wires everywhere Ali?"

"I noticed you looking at them effendi. But there's nothing to be done about them. It would cost a great deal of money to have the apartment properly wired."

"But why wasn't it done when the block was built?"

"In the 1870's, Shari El Khadre was a most fashionable street in which to live. My father said many famous writers, poets, singers, and artists lived in this block. In those days, the rooms were lit by gas. But at the end of the century, electricity came to Cairo and gas was seen to be dangerous, although people were still allowed to use it for cooking. In those days, and even now, the owners of the building were Jews, so when it came to installing electricity, they did it cheaply."

"By not chasing the wires into the walls or under the floors and ceilings."

"Exactly effendi."

"But that's more dangerous than gas brackets. Surely it's not the same in all the apartments?"

"Mostly effendi. Those who own, and can afford, have done the work. But mother and father rented, so after he died there was never enough money."

A girl wearing a school uniform entered the room carrying a tray, on it two glasses of mint tea.

"Effendi. Please meet my sister Fatimah. Fatimah, may I introduce Captain Fry."

Shyly, Fatimah offered me a glass on a saucer, which I took, balancing them both on my knee, until Ali moved a small table to the side of the sofa, doing the same with another for himself.

"Have you told your mother about your race winnings?" I asked when we were alone once more. "Just to let you know, before Mervyn and I left for Giza I opened an account for you at the Bank of Egypt."

"Thank you effendi. Yes I did. But you know what mothers are. She scolded me for risking my money. But I think she's secretly pleased that the family's a little more secure."

"How do you feel about joining us on our trip?"

"I am honoured effendi. You are very kind to think of me. I will try not to be a bother."

"Ali! How could you possibly be a bother? The honour is mine. See it as a thank you for the assistance and pleasure you've given Mervyn and I. I've also taken the liberty of booking us on the Sunshine Express, leaving Cairo tomorrow night. But in the morning, I'd like us both to go to the bank because you need to sign a few documents."

"Very well effendi."

"I've an idea. Afterwards, let's visit Tirings and get you a suit of clothes for the trip. I know you're proud to be a dragoman, but if you wear European clothes, people will see you as more of an equal and treat you as such. I know it sounds terribly snobbish, but things like that are important these days.

"You are most kind effendi."

"And from now on, how about calling me Ron? After all, we're friends, and friends call each other by their first names."

"Very well effendi. I mean Ron. But I'll begin tomorrow if I may. Mother wouldn't understand the familiarity."

Ali suggested we visit the bathroom to wash our hands. When we returned, Fatimah was there and beckoned us into the dining room, where the table was laid with a white, lace-trimmed tablecloth, glittering cutlery, and glasses, along with shining china plates. But it was the bowls containing various colourful and delicious looking concoctions of salads, vegetables, beans, rice and breads, which really caught my eye.

Ali stood at a chair and motioned me to do the same, although it seemed I was to take the chair at the head of the table. Shortly, another girl, again dressed in school uniform, came to the table, carrying a large china tureen, setting it down in the centre.

"My younger sister, A'ishah, effendi," Ali said. "Both my sisters are home from school for their lunch. A'ishah! This is my friend Captain Fry, who I've told you about."

"Good day Captain," said A'ishah. "We are honoured to have you as our guest. Mother is with our little brother. She will be here in a moment."

Lunch was formal. Because, in true Arab custom, as Ali's family began to eat, the lack of personal cutlery made me realise, it was a requisite I eat with my fingers using only my right hand. By this time, I had watched Ali perform the custom many times, but never thought that I would do the same. However, keeping a close eye on my friend, and without too many mishaps, I began shovelling rice, lentils, and a savoury tomato sauce, topped with crispy fried onions into my mouth. I knew this dish to be Kusharie. Which, by now was a particular favourite, deciding to ask Ali for the recipe, so Mrs Lanesome might make it for Mervyn and I when we return to England.

Unless spoken to by Mrs Rashid, as the meal began, except for joining everyone in saying 'Bismillah', before we sat down, Ali's sister A'ishah failed to speak, Ali and Fatimah speaking rarely. This then left the conversation strictly, and a little stiffly, to be conducted between Mrs Rashid and myself.

"I hope your son is feeling better Mrs Rashid," I said after yet another long pause, during which I helped myself to more Kusharie, as wells as feta salad.

"Thank you Captain. Just now, Ahmad managed to eat a little food. He says his throat is very sore. For a while, I was worried. There's a great deal of diphtheria in Cairo. But the doctor has reassured me it is the beginning of a cold."

"May I say Mrs Rashid, how impressed I am with you and your children's power of English?"

"Thank you Captain. Ali's father was keen for his children to get the best education. He worked hard to keep them at the English School in Shari Al Tura Bulaqiya. The annual fee for my three elder children was one hundred and thirty five pounds. By the time Ali left to go to Fuad University, little Ahmad was attending the infant school."

"So girls are also able to enter the school?"

"Certainly Captain. I attended as a girl of sixteen when the war was two years old. Sister Margaret Clare and Archdeacon Horan founded the English School in 1916. My father was Coptic and keen for his children to get a good education."

"But you, Ali and his sisters, are Muslim."

"My husband was a Muslim. I converted to Islam in order we might marry."

"Was that normal?"

"No Captain. My family disowned me. Hamid, my husband, was more fortunate to have less orthodox parents. Ali and his sisters and brother have never known their maternal grandparents."

Ali nodded gravely.

"My teachers were the best in Cairo effendi," he said, while glancing at his mother for permission to speak. "Most were English. Mr Grose, the headmaster, has been at the school for nearly twenty years. He used to be an administration official, with a promising career in Government. But when the education department transferred him to the post of temporary headmaster, he so loved the school, he gave up his job to undertake the position full time, despite taking a huge dip in wages. He is a wonderful man, and became a good friend as I passed through the school. Mr Grose is very encouraging, and dedicated to seeing his pupils achieve their goals in life."

***

Reading this chapter after several months have passed, I feel sad because several weeks later Ali's mentor friend and headmaster, Mr Grose, was killed in an automobile accident on the Cairo-Suez road.

***

"If you don't mind me asking," I said. "If it's called the English School, how did you manage, being of the Muslim faith?"

"When the war began," Ali continued, "because of submarine activity in the Mediterranean, British government officials and their wives became reluctant to send their children back to school in

England, where they might very well remain for the duration of the war. And as mother has already mentioned, Sister Margaret Clare and Archdeacon Horan of All Saints Church began the school. Mother was one of its first pupils."

While Ali recounted the history and guidelines of his old school, I secretly took a moment to glance around the table at his mother and sisters. All were gazing at him tenderly and listening intently. Despite his tender years, Ali was definitely the man of the house.

"I entered the school at five years of age," he continued. "Of course, I didn't know that I was only allowed to be there because the school was going through a financial crisis at the time, and needed to increase its revenue. For this reason, the committee changed the 'only European' policy to allow Muslims, Greeks, and Jews. Our religions were accommodated for accordingly. The Muslim children went to the hall at midday for the Dhuhr prayers, and by Asr we had finished school and at home."

"What year are you in Fatimah?" I asked Ali's older sister.

"My final year Captain," she answered shyly, glancing in my direction, her brown eyes shining beneath long dark eyelashes

"What will you do when you leave? I imagine you'll try for university."

Fatimah blushed and glanced at her mother for approval. However, Mrs Rashid answered for her daughter.

"My husband and I planned for Fatimah to study medicine. But as I am now a widow, the medical school fees are too high."

"What a shame," I said.

"It is God's will Captain. There's a perfectly good secretarial college now in Cairo. Isn't there Fatimah?"

"Yes mother," answered Fatimah. Although her voice betrayed disappointment, giving me the impression the issue was a bone of contention between mother and daughter.

Suddenly, it was clear this family needed help. Not only were they living in a potential death trap, but also the future of each child was frustrated by their poverty. The money in Ali's account would grow interest, should he leave it there. But with everyday expenses, rent and power bills, it would not sustain the Rashid family forever.

In true Fry fashion I began to hatch a plan that might see Ali and Fatimah's ambitions realised, and guarantee A'ishah's, Ahmad, and Mrs Rashid's future life. In addition, my scheme would also need to take into consideration the work necessary to replace the dangerous electrical wiring.

Mrs Rashid's dessert course caused me to break the resolution I made only the day before, and half way up the little Pyramid, where I promised to cease eating sweets and biscuits, since the table suddenly became the bearer of numerous silver gilt trays, each containing a different and delectable Egyptian dessert.

We began by consuming Cinnamon Date Cake, along with strong, sweet, frothy coffee, of which I was now careful not to drink the sludge at the bottom of the cup.

Also, small crispy, fried, honey coated, dough balls called Awamat.

Then chocolate-coated dates, as well as Halva, which Ali said was toasted sesame seeds pounded into a paste, then mixed with something called tahini; an oily cream made from the same seed. Halva is made by adding honey, cinnamon and spices to the tahini.

In conclusion, my favourite sweet Baklava appeared, which needs no description.

In truth, how I ever got up from the table once we had said 'Alhamdulillah' was a miracle.

After thanking Mrs Rashid and saying goodbye to Fatimah and A'ishah, Ali accompanied me down the stairs and into the street.

"Thank you Ali," I said, as we shook hands. "That was wonderful, and so unexpected. But such a trouble for your mother. All that food. With you as the only breadwinner, how on earth can you afford to eat like that every day?"

Ali laughed. "We don't. The meal was for you. It is the manner of Islam to honour our guest and see he is well treated. Should we have unexpected visitors, Mother has always something put aside."

"I didn't mean her to go to so much bother."

"It's never a bother. We see it as an honour to be hospitable."

"Well it's an admirable characteristic that I wish some of my own countrymen possessed."

"For a man who is so kind, making you happy is the least my

family can do. Think of us as your family."

"I'm honoured Ali. Truly I am. I'll see you at the hotel tomorrow morning at about nine o'clock. Is that alright?"

"Of course Ron."

For a moment, hearing him say my name, instead of the very formal effendi, touched my heart, and I quickly crossed the street for fear he would see the tears in my eyes.

Chapter Twenty Nine
Suddenly I felt I was back in the army and sharing the toilet block with my comrades

Most undignified wolf whistles issued from the terrace as the caleche deposited me on the steps of Shepheard's, where immediately I saw the origin of the gaiety. Mervyn, Harry, Trooper Harding and Trooper Shaw, were sitting at the railing, showing signs of having been there a considerable time, judging by the number of beer bottles on the table.

Not being too keen to join in the frivolity, I crossed the pavement until I was looking up at them.

"Here you are!" Mervyn said, getting up and leaning over the rail. "I was beginning to worry. Where've you been?"

He was well on the way to being drunk, and I wished I could have persuaded him to go to our room and lay down, but realised the suggestion would be regarded as most inappropriate in present company.

"I met Ali. And his mother gave us lunch," I said instead. "Have you had lunch?"

"No. The lads and I caught the tram from the barracks and got stuck into the beer as soon as we arrived."

"Obviously," I said, feigning amusement. "How are you boys?"

"Fine Captain Fry," Harry, Peter, and Jim said in unison. "Getting a bit squiffy."

"If we're going to the Kit Kat Club tonight you'd better slow down. Why don't all of you come up and lay down for a while?"

"Now that's an invitation ain't it Pete!" Harry exclaimed, nudging Trooper Harding in the ribs. "What do you say lads? Do you feel like doing a bit of, lying down?"

By his intimation, along with Trooper Shaw and Trooper Harding's raucous laughter, I became convinced my cover was blown. Nonetheless, I believed no malice was intended. In addition, Mervyn seemed to take the insinuation with a pinch of salt, indicating, that sometime during my absence, the whole affair had been an issue of discussion, in which some rational decisions had been reached. If truth were told, I felt relieved instead of confronted, recognising that from henceforth, with these men at least, Mervyn and I could be ourselves. To my surprise, Harry responded to my suggestion in the affirmative.

"Ron's right," he said. "I don't know about you blokes, but I could do with a nap. By the look of things, it's going to be a long night."

The Troopers appeared extremely smart in their dark blue dress uniforms, instead of the usual khaki jackets, jodhpurs, and leggings. As a result, once they were in the room, it was quite an experience when they decided to strip down to their vests and underpants, reminding me of the night at 'Les Dancing Dubois' in Toulon.

Mervyn was equally tipsy, so he also decided to remove his clothes, and flopped on his bed, quickly joined by Jim Shaw. While Harry and Harding occupied mine. Where, after a boyish bout of Greco Roman wrestling, they fell asleep, and in no time, all four were snoring happily. Convinced that nothing would disturb them, I ran a bath and looked forward to a long wallow in its depths.

Like most, I do my best thinking in the early hours, before either rising, or lying in a warm bath. So it was here I began to plan a means to allay the predicament of Ali's family.

Since leaving England, it has been my habit to check backdated copies of The Times in order to keep track of the share prices. At the last count, my shares in the firm are valued at one hundred and seventy eight shillings and sixpence each. The overall previous year's profit for Fry Sugar, as announced in The Times the preceding week, being a cool ten million six hundred and forty three thousand pounds. The amalgamation of my great uncle's company with other smaller sugar manufacturers at the beginning of the century was a protective measure against the monstrous American Sugar Refining Company that threatened to destroy the British sugar industry. This resulted in the Fry Sugar Company becoming the fourth largest single corporation in the world.

As you are well aware, I have few financial worries. My donations to charities and organisations in England, the gifts I often give to friends, the donation to the Abbassia hospital for a new operating theatre and recreation facilities, as well as Mervyn's monthly stipend, hardly make a dent in my substantial fortune.

Therefore, one more arrangement would barely alter the status quo.

Accordingly, I resolved to wire my solicitors, Thring, Sheldon, and Ingram, requesting they create a standing order at Lloyds in Milsom Street, in order that each month an appropriate amount will enter Ali's account at the National Bank of Egypt. In fact, I was pleased I had taken the initiative to open the account, as it made the arrangement much easier to put in place. Also, I decided to ask Mr Thring to ensure my identity remain secret. Naturally, at some point, Ali will notice his account growing, rather than receding, and put two and two together as from whom the sum derives. Yet it has always been my custom, and the practise of my family, that we remain anonymous when gifts are given.

I realise I must reveal myself at some stage. How else will I see Ali resume his university life, and Fatimah, her place at medical school? So I made a decision to present them each with a cheque, sufficient to cover Ali's last year and Fatimah's seven.

With my plan in place, I shut my eyes and dozed, occasionally becoming conscious enough to turn on the hot tap in order to increase the temperature of the bath water.

Had it not been for the five o'clock call to prayer I think I might have spent the remainder of the evening in the bath. However, the doleful drone of the Muezzin calling from the minaret of Barquq

Mosque in the Musky was not entirely responsible for my waking, but also Harry and Peter Harding sharing the toilet in the corner of the bathroom.

"Sorry Ron," Harry said, turning and grinning. "We both woke up fit to bust. You'll look like a prune if you stay there much longer."

"Don't worry," I said, pulling the plug. "I'll be out in a jiffy. Are Mervyn and Jim awake?"

"Just about. Can Pete and I take a shower? I sweat to buggery when I'm asleep."

"Of course. Hand me a towel, and I'll get out and leave you boys to it."

Suddenly, I was back in the army, and sharing the toilet block with my comrades. It was really quite heartening.

In the bedroom, Mervyn and Jim Shaw were lying on the bed smoking cigarettes, the scene resembling an illustration I remember seeing in a novel entitled 'Le Livre Blanc'.

A friend told me about 'Le Livre Blanc'. As a consequence, when next in Paris I searched and found a copy in a bookshop on the left bank. In Paris a decade ago, it was easy to purchase books of a somewhat risqué nature. This book, a treatise on homosexual love, was written anonymously. However, the famous poet, dramatist, writer, and designer Jean Cocteau, in his preface to the book, did hint he might be the author. As my command of the French language amounts to the linguistic heights of 'Oui, No, and Pardon', my interest in the novel was solely visual and artistic. It was the eighteen explicit illustrations that fascinated me. The simple line drawings of naked young men in various positions, and states of excitement, have given me immense pleasure on cold winter nights throughout the subsequent years.

From its hiding place in the bottom draw of my bedside table 'Le Livre Blanc', beckoned to me, tempting me to take French lessons in order I might fully appreciate the message contained within its tantalising pages.

***

Everyone having dressed, shaved, showered, suitably coiffured, sprinkled with Eau de Cologne and toilet water, Mervyn and I followed troopers, Watson, Harding, and Shaw, down the hotel stairs and into the Long Bar.

"And what's it to be?" said Joe the Canadian barman. "The usual Captain Fry?"

"Thanks Joe," I said. "What about you lads? Scotch and soda Mervyn?" he nodded. "Harry?"

"I'll have a rum, if I may Captain."

Harding and Shaw also agreed to rum. Therefore, once fully armed with drinks, we found a table in the corner and sat down.

"How've you been Harry?" I asked, "I mean, since last we saw you."

"Funny you should ask Captain. I was about to tell you earlier, upstairs in the bathroom. On Monday, I was ordered to the office of our Division Head, Captain Chichester. I was truly nervous sitting in the waiting room. I'd no idea why I'd been called. I shouldn't have worried though, because as soon as he came through the door, he was all smiles and shook my hand."

"What did he want?" I asked. "Don't keep us in suspense."

By the smug look on Mervyn's face I could see he knew what his brother was about to say.

"I reckon the CO's had a hand in it," Harry continued. "Because they've decided to send me home to join the Army Physical Training Staff. I begin training at the college in Aldershot as soon as I get back. They're even going to write an article about me in the 'Charger'."

"That's splendid," I said. "That's your problem solved. What a stroke of luck."

"But hang on. Last Sunday, when we spoke in the lav, you told me you were going to see the C.O. Did you?"

"With all the spur of the moment arrangements when your brother and I decided to cut it to Giza on Monday afternoon, I clean forgot. I'm sorry Harry. It was my intention to see him tomorrow afternoon, before Mervyn and I catch the train. But now it looks like I won't need to."

Harry gave me a quizzical look, although my expression must have convinced him that I was telling the truth, because he shouted drinks to celebrate his transfer. When Mervyn and I were alone however, and while the boys were at the bar collecting the drinks, he challenged me.

"You're fibbing."

"Just a bit. But don't tell him. All this Kowtowing is embarrassing."

Once we had finished Harry's round, and after thanking Joe, we made our way to the front steps where we hailed a caleche.

Chapter Thirty
Dinner at the Kit Kat Club - George Calomiris exposed - Pranks with PO Evans

The downtown streets thronged with life, the pavements teeming with last minute shoppers, office workers hurrying to the tram stops, while the road traffic crawled at a snail's pace. The automobiles, trucks, donkey carts, and camels, either jostling for position, or drifting lazily out of the path of any approaching tram. By now, Mervyn and I were so accustomed to Cairo life that we let it pass almost unnoticed, as did Troopers Harding, Watson, and Shaw, squeezed together in the facing seat of the caleche.

Our trip took us through Bulaq, a district now entirely familiar to me, across Bulaq Bridge, through the elite district of Zamalek and over the Imbaba Bridge, where I was reminded of the naughty boys selling themselves on the walkway high above. My reverie was interrupted however, by a recognisable rumbling behind us, and looking at my wristwatch, my assumption was confirmed.

"The Sunshine Express!" I shouted over the noise. "It leaves Rameses Station at seven thirty."

"That's our train then!" yelled Mervyn as it passed within feet of us. "We'll be on it this time tomorrow lads."

Kit Kat Square was bursting with activity, the collection of tables and chairs occupied by mainly Europeans, either long-term Cairo residents, or foreign tourists, as well as army officers and lads from the ranks. The inner sanctum of the Kit Kat Club was comparatively quiet, since it is situated on a platform and separated from the main body of the club by steps on each side, also encircled by brass railings. Here, the tables were reserved for the influential and elite of the audience. Therefore, it was to this area I led my party, where the Maître D greeted us.

"A table for five please," I said, tipping him a pound.

The financial incentive seemed to do the trick, since he led us to a table facing the stage, even holding out my chair as I sat down.

As it filled with the who's who of Cairo, the troopers appeared entirely comfortable sitting in the exclusive section, despite being frequent visitors to the Kit Kat and accustomed to occupying seats in the main body of the club.

A Nubian waiter passed us, so I ordered a bottle of champagne and everyone lit cigarettes

"What's to eat?" asked Mervyn, taking a menu card from the centre of the table. "What's Consommé au Riz?"

"I think riz means rice in French," Jim Shaw said. "I've seen it written on the side of sacks in the barracks kitchen."

"Consommés is soup," I said. "But I've never heard of it containing rice."

"How about, Darnes de Barbues?" Harry asked, frowning. "What on earth's that Ron?"

"We'll ask the waiter when he comes back."

It was slightly odd to sit in the open air, under a virtually black sky, while around us the sparkling women's gowns attempted to out-dazzle the millions of stars overhead. No music played, only a gentle ripple of conversation was heard, along with the clink of glasses and the occasional burst of raucous laughter from the groups of squaddies below in the main area beyond the rail.

As the champagne started to take effect, Harry, Peter and Jim began to regale Mervyn and I with a few stories of army life, some more repeatable than others. Although one, I really must relate.

"A wily Greek owns this place," began Jim, lowering his voice mysteriously. "He's notorious. Most of us lads are careful to steer clear of him, and the men he employs."

"Why's that?" Mervyn asked.

"Hey! I hope you both won't mind us telling you this?" interrupted Harry. "He's a bit like you two, if you know what I mean."

"But we wouldn't imagine either of you would do anything like the things he does," added Peter Harding.

"Tell us! For heaven's sake," I exclaimed, laughing, and once more filling our glasses.

"His name's George Calomiris," Jim said, taking up the story again. "They reckon he's a millionaire, and one of the richest men in Egypt. But he uses his limitless fortune to satisfy his unusual desires."

"Come on Jim," Harry whispered. "Don't pussy foot. He likes it up the arse Captain, plain and simple. Calomiris sends out a tout to find him a handsome young soldier. The tout promises the chap a general's salary, any girl he desires and a life of luxury, just so long as he remains available to service Calomiris' needs."

Mercifully, as the character Harry painted came to life in my mind, the dimly lit club, as well as the rosy glow of the candle on the table, hid my blushes. Mervyn too was unusually quiet, perhaps unaccustomed to hearing his brother speak so candidly.

"Once the handsome young soldier is found," said Peter Harding. "He's installed in a suite at the National Hotel, also owned by George, and given the choicest food and drink, along with a harem of dancing girls, mostly pulled from the chorus line of this club. Then, all the lucky chap need do is leave a little of himself for Calomiris when he calls."

"How extraordinary!" I exclaimed, endeavouring not to display too much envy in my voice. "How long does this go on? Surely the soldier's absent without leave."

"Exactly Ron!" Harry exclaimed. "But George is always caught in the end. The rumour is that the manager of the National Hotel, who's also a Greek, has a conscience about how George treats the young soldiers. So, when George is paying a visit he gives the game away to the CID, who raid the suite, catch George and the not so unfortunate chap, 'at it', so to speak. Although, the odd thing is buggery, if you'll excuse the expression Ron, is not a crime in Egypt, but harbouring a runaway is a prisonable offence. How come Calomiris only ever pays a fine? The word is the CID takes his bribes and as soon as the coast's clear, George is up to his old tricks again."

"A mate of mine told me," put in Peter Harding, "Calomiris is very funny when he gets caught. Apparently, he puts on a pitiful display, clutching his arse, saying it's his downfall."

Although the story had been extremely frank, also rather shocking coming as it did from the lips of heterosexual men, I joined everyone in laughing wholeheartedly.

"Hey! How come your mate knows that Pete?" Harry asked when we had composed ourselves. "He must have been there at the time."

"Do you know! You're right Harry. I've never thought of it that way. Mind you, I've always thought him a bit of a bender. He hangs around the bogs a lot, combing his hair in the mirror."

The drink was obviously taking effect because, once again, we all burst into boisterous laughter, causing heads to turn, and frowns from the occupants of the surrounding tables.

How astonishing I thought. Here I am, a man of my years, completely at ease, sitting with three young lads, while exchanging conversation of such a nature. Finally, I felt accepted, no shame marring our friendship, and by his expression, I knew Mervyn was feeling the same.

"What shall we have then?" I asked, once order was restored. "I'll grab that fellow over there. He might be able tell us what's on the menu."

A tall Nubian waiter approached, wearing the customary baggy, dark blue pantaloons, red embroidered bolero jacket, and red tarbush. He bowed austerely when he arrived at the table.

"Excuse me," I said, trusting he understood English. "Can you tell us what 'Darnes du Barbues' is?"

As if he were about to make a speech, the Nubian coughed and cleared his throat.

"Fish steaks sir."

"What kind of fish?" Mervyn and Harry said in unison.

"Sometimes Catfish. But tonight, brill. The dish comes with French fried potatoes and a remoulade sauce."

For a man with a face as black as pitch, thick lips, and a bulbous, flat nose, he spoke awfully good English, complete with an accent that would not sound out of place at any English public school. I wondered what environment had prompted this somewhat refined, slightly affected, enunciation.

"What's in the sauce?" Jim asked.

"I am only the waiter sir, not the chef," replied the Nubian stiffly. "I'm afraid I have no idea."

"How about the 'Grenadins Du Veau'," I said. "Veau is veal is it not?"

"Correct sir. Veal steaks, cooked in pork fat, vegetables and Madeira."

"That sounds nice," Mervyn said.

Harry was endeavouring to pronounce the French.

"Poulet Au Fayoum Rotis," he said. "Doesn't poulet mean chicken, and rotis roast?"

The Nubian nodded gravely.

"Then I'll have roast chicken. But I don't know what the Fayoum means."

"I believe sir, Fayoum is a town about eighty miles southwest of here. It is the site of Crocodilopolis, the oldest city in Egypt. Also, I believe the Roman portrait mummies were discovered there."

For a moment, no one spoke, clearly stunned by the Nubian's answer. Furthermore, had my camera been equipped with a flashbulb, the expressions on the faces of everyone would have made a photograph well worth keeping. It was obvious the Nubian was slumming, perhaps earning cash on the side to aid his progress through higher education. Unfortunately, we never had the opportunity to find out.

In the end, I ordered the fish, Harry, Mervyn, and Peter, the chicken, and Jim the veal, no one fancying the consommé. I made sure there was salad, plenty of fried chips and Pommes Chateau, which, according to our intelligent waiter were peeled potatoes, turned into an oval shape, and then roasted in butter.

All of a sudden, a commotion in the main auditorium drew our attention, and standing to look over the railings, we saw a donkey cavorting between the seated guests, a young airman riding on its back, jokingly whipping the animal with a stick of celery. To the cheers of his mates, and the shouts of the donkey's owner, the young man proceeded to mount the steps leading up to our section of the club.

"That's P O Evans!" shouted Peter Harding. "He's a Pilot Officer with 112 Squadron. But in his other life he's a professional jockey. He races at Heliopolis. We've put money on him many times, haven't we lads."

The donkey was small, and so was P O Evans. How he ever saw out the cockpit window to fly a plane, I found hard to imagine.

"Ride him cowboy!" Harry yelled, causing a spatter of laughter from the people sitting in our vicinity.

P O Evans and the donkey clambered onto the stage, where they performed a floor show all of their own, going backwards and forwards along the footlights to the cheers of the crowd, which by now had fully entered into the spirit of things. This cabaret might have continued had it not been for the interference of two burly henchmen, undoubtedly employees of George Calomiris judging by their size and smarmy appearance. With the crowd whistling for all its worth, both men climbed the steps at either end of the stage and advanced on Evans and the donkey, one grappling the animal's head, while the other hauled Evans off its back. Evans was plainly the worse for wear. But he bravely made a play for one burly brute, although he stood little chance against the henchman, who simply put his hand on the young chap's forehead, while Evans flailed uselessly with his fists. One such performance I remember seeing in a Charlie Chaplain film, and so had the rest of the audience by the way people laughed and applauded. Furthermore, and as if the entire sketch had been meticulously rehearsed, while the other henchman led the donkey across the stage to the top of the steps, the petrified creature urinated over the footlights, causing them to short out. Mercifully, donkey and henchman appeared a little singed, but unharmed.

Had the evening ended there, I would have been entirely happy, because I was unable to remember a time when I had laughed more.

Then our meals arrived, so everyone adjourned to the serious business of eating.

I recollect remarking that my fish tasted slightly muddy. Then, I suppose a brill would, seeing it is a bottom-feeding type of fish. Harry, Mervyn, and Peter said their chicken was delicious, although they were unable to see any link between a roast pullet and a load of Roman mummies. Jim enjoyed his veal in Madeira, nonetheless said it was rather rich.

To finish everyone chose fruit salad, refreshed with Kirsch, and a board arrived containing the most interesting collection of cheeses I had yet to see. Had Ali been present, he would have told us that the cream coloured, textured cheese was Roumy, the salty white and creamy one, Domyati, and the crumbly white cheese, Areesh.

He would also have warned us, that the cheese in the clay pot was Mesh cheese, a collection of old cheeses and yoghurt, mixed with red chillies and any other fitting ingredients. Left to ferment, the older it was, the better it tasted. He would also have cautioned us to look carefully for live worms, which may have invaded the cheese over time.

Our appetites suitably satisfied, we settled back with a bottle of Taylor's and five good Havana cigars and waited for the cabaret to begin.

Chapter Thirty One
Farid Al Atrash - Badia Masabni and Naguib Al Rihani - The Sultana of Romance Hekmet Fahmy

Not only was the seating area of the Kit Kat Club unique, but also at this point I feel I should spend a moment to describe the stage, as it certainly warrants a mention. With the Egyptian weather being as it is, there is little risk of rain spoiling the show, as a result, many venues in Cairo are open to the sky. Accordingly, the stage was more akin to a large podium, an array of tall white classical columns, making it appear like a Grecian temple, although minus a roof. Overall, it was remarkably plain given the typical decoration seen around Cairo.

Spotlights, on the top of high metal poles, trained pink light on fine gauze suspended between the two central columns, while green light shone upwards inside niches at either end of the podium. Presumably, the middle opening was the performance place, while the side positions were for the orchestra. My guess was proven correct when shadowy, ghoulishly green figures, carrying musical instruments, appeared in each niche.

Once settled in their seats, and without a moment to tune up, a haunting melody began to emanate, reminiscent of our night at Café Riche. Then, as if from nowhere, a young man appeared in a spotlight, and judging by the applause, he was a popular performer at the club.

"You're regulars lads!" asked Mervyn. "Who's he?"

"Farid Al Atrash," Harry said. "He's a singer. You wait until you hear him. He has an unusual voice. Not a bit like yours Mervyn."

This was the first time I had heard Harry speak of his brother's voice, signifying that he too was aware of Mervyn's talent. If what Harry said was true, I waited expectantly for the young man to sing.

While the orchestra continued, Al Atrash came down from the stage in order to kiss the hands of several European society women seated amongst the front tables, to the obvious annoyance of their male escorts.

"He's a real ladies man," Peter said. "Lucky devil. He can have any girl he pleases."

"I can see that," I said. "With his looks I'm not surprised."

Dressed immaculately in a dinner suit and black bow tie, Farid was indeed handsome, with thick, jet-black hair, unusually pale skin for an Egyptian, and the sultriest eyes I had ever seen.

At last, the orchestra finished a long, elaborate phrase and Farid was allowed to sing. And sing he did, like a bird, albeit an Egyptian bird, bearing in mind the honey like quality of his voice and the dexterity of his warbling. Except, I had to agree with Harry, since Mervyn's voice was entirely different to Al Atrash, due to their opposing cultures and influences. But that is no reason to decry either, as each warrants praise for their beautiful quality and masterful control.

The lads were keen for the entertainment to move on apace. However, they began to fidget as Farid's song took yet another diversion into improvised poetic segments, sometimes lasting as long as five minutes.

Beyond the railing, in the plebeian section of the club, the squaddies were less patient, becoming restless. They were here to see the dancing girls after all, and not to hear some young man crooning in Arabic. Therefore, despite loud appeals to be quiet from people wishing to appreciate the singing, the young soldiers in the lower section began a chorus of, 'Why are we waiting?' to the tune of 'Oh Come all ye Faithful'. It pleased me that even though they could plainly hear their colleague's caterwauling, Harry, Peter, and Jim refrained from joining them.

Farid's song did eventually end, and he approached the microphone.

"Ladies and Gentlemen," he said, his voice reverberating between the loudspeakers positioned around the square. "Welcome to the Kit Kat. It is my great pleasure to be your host for the evening. Tonight, we are honoured to have as our guest the creator of the Kit Kat club, as well as the Opera Cabaret."

A follow spot emanating from a platform behind us flashed on, the operator trailing its beam across the gathering, clearly searching for the honoured guest. It finally alighted on the small glittering figure of a woman seated at a table, beside her, a distinguished gentleman sporting a moustache and beard, dressed in an immaculate dinner suit, crimson tarbush, and tassel.

"Ladies and Gentlemen," continued Farid. "I am proud to present the elite of Cairo show business, Badia Masabni, and our Kesh Kesh Bey himself, Badia's esteemed husband, Naguib Al Rihani."

Rihani got to his feet and bowed, while Badia remained seated, nodding to her left and right, as a European aristocrat might do as her carriage passed the cheering crowds.

Naturally, I knew of Opera Cabaret, or Madame Badia's Cabaret, as it was more commonly called. It was already well established during the war years, and extremely popular with the British Tommies. Also with Australians and New Zealanders, the former anticipating action in Palestine, or relocating to France, while the latter would face the madness of Gallipoli.

Badia Masabni is responsible for originating the image and costume worn by the Oriental Dancer, which European artists like Austrian, Rudolf Ernst, and American, Charles Godfrey Leland, created in Victorian times. Realising that Europeans were the most frequent visitors to Egypt, to please a potential audience, Badia dressed her dancers accordingly.

With her innovative choreography, Badia is famous for changing the style of Oriental Dance. A Belly Dancer, incidentally a title invented by the French not the Arabs, with Badia's new steps, can now use the entire performance area. She gyrates her hips and moves her arms in a choreographed way, not improvised, as was the custom for hundreds of years.

Because of the increasing size of modern Middle Eastern clubs and cabarets, it was necessary for the dancer to be seen at a greater distance. As a result, and as a way of drawing the attention of the audience, Badia introduced props into the routine; for example, veils, tambourines, finger symbols, canes, drums, scimitars, and even live snakes.

Badia's Casino became the haunt of Cairo's 'le beau monde', everyone wishing to be seen at Badia's cabaret. As a young Captain in the Royal Flying Corps, I recollect feeling extremely important walking through the lobby amongst the 'mieux dans la société'. Then, taking my seat with my fellow officers and ordering a bottle of the best French champagne.

The only disparity between my flying corps chums and me was that they were there to ogle the wobbly bits of girls dressed in chiffon and wearing bangles, coins, and veils. Whereas I was craftily leering in the other direction at handsome young Egyptian men, or the muscular chests of Nubian waiters dressed in nothing but baggy pantaloons, and sleeveless, gold braided boleros.

"Have you ever seen a Naguib Al Rihani's film Ron?" Harry asked, catapulting me back to the present. "He's quite funny. A while ago, Pete and I went to see Errol Flynn in 'Charge of the Light Brigade', at the Metropole, and Rihani's was the B picture. It was all in bloody gyppie. But if you were quick you could pick up the story from the words going along underneath."

"He reminded us of Will Hay," Pete said. "All facial expressions. You know the sort. You don't need to understand what he was saying. Just his face makes you laugh."

"Mervyn! Didn't we eat at his restaurant the day we first met Ali?" I asked, but received no response, because at that moment the lights on the stage went out, and except for the candles on the tables, everywhere was dark.

"And now ladies and gentlemen," Farid said, from out of the darkness. "Straight from her latest triumph in Beirut, I give you 'The Jewel of the Nile', 'The Sultana of Romance'. Cairo's one and only,

Hekmet Fahmy."

For a moment, I looked away from the stage, turning my attention instead to my table companions, seeing their faces illuminated by candlelight, each man eagerly anticipating the appearance of their object of desire. Even Mervyn appeared expectant.

The sound of a drum penetrated the gloom as a pinpoint of light pierced the smoky room like the beam from a lighthouse searching the fog. Settling on the sheer curtain across the centre of the stage the light grew in size as the rhythm quickened, revealing the misty figure of a woman thrusting her hips forward to the beats of a Darbuka drum. Slowly the curtain parted as the distinctive sound of an oud joined the tempo, the spotlight turning our attention to the oud player, who was none other than, Farid Al Atrash, obviously not only a singer, but also an accomplished oud player.

Hekmet, now silhouetted against a ruddy backdrop depicting a sunset over the pyramids, shimmied towards the front of the stage, the coins on her belt jingling to the rhythm of the drum and the oud. A glow from the footlights began revealing her sinuous legs, swaying inside her pink, transparent harem pants. With her hips and belly materialising, light sparkled from the jewelled belt and a diamond brooch she was wearing in her navel. Her breasts were next to appear, large, encased in an elaborately embroidered and beaded brassiere. Lastly, we saw her face, and the crowd went wild.

Totally astonished by what I saw, I nearly fell off my chair. Believe it or not the sensuous creature shaking her shoulders, undulating her stomach and chest, all to the beat of the Darbuka, was none other than the beautiful siren I had encountered on the houseboat earlier that morning.

"It reminds me of riding a camel!" yelled Mervyn, over the cheers. "It's the same sort of movement."

Getting up from his seat, he demonstrated what he meant by thrusting his hips back and forth, to the amusement of everyone around the table. My attention however was fixed on Hekmet Fahmy. Her sultry eyes, the same I had seen peering through the jasmine; the raven locks now falling carefree about her shoulders, arms, snakelike, entwining in the air, her gently twisting fingers, this time holding not a cigarette, but tiny cymbals.

"I met her earlier today," I said to no one in particular.

At first, the lads appeared not to have heard over the drumming and applause. Then suddenly the realisation of what I had just said sunk in.

"You what?" Harry gasped.

"Hekmet and I met this morning," I continued. "She lives on a houseboat."

"However do you know that?" Mervyn asked. "What have you been up to Ron?"

"When I dropped you off at the Gezira Club this morning, I went looking for Ali's houseboat. Well hers is next door but one."

"You spoke to her?" Peter said, keeping his eyes on the stage, clearly not wishing to miss a single pulsating moment. "What did you talk about?"

Plainly, I was becoming the main attraction simply because I had exchanged conversation with the floorshow.

"She asked me aboard for a drink?"

"What did you do?" asked Harry.

"Well you know me lads. I took her up on her offer."

For a moment, each man took his eyes off Hekmet and looked at me, puzzled by my answer. But seeing my innocent expression, they burst out laughing.

"You're kidding of course," Mervyn said. "That would be the day."

"It certainly would my boy," I said. "Old Ron knows too well what side he bats for."

Pleased to see the merriment my joke produced, and aware there was increased light around us, I signalled our Nubian and ordered another bottle of champagne.

"But really Ron," Harry said. "What happened?"

"I asked her if she knew where Ali lived. She said she thought it might be two boats along. She said she liked tall men. They always met her expectations."

"Well that lets you out then Mervyn old chap."

"Then she invited me in," I continued.

"You don't say!" said Jim. "I would have been there like a shot. Mind you, they reckon she's not partial to the likes of us common troopers, but most of the officers in our unit have had her. The talk is she gets them tipsy and then wheedles information out of them, passing it to whoever's interested."

"I've heard she's a nationalist, and not a great lover of the British," Peter said.

"She didn't give me that impression. She was really quite pleasant."

Throughout this conversation, Hekmet twirled and pivoted about the stage, the rhythm becoming faster as the orchestra attempted to keep pace with her increasing choreography. At one point, she shimmied towards Farid, who took over the melody with his oud, improvising dexterously to her every move, until the air was full of trills, jangles, twangs, and beats. Then all of a sudden, it was over. The spotlight and footlights went out, and the audience rose to its feet to show its appreciation.

Chapter Thirty Two
Hekmet Fahmy, belly dancer, and international spy - Royal command performance

"Wow!" Harry shouted. "That was fantastic! They sell postcards at the entrance. Photographs of the dancers. Do you think she'll autograph one for me? If she knows you Ron, she might."

The lights switched on to reveal Hekmet standing at the top of the steps, deftly avoiding the coins that were showering onto the stage. Then the orchestra began to play again and Farid Al Atrash began another tune. Hekmet commenced to gyrate, shimmy, and pump once again. Although this time, she descended the steps into the audience, her arms twisting in the air like a pair of snakes, while her hips popped back and forth.

Reaching the first table, Hekmet swivelled up to an old man who promptly leaned forward and tucked a wad of Egyptian pounds into her belt, while more paper money and coins showered from the surrounding tables, resounding and fluttering around her feet.

Subsequently, and completely unashamedly, she turned to our table and began sensuously undulating towards us, shaking her shoulders in time to Farid's oud. Once within touching distance she recognised me and smiled.

"Ron! It's your lucky night," Mervyn shouted over the music. "Give me some money. We should give her something."

With her shoulders quivering, causing her breasts to wobble,

Hekmet pushed the pair towards my face, causing Harry, Pete, and Jim to jump to their feet and clap furiously.

She was so close I could see her glistening belly and smell her sweat, musky, slightly reminiscent of Nile water, yet tinged with a hint of jasmine oil.

"Ron!" yelled Mervyn. "Give me the money!"

Positively tearing my eyes away from Hekmet's juddering bosom, I reached into my jacket pocket, and finding my wallet, took out a few pounds. I had no idea how many. Mervyn snatched them, and rotating his way around the table, all the while mimicking Hekmet's arms, and hip thrusts, he rolled up the notes and stuffed them into the chasm between her breasts, producing a huge burst of applause from the audience.

Hekmet returned to the stage, shimmying, twisting, thrusting, and coiling, until suddenly, in one last spiralling turn, the orchestra stopped, the lights went out to the whistles and stamps of the crowd.

"I'm going to run to the kiosk to buy some postcards," Harry said. "With any luck she'll come out in the interval. She usually does."

"I'll come too," Mervyn said.

"Me too," said Jim.

As they hurried away, our Nubian friend arrived holding a bottle of champagne, which he duly opened, placing it in the ice bucket beside my chair.

"That's why we like this place." Peter said, as I filled his glass. "You never know what you're going to see. There's never a programme. Last time, one of Badia's girls began her dance lying on her back on a platform covered in carpets, where she squirmed around like a snake, wearing a crown of lit candles on her head. But it's never been as good as tonight, because down there you don't get such a good view."

He gestured to the plebeian section of the club.

"You've spoiled us Ron. From now on we'll never want to sit anywhere else."

Peter Harding was a pleasant chap. I liked him from the moment we met at the barracks almost a fortnight ago. Was it really just two weeks? So much has happened. It seemed a lifetime since Mervyn and I stepped off the ship.

Pete was older than the other men. Older and wiser as the saying goes. Fond of his pipe and taking a back seat, he allowed the younger chaps to let off steam and dominate the conversation. There was also a gentleness about his manner. A way one finds in people brought up in the countryside, where life is simple and slow. Not that Peter lacked courage. One could see in his eyes that he was stalwart and loyal, and would defend a friend right up to the bitter end. Just the sort of chap one would be proud to call your offsider.

Harry, Jim, and Mervyn returned, each holding a picture postcard of Hekmet Fahmy.

"In mine, she's dancing with a sabre," Harry said, sitting down next to me and pouring himself a glass of champagne.

"Mine has her posed on a couch," Jim said, offering Harry his empty glass. "She looks really lovely."

"My photograph has her wearing a candleholder of lit candles," Mervyn said, giving me the impression he was rather more interested in the candleholder than any other apparatus Hekmet might possess.

A murmur in the crowd drew my attention to a door at the side of the stage, which opened to reveal a young man, followed by one of the henchmen who entertained us previously. Standing over him, the burly fellow waited while the young man collected the coins and notes scattered around the stage and the front tables, ours included. Then they disappeared through the door. However they left it open as a young woman slipped through, dressed in a stylish, crimson, worsted two piece suit, which appeared to be fresh from a Parisian couturier.

Of course, the woman was Hekmet Fahmy, and to my amazement, she headed directly towards our table. Immediately, Harry jumped up as he saw her approach.

"Please Miss Fahmy," he said, holding out his chair. "Please sit down."

"Thank you young man. And we'll need another. I've asked Mr Calomiris to join us. I know he won't want to miss the second half of the show."

Hekmet gazed at me from under her long black eyelashes, at the

THE MERRY MILLIONAIRE

same time darting her eyes to the bottle of champagne in the bucket. Then our Nubian friend was at my side and I was ordering two more bottles, plus two extra glasses, one for Calomiris and one for Hekmet.

"Darling! How nice to see you again," she purred. "So soon since our last meeting. This time it is you who is offering me a drink."

Out of the corner of my eye, I could see the reaction I would have expected from the lads.

"Miss Fahmy, I'm sorry I was unable to take you up on your kind proposal this morning. It was rather early, and I was actually quite busy."

"Ah yes! Did you find your friend?"

"I did Miss Fahmy. Thank you."

"You know my name. What is yours, may I ask?"

Harry, without a chair of his own, and mesmerised by the close proximity of his pin up, had perched on the edge of Mervyn's seat, almost sitting in his brother's lap. All the while, spell bound, Peter, and Jim had their elbows on the table, their heads resting in their hands.

"Ronald," I mumbled as I too succumbed to Miss Fahmy's magnetism.

Surprisingly it was Jim Shaw, who summoned up the courage to speak first.

"Excuse me Miss Fahmy," he stammered. "Would you be kind enough to autograph my photograph please?"

"Show it to me darling."

Jim held it up for her to see.

"I remember that," Hekmet said, laughing. "A cheetah was supposed to be in the shot. They wanted it to lie on the floor beside me. But whatever they'd given it to eat that morning must have disagreed with it, because it was forever passing gas. We gave up in the end, and I did the shot alone."

Jim darted around the table, and giving her his fountain pen, waited for Miss Fahmy to sign the postcard. Harry was next, and lastly Mervyn. Consequently, as other gentlemen saw a queue forming at our table, they left their own and joined the line. As she signed postcard after postcard, Hekmet chatted to me quite casually.

"How long have you been in Cairo Ronald?" she asked as I lit her cigarette.

"Several weeks Miss Fahmy."

"It is a beautiful city. Is it not? Have you been up the Nile?"

"Not as yet. Mervyn and I are leaving for Luxor by train tomorrow night."

"Mervyn?" she asked, looking around the table.

"I'm Mervyn," Mervyn said modestly.

"Ah! The boy who gave me money. You are very brave Mervyn for one so young."

Mervyn blushed so deeply, even the rosy glow from the candles failed to hide his embarrassment.

Once the eighth autograph hunter was suitably satisfied, by a wave of her hand Miss Fahmy made it quite plain she was finished signing for the moment. And taking a glass from our Nubian, she held it while he filled it with champagne.

"And you boys," she said, directing her question to Harry, Jim and Peter. "Which unit are you from?"

"The Seventh Queen's Own Hussars Miss Fahmy," answered Harry.

"Ah! Yes. 'The Saucy Seventh'. I know it well. I'm well acquainted with Captain Chichester. Maybe you know him?"

"We do Miss Fahmy. He's captain of our division. A very fine gentleman."

"He is indeed. And well equipped for the service. You're soon to leave for the Canal Zone. Am I correct?"

It was then that I noticed Peter Harding imperceptibly nudge Harry, completely understanding his motive. Who knows where information given most innocently might eventuate?

"I've no idea Miss Fahmy," Harry said. "We're the last to hear these things."

If the boys were unaware of such arrangements, then I wondered how Miss Fahmy was acquainted with such knowledge. Obviously, she is on relatively intimate terms with someone within the Saucy Seventh, and it was not difficult to fathom out with whom.

"May I have another darling?" Hekmet said, draining her glass. "I get so thirsty after a show."

"I can well imagine," I said. "It looks most energetic."

"Sharqi must be spirited darling. We must keep the customers happy. Otherwise, we'd make no money.

"Then the money we saw thrown is yours. The club doesn't pay you."

"Bahia doesn't pay us darling. We dance for our money. And what you saw is not all mine. Half goes to the orchestra."

"You mean they don't get paid either," said Mervyn.

"No darling. The Nubians, the doormen, and the barmen are the only men who receive a wage. All the same, we girls get a commission on how much champagne the customers drink."

"Do you invent your own movements," said Harry, clearly itching to get into the conversation.

"Partly darling. Bahia choreographed my floor work. But the Sahara, the dance I began with, and the Tamr Henna in the second half, are set pieces I learnt as a girl."

"You moved so fast in the second dance," I said. "The musicians found it hard to keep up."

"In Sharqi cabaret dancing, the dancer conducts the band. She is the inspiration that directs the music. Tonight the Magency was too slow, so I needed to speed it up."

"What's Magency?" asked Mervyn.

"In England, I think it would mean overture."

Gradually, I was becoming aware that a style of dance I previously regarded as close to eroticism, simply aimed to titillate the palates of heterosexual men, was as classical a form of dance as the ballet. In fact, oriental dance was far older than most others.

"Does Badia supply your costumes?" I asked.

Hekmet laughed.

"Of course not darling. No girl wants another to have anything to do with what she wears. We make our own, or there are women in Cairo who do nothing else. Back on the boat, I have racks of costumes. In one year a Sharqi dancer must never be seen in the same costume twice."

As I mentioned earlier, on my jaunts with the lads from the Aero Factory to Madam Bahia's Cabaret I had never given belly dancing much thought. Rarely had I given the girls much attention. The male Nubian dancers were more to my taste, dressed in feather skirts and nothing else. Another attraction was Moussa, the famous snake charmer, playing a tune on his bungi, at the same time, coaxing an asp out of a basket. Badia also employed a rather handsome sword swallower, his act so terrifying I could almost sense his weapon down my own throat.

My recollections were interrupted by a commotion coming from the outer periphery of the club.

"There's a carriage pulled up at the entrance," Harry said, standing to get a better look. "Also a cavalry escort."

"It's the King," said Hekmet. "Trust him to miss my show. Tahia's the lucky one tonight."

Shortly, I noticed a squat, middle-aged Greek standing at the table next to ours. He was speaking with the occupants, seeming to be causing some consternation. However, the man and the woman quickly became resigned to their fate and capitulated, collecting their glasses, cigarettes, and lighters, following our Nubian carrying their champagne bottle to another table.

This hurried preparation could only mean one thing; we were to be table neighbours to King Farouk the first, and his entourage. This was certainly turning into a night to remember.

Chapter Thirty Three
In the presence of a King - Moussa, the snake charmer - Tahia Carioca

Any talking and laughter ceased as the orchestra hurried onto the stage and took their places, while Farid Al Atrash appeared in a spotlight, frantically gesturing to the operator to train the light on the royal guests and not on him.

Without warning, the orchestra began to play the Egyptian National Anthem, the jolly, um papa, music causing everyone to stand and place their burning cigarettes in their ashtrays. Then, to the cheers of the inebriated soldiers in the crowd, and with the follow spot lighting the young King's procession through the outer seating area, King Farouk climbed the steps and approached the area closest to the stage.

"We're lucky," Hekmet, said into my ear. "Had I not been sitting with you, Calomiris would have moved you instead of Lord and Lady Castlemaine."

"Was that Lord and Lady Castlemaine?" said Mervyn. "They were with us on the ship. Ron and I met them in Toulon. The old boy must have persuaded Lady Castlemaine against Khartoum."

"Calomiris troopers!" Harry whispered to his pals. "I wouldn't be bumming that greasy dago. You'd more than likely get a dose of the pox."

Low and behold, no sooner had his name been mentioned than

George Calomiris appeared, this time arriving at our table, standing stiffly as the National Anthem went into a second verse. It was a jolly tune and I wondered at the time who wrote it.

As the young King, his uncle, Mohammed Ali Tewfik, and several suited gentlemen reached the table beside ours, the orchestra played the last chord, and not until the royal party was seated did we resume our seats.

"Don't let him see you cross your legs," Calomiris said, as he sat in a chair hurriedly found by our Nubian, "It's against royal protocol."

Mervyn made a face at his brother, causing Harry to snort and stifle a laugh. However, there was no time for further reaction as the lights in the club dimmed and we heard the whining sound of a Bungi. If you are wondering what a Bungi is, then I will relieve your curiosity by explaining that it is a reeded pipe a snake charmer uses, the bulbous gird section half way along the wooden tube, acting like a reservoir, similar to that of the Scottish bagpipe.

Slowly, a patch of light appeared on the stage, and crouching within it, a man playing the very instrument, waving it rhythmically above a basket made of reeds. With the hypnotic melody filling the auditorium, the tiny black head of a snake appeared and slowly crept over the edge, even its flicking tongue clearly visible from our front row seats. The snake charmer was Moussa; the man I remembered seeing nearly twenty years earlier. It was definitely him. I recognised his face instantly, despite his increased waistline. Furthermore, in all the years, his performance remained unique and unaltered. The reason for Moussa's fame is because he differs from all other snake charmers, since, instead of sitting in one spot and luring the snake from the basket, he gets to his feet and dances.

Still playing the haunting tune, Moussa sways and twirls, while the snake mimics his movement.

That evening, not only were we treated to Moussa and the snakes routine, but also the lights on the backcloth grew brighter to reveal the sinewy curves of yet another creative creature, Tahia Carioca, possibly the most famous belly dancer in the world.

Although Tahia remained motionless, our table joined those

around in applauding, even the young King, clearly visible a few feet away, being one of the most audible. Despite the adulation of the crowd, Hekmet sat smouldering, reacting typically to the presence of a rival.

"Let's have another bottle darling," she growled. "Seeing her dance makes me thirsty. She puts so much effort into it."

Our Nubian was there instantly and I began losing count of the number of bottles I had purchased. But their effect on the lads was becoming apparent. Especially Harry, who whistled loudly as the spotlight lit up Tahia's face.

Her music differed from Hekmet's, having a somewhat European rhythm, perhaps even a South American tempo similar to which Carmen Miranda sings and dances. Even so, as she began to stroke the air with her hands and pump her hips, Tahia's movements were identical to Hekmet's.

Although Harry, Pete, Jim and sometimes Mervyn, were voluble at the beginning of Tahia's performance, other people sitting nearby were markedly restrained, obviously aware of their close proximity to the young King. By shimmying her coin belt and chinking her finger cymbals however, Tahia made it clear she was about to approach his table. As a result, Farouk began to whistle, joining Harry and the lads.

Evidently, seeing their King intended to enjoy himself, the patrons around him soon lost their inhibitions and began to cheer and whistle, everyone, however except me. I have never been one to overdo my enthusiasm, more than likely reflecting my non-conformist upbringing, which encourages self-control. In this respect, perhaps I take after my father.

Although, her eyes betrayed lust and longing, Tahia's mouth was fixed and expressionless. And while jabbing the air with her hips, she arrived at the Kings table, her arms twisting like Moussa's snake, which continued to follow the lone pied piper up on the stage. Then, with her ample bosom heaving inside an embroidered, golden sequined brassier, she shivered her tawny breasts towards the King, Tahia's every movement inviting his attention. Moreover, it was at this moment she received it in a way she least expected.

All eyes were on the spectacle, consequently, what happened next has become legend and fixed in the memories of all who witnessed the event. Yet, I will refrain from keeping you in suspense any further, only to tell you that the King suddenly reached into his glass, plucked out an ice cube, and popped it into Tahia's yawning cleavage.

People gasped, and quite audibly over the music. Then Tahia, completely affronted by the outrage, and clearly forgetting for a moment who Farouk was, slapped him hard across the face, and then ran up the steps and onto the stage, disappearing presumably into her dressing room.

Everyone was stunned, unable to decide whether to cheer, which might be construed as condoning Tahia's actions. Or instead to remain silent, which might be seen as disapproval of the King's actions. Instead, everyone began talking excitedly, congratulating one another at having been present at such a momentous occasion, a moment that more than likely would make the Egyptian history books.

No one was more delighted by what she witnessed than Hekmet Fahmy, and she clapped her hands in delight, causing King Farouk's attention to be drawn to our table. He leaned towards a burly bodyguard standing close by and placed a small package in his hand. The bodyguard then sauntered across the divide between us, and reaching Hekmet's side, bent and whispered in her ear, at the same time placing a soft-skinned pouch on the table.

"Tell the King I'll be at the gates at midnight," I heard her respond. "And thank him."

As the man returned with her message, Hekmet pulled the gold braid drawstring of the blue doe skin pouch, drawing forth a sparkling diamond bracelet which she held up for everyone to see, at the same time nodding her thanks to the smiling King.

Undoubtedly, this boy of seventeen was in for an interesting night, since, as soon as he acknowledged Hekmet's acceptance and approval, he stood up, bowed to the crowd, who had also risen, and to yet another rendition of the National Anthem, left the table followed by his uncle and body guards.

"Don't worry darling, they're fake," Hekmet said, as she slipped the bracelet around her tiny wrist. "He's a pocket full. He's learnt from his father. King Fuad was notoriously mean, amassing a fortune from swindling property out of poor unfortunates who felt obliged to give him whatever he demanded, all the while spending his ill-gotten gains and Government funds building palaces and buying fast cars. The boy King will do the same."

"Perhaps you're right," I said. "He's already got quite a reputation for acquiring the rare and odd. But always manages to get them at bargain prices."

"A pawn of the British darling. Allowed to reign to keep Egypt ignorant, while they plunder her wealth."

Hekmet's fifth glass of champagne had plainly loosened her nationalist tongue. She obviously detested the British, yet I felt no animosity from her. It was the establishment she hated, not the individual. Had I known how far her patriotism would take her later in her life, I would have held an entirely different opinion of Miss Hekmet Fahmy.

"In all the excitement I neglected to introduce myself," said Calomiris. "George Calomiris. Very pleased to meet you all."

"Pleased to meet you too, Mr Calomiris," everyone mumbled.

"And you, young man, what's your name?"

Lighting a cigarette, Calomiris directed his question at Harry, who happened to be sitting in the chair beside him.

"I notice you're in the Hussars. You appear very fit. May I say, tight? You exercise, of course. I admire a chap who looks after himself."

All the while Calomiris was speaking, he was deliberately edging his chair towards Harry's, who responded by moving his away, until he was backed up against Peter Harding and trapped.

"You're one for the ladies I can see," continued Calomiris. "I'm sure you've dozens falling for you."

How the little Greek was able to discern Harry's ripped torso through his tunic, I failed to see. Nonetheless, Harry was receiving the full seduction treatment, which he was clearly not enjoying.

"Thank you Mr Calomiris," he said. "But I've a regular girl. She's a nurse at the British Hospital. But Jim is always looking for a bit of skirt. You're free now, aren't you Jim."

Jim Shaw's mouth dropped open as he suddenly became implicated in Harry's defence scheme.

"No! Mr Calomiris," he stammered. "Harry's having you on. I'm not keen on girls. I'd rather stay in the barracks and read a book, or play ping-pong with my offsider Cecil. But Pete on the other hand; he's a right ladies man."

"Hey!" Peter Harding exclaimed. "Not on your nellie Mr Calomiris! But if you'll forgive me, a suite at the National Hotel, along with a bevy of dancing girls, all the champagne I can drink, and a general's pay, might suit some lucky chap. But I'm a simple bloke Mr Calomiris, with simple tastes, and would never allow myself to be swayed otherwise; if you get my meaning."

Touché! Peter's remarks certainly stopped Calomiris in his tracks, who, rather than pursue the conversation further, poured himself a glass of champagne and lit another cigarette.

Now that our surprise guest had driven away, and with order resumed, Farid Al Atrash returned to the stage and took his place at the microphone.

"Ladies and Gentlemen," he began. "I'm sure you will agree with me when I say, you never can tell at the Kit Kat. And now for the moment you've all been waiting for. The finale of our show. We know that the Kit Kat Club wouldn't be here had it not been for one person, since it was she who created Raq Sharqi and put Cairo on the dance map of the world. Therefore, without further ado, I have the great pleasure to present, Miss Bahia Masabni and her Opera Casino dancing Girls."

Farid gestured to the follow spot operator and we were plunged into darkness, drama created again by the appearance of perhaps a dozen veiled figures, silhouetted against a glowing turquoise screen.

As the stage became brighter, more females appeared above previously unseen trapdoors, all the while the orchestra playing a lilting melody, reminding me of Umm's university song we heard at Café Riche.

A disconnected voice, singing in Arabic, joined the music, while the follow spot, lit up a face in the centre of the stage who I recognised as the women who had been sitting beside Naquib Al

Rihani. Instantly, the audience began clapping and calling out to Bahia, the way only Middle Eastern people do during songs. Despite her obvious maturity, Badia had not lost her charms; her form still beautiful; shrouded in veils of sheer chiffon; harem pants festooned with gold chains, silver braid, and a jewelled, jingling coin belt.

Singing the peoples popular choice, while backed by a chorus of vestal diaphanous females, Badia fronted the hypnotic parade, moving forward into the auditorium. Hekmet, sitting beside me, suddenly became serious in the presence of her mentor.

"Badia will be remembered forever," she whispered as I lit her cigarette. "She's the woman who brought oriental dance into the twentieth century. We must thank god for the marvellous gifts she's given the world, and hope her memory lives on in the hearts of everyone in the present, and in the years to come."

For a further hour, Badia continued to sing and dance, all the while backed by her Opera Casino Chorus; the same song, of course, with breaks for innovative improvisation from various orchestral instruments, together with Farid Al Atrash, either singing or playing the oud. Eventually, the spectacle peaked with a pyrotechnic display issuing from the top of each column at the rear of the stage. Thus, declining many appeals for an encore, Badia and her girls left the stage, and the lights came up to reveal Mervyn, Harry, Jim, Peter, and myself, entirely alone. Hekmet no doubt, at a convenient moment, left the table to keep her tryst with a King. Calomiris, slipping away, anticipating a clandestine meeting with yet another young soldier, ensconced in his suite at the National Hotel.

"That was something. Don't you agree lads?" I said, pouring the last of the champagne from the final bottle into each of our glasses. "And it wasn't only the stage show which was entertaining. I think the night calls for a toast. Look! There're four menus still on the table. Let's sign them, so we can each keep one as a memento of this very special night."

Chapter Thirty Four
Peril on Imbaba Bridge - New clothes for Ali

Wherever one may be in the world, whether in the West End of London on a frosty morning, a muggy dawn in downtown New York, or a street filled with the song of a lonely blackbird in Quartier Pigalle, leaving a club in the small hours is always an enjoyable and relaxed experience.

Having been visibly and audibly stimulated for perhaps eight hours, the peace one encounters walking along the dark and silent streets is rejuvenating. As you step into a brand new world after being suspended in time for a period, one's soul inevitably feels refreshed and reborn. This was exactly so for my companions and myself as we shunned the endless queue of caleches and taxis waiting expectantly outside the club, opting instead to walk the road leading away from Kit Kat Square towards the river and the Nile houseboats.

"So it's Luxor tomorrow for you and my brother," Harry said, as he and I let Mervyn, Peter and Jim walk ahead. "Ron, in all the excitement of the last week, I hope you don't think I haven't wanted to thank you for everything you've done for me. Mervyn told me this afternoon that you pulled strings to get me home. He spilled the beans after his third glass of beer. I can't tell you how grateful I am."

"Now don't be soppy," I said. "I enjoy making people happy. What else is there in life?"

"That's a tremendous sentiment. How my family would have got on without your help I'll never know."

He was still a little drunk, because he suddenly put his arm through mine and I experienced tenderness yet experienced between men of otherwise opposite persuasions. To be honest, I loathe sentimental reactions regarding my acts of kindness. As a result, I rapidly changed the subject.

"Has anyone approached you regarding the article in The Charger?"

"Not yet. Although Chichester did say I still might have to go with the chaps when we leave for the zone. He said there's a lot of paperwork before they can officially transfer me."

"Can I ask you a favour? When you do the interview, please don't mention me. And certainly don't give my name."

"Definitely Ron. Whatever you say."

Taking his arm out of mine, he flung it over my shoulder, although the disparity in our height meant we must have appeared quite ridiculous.

"Come on you two!" Mervyn shouted from up ahead, "What are you up too?"

Our route took us north, along the river and through Imbaba, the Shari el Bahr el Ama quiet due to the early hour.

Yet the dawn had barely defeated the darkness. And as we walked, we were treated to a glorious panorama of the affluent villas and apartments of Zamalek, shining golden in the first rays of the rising sun. While the navigation lights still twinkled, reflecting in the languid waters of the Nile.

"Do you know how deep it is?" asked Mervyn, once Harry and I had caught up with him and the others.

"Maybe thirty feet," I answered. "We'll have to look it up. Perhaps there's a gauge on the bridge."

Once again, I was encountering the Imbaba Bridge, though this time at night, and suddenly I remembered the taxi driver's warning. 'Do not go alone effendi. Bad boys up there.'

Our earlier decision to walk the distance between Kit Kat and Ezbekiya meant there was no alternative but to cross the bridge on foot. Surely five grown men were sufficient to stem off any assault they might encounter. However, I was the only one aware of the bridge's notorious reputation, so decided to keep my knowledge to myself, for fear of provoking a situation that might otherwise be ignored by innocent parties.

It was necessary to climb five sets of stone steps before we could reach the walkway, and climbing the first flight, we were entirely alone. However, arriving at the road and rail level, we discovered several couples clinging to the granite walls like mussels on a rock, their dark shapes glued together in the shimmering reflection of the water below.

These clandestine encounters are unusual in the world of Islam, as the coupling of men and women in a casual, covert way is a sin in the eyes of Allah. So might these women be prostitutes? There must be a need for such a profession, even in a predominantly Muslim country, where such an occupation is frowned upon.

No one spoke while we climbed the following flight of steps, with only the occasional clatter of a caleche or buzz of a motor vehicle passing below to break the silence. As we proceeded, we encountered further shadowy couples, either huddled on the steps, or leaning over the parapet, gazing at the limpid water passing beneath.

When we reached the walkway however, the activity around us altered dramatically.

"Have my arse for three piastres soldier," someone muttered from the shadows. "Want it sucked trooper?" said another. "Give me five and I'll be a woman for you right here against the wall."

Harry, Peter, and Jim were still quite drunk, and ordinarily would be full of Dutch courage, as the saying goes. But they were unusually quiet, refraining from the normal banter one would expect from a bunch of soldiers in a similar situation.

It was obvious they were intimidated by the threatening, penetrating atmosphere.

The voices I concluded belonged to boys of fifteen or sixteen, and no older, since they possessed a squeakiness particular to the post pubescent.

Unable to speak for Mervyn, personally, I felt equally endangered, as well as disgusted by their open and lewd invitations. They were sordid creatures willing for a stranger to brutalise them for the sake of a few coins.

Hurrying on, we fixed our eyes on the way ahead, well aware of the fact that at this point the river was extremely wide, there being a considerable distance between us, and the relative safety of the opposite bank.

Periodically, along its span, several gangways allow a person access to the opposite walkway. As a result, by crossing from one side of the bridge to the other, a sightseer might be afforded a view up the Nile as well as down. Several such gangways positioned at intervals between the east and west banks proved most convenient a few moments later.

To our great relief, the sexual harassment seemed to diminish the further onto the bridge we went, as if we had left the territory of the predatory youths and entered a quiet 'no man's land'. Yet, our relief turned to apprehension as, maybe a hundred yards ahead, a group of shadowy figures stood barring our way, lit only by the shimmering river below. Uncertain as to what to do we stopped walking.

"Don't let them see we're afraid," Peter whispered. "I count nine. What about you Harry?"

"Yes. Nine Pete. The one in the middle's pretty big. I'll take him. The rest of you tackle the others."

"You're not thinking of fighting them?" muttered Mervyn. "I've never been good at that sort of thing, let alone Ron."

"Hey!" I said in my defence. "You speak for yourself young man. You forget my Greco Roman wresting forays at Bath Boys Club and Wildsbridge Scouts. I used to take on the best in my day."

"That was when you were a few stones lighter. These lads are twenty years old or more, and packing knives I shouldn't wonder."

"I say we beat it across to the other side and run," Pete said. "We're lucky to have stopped beside a crossing place. If they're equally spread then there's not one behind them for a considerable distance. If we run we can get a good start on them."

"I'm surprised Pete," said Harry. "I've not known you to turn and bolt in a crisis."

"You're right mate. But I agree with your brother. It's better we give them the benefit of the doubt, and after all, he and Ron are civilians. We've a duty to protect them."

Jim agreed with Peter. So the consensus was that we go with Peter's plan. Therefore, slipping into the shadows under the central parapet, we began traversing the crossing point, and once gathered on the southern walkway, either Harry, Jim, or Peter, I am unable to remember who, began to jog, the rest of us following, until we were abreast of the men bunched on the other side of the bridge.

"Baksheesh!" one shouted. "British give baksheesh. Egyptians poor. British rich. Give baksheesh!"

"Just a nice way of saying you're going to fucking rob us," shouted Harry as we passed them at speed. "We know your game mate. Catch us if you can."

The mob began to run, keeping pace with us along the other walkway, matching us stride for stride.

"Come on everyone!" Harry yelled. "It's critical we get ahead of them at the next gangway, otherwise they'll catch us for sure."

Never having been good at running, unless in short bursts, like the hundred-yard dash, or the four forty yards, I lose my puff if I am running a longer distance, tending to stop to catch my breath, or relieve a stitch. Therefore, cross-country running was a complete impossibility. In this case however, and despite my lack of stamina, I stuck out my chin and ran for all I was worth, even passing Mervyn and Jim at one point, my long legs finally doing their stuff.

"Wow Ron!" cried Harry as I drew up beside him. "Not bad for an old chap."

Unable to respond to his cheeky remark for fear of losing my stride I battled on, only to see the crossing point, marked by a shimmering gas lamp, getting closer every second. Aware that the distance between our foes and us had become considerable, we arrived ahead of them.

"Keep going," panted Harry. "If we get across the next section we'll beat them well and truly."

The centre section of the bridge to which Harry referred was different to the others, since the middle possessed a watch house, along with moveable iron barriers at either end. But these were not in position, meaning the five of us were able to continue without interruption until we reached the far end, and another crossing point. With our pursuers now directly behind and getting closer by the second, miraculously a klaxon sounded and the barriers unexpectedly slammed into position, as the entire section began to shudder sideways, trapping the robbers beneath the watch house.

"It's the swing bridge!" I shouted, hardly able to say the words. "Of course! What a stroke of luck. They'll be stuck for at least half an hour."

Laughing and jeering like triumphant schoolboys at a rugby game, we claimed the victory, while the sails of a ghostly flock of feluccas slid past beneath us.

"It's way past midnight," I said, as we walked the streets of Bulaq. "You're going to be AWOL lads."

"It's okay Ron," Jim said. "We've twenty four hour passes. We're booked into the European Club. Just hope they'll be someone at the desk to let us in."

Fortunately for them there was. So, after saying goodnight, and arranging to see them on our return from Upper Egypt, Mervyn and I crossed Opera Square into Sharia Ibrahim Pasha and arrived at Shepheard's Hotel safely and no worse for wear.

***

The following morning, and leaving Mervyn soaking in a hot bath, I took breakfast in the dining room. Then, collecting my hat from the cloakroom, I found Ali waiting across the street as arranged. Seeing there was time before the banks opened, I suggested we take a stroll in Ezbekiya Gardens, where we might take tea in the teahouse.

"We had rather a time of it last night," I said, as we crossed the road, dodging the traffic. "Firstly, I met Hekmet Fahmy the famous belly dancer. In fact, I met her twice yesterday. Extraordinarily, and unbeknown to me, she helped me find you by guiding me to your houseboat."

"She lives almost next door," Ali, said laughing. "Hazim and I watch her practice her moves on her balcony."

It was tempting to ask whether he and his friend witnessed other less public moves on her behalf. I also resisted telling Ali of her midnight tryst with his sacrosanct and illustrious King Farouk.

"Afterwards," I continued, as we entered the teahouse, finding a table and placing an order with a waiter, "on our way home, Mervyn, the lads, and myself, were almost set upon and robbed by thugs on the Imbaba Bridge."

"Christian boys Ron. No Arab would dare do such a thing. It is forbidden by Allah to steal. Anyway, what were you doing on the bridge? It is a very bad place, not only at night, but even in the day."

"I know. But it was such a nice night; we thought we'd walk back to the city."

"Please Ron! You must be careful. Cairo is different at night. And the British are not popular. It is not safe for you to walk about unprotected."

"Thank you for your concern Ali. I promise to be more careful in the future. Now, changing the subject, since meeting your family yesterday, I've been thinking."

Our waiter arrived with a pot of tea, plus Ali's coffee, and I paused while he laid the table.

"Understandably," I continued, once we were alone. "The race winnings in your account won't last forever. But I believe it's important you return to university and resume your studies. Also, Fatimah should enter the city medical school. You remember I opened an account for you at The Bank of Egypt. Well it's also my wish to sponsor you both. As a result, I've made out a cheque in your name for two thousand Egyptian pounds, which I believe is the correct sum to cover your remaining fees. In addition, I've another for five thousand for Fatimah, so she may open an account to pay for her keep and fees for seven years of medical training."

"Effendi!"

Ali took my hand just as I was about to spoon sugar into my tea.

"Ron!" he said, gripping so hard it was impossible to move. "I don't know what to say. My sister won't know what to say. Also, mother will be angry that you're doing this. She's very proud."

"Of course! I realise that. But she'll be even prouder, as will I, to see you both achieve your ambitions. Unless I step in and take control there's no other way this will happen."

"Very well Ron. I'll speak to mother and tell her what you've said. She'll understand in the end. You're an angel Ron."

"Now stop it!" I said, gently easing his hand from mine. "I'm not finished. All that dreadful wiring hanging around your mother's apartment. This afternoon, before we catch the train, I want you to find a local electrician, and instruct him to begin working on making the electrics safe. Tell him money's no object. Now come along. Drink your coffee. I've had my say. Let's talk about something else."

With formalities at the bank completed and Ali's race winnings safely deposited, it was time to take a trip to Tirings Department Store in order to kit him out for the excursion. Although I had never seen him in anything other than a gallibaya and turban, Ali must have been secretly longing to wear European clothes, because as soon as we were through the doors of the men's tailoring department, he went straight to the off the peg white suits, raking through them like a veteran.

"Choose anything you like," I said. "And don't forget a hat. Panama of course."

Despite being somewhat surprised, the assistant was most helpful, immediately assessing Ali's measurements and recommending this suit or that, until Ali made a choice of two, the assistant directing him to the changing room where he could try them on for size.

When he emerged from behind the curtain, I swear my heart missed a beat, because the young man standing before me was no longer a lowly dragoman, traversing the dusty streets in sandals, gallibaya, and tarbush. In a matter of minutes, he had been transformed into a gentleman about town, looking chipper in a pristine white three-piece suit, shining brown leather shoes, starched white shirt collar and cuffs, snappy crimson and blue necktie, together with a crisp creamy Panama, complete with a black silk band.

"Thank you," I said to the assistant. "There'll be two of everything. My friend will also require two pairs of cuff links, a tie pin, collar studs, a wrist watch, and alternative neck ties."

As he suddenly realised the magnitude of the order, the assistant hurried away to call a colleague.

"We'll be dining and dancing," I continued. "So it'll be important you have a suit for the evening. Also, we may as well kit you out for university with a couple of plain jackets and trousers, along with a few shirts. We mustn't forget vests, underpants, and pyjamas, something you'll need to become used to wearing."

As I had already achieved individually for Eric, and then Mervyn, here again I was doing what I loved to do best; taking an ordinary chap and changing him into a prince, or a sow's ear into a silk purse, not that I said as much to Ali, knowing the Muslim regard for pigs.

When on holiday a young man requires a trunk. Therefore, leaving our busy assistant to collate Ali's collection, we made our way through the extensive store in search of the luggage department, finding it in the basement.

An 'Oshkosh' trunk, I have always considered the best, especially the 'Chief,' which is roomy enough to hold the complete wardrobe and accessories of the modern gentleman. The Oshkosh can open like a wardrobe, having the convenience of hanging space, drawers, as well as compartments for everything a gentleman might need on his excursion.

With my extensive travels abroad, I have never had cause to complain about mine. The Oshkosh is advertised as being built to withstand the rigours of the voyage, and guaranteed for the lifetime of the purchaser. Besides, who knows where else Ali might travel in the years to come.

Once Ali's wardrobe and luggage were bought and paid for, plus instructions given to deliver everything to Shepheard's; with Ali, wearing his new clothes, and me in a new pair of lightweight plus fours, we stepped into the sunny street and hailed a caleche that would return us to the hotel.

Had I my camera handy that afternoon when Ali and I walked onto Shepheard's famous terrace, I would dearly love to have captured the expression on Mervyn's face.

"Well don't you look something Ali," he said, glaring at me sideways. "Up to your old tricks again I see Ron. You can't resist it can you?"

"You're right. I can't, as you know too well."

Ali and I sat down, and while I caught the attention of a waiter, I saw Mervyn had turned bright red, and returned to reading his copy of the Gazette.

"You'll need to pray in half an hour Ali," I said, hearing a huff issue from behind the newspaper. "Ask them at the desk for my key. You can use our bathroom. But there's still time for coffee."

"May I have a cordial Ron?"

"Of course. How about you Mervyn? Another scotch and soda? If that's your poison."

"It just so happens it is Ron," Mervyn snapped. "And thank you. Make it a double."

At this rate, and in his present mood, seeing it was not quite noon, Mervyn would be well on the way to being nine tenths to the wind by the time we board the Sunshine Express. Clearly, it was necessary to distract him from imbibing for the remainder of the afternoon with some activity requiring complete abstinence from alcohol.

"This afternoon Ali needs to see someone about certain work required inside his mother's apartment," I said, once Ali had gone upstairs to pray, and Mervyn and I were alone. "How about we go to the club? You could have a swim."

"What's come over you all of a sudden?" said Mervyn, glaring at me over the newspaper. "Thinking of me for a change. I was beginning to think I didn't exist. You're so preoccupied with Ali it's sickening.

This outburst had been waiting to happen, spurred on no doubt by a combination of several more drinks than I had anticipated, plus a hangover from the previous night.

"I'm not going to argue with you Mervyn. We've had this out before. Come on. You'll enjoy a swim and a sun bathe."

"We haven't time," he said, grumpily. "We haven't begun packing yet. And don't expect me to share a sleeping compartment with your friend."

"Alright. We'll change the sleeping arrangements. So let's go and pack. But lay off the booze for a bit. Otherwise you'll be passed it on the train."

Once Ali had finished praying and left to find an electrician, Mervyn agreed to return to our room, where we spent an hour packing for the trip. Thereafter we spent the remainder of the afternoon listening to the band playing in the hotel garden, a pleasant oasis of flowering shrubs, gentle fountains, and shady palms. While enjoying a selection of tunes from, 'Swing Along' and 'This'll Make You Whistle', two West End shows currently running at the Gaiety and Palace theatres, I caught up with The Times, while Mervyn pondered over a hand or two of Patience.

Presently, Ali having returned, and with the sun dipping behind the Thomas Cooke offices on the far side of the garden, it was time to return to our room to freshen up, then make our way to the hotel steps where a caleche waited to convey us to the station. The three of us were about to exchange our world of trams, trains, caleches, bustling dusty streets, minarets and mosques, with mysterious mummies, ancient religions, timeless monuments, Pharaohs, temples and tombs, as yet another adventure begins.

*The Merry Millionaire's adventures
continue in Book Two
Pomp and Circumstance
Memoir of Captain Ronald Willington Fry
Volume Two*

The Merry Millionaire's adventures
continue in Book Two

Pomp and Circumstance
Memoir of Captain Ronald Willington Fry
Volume Two

In this second book of his duology, J.A.Wells utilises his finely tuned sense of period and historical fact to transport us to a world of caleches, feluccas, mummies and mosques, through which his masterfully drawn characters cavort with gay abandon, caring little for what might be around the corner and naively ignorant of the catastrophe which would end a decade of decadence and depression.

Played against a backdrop of spy-ridden Egypt, pre war England, abdicating Kings and unexpected coronations, we continue to share further travel adventures with our intrepid explorers, Ron and Mervyn, as they discover far more than simply the mysteries of the orient.

After a venturesome jaunt up the Nile, back in Cairo we find Ron and Mervyn at Shepheard's Hotel, where the fascinating Lee Miller has invaded the Long Bar. A flamboyant party at Baron Empain's Palais Hindou serves to whet their appetites for the supernatural. Then joining the luxury ship that will take them home, they rub shoulders with Egyptian royalty, learning more than they should regarding the secrets of the palace. Using his newly found entrepreneurial skills, Ron organises an on board concert, Mervyn's angelic voice and good looks stealing the show. Ghosts are on the agenda once more at an overnight stay at London's Great Western Hotel.

What may become of the pairing of Ron and Mervyn, poles apart in age and class, yet similar in inclination?

Find out more

BUY J.A.Wells' books worldwide at:
Amazon.com
Amazon.co.uk
Amazon.com.au

VISIT   J.A.Wells Author Website
www.johnwellsmurals.com.au/author

LIKE   J.A.Wells on Facebook
www.facebook.com/JAWellsAuthor

FOLLOW   @jawells6661 on Twitter

FOLLOW   john.wells6661 on Instagram

Printed in Great Britain
by Amazon